HAD TO MAKE YOU MINE

A SEXY OFFICE ROMANCE

Southern Charms Book One

Kat Long

Cover Design: Kris Guiao
Editing: Rebecca Colvin of Just Ask Her Production, LLC
Proofreading: Brett Mahaffey
Formatting: Kris Guiao

*"Tell me every terrible thing you did
and let me love you anyway."*
~ Edgar Allan Poe

*"In the end, the love you take is equal
to the love you make."*
~ Paul McCartney

CONTENTS

PROLOGUE: SIX YEARS AGO
Annaleigh

The blue lights of the bar washed over my body like warm waves at the beach in summer. Nothing in the world was better than the electric feeling moments before a show: breathing in the scents of beer, sweat, and polished wood. Something was different tonight as the four of us prepared to take the small stage at B's Bar. The air crackled with the intensity of the crowd, and my pulse hammered in time with the steady beat.

I stretched my muscles and ran my fingers over the fretboard on my JIVA10 guitar, palms itching, ready to play. Alex anxiously tapped her drumsticks while Bird finished a drink. All of us were immersed in our own rituals to prepare. The noise faded to the background as our eyes met, and we smiled. We knew this was going to be memorable.

"And here they are...Alice's Monsters!"

My uncle's voice cut through the noise as the applause got louder, and we put our hands together and yelled:

"Do it right!"

"Or not at all!"

"Own the stage!"

"And chicks dig scars!"

Breaking away, Alex ran out first, took a seat, and flipped her drumsticks in the air. Bird and I followed next with our guitars. Taylor strolled up to the mic last, waving to the crowd. His shirt reflected the colors that bounced off the mirror ball above the stage. He turned and nodded, and I started the opening riff to Alice Cooper's *Spark in the Dark*.

We played song after song, getting lost in the music and the crowd's magnetic energy. The bartender kept our drinks flowing, and we were sticky and sweaty under the sparkling lights.

I took center stage for my bass solo during a Pearl Jam song and met Bird's eyes. They were bloodshot, and Bird was sweating heavier than anyone else. Taylor's attention also turned when Bird's foot started tapping offbeat to the music.

I glanced at Alex, wondering if we should cut the set short, when her drumsticks fell with a clatter that echoed across the stage. Turning back, we watched in horror as Bird collapsed and hit the floor hard, the guitar splintering in every direction. A roar filled my ears, drowning out everything but Taylor's scream and Bird's vacant expression.

MY KNEES FELT WEAK

Annaleigh

I snapped my eyes open with a start, not realizing I had dozed while on the beach. Rush softly played in the background as I dug my toes into the gritty sand and hummed along. The weather was a balmy eighty degrees, and the reason I fell asleep in the first place. The sun had reminded me of the stage lights from six; no, seven years ago.

Lyrics drifted around my mind, something about blue skies, bright lights, and memories. But before I had time to jot them down, they flew away, like the seagulls screeching by. That was my new norm. The lyrics that came like second nature were now almost nonexistent. Maybe time didn't heal everything.

Baxter, my boxer, hogged more space underneath the umbrella than me and was doing his best to stay far away from Jenna, who had been my friend since middle school. We had braces at the same time, sang in the same choir, and lived in the same neighborhood.

We spent at least one Saturday a month with our other two friends, and the beach was the perfect choice for today. I smiled at the cover of my romance book before grabbing a beer from the cooler behind me and looking at the four of us. We affectionately called ourselves the *Southern Charms*. I voted for *Bourbon Babes*, but the girls vetoed it, and *Southern Charms* stuck. The beach, my girls, a book, and a beer, nothing could be better.

"Your crazy dog still hasn't forgiven me, Annaleigh," Jenna said, while tentatively sticking out her hand for him to sniff. Baxter looked up with his big brown eyes and scooted closer to me before laying his head back on his blue beach towel.

"You know, Jenna, you wouldn't be my favorite person either if the last time I saw you, I got two shots, and something stuck up my butt," I said with a smirk.

Jenna smiled and stood up to stretch before she motioned for us to do the same. "Let's go cool off before we all turn into lobsters. The sun is killer today."

I gave a half shrug and stood, stretching my legs and bookmarking my page. The sand wasn't scorching like it would have been in the middle of summer, but we still took our time heading to the shoreline and splashing in.

The water felt amazing as I swam up to my waist before laying back and looking at the clouds drifting across the sky. Jenna and Olivia floated beside me while Addison dragged her chair behind us and sat in one inch of water, keeping an eye out for an elusive shark she was sure was lurking just beneath the surface. I mean, we were more likely to get struck by lightning than attacked by a shark, but to each her own. I believed in signs from the Universe, and Addison believed *Jaws* would attack her in four feet of water.

"I have a new recipe I want y'all to try," Olivia said, dunking her head under the water and coming up with a grin. "It's a lavender scone with tart, lemon glaze."

"Um. That sounds…" I said, trying to find a friendly way to say that sounded gross.

"Weird? I know, but I think it works."

"Hum. Lemons are toxic to animals," Jenna said. "But I wonder if it so I went with it, pretending that running into beautiful strangers on the beach was my norm. We still stood close, close enough for me to see the flecks of gold in his eyes. He dialed the smile back to a smirk and reached out to shake my hand.

"Nice to meet you, Annaleigh. I'm new to the area."

The way my name rolled off his tongue, with his midwestern accent, made me think of the other seductive, tantalizing things he could do with that appendage. It also reminded me that I was going home to an empty townhouse with a judgmental boxer.

"What brought you to Charleston? New job? Parents? Girlfriend?

So much for my two-word vocabulary.

Why did I say, girlfriend? I could have said, what brought you to the beach or offered to lick the sweat off his six-pack, or even offered him a freaking orange slice. It was like desperation oozed off me. Usually, I was calmer and much more collected, but orbiting around that level of manliness had me tongue-tied.

"You ask a lot of questions, Blue."

Blue? He said that before, and it sounded even sexier than my name.

"And you avoid answers like it's your job." I bit my lip and reached down for my beer, taking a long pull, hoping it would break the tension.

"Yeah, it's my only redeeming quality." He rubbed the back of his neck and stepped closer. "I accepted a job and moved here last week." His eyes dropped to my mouth while I struggled to keep the calm and collected facade going.

"You should join us tonight," Jenna said, glancing up from her book. "We're heading to *B's Bar* later on this evening to listen to some local bands and do karaoke."

"Do you sing karaoke, Blue," he said, without a glance to Jenna.

"Sometimes, but it involves copious amounts of liquor and bad decisions."

"Hmm." His smile was back, showing one glorious dimple that was so deep I could've moved into it and lived there happily ever after. "Do I look like a bad decision to you?"

I sighed, "Yes," and took another drink, praying he didn't hear.

I was suddenly aware of the uncomfortable amount of sticky, under-boob sweat my body was producing. Ugh, to be one of those girls that looked dewy when they sweat. I looked straight up like a half-melted popsicle on a hot cement sidewalk.

"Thought so, Blue. Thanks for the offer, ladies, but I have plans later." He lowered his eyes to mine and dropped them down. I felt exposed, as if he could see straight through me.

"Plus," he added in a whisper only meant for me, "I'm not looking for a casual fuck."

What the hell?

He put his sunglasses back on and jogged away, leaving me open-mouthed and staring.

I dropped to my chair to get my heart rate under control while Olivia handed me a fresh beer, ice-cold and already opened.

"What just happened?" I took a drink and looked down at Baxter. He looked back as if to say, "what do you expect when you get too close to that amount of sexiness wrapped up in trainers and board shorts?"

Baxter was *a boss* at silently judging my life choices.

"Tell us again, Annaleigh, how you want to take a break from dating?" Olivia said with a smile. "One minute, you were eye-fucking each other, and the next, your cheeks turned purple, and he jogged away."

Jenna shook her head and filled up Baxter's water dish, then stood up and looked up at the clouds that were getting darker.

"See, you just need to meet a guy like him, one that leaves you speechless. Minus the asshole personality."

Baxter took a tentative sniff of the water before lapping some and adjusting his position to keep Jenna in his line of sight.

"No thanks, Jenna. I'm pretty sure I just solidified why I'm done with casual dating, no matter how tongue-tied I was around that man. We can't just invite a guy to a bar without him thinking I was looking for a hook-

"Maybe. And I would make a your-mama joke right now, but you'd probably hurl," I said, laughing at the irony.

"Yeah. Gross, asshole. You ready for Monday?"

I put down the orange and picked up my shirt, rubbing it across my face and chest, before tossing it in the general direction of the stairs. Was I ready for Monday? Looking at our picture again, I picked it up and put it on the kitchen island. *Fuck yeah, I was.*

"Yeah, man. I'm having dinner with the Bank President and his wife tonight, and then I have to make some progress on these damn boxes. How are you? Still plan on visiting in a few weeks?"

"Good to hear, Maxie. Tay keeps me sane by dragging my hairy ass out of the basement every day to join the day-walkers. But hell, I make my own hours, so what could be better?"

Giving in, I picked the orange back up and smelled it before digging my thumb into its smooth skin. "I still can't believe I haven't met Tay," I said, with a mouthful of oranges.

"Me too, Bro. We haven't been to Charleston in forever and are long overdue for a visit. You better plan some fun shit because I'll have a delightful surprise for you when we get there."

"Delightful?"

"Yes, positively delightful. You heard from them since the move? Or her?"

It went without saying he was talking about our seemingly perfect parents that chose social status over a relationship with both their sons and my ex. There was not enough alcohol at my place to open that can of worms, and I was trying to keep her the hell out of my head.

"No. Thank fuck. Radio silence. I keep waiting for a letter from father's firm saying I was in breach of contract or something. You know he's bound to pull some stunt like that."

"Not really, man. Not anymore."

"Oh, damn. Warren, man. I'm sorry."

I hung my head and looked at the floor, noticing the steady stream of orange juice dripping from my arm. The orange in my hand was a squeezed, messy pulp. And I now had a mess to clean up on top of everything else.

"Dude, you gotta quit apologizing. No one knows the mind fuck our parents play better than me. I'm just glad we're finally talking again."

"Me to Warren, I never should have let this much time go by."

Grabbing a handful of scattered napkins on the kitchen island, I mopped up what I could before tossing everything in the garbage.

"Water under the bridge, man. Now tell me, have you fucked her out of your system yet?"

"Ha! Not looking. Gotta at least unpack and have something in the fridge besides takeout."

"I guarantee it will make you feel better, especially after you caught her in the act."

"Don't remind me. That image is not something I've been able to forget. I'm glad it happened before we got married. Can you imagine the scandal we would have caused when I filed for divorce? Or if it had made the papers? She is just the sort of person who would cause as much drama and trouble as possible."

"Way to look on the bright side. Still, you should at least go on a date. Remind yourself that not all chicks are cheaters."

I turned on the water in the sink, ran my arm underneath, and thought about Blue, wondering how tonight would have gone if I had agreed to meet her. Would we have made another date? Realized we were better off going our separate ways? Or gone at it like horny teenagers in the parking lot? Our five-minute conversation had me worked up more than my entire relationship with Nicole.

I'd always attracted a certain type of woman. It was inevitable with who my parents were, and I never thought I'd tire of the dark-haired beauties who wanted to be on my arm. But their personalities were as fake as their boobs, and I foolishly listened to my parents when they said I made a suitable match with Nicole. I couldn't imagine marrying someone like her now. She was like a black widow disguised as a butterfly, ready to strike as soon as my guard was down.

"You there, Maxie? Did you die?"

"Yeah, sorry. I met someone today at the beach, but I was a complete dick to her."

"What the hell for?"

"Who knows? I couldn't get Nicole's cheating face out of my head. She's buried herself in my brain like a fucking carpenter bee. No matter how much I try to stop thinking about her, I can't."

"Well, that's understandable considering you walked in on her spread-eagle on your bed. But don't sweat it. Just do better next time. Eventually you'll meet the right girl, and when you do, trust me, you'll know, man. You'll know. Maybe that girl was someone to get your mind off Nicole, even if it was just for a little while."

I missed Warren's straightforward logic. We were going to have a great time when he visited.

We talked a little longer before I bowed out. My sweat from the run was permeating the townhouse. I had to shower.

After I hung up, I sorted through the growing pile of takeout menus on the counter and added grocery shopping to my growing to-do list. I grabbed another piece of fruit from the welcome basket Jake sent, glancing at the oranges in the basket and thinking of Blue. I headed up the stairs to take a shower, thankful the city seemed large enough that the chances of seeing her again were next to nothing.

After my shower, I found one of my Tom Ford suits in the back of the closet still in the dry-cleaning bag. I paired it with a muted blue shirt, maroon tie, and Brioni loafers. Once dressed, I grabbed my phone to see where the Country Club was, and surprisingly, it was close to home. When Jake first mentioned the club, he saw my hesitation but assured me the restaurant was one of the best in the area, and he had an *in*. He laughed when he told me his *in* was Katie, his wife, and the Head Tennis Pro

I pulled under the awning and handed the valet my keys, taking in the vastness of the Country Club while waiting for Jake outside. I caught the tail end of a tour, remembering Jake had told me this used to be a working plantation.

> *"This Plantation House turned Country Club has been around since the 1800s, on almost a thousand acres of plantation land near the Cooper River, complete with an eighteen-hole golf course. Notice the tall white columns and balcony that runs along the outside edge, and the towering oak trees hanging heavy with Spanish moss and bright, perfectly manicured flowers and shrubbery."*

Half listening, I spotted Jake and his wife walking towards me, and I waved my hand in greeting. After introductions, we walked inside and made our way to the restaurant. The inside was impressive, with open staircases that led to the upper levels and skylights to showcase the house's natural light.

I nervously removed my glasses and cleaned them on my tie but was put at ease with how laid-back Jake and Katie were. They both stopped to introduce me to several people, and Katie greeted the server by name, asking about his daughter, and ordering a white wine. Jake ordered a gin and tonic, and I got a bourbon on the rocks.

As the evening went on, I found myself enjoying their company and looking forward to Monday. Katie was an absolute delight, and I found out Jake was an avid golfer and in a jam band. We talked about music and planned to come back and play the course in a few weeks.

As Katie finished her dessert, our conversation turned from music and golf to work.

"So Max, these first few weeks, take time to familiarize yourself with your clients. Make calls, set up meetings, and most importantly, utilize your assistant. She'll be invaluable and answer questions."

"Absolutely, Jake. I look forward to working with you both."

"Plus, Max. She's a stunner," Katie added, earning a stern look and then a grin from Jake.

I wasn't sure how to answer Katie, so I stayed quiet, earning a respectful nod from Jake. Not that I minded having a hot assistant. I'm sure she'd make the long days go by faster, but I didn't need any distractions. Like I told Blue on the beach, I wasn't interested in a one-time fuck.

And Nicole was still taking up too much space in my head. I was done with drama and done with my last name. I dropped it with the move and went by my middle name now.

Katie looked between us both and backtracked quickly, "So Max, you practiced Law in Chicago? What made you want to switch to Commercial Banking?"

"Yes. I practiced at my family's firm for just over seven years but was ready for a change. It will be nice to put my MBA to good use."

"So, you are extremely motivated?" she asked, making me shift in my seat and wish I had ordered another bourbon.

"Um. Career motivated, yes."

Jake brought the conversation back around to the upcoming Whiskey Gala next weekend, and I breathed a sigh of relief. As we said our goodbyes a few hours later, I felt lighter than I had in years.

New city.

New job.

New life.

No distractions.

When I got home, I poured another bourbon, added some ice, and turned on the TV, trying not to think about Blue or the unopened boxes.

- *3* -

YOU SOON LINGERED

Annaleigh

I wish I could say I was a confident sex goddess and forgot about Broody McAsshole when we got back to my townhouse. But that would be a big fat juicy lie. I felt like the lead in a bad sitcom, thinking of super insightful zingers after the fact. I wish I would have said something witty while flipping my hair and strolling off into the sunset. But no, I stood there, dumbfounded, with my mouth open while he jogged away.

Broody kept entering my mind at the bar and through karaoke. And he was still lingering the next morning at the Farmers Market, and now, during the last set of my tennis match with Jake's wife, Katie.

Katie and I found each other at the bar one evening at a work event, bonding over bourbons—bourbon that was the exact shade of Broody McAsshole's eyes. And there I went thinking about him again. *Damnit.*

"Mister McHottie?" Katie said, pulling me back to our tennis game and giving me a high-five.

"No, Broody McAsshole," I corrected with a sigh, walking towards the bench where our towels and water bottles were.

"Right, then Broody McAsshole called you out for maybe, but not definitely, wanting a booty call and bailed before you could answer?"

Katie retied her blonde hair and took a long drink of water, putting her hand on her hip and looking at me like she knew something I didn't.

"Yep, that about covers it. Did I mention how mature I'm acting about the whole five-minute conversation?" I said, running the towel over my face.

I didn't know what was worse, not getting Broody out of my head or letting Katie cream me again in Tennis.

Giggling and shaking her head, Katie took another drink before continuing.

"You might have mentioned that once or twice and told me again and again how sexy he was. Come on, Jake will be here shortly for the kids' lessons, but we have time to head to the club for lunch."

"Sounds great. I'm in the mood to eat my feelings."

We packed up our rackets and headed to the clubhouse, following the golf cart path past the water hazard and through the shrubbery.

"I feel like it's my job to point out this is the most we have ever talked about a guy, Annaleigh. And I've known you for, what, five, six years now?"

"Tell me about it. It's hard to believe it's been that long. I remember almost falling on my face that weekend I ran into y'all at the soccer field."

I shook out my shoulders as we walked, thinking about that day.

"I know, right. Your eyes were so wide when you stopped on the jogging path and saw Jake and me on the bleachers."

"I think the wide eyes were from seeing the Bank President when I was a sweaty mess and then drinking half of your screwdriver before I realized it wasn't water!"

"Hey, we have three kids who play three different sports on Saturday. That requires a little liquid motivation," Katie said with a smile, opening the outside gate at the restaurant and motioning to a server that we were going to sit outside.

"No judgment here, lady, especially not about something with oranges in it. But after running two miles and taking a huge swig of that, it took me, what, a good few minutes to stop coughing."

"I remember Jake was so worried. He didn't know there was vodka in there."

"And you wouldn't stop laughing, Katie!"

"I know, I was a bad friend. Speaking of oranges, how are you feeling?" Katie said, sitting down and passing me a menu.

"I'm feeling okay. Haven't had any bad symptoms for a while. And I did start on Vitamin D supplements."

"But doesn't hypocalcemia require more than just supplements?"

"Sometimes," I said, looking over the menu. "But with extra calcium in my diet, I'll be fine."

"Hmm, if you say so," Katie said, biting her lip like she wanted to ask me more. "So anyway, tell me more about this guy."

"Oh, there's not much left to say. The girls see it as a good thing a guy has gotten under my skin, but I see it as an affirmation to take a break to prioritize work."

I shrugged my shoulders and glanced at the menu, not believing the words coming out of my mouth. The truth was a five-minute conversation with Broody, and his bourbon eyes had occupied my thoughts more than all my dates in the last several years. The tiniest spark took shape as we sat, a lyric. *Wait, a lyric?*

> *"A moment of time, will I ever be ready? Heart beats out of sync, will it ever be steady?"*

It stuck in my head long enough for me to take out my phone and jot it down. *Strange*, I couldn't remember the last time one stayed with me long enough to do that.

"Hmm, I don't agree with you," Katie said, bringing me back to our talk. "But I guess it's a good thing Jake said your department was going to be pretty busy these next few weeks getting ready for the conference in Tennessee."

"Right," I said, thinking of the week ahead.

Between the new Senior VP, renovations on our floor, and planning for the upcoming trip, I knew I'd be at the office long past five o'clock each day.

"We had dinner here last night with the new SVP. Jake is pleased with him. Once they started talking about Business Risk Ratings, I tuned out. But he seems like a good guy. Quiet and distant, but good."

I ordered a salad and club soda like Katie, and her eyes stayed glued to the menu, baiting me perfectly before I realized what she'd done.

"Why do you say distant? Did he not want to get to know you both better?"

A sly grin spread across her face as she passed the menu to the server. I could tell she was itching to tell this story. All she needed was the opening I gave her.

"It's a pretty interesting story since you asked. Jake met him a few months ago when he went to Chicago. They were the only two guys wearing suits at this little dive bar and stayed in contact when Jake came back. It turned out, Max was looking to move, and Jake was looking for an SVP. Max said he loved the area and was ready to be finished with the snow in Chicago. He's very good-looking and very motivated. It could be destiny."

"Destiny is something we've invented because we can't stand that everything is accidental," I said, sipping my club soda and looking towards the eighteenth hole.

"Wow, Annaleigh. That's really deep."

I did my best to hold in a grin, biting my lip to keep it from turning up and twirling my ponytail innocently.

"Wait! You just quoted a movie or something, didn't you? Plus, you twirl your hair when you're nervous," Katie said, waving her hand.

"What? No, I don't," I said, letting go. "And it could be an Annaleigh original! Besides, it's true."

"So says you," Katie said with a wink.

"You know I'm a big believer in signs Katie, but no thanks," I said, taking another sip. "I mean, even if I wasn't working under him, I'm without a doubt not dating someone from the bank. Oh! I almost forgot to ask, how was your niece's wedding in Slippery Rock?"

"It was beautiful, thanks for asking. Gabe and Noelle are so happy together."

"He owns a bar, right?"

"Yes, and she works for an accounting firm. They had the wedding and reception at her parent's Country Club in Butler. They are going to be so happy together. Like you will be one day," she said.

"I am happy, Katie."

"Oh, stop. You know what I mean."

I pushed my salad around my plate, wondering if taking a break was the right path. Dating equaled relationships. And relationships equaled trust, honesty, and intimacy, all the things my life seemed to lack. But relationships also meant mistakes. And mistakes could have devastating effects. *Nope, I was good.* Single was definitely better, no matter how much Broody had gotten under my skin.

"I could always set you up with one of the tennis pros here."

"Oh, No way! I know you mean well, but three strikes with you and Jake setting me up is my limit for embarrassment."

"Oh, come on, Jake's buddy from the club wasn't that bad."

"You mean the one that suggested we go to a strip club afterward because it was amateur night, and he wanted to see me in action before another date?"

Blushing and almost snorting into her club soda, Katie took a moment to wipe her face before continuing.

"I forgot about that. Jake hasn't played a round with him since. He mentioned something about him bringing down the group score."

"Well, good riddance," I said, clinking my glass to hers.

A half-hour later, Jake brought the kids over to grab Katie before their tennis lessons.

"Hey, ladies," he said, leaning down to kiss Katie. "Have a good game?"

"Sure did, babe, thanks."

"Your lovely wife beat me as usual," I said with a smile. "But one of these days, I'm going to win a set."

"Aw, come on, Anna, you have made mad improvement since we started playing."

"Don't I know it, but I'm pretty sure it would be bad for business if I beat the best Tennis Pro here."

Jake shook his head and reached down to take a sip of Katie's club soda.

"Annaleigh. Did you get a chance to..."

"Yes, I finished up the access requests for the SVP yesterday and connected his laptop to JMS's network."

"What about..."

"Yes. I made sure maintenance moved all the nonessential furniture out of the office until he meets with Elise and called the hotel to add his name to our table for the Gala."

"And also..."

"I confirmed that his welcome basket was delivered earlier and have a few plants ready for pickup tomorrow to brighten his office. I'll grab them when I run out for lunch."

"Have you asked him for a raise lately, lady? Because that freaky mind-reading thing the two of you do probably deserves more money," Katie said with a smile as she stood up to give Jake another kiss and ruffle her youngest's hair.

"That gets funnier every time, wife," Jake replied with a wink to her and a nod to me.

After so many years of working together, I was almost always a step in front of what he needed.

"I'll put something on our calendars Monday to go over expectations and commitments and bring extra coffee and pastries in the morning."

"Perfect, I wouldn't say no to an extra blueberry muffin. See you tomorrow, Annaleigh. Come on guys, let's head down for your lessons."

Taking his youngest's hand, he waved and turned to head to the courts. Katie and I said our goodbyes, knowing we would see each other next weekend for the Gala. I headed to the locker room to change before going home, and another lyric pushed its way through my thoughts.

"Eyes so deep I'd gladly drown. Would you save my breath or sink me down?"

The lyric stayed long enough for me to put it in my phone *again*. I shook my head. It had to be a fluke. My writer's block had been going on for far too long to be cured in a weekend.

Closing my locker, I zipped up my duffle bag and added a note to stop by *B's* this week for the financials. I had more important things to focus on than a temporary cure of Writer's Block.

- *4* -

A SUDDEN SPARK

Max

Why *the hell was I still smelling oranges?*
Either the orange juice had permeated the tile, or I had phantosmia. Maybe this damn fresh air had given me a sinus infection. Or I was going crazy. It was the only explanation for why I was still obsessing over a five-minute conversation where I was nothing but an asshole. *What the fuck was wrong with me?*

My house was almost unpacked, and my fridge had more than takeout boxes. I wasn't sleeping on the couch and planned to make a trip to the design district and hardware store this week. There were more important things for me to think about than Blue.

I put on my vest and straightened my slacks over my Officine Creative Anatomia loafers before locking the door and getting in my truck. Van Halen played as I turned out of my neighborhood, and I turned it up and focused on the day ahead. I got to the bank with time to spare and found my assigned spot in the garage beside the building. I grabbed a box with a few personal effects and walked out of the garage, taking in the architecture of the three-story brick bank.

It had two large white terraces on the upper levels, and green ivy hung around the railing and trailed down one side. The third floor had big bay windows, and I could see several restaurants and a bakery down the street.

Inside, the large lobby had a tall, recessed ceiling, and the floors were light, like driftwood. The chairs were a pale blue and looked comfortable. The southern designs were so different from the cold, dark Chicago buildings. Frosted glass windows separated the offices, and the elevator was on the right side of the receptionist's desk. Looking up from his computer, the uniformed guard stood and greeted me with a smile.

"Good morning, Sir. May I help you?" he said with a southern drawl and a smile.

"Yes, good morning. I'm Maxwell Jackson."

"Yes, sir, the President said to expect you. I'll just document your driver's license and plate number while you're waiting on your access card, and you can head upstairs."

"Thank you." I handed over my Illinois driver's license and took out my phone, adding a trip to the DMV to my to-do list.

I nodded my thanks to the guard and stepped into the elevator. I'd ask my Executive Assistant to compile a list of customers to contact and ask her to lunch. Having a good relationship with her was essential. I remembered Katie's comment about her being beautiful, but that didn't matter. The only thing that did matter was her competency, and Jake certainly thought highly of her. But anyone would be better than my old assistant. She spent her days criticizing my every move.

The elevator doors opened to a large lobby with a receptionist sitting in the same styled desk as below.

"Good morning, Mr. Jackson. Welcome to JMS. I'm Elise Baker. It's a pleasure to meet you."

Her skin was a dark bronze, and her hair was cut in a short, severe bob. She had kind eyes and looked to be about ten years older than me, not that I'd ever say that.

"Good morning, Elise. Please call me Max. Nice to meet you too."

I smiled back and shook my head slightly as she blatantly gave me a once-over. Not the first time I'd gotten that reaction, but it was refreshing to know it wasn't my last name that made Elise do a double take. Something in her eyes didn't sit well—as if she'd already formed her opinion about me before my first words, and it wasn't a good one. Regardless, it was nice not being a Smerdon here, just Maxwell Jackson.

She led me through the lobby and past several open offices to the far end of the floor. In the middle was a boardroom surrounded by glass, and through the open door, you could see floor-to-ceiling windows with that a view of the Cooper River. The room had a large oval table and several plants.

On the far side of the floor were two large offices. The corner one looked to have a door leading directly into the boardroom, and the other was just as impressive but looked spartan in comparison.

There was an L-shaped desk in between the two offices. I assumed this was where our assistant sat. The desk had lots of small succulents, two computer monitors, several personal pictures I couldn't make out from here, and smelled like citrus.

Wait. Citrus? Great. The last thing I needed was a reminder of *her* today.

"Mr. Rosenberg?" Elise said, knocking on his partially open door, "Max Jackson just arrived."

"Thanks, Elise." Jake stood up from behind his desk and walked over to shake my hand. Elise gave me one more obnoxious glance before walking away.

"Hey man, welcome. Please have a seat. Anna will be here shortly with coffee and muffins."

"Thanks, Jake, glad to be here."

The second he said the name Anna, I got an uneasy feeling. Why did that sound familiar?

"Like I was saying at dinner, take some time to review your portfolio these first few weeks. We have several introductions and lunches planned, and Anna will schedule a time for you and Elise to sit down and go over options for your office. I thought you would like the one by mine and closer to her, but you are more than welcome to the other corner office. Here, let's look," he said, standing up and motioning me to the door.

We walked to the office beside his—even though it was nearly empty— it was pleasantly inviting. A large black sleek desk was by the far wall, and the opposite side had a small table with two chairs, a door leading to a private bathroom, and a cabinet that opened to a copier and shelves.

"Anna kept some original furniture so you could get a feel for the layout, but please feel free to change anything you like. The office on the other side is empty, so anything you don't use can be moved back. Here, let's walk over to the other."

"That's unnecessary, Jake. This one is perfect. You can't beat that view."

Putting my box on the desk, I looked around. I could see myself happy here.

"Sounds good Max, your computer is being delivered from IT this morning. Anna will help get you set up to the network."

"Thanks for the welcome, Jake. And all the plants are a nice touch," I said, following him back to the lobby and taking in all the green.

"Oh, that's all Anna. I do not have the patience to keep up with all the plants around here. I'll let you get settled. Let's grab lunch today. Oh, I almost forgot. Be right back."

I nodded, and Jake went back to his office, coming back and tossing an orange above his head before catching it.

A strange feeling of panic caused my palms to sweat and my tie to feel too restricting.

Oranges? Anna?

It couldn't be the same person. She had a double name, right? Anna Grace? Anna Marie? Anna Lynn? Thoughts buzzed around my brain like frenzied murder hornets on a mission while Jake walked over and put the orange beside her keyboard. Charleston was a decent-sized town, too big for it to be the same person.

"Her friend owns the bakery down the street, so she brings coffee almost every day. The least I can do is bring her favorite fruit," he said with a smile, putting his hand in his pocket to take out his phone.

"What did you say her name was again?" I said, dreading the answer. *Please no.*

"Anna. Annaleigh Mackey."

Oh. Fuck. Me. This was bad. This was a nuclear explosion from a volcano under Yellowstone National Park. *Oranges. Blue.*

"You alright Max," Jake asked, pulling me out of my panic.

"Yeah, sorry," I replied, my throat dry and scratchy. I needed water or a shot. Possibly both.

"Alright, I have an eight o'clock call. Boardroom at nine for introductions."

And with that, Jake walked back to his office and shut the door.

I stood in the spot between our offices for what felt like an eternity, staring at that stupid orange. It was mocking me. There was now an almost blinding panic making my pulse race and my throat get impossibly drier. I did the only appropriate thing I could think of to do. I went to my office and shut the door.

Oranges.

I swear I could still smell them through the shut door while trying to get my panic under control. But that was stupid—you couldn't smell unpeeled oranges. I paced back and forth, pissed that I had to adjust my cock twice in the process. He must have missed the memo that she was off-limits. So off-limits. Suck it up, apologize, move on. Don't think about seeing her, being close to her, touching her.

Goddamnit, there went my cock again. I grabbed a water bottle from the table and drank it down, then cracked my neck and walked to my office door. It might not be her. This was the South. Everyone had a double fucking name. I started to doubt my sanity as I slowly opened the door, praying I was wrong.

Nope. I wasn't wrong.

Not. At. All.

There she was—a vision in a black pencil skirt, white blouse, and sapphire blue heels. She stood with her back to me, putting away something in the cabinet behind her. Her blue bikini was nothing compared to how her ass filled out that skirt. The curve of her neck was beautiful, and I was mesmerized by the gentle sway of her hips as she moved around her workspace. And was she wearing thigh-high panty hose? *Oh God*, sheer black thigh-highs with a back-seam.

I was teetering between anger and arousal. How could the woman I haven't been able to get out of my head be here? It had to be some sort of sick test of my willpower, my willingness to take this new opportunity seriously. I should be indifferent and standoffish. She couldn't know how much she'd gotten under my skin.

Her light blonde hair was in a low loose bun, and when she turned around, I saw the moment she made the connection. Her smile went from welcoming and warm to confused, and finally, her eyes narrowed, and she stepped towards me with a stern, unreadable expression.

"Good morning, Annaleigh. I'd like to introduce myself."

I held my hand to hers, unashamed to admit I was looking for an excuse to touch her. She had the most adorable crinkles between her eyebrows as she looked back at me, taking her lower lip in her mouth again, just like at the beach. It made me want to bite that lip and taste her mouth.

What? This was going to be a problem. A big fucking distraction. I had to apologize, then shut it down and push whatever feelings I had away.

But her eyes. All it took was one look at her eyes, and I lost my train of thought.

"Hello," she started, tilting her head to the side and meeting my eyes.

Jake chose that moment to walk over and break up whatever the fuck was happening. He eyed the bakery bags on her desk, unaware of the sheer panic on my face.

"Morning, Anna. Good weekend? Would you please…"

"Hi, Jake. Yes, thank you. I'll head down to IT to pick up Mr…"

"Maxwell Jackson, but please call me Max," I said, putting as much emphasis on the please as humanly possible. I gritted my teeth as she took me in, and her eyes narrowed, with an emotion I couldn't read. Not that I should be able to read any emotion she had.

"Mr. Jackson's computer."

She paused as if she was deliberately ignoring me. Her gaze was focused and intense and on anything but me after she gave me that initial once over. Clearly, she was not intimidated by an asshole in a Tom Ford suit.

"Here's your tea, Jake. Liv got in a Rose Earl Grey I thought you would want to try. But I brought an extra Maharaja Blend if you're not crazy about it."

She gave Jake that welcoming smile that I wanted all to myself as she handed him the tea.

"Mr. Jackson, I brought an extra latte for you. Please let me know your morning beverage preference for tomorrow. Jake, here's a blueberry muffin."

Handing him the bag, he gave her a big smile as he sat the bag on her desk and took a sip.

"This is good, but do you have your…"

"Sure, here's the orange blossom honey," she said, reaching in her desk and still looking anywhere but at me.

"Thanks," Jake said, taking the bag, tea, and honey back to his office. He shut the door, bringing the tension back up to nuclear.

"I have an orange scone and danish. If you're interested, please help yourself."

She turned, shook that beautiful blonde hair I wanted to tangle my fingers in, and walked away.

"Wait, Annaleigh," I said, but she stepped around me and kept walking.

I followed her as she walked, keeping my eyes on those blue heels. Reaching out, I touched her shoulder, startling her as she walked inside an empty office without turning around. When we both were in, she turned to look at me and opened that sweet mouth.

I interrupted, knowing I needed to get this out before she could say anything. My father always said apologizing was a weakness, but she deserved one. This was the last thing I needed my first day, and the last thing I needed with this move, a distraction.

"I owe you an apology. I was out of line that day at the beach and shouldn't have insinuated you were only after a casual fling."

"Fuck, Mr. Jackson, a fuck."

"Right, a casual fuck. Fuck, Blue. Anna, please call me Max. I apologize for the way I acted on Saturday. I've been looking forward to starting here, and I hope we can move past this and have a mutually professional relationship without being immature. My being immature, I mean. Not you. You were not immature. I mean, if we can't move past this, we both would be immature, right?"

I was rambling now, trying to build a bridge between our new working relationship. But I was clenching my jaw so hard my teeth were going to crack. Hearing her say *fuck* had my cock twitching *again* in my pants. I shouldn't have said immature, but this had to stay professional. If that meant bringing my asshole out, so be it—anything to keep her siren's call from tempting me.

She was the picture of confidence in those ridiculous sky-high heels but still had to look up to meet my eyes. It was hard not to smile, so I did and could immediately see the mistake as her eyes flashed fire.

"Immature? Immature? You know what, Mr. Jackson? Max."

She paused in her brutal word assault, and I knew she hadn't heard my rambling. "You don't owe me a damn thing. I may have been quiet Saturday, but I wasn't blind. Our relationship will be strictly professional, and seeing you on that beach has already been forgotten. I'm going to head down for your computer. I'll have it set up shortly. Please help yourself to the latte. And Max, call me Annaleigh."

She turned around and walked away, leaving me speechless. Well, almost.

"I should have gone out with you that night," I called after her. *Where had that come from?*

She stopped and bowed her head before looking over her shoulder. She opened her mouth to respond but didn't. Turning back around, she took the scent of oranges with her as she walked away. I wasn't sure if I was relieved or disappointed, but I had the sudden urge to call after her again and tell her she was all I'd thought about this weekend. But like a stubborn asshole, I let her walk away.

- 5 -

LET ME PERISH

Annaleigh

A *nd all I could say was, hello...*
       Damnit. Damnit. Damnit.

It was a sign.

And not just a sign. It was a neon pink flashing sign on a dark, starless night that said, *look here, dumbass.*

His voice was growly and deep, like sleet on a tin roof, and his suit was perfectly tailored to every inch of his body. How was he here? How was that him, just as attractive as I remembered. And what did he mean when he said he should have gone out with me?

I was normally not one for fantasizing, but that was exactly what I did all weekend long. Broody McAsshole. Max. Maxwell. The name suited him. He smelled like spicy sandalwood and was wearing a vest that hugged his broad chest and sexy, round, tortoiseshell glasses that framed his face.

He was exactly the kind of man I didn't want to deal with, an asshole, a bad attitude, an alpha. But then he said he should have gone out with me, and I melted. *Melted.* That neon sign was back and flashing again, this time with the words *Danger Ahead*, but all my stupid brain could see was the vulnerability in his eyes.

I took a few deep breaths, twirled my hair around one finger, and put a hand on my stomach, trying to calm my pulse while I walked down to IT. I had to stay professional. There wasn't another option unless slapping the word immature right out of his mouth counted. I needed to put on my big girl panties and step up the civility after I stopped sweating and unstuck my skirt from my butt cheeks. A thong was *not* the smart choice today. Was butt deodorant even a thing? *Probably not.*

Maybe he was a narcissistic asshole with the personality of a wet mop and a dick the size of a Tic-Tac. Immature my ass. At least I wasn't an uptight jerk with a smart mouth. But it didn't matter, and we needed a hard reset. We were going to be working closely together, so we had to have an open line of communication. We couldn't spend each day tiptoeing around each other.

With my pep-talk complete, I got back to Max's office while he was still meeting the board members and executives. I connected his laptop to the docking station, put an extra monitor in his office, and then linked his calendar to my phone. I set a daily recurring morning meeting with the two of us then another to include Jake every afternoon.

My list of customers Max needed to reach out to this morning was almost finished when the meeting ended. Almost everyone looked pleased and was shaking Max's hand. Except for Raymond, but that was a whole other can of worms. Max walked by and hit me with a panty-melting smile, motioning me to his office. I plastered a professional one on my face and stood up with a nod, grabbing my tablet.

"How were introductions?" I said, following him in and partially closing the door.

"Mostly positive, except for one. Roger? Ruban?" he said, walking toward the small table and chairs that were in his office.

He pulled out one of the chairs and motioned for me to take a seat. I crossed my legs, pretending not to notice how his eyes glided down my body as he was pulling out the opposite chair.

"Was it Raymond?" I said, trying to dissipate the desire I felt from his gaze.

He nodded, taking off his glasses to clean them on his tie. *Clark Kent had nothing on Maxwell Jackson.*

"What's Raymond's deal? Does he always act like a dickhead to new people in the office, or should I feel special?" Max said, leaning forward to put his elbows on the table.

It was important for people to make conclusions on their own, but Max needed to know about this guy since he was already picking up on the negativity and got a less than warm welcome.

"How honest would you like me to be?" I said, biting my lip and tapping my stylus on the table.

"Give it to me straight, Blue." Raising my eyebrows with the nickname, he quickly backtracked and said, "Um, Annaleigh. Please."

"Okay. Raymond was hoping his son, Benjamin, a Junior Credit Officer, would get your position. He constantly questions all of Jake's decisions and generally opposes anything he puts to a vote. Raymond thinks because he was one of the board's founding members, his son should be guaranteed a place, and everyone should give them both special treatment."

Max's eyebrows got higher as I spoke, nodding with the words. "You look like you want to say more Annaleigh, what else do I need to know about him?"

"Well," I said, "He's a sexist jerk to all the admins. And his son is a twatwaffle."

Max snorted. It was an extremely unsexy sound, and I was going to have to remember it the next time he had me all hot and bothered.

"A twatwaffle? Wow. Is that a technical term?" Max said, leaning towards me and spreading his legs to put his elbows on his knees.

"No, an immature one," I deadpanned, looking at him for a reaction.

I gave him a big smile, and before I knew it, we were both laughing. *Oh my, his laugh.* Forget the way he filled out that suit or the golden-brown shade of his eyes—his laugh had my clenching my thighs and blushing like a teenager with a crush.

"Good to know, and thank you for the honesty. It's a shame to say I am extremely familiar with his type. And now I know I wouldn't want to get on your bad side, especially when you throw around words like twatwaffle."

Max let out a barely-there sigh and shook his head with one more smile. "Do you normally talk about executives like that?"

I smiled and took a breath. *No.* I most definitely did not talk about executives or board members like that. But something about Max made me want to open up, warn him about Raymond, and protect him. Plus, I would do about anything to see him smile like that again. Something told me he didn't do that nearly enough.

"No. But I think honesty is important for our working relationship, and if that means giving you my opinion in less than professional terms, so be it. Would you rather I tell you to ask Raymond to lunch to try and win him over?" I said, crossing my arms.

"No, I'm glad for the honesty. But I hope I never get on your bad side."

Checkmate. He narrowed his eyes and mimicked my pose, crossing his arms and leveling me with a glare that brought the temperature in the room down ten degrees.

I narrowed my eyes, preparing to put him in his place, but then stopped and put my hands up.

"Before this gets out of hand, let's do a hard reset. We are going to be working closely together, and we can't spend every day in a verbal sparring match. I get that we had a less than stellar start, but seriously, Max."

I could see him mulling the words over and grinding his jaw. He wanted to say more. He looked like he was itching for an argument, itching for a way to keep me at arm's length. I didn't blame him, it was the smart thing to do, but something kept me from pushing back.

"I agree," he said, holding his hand out for me to shake. "My name is Maxwell Jackson. I left Chicago and moved down here a few weeks ago. I enjoy building things with my hands, listening to classic rock, and running on the beach. I prefer coffee to tea, books to movies, and my biggest pet peeve is dishonesty."

I smiled. It was hard not to and took his hand. "It's a pleasure to meet you, Max. My name is Annaleigh Mackey. I'm a South Carolina native and dog-mom to a judgmental boxer named Baxter. I listen to all music with a particular love for Shock Rock and Country. I'm a damn good assistant, and I'll do everything in my power to ensure you are successful here. I also enjoy both tea and coffee, gardening, romance books, and my biggest pet peeve, I guess, would be the same. Oh, and people who chew with their mouth open."

"The pleasure is mine, Annaleigh," he said, emphasizing the word pleasure and looking down to where we were still shaking hands. With one gentle squeeze, he let go and met my eyes.

"Here," I said, holding out my hand. I needed to keep my hands busy, or else I'd reach out and touch him again. "Give me your phone. I'll sync everything for you."

"So, you're saying you want to keep tabs on me?" Max said, adjusting his cufflinks.

"Pardon?" I said, not looking up.

I added my number and sent myself a text so I'd have his. I couldn't meet his eyes, biting my bottom lip as my fingers flew across his screen. All I could think about was how he said the word *pleasure.*

"Nothing," he replied.

Wait. What did I miss? Two hours into working with him and I was already distracted.

Once it was synced, I handed the phone back to him, and it rang. He looked down and said with a frown, "Please excuse me. I need to take this."

Nodding, I stood up and walked out, shutting his door. I sat down at my desk and could see him pace the office through the frosted glass

Gah! While he was occupied, I grabbed my phone and quickly fired several texts to our group chat.

Annaleigh: MAYDAY MAYDAY!

Olivia: What happened, all okay?

Addison: ...

Annaleigh- BROODY MCASSHOLE is the new Senior VP!

Addison: This is GREAT NEWS!

Addison: Holy Shit!

Annaleigh: WHY IS THIS GREAT??

Olivia: What the hell?? Hot beach guy with the drool-worthy six pack and personality of a douchecanoe?

Addison: You were JUST saying how much he got under your skin… Now's your chance to get under him!

Annaleigh: NO NO NO NO NO!! HE IS MY BOSS!! My VERY distracting Boss!

Olivia: If that isn't the most fucking adorable thing EVER Anna!! This is the beginning of your love story!

Addison: Your very own dirty, sexy love story Annaleigh! Yes, sir.. I'll be glad to DICKtate that for you

Olivia: GIF of someone spitting out a drink

Annaleigh: GIF of head exploding

Addison: GIF of dancing eggplants

Addison: Right away, Sir, I'll be glad to CUM to your office.

Jenna: Sorry, dealing with an asshole cat. I agree with Adie. Go for it!

Annaleigh: GIF of cat filing middle finger

Olivia: I'm calling it. You are gonna screw each other senseless.

Annaleigh: YOU ARE NOT HELPING!

Jenna: We demand details when it happens. Explicit, graphic, dirty details.

Addison: YES!

Annaleigh: NO!

Jenna: YES!

Olivia: YES!

Annaleigh: DAMNIT. Y'all are NO HELP!

Olivia: GIF of dancing hearts
Addison: GIF of bunnies humping
Jenna: GIF of facepalm
Annaleigh: GIF of eye twitching

I shook my head and put my phone back in my top drawer before taking a bite of the lavender lemon scone from Olivia's bakery. *Wow, this was a great creation!*

Our department had a funding meeting next. I took notes but forgot to upload them and spent an hour trying to remember what happened. A half-hour later, I collated an expense report incorrectly and sent the same email twice. I had to get out of the office. I was so damn distracted. The man I had spent the last seventy-two hours obsessing over was here, in the flesh, and all I could think about was him saying he should have gone out with me that night.

I closed my laptop and grabbed my purse. I needed my happy place to regroup and reset. The fresh air helped, and I rolled down the windows of my Highlander and turned up the radio. I ordered lunch from a cafe close to the outdoor nursery and finished my sandwich before walking inside. I had already chosen plants for Max's office, but I spent time walking through the rows and rows of plants and flowers. I found a Tiger-Claw Aloe that would look great on my desk and matching pots for Max's plants.

I left feeling content, ready to finish the day with no mistakes. But the closer I got to the bank, the more nervous I was. I headed back upstairs and greeted Charlie, the security officer, and Elise. She gave me a knowing look as I tried to walk by her.

"And how are you enjoying the new Senior Vice President," Elise said, hoping for a juicy tidbit of information.

I put the plants down and smiled, taking out a double chocolate chip cookie from my purse and passing it to her.

"Hey Elise. He's adjusting well and will be an asset to the bank."

She smiled and opened the bag to take a bite.

"I don't think I would be able to concentrate with that Man-Candy sitting so close."

Elise leaned forward and wagged her eyebrows. I didn't answer but felt the color rising in my cheeks.

"I wouldn't mind getting under him if you know what I mean," she said with a wink. "You're blushing, Annaleigh. I can't imagine why."

I rolled my eyes and picked up the plants. Elise was married with two boys in college but enjoyed pushing my buttons, along with everyone else's.

"Elise, I'm not going to answer that. Mr. Jackson is my boss. How's Randy doing?"

"Screwing his secretary, thanks for asking. And thanks for the cookie Anna, you must have known I needed an afternoon sugar boost. By the way, here's the information for furnishing the new office," Elise said with a tight smile.

How the hell do you respond to that bombshell?

"Um, thank you. I sent you a meeting request for you to go over everything with him."

"No, that's okay. I'm sure the two of you can put your heads together to get his office done," Elise said, giving me a mischievous look.

She was always looking to cause issues.

"Get that idea out of your head," I said with a tight grin on my face, grinding my teeth. No way was I going to give her anything to gossip about now.

"I don't know what you mean," she said, smiling and taking another bite.

I didn't have time to play any more of her games, so I walked away and sat the plants by my desk. Needing an afternoon caffeine boost, I went into Jake's office to use the hot water on his coffee maker. I filled up my *Executive Assistant, Because Badass Miracle Worker Isn't An Official Job Title* mug, he got me for Christmas when the two of them walked in together.

"Hi Anna, good timing, let's go over details for the Whiskey Gala and Tennessee, please," Jake said, walking over to hand me an orange.

"Of course, I'll get my tablet. Would either of you like coffee or tea?"

"I'll take an Earl Grey please, Anna. Max?" Jake said, looking at Max.

"Coffee please, just cream," Max replied, the corner of his mouth ticking up. He met my eyes and smirked just enough to show one glorious dimple. *Yep, he was going to be a problem.*

"Not a tea drinker?" Jake said, not noticing my foot tapping nervously on the carpet.

Jake brought his coffee cup over and handed it to me. I busied myself making coffee for Max and tea for Jake and me, pretending I didn't feel Max's eyes on me.

"Never had a cup of tea I liked actually," Max said, taking off his glasses and cleaning them on his tie, again. *What was with that?* I made a note to pick up a lens cleaner and a lint cloth for him.

"Ah, well, if you ever want to venture to the dark side, ask Anna to make you a cup. She picks the best blends, and now, it's all I drink."

I smiled at Jake's compliment and plated everything before we began. We sat at his table, each taking a sip before I started, "Raymond sent me an email today asking to be moved to your table at the Gala. I said the table was full, so we need to adjust the seating chart."

"Good call, thanks. I'll see if we have any prospects to invite," Jake replied.

I nodded and made a note before continuing. "Great. Also, your tux will be ready Thursday. I sent it to the same place as Katie's dress so you can pick up both that afternoon. And remember, everyone needs a mask, and there's a cocktail hour before dinner. The car will be at your house at seven o'clock Saturday."

"Perfect, please plan on riding with us, Anna. You too, Max."

'Umm. I have a tux but not a mask," Max said, taking the extra cream from the table and adding what could only be described as an *obscene* amount to his coffee. He might as well be drinking milk.

"No worries, Max. I'll pick up several options for you this week." I clenched my thighs under the table, not able to shake the image of Max's lips wrapped around his coffee cup.

What was wrong with me?

"Thank you, Anna," he said, as his thigh lightly brushed mine.

When it did, a jolt of electricity shot up my leg like I'd been given an electric shock, and a shiver ran up my spine. I took a deep breath, taking in his spicy scent all over again while goosebumps pebbled my skin. His eyes narrowed, and he cleared his throat.

He felt it too, this desire. This pull. This spark. Didn't he?

Seven hours.

We had been around each other for seven hours. What would happen tomorrow? Next week? Next month? I'd spent half of today fantasizing about him and the other half worrying because I was fantasizing about him. His thick, muscular thigh brushed mine again as he listened intently to whatever Jake was talking about now.

Whatever Jake was talking about… *Shit!*

"....Atlas Hotel?" Jake finished, looking to me for a response that I didn't have because I wasn't listening.

It had taken close to three years for Jake and me to develop the working relationship we had. I could predict what he needed before he realized he needed it, and I could usually answer his questions before he asked them. Now, not only *did* I not have an answer, but I had no idea what he'd just said.

"So, a connecting suite," Max said, jogging my memory enough to jump back in before Jake was the wiser.

"Yes, you and Jake will have a two-room suite with a common living and conference area. I'll be on a floor below with our Retail, Credit Management, and Treasury partners. I'll spend most of the week in the shared conference space working remotely while everyone is attending lectures. Two evenings have scheduled events, and two are free. I'll have an updated itinerary as we get closer."

"Great. Thank you both," Jake said, standing up and adjusting his jacket. "I'm heading to pick up Caleb from baseball practice. See you both in the morning."

He patted his pockets, and I picked up his phone and handed it to him.

I stood up, smiling awkwardly at them both, and took my tea to my desk. Sitting down in a haze, I adjusted my new succulent and looked over my notes. I tried to gather my thoughts but was interrupted by a quiet throat clearing. Max was standing in front of my desk with his arms crossed.

"Thanks for that. My mind had drifted," I said, fanning myself with the tablet and wondering why I'd opted for hot tea instead of a cold-brew.

"Why?" He didn't try to fill the silence with unnecessary chatter. He merely waited for me.

"I don't know."

And I didn't. Something was happening to me—something I didn't understand and didn't like.

"I should have gone out with you that night," he said, with a voice so low I could barely hear him.

"And then what?" I said, looking down at my hands and talking just as soft. "We would have gone out? Danced? Kissed? Fucked? Imagine, just for a second, Max, if that had happened, and then gotten out here? I'd become the office slut overnight. I'm behind with my work already and so distracted. Today has been a disaster, and no matter how much I wish it could be different, it can't. So please, Max. Walk away."

A wave of exhaustion crashed over me, and I finally looked up with flushed cheeks and a sad smile. His pupils got dark, and he straightened his tie, taking a step away from me.

"Forget what I said. Consider it done. Don't disturb me for the remainder of the afternoon." His voice was cold and harsh, and he pushed up his glasses, walking to his office and taking a seat. His eyes met mine, those bourbon eyes unyielding until I looked away. I put in my air pods and got back to work, pretending what I said was what I wanted.

6

STARS IN THE SKY

Annaleigh

I contemplated not going into work all night, tossing and turning, before finally giving up and getting out of bed at three to make coffee. My nerves were shot. I prided myself on being good at several things. I had a kick-ass voice, moderate dance skills, and could make a damn good strawberry shortcake. But above all that, I was good at my job. I was great at my job. And Max made me so distracted I couldn't concentrate.

I'd almost thrown up Tuesday morning and only managed to choke down half a banana before I felt sick again. My shower didn't help, but I did manage to eat the rest of the banana before picking up Max's coffee with extra cream.

I sat behind my desk, pretending to work and tapping my heel nervously on the carpet. The office was quiet and empty when I'd shown up, and I was grateful for the solitude. I felt like such a failure yesterday. I was unprofessional and allowed my emotions to get the better of me. And today wasn't shaping up to be any better. I exhaled and adjusted my necklace. Each time I heard the elevator ding, I turned around to glance toward the lobby.

I couldn't decide what was worse, hoping that he had quit or hoping he would show up with a smile.

But by eight-thirty, Max hadn't shown up. I tried not to worry and made three circuits around the office to water the plants and peek out the window before I gave up and sent him a text.

Annaleigh: Your coffee will be cold by the time you get here.
Max: Good Morning to you too.
Annaleigh: Will you make the 10am call?
Max: Yes. I'm in line at the DMV.
Annaleigh: Unless you're close to the front of the line, leave and go back Thursday. You're more likely to get in then. I can download the change of address forms ahead of time.
Max: Thanks. Wish I had known that yesterday. Leaving now, be there in 30.

I dropped my phone on my desk and smoothed my hair. *Thirty minutes.* I had thirty minutes to get my life together.

Twenty-eight minutes later, I heard the elevator ding. Max walked through the office all confident in a navy pinstripe suit and matching vest. His dark brown hair was artfully messy, giving him a casual but professional look. I'd bet my right kidney he spent a half-hour in front of the mirror perfecting it. Maybe that was the real reason he was late, and the DMV was just an excuse.

Max walked by me with a curt nod, not even saying good morning. He stonewalled me. I get it, we had a less than perfect start, and he was keeping me at arm's length. Why would he do anything different? I told him to walk away. It was for the best.

When I got to the office Wednesday, Max was waiting with a smile and an orange. He looked stylish and handsome in a black suit and blue vest. His mood swings were giving me whiplash, but I returned his smile and sat down.

"Thanks again for saving hours of my life yesterday. Here, someone told me these are your favorite. Consider it a peace offering for my attitude," he said, passing me an orange.

I smiled and opened my desk drawer, taking out one I had left yesterday. He shook his head and rubbed the back of his neck, clearly unsure of what to say. I reached out and took his, tossing mine back in the still-open drawer.

"Yours looks tastier. Thank you, Max. And here," I said, taking a handkerchief from my desk drawer. "This will work better than your tie."

He looked at the handkerchief and then back to me. I stood up, walked around to him, folded it into a triangle, and tucked it in his front jacket pocket. Max tracked the movement with his eyes and put his hand over mine.

"Thank you," he said, removing his hand.

He gave me a tight smile and cleared his throat, turning around and walking into his office. I sat back down and peeled the orange, confused as hell.

Max: Reminder for tomorrow. I'll be at the DMV first thing.
Annaleigh: Noted. See you shortly.
Max: I heard a song this morning and thought of you. Blue by Beyonce. Have you listened to the lyrics?
Annaleigh: Didn't take you for a Beyonce kinda guy. Will give it a listen.

I put in my air pods, downloaded the song, closed my eyes for a minute, and listened to the lyrics. Before Queen B even got to the chorus, my heart was racing.

Annaleigh: I enjoyed the song. Have you heard Complicated by Fitz and The Tantrums?

Max: I'll give it a listen.

Annaleigh: I came back from lunch to find a beautiful blue planter for my Tiger-Aloe. Any idea who I should thank? My Tiger Aloe is happy. So am I. Meetings scheduled, calendar updates to follow. New song for you, You Can't Always Get What You Want by The Rolling Stones.

Max: Glad you like the planter, no idea who you should thank. I prefer Crossfire by Brandon Flowers. Out of the office this afternoon and early meeting tomorrow. Will be in late. Please have a Nitro cold brew with extra cream ready for me at 10:00 am.

I attempted to distract myself after he left that afternoon by answering a few emails, but my attention span was nonexistent. I pinched the bridge of my nose and sighed, picking up another orange to peel and ignoring a notification on my phone to call my doctor and schedule bloodwork. For the first time in I don't know how many years, I was ready for the week to end.

7

YOUR AESTHETICS

Max

After infinite distractions later, my concentration was nonexistent. I'd spent this last week irritated and blankly staring at my portfolio, only thinking about her. Today and tomorrow, I had to be productive. Jake and I had conference calls all morning and two meetings with clients that would take me out for most of the afternoon. Tomorrow should be a breeze and give me time to get my head on straight before the Whiskey Gala Saturday.

Blue. Anna. Annaleigh: I loved saying her full name, letting the syllables roll off my tongue. I loved texting her, knowing that smart mouth would put me in my place with a quick-witted, sarcastic comment or a very subtle innuendo—and the flirting, the presents, the skirts. And I couldn't let go of the fact that I'd never been drawn to someone as much as I was to her.

But at the same time, I was damn pissed that work didn't have my full attention. It was her fault. I went between ignoring her to not being able to keep my eyes off her. It was maddening.

I ran my fingers through my hair while I stood under the hot shower, willing myself to not think about the way she nibbled on her bottom lip when she concentrated, or the delicate curve of her neck when she pushed her blonde hair over her shoulders. Or those damnable back-seamed thigh highs.

Shaking my head, I gave in, angrily gripping my cock. My thumb brushed over the swollen tip, and I stroked down hard. Bracing one hand on the shower wall, I moved my hand faster, knowing this was going to be quick and rough.

I closed my eyes, and there she was, under my desk with her knees spread and a red-painted finger held to her lips. She bent forward to unzip my pants, and I got a teasing peek at her cleavage. My eyes squeezed harder, imagining her taking my cock to the back of her throat in one smooth, wet motion. My hand moved faster, tightening the grip to the point of pain, almost hearing the sexy little moans she would make while bobbing up and down. I would thread my fingers through her hair and pull, urging her to go deeper. And she would.

Her tongue would lap and swirl over the head, and I mimicked the motion with my thumb, stroking harder, faster, right to the edge. My balls went tight, and I ground my teeth, groaning her name loudly until hot, sticky ropes of come coated the shower wall. My hand slowed down as I squeezed out every drop of pleasure.

I dropped my shoulders under the hot spray and breathed deep, fucking my hand would never be as good as feeling her under me, on top, on her knees, on my desk, or in my bed.

Goddamnit! I rolled my shoulders and turned off the spray, stepping out and wrapping a towel around my waist. My phone was still charging, and I picked it up when I heard it vibrate, running a hand through my damp hair. There was a text from Warren that I missed last night, and a text from *her* with several reminders. I replied to Warren, saying I'd call him later before focusing on what had my attention.

Blue: Reminders synced to your calendar, coffee with extra cream?
Max: Yes, thanks Blue.
Blue: Annaleigh at work, please.

Max: Blue suits you.

Blue: You're going to be the reason I drink today, aren't you?

Max: Then should I bring the coffee?

Blue: I got it, but do you want to explain that nickname to Jake or ELISE?

Max: Fair point, but we're not there, are we?

Blue: Touché. See you at work. I'll be the one in blue.

With that one sassy remark, my frustration turned to irritation, then anger. She was trying to be professional by insisting I call her Annaleigh but threw in the blue comment like a tease. I finally had the catalyst to move from Chicago, and this distraction could not jeopardize my job. But regardless of how angry I was with my inability to focus, the flirty banter bullshit was proving to be the highlight of my day.

When I tore myself away from the fantasies and made it to work, I rushed up the stairs, pretending I didn't see her silhouette in Jake's office and shut my door.

Annaleigh walked in a little later with a coffee while I held up a picture, trying to figure out where to hang it, oblivious to the pull she had, which pissed me off even more. She didn't knock, just swept into my life like she had always belonged there.

"Good morning, Max. Why not center it over there? If you plan on keeping the table, it will draw the eye, especially if the frame is the same shade as the table. Here," she said, walking over to show me and placing a mug on my desk.

There was a noise I couldn't place. It took me a second to realize she was humming quietly, unconsciously, like there was a song playing in the background of her mind.

Pushing the sappy thought from my head, I saw she had brought me coffee in my mug. That coffee mug was a present from Warren and said, *MBA...When Your BS Can't Take You Any Further.* She took it upon herself to come into my office and get my favorite mug. It was thoughtful, sweet, and something she had done every day. And that small gesture, for some reason, had me furious.

I couldn't explain it, but the need to lash out at her was overwhelming. I felt like if I didn't push her away, I would pull her into my arms and drown myself in her blonde hair and citrus scent.

"What do you think, Max?" she said, turning to me with a smile. A smile that lit up her face and made her jade eyes sparkle.

"Why don't you just do the rest of it?"

"I'll be glad to sit with you and Elise."

"Why don't you just do it? I don't have time to worry about petty decorating."

"Petty decorating?" She shook her head and crossed her arms, taking a step back and looking at me. Her posture stiffened like she was ready for whatever I was going to say. *Good.* If she hated me, I wouldn't be tempted to spend my days working to see her smile.

"Yes. Did I stutter, Annaleigh?" I purposely spit out her name, pushing the coffee to the end of my desk.

"Excuse me?" Her eyes bored into mine before she rolled them, stepping forward like she was up to the challenge of calling me out for being an asshole. Maybe I was, but her hold over me was infuriating.

"You're the assistant, right, so assist and handle it." *Yep, I was an asshole.*

"Why don't you keep the dumbfuckery to a minimum today and focus on your job and not lame attempts to pick a fight, Maxwell."

She stressed my full name, and damn if it didn't turn me on. And I was sure she used another immature word just to goat me.

"Dumbfuckery?" I narrowed my eyes.

"Did I stutter? I'm sorry, Max, you seem to have mistaken me for a woman who will take your shit."

"You could have just said yes. There was no need to release the flying monkeys. You are my assistant."

I stressed the word assistant, and she put one hand on her hip, not chair. Without her heels, she only came up to my shoulders and looked like she would fit perfectly in the crook of my arm.

"Trying to get rid of me already?" I said, stepping to the side and cuffing my sleeves.

I took off my glasses and pulled my tie from the vest, cleaning them. She tracked the movement, and one corner of her mouth ticked up. Bending down, she opened my bottom desk drawer, took out another handkerchief, and handed it to me. I looked at it, then her, before tucking my tie back in my vest and taking it.

"Not likely," she said, smiling as I tucked the handkerchief in my pocket, "I need to switch out your docking station and plug everything in, and I'm not bending down here with you standing next to me."

Bend down? Bend down? Christ, she was going to crawl under my desk in a skirt. Visions of this morning popped before my eyes, making me curse quietly and move towards her, despicably hoping for a peek.

"I'll be glad to..."

"No, I don't want to risk you scuffing those Ferragamo's, excellent choice in shoes, by the way. And love the vest."

She bent down and got to work. I stood back and watched, useless. I needed to keep arguing, needed to stop glancing down at her, needed to buy a thousand more vests, so she kept looking at me like she had, and I needed to lock myself in the bathroom and take care of this persistent hard-on.

"Max, ready for our call?" Jake said, walking in just as Annaleigh popped out from under my desk like a sexy as hell jack-in-the-box. A wisp of hair came free from her bun, and I wanted to reach out and brush it behind her ear.

"Jake, I'm going to finish setting everything up here. Am I good to sit this one out?"

"That's fine, no new business, just more introductions," Jake replied, looking to her on her knees and back to me. I took another step back, keeping my eyes anywhere but on her.

"Thank you for your help, Annaleigh," I said, meeting her eyes as I followed Jake out of the room.

"You're welcome, Max. I'll have your mask choices when you get back. Oh, and Jake, I picked up a new one for you. The one you had doesn't match Katie's."

"We can't have that, can we? Thank you," Jake said, smiling and walking out. He motioned for me to follow. I looked back one more time, but Anna was already looking away, setting up something underneath my desk.

The call was a welcome distraction, and an hour later, she walked back in with a box, removing the tissue paper to show me four masks. One was gold with black, covering close to half of the right side of my face, very *Phantom of the Opera*, and a silver mask, barely covering my eyes that tied with a black ribbon. There was also a wide black metal filigree mask with dark gray detailing, and another one colored a deep metallic navy with detailed silver fleur-de-lis' on it.

All four were great finds. I wondered if she had a secret mask connection within the city, meeting someone in a back alley at three o'clock in the morning for the deal to go down. My eyes moved back to the gold and black design.

"I agree," she said, following my eyes and not missing a detail. I could see why Jake speaks so highly of her—her ability to read people was second nature. Or maybe that was just her ability to read me.

"Pair this one with gold cufflinks. You'll also be able to wear your glasses comfortably." *Wow*, I couldn't believe she took my glasses into account.

"Great options, Annaleigh."

"Thanks, Max. My back-alley mask connections always come through before events."

She winked and ran her hand over the black ribbon of one mask. I guess we were back on a level playing field.

Wait. What? Her back-alley connections? She was too far in my head, creeping into my brain like my favorite song on repeat.

"Damn," I said, touching the buttons where my cufflinks would normally be.

"What?"

"My gold cufflinks, I didn't bring them with me."

I knew exactly where they were, still in my top dresser drawer back in Chicago, or maybe at the bottom of Lake Michigan by now. I'd almost prefer Lake Michigan. I'm pretty sure those were a gift.

"Can someone overnight them for you?"

"No, absolutely not. Not worth the trouble," I said.

Her eyebrows drew together, and I sighed, knowing this would come out eventually—the fewer words, the better when it came to my past.

"The cufflinks are residing in my old house, with my ex, who I have no desire to speak to, ever."

"Ah, I see. In that case, I'll pick up new ones for you before Saturday."

"That's unnecessary, Annaleigh," I said, taking off my glasses and reaching for the handkerchief.

"Max, this is my job. I'll be happy to pick some up. Is there anything else you are missing?"

"Um, well, yes, but personal errands are not part of your job description."

"They are, actually. I assist with anything that makes your life easier. I won't even go into everything I've done for Jake these last few years. What else do you need?"

She said that last part with a reassuring smile, letting me know she didn't mind.

I'd doubt she'd be smiling if she knew the dirty thoughts going through my head on all the ways she could make my life easier. Starting with relieving the pressure in my cock.

"I need dress socks. My washer and dryer were just delivered, and I haven't hooked them up. And where did you get the Chinese evergreen? I'd like another for the opposite corner over there," I pointed, and she followed my finger to the empty space in the office.

"There's a nursery close to my house with a great selection. I'll take care of everything. What's your shoe size, and do you prefer a particular brand?" she asked, pulling her phone out to take notes.

"No, and twelve," I said, glancing at my computer and seeing it was time to leave for my meeting.

"Of course, they're a twelve," I heard her quietly say under her breath.

I should let it go. I shouldn't instigate, but once again, my body seemed to outwit my mind. "What was that?"

"Oh, nothing I should have said out loud. I'm sorry, Max. Honestly, I'm still distracted."

"Why? You still haven't told me why, Blue."

"Max, you know why."

"Do I? Tell me."

It was a command, a plea on my lips. I was back to my basic instincts, needing her words like oxygen. I wanted to crowd her space, tangle my fingers in her hair, and make her yield, make her mine.

"The only way to get rid of a temptation is to yield to it, Blue."

"No, Max. Don't do that. Don't use someone else's words."

Once again, she called me on my bullshit, this time picking up I was quoting Oscar Wilde. Damn this woman.

"Aren't you tired of this? The back and forth, the bickering?" I said, moving closer.

"How do you expect me to answer that? Nothing has changed, Max. You're my boss."

"But what if I wasn't?"

Her mouth opened to respond, but I stepped back and held my hands up, not wanting to hear her justification. I got it. *I did.* But some unexpected force kept pulling me to her. I'd never ask her to break the rules or compromise her job, but I also couldn't pretend that I wasn't attracted to her. I couldn't pretend that I didn't want more.

I put distance between us and crossed my arms. With a shake of her

Max and me.

"I'm glad you stopped by again, Annaleigh," he said, pushing the envelope closer. I shook my head and pushed it back.

"Of course," I said. The burger hit the spot, and we said our goodbyes shortly after, somewhat successfully giving me the distraction I needed.

Their words about Bird and music stayed with me for the rest of the day and when I took Baxter for his evening walk. I did my best not to think about Max, relieved he was out of the office for most of the afternoon. The trees swayed with the summer breeze, and the streetlights were just starting to come on when I got back to my townhouse.

I needed to check on my succulent garden and strawberries on the terrace, but Baxter had a hard time climbing up the spiral staircase. I'd have to bribe him with bacon so he wouldn't whine, but for now, I poured a glass of red wine and sat on the porch outside the master bedroom.

What Uncle Bob and Alex said made sense. I wanted to give Bird a call but had a feeling if I did, we'd be up late, and not even a latte from Olivia's bakery would be able to keep me alert.

Something needled in the back of my mind about Max. He'd gotten more under my skin than any guy had before, which was stupid since we'd just met. I had an overwhelming desire to call him just to talk but pushed the thought away and poured another glass of wine.

- *9* -

IGNITE MY FIRE
Max

As unhappy as I used to be, I remember when life was simpler. I'd wake up, go for a run, put in a solid ten hours at the office, go to whatever event was planned, and go to sleep. I didn't worry about anything but my family, my job, and myself. I wasn't happy, but everything was predictable. Structured. Organized.

But since Annaleigh Mackey entered the picture, my life had been turned upside-down. Each day was an unending exercise in self-control. I never knew what she would do to piss me off or turn me on. *I was a walking contradiction.*

After my afternoon meeting ran late, I got back to the bank and took the stairs two at a time to finish my day with no interruptions. I walked around the corner in the all but empty office, when a whiny voice cut through the silence. The voice was high and squeaky, sounding like nails on a chalkboard. I deliberately tuned it out until I heard the words, "... uncooperative bitch."

Stopping in my tracks, I glanced up and saw Raymond sitting in his office with someone else. He looked irate and slammed his fist on his desk and pointed his finger at the person with him. His whole face an angry shade of red. Staying out of view, I held my breath and listened.

"She'll fall in line," Raymond said, like someone with a serious vendetta. "Once I pressure the board to vote Jake out, she'll thank you for the opportunity."

"On her knees," the squeaky voice replied.

Who the hell was this prick? I slowly inched closer, straining to hear the conversion to see who the fuck they were discussing.

"Quiet, idiot. You never know who's still here. I have it on good authority that she fucked her way through the club. Are you sure she's even worth your time?"

What the hell? Were they talking about Annaleigh? Or someone else—either way, unacceptable.

"Annaleigh said no. No one says no," the voice replied.

"Just like your dad, Benjamin. Pack it up, time to head out," Raymond said with a dismissing wave. He stood up and tramped to the back staircase, practically closing his office door in his son's face.

So, this was the creep Benjamin who thought he'd get my job, that undeserving weasel. My fingernails dug into my palms, and anger coiled hot in my gut like a blinding inferno. I purposely moved into his line of sight, daring him to look my way.

Benjamin walked with his shoulders hunched, beady eyes meeting mine, then darting away. I strode up to him, glaring, and bumped his shoulder hard enough to make him stumble.

"What the hell, man?" he said, shaking his head and trying to walk around me to the backdoor. Sweat beaded across his forehead, and he pressed his back to the wall as he tried to slide by me. I had a good couple of inches and twenty pounds on him. It wouldn't have mattered if it was the other way around because no one talks about my girl that way. No one.

Wait. My girl? Christ.

Growling through my teeth, I squared my stance and met his squinty eyes, "I don't believe we've met. My name's Maxwell Jackson. And make no mistake, I will end you if I ever see you near her."

I didn't yell or raise my voice. I only growled the words out, making him turn toward me to hear the threat. *Yes, a threat.* This punk was used to riding his daddy's coattails and being all too familiar with that—it was going to stop here.

"Whatever, I don't know what you're talking about." He tried to push away but slipped on the carpet. I grabbed a fistful of his shirt to keep him from falling on his miserable face.

I tightened my grip and leaned in closer. "Yeah, you do. From now on, you don't even think the name Annaleigh."

"Or what?" He bowed out his chest in a feeble attempt at intimidation.

"Or this." I drew my fist back and popped him in the jaw with just enough force to make his head bounce off the wall. It wasn't a haymaker, but it gave me significant gratification to watch the blood drip down his split lip. I let go and stepped back, adjusting my tie and giving him space to wipe his lip.

Dick move? Absolutely. But this guy filled me with rage, blatantly talking about taking advantage of women like it was common practice.

"You'll pay for that!" Benjamin raised his voice, eyes darting around as if someone was going to come running out to back him up. He didn't know I watched his piece of shit father walk away and was confident no one else was here. He attempted to smooth his hands over the wrinkles in his shirt but only smeared the blood.

"This isn't over, Jackson, just wait till…"

"Your father hears about this," I interrupted with a condescending smile. Just like a spoiled, rich kid running back to daddy to fix his issues.

"Exactly. Watch your back," he said, looking at me and wiping his lip again.

"And you remember what I said." Not waiting for a response, I shoulder-checked him and left him bleeding in the hallway.

It was easy to figure out his end game, but what part did Annaleigh play in his sick chess match? I didn't want to believe what he said about her and sleeping around, but why would he make it up?

There was no way I could concentrate after that, so I packed up my laptop and left the way I came. I sat in my car and swallowed down the irritation bubbling in my stomach, wondering why the hell I was so concerned with their conversation. Home was not where I wanted to be, so I pulled out and veered to the left, pulling into a bar called *Cooper Dog Ale House* a short while later. My knuckles throbbed and were split, but I didn't care as long as Benjamin got the message. I was tempted to check out that bar Blue mentioned, but with the way my luck was going right now, I'd run into her.

Since Warren was planning a visit in a few weeks, I looked up *B's Bar* the other night and saw it was a local's favorite. If you were in a band and need practice space, you could go during the day. It sounded like a spot I would love, and a place Warren would want to check out.

But tonight, I settled for *Cooper's*, getting out of my truck and walking across the parking lot. When I stepped in, my nose was assaulted with the delicious smell of fried food. I took a seat at the bar and ordered a draft and sandwich. Peanut shells littered the floor, and vintage license plates hung on the wall, giving the dive bar character. The bartender sat a bowl of nuts in front of me with the draft, and I took a long pull of the bitter porter, scanning the people.

My eyes fell on a tall blonde with short cut-offs and a pink tank top. Her hair was in a high ponytail, and I could see her red lips from my seat. She was hot, but I felt... nothing, not a speck of interest. I squeezed my eyes shut and downed the rest of the beer. When my sandwich arrived, I signaled for another draft and took a bite, not having an appetite but needing to keep my hands busy, so I wouldn't text *her*.

I wasn't sure if I was up for drowning my troubles, but before I could decide, I saw the blonde leaning over the bar, putting her tits on display. I got an eye-full, but again my cock took no notice. He was too hung up on Blue. Like me.

"Hey, Sugar. Why don't I sit down here so you can buy me a drink?"

She had a sweet, thick southern accent and dark eyes, exactly the type to help me out of this funk.

"You look upset. Want to tell me why?" I glanced behind me as she traced her fingers up my arm. There was a massive guy by the pool tables glaring with his arms crossed. He cracked his knuckles and stared harder. My body was itching for a fight, looking for a way to burn off this adrenaline, but I wasn't about to walk into that hornets' nest.

There were two other guys just as wide, flanking him, waiting to see what happened next. I could hold my own and would have had no problem dropping one, maybe two, but there was no way I could take all three. I didn't have a death wish, no matter how shitty I felt.

"Not looking for company tonight. But it seems like someone back there is." I tilted my head in the guy's direction, and she nervously looked over, not removing her hand.

"You sure you can't help me make him jealous, Sugar?" She leaned over further, tilting her head and running her tongue over her lips.

"Maybe another time." I didn't meet her eyes, focusing on my sandwich.

"Your loss," she said, shrugging her shoulders and walking back to the pool tables. The big guy followed her the whole time. I finished my draft and paid the tab, walking out to see the blonde standing with the pool-table guy. At least I had made one right decision today.

As I drove home, my mother's name flashed across the caller ID, but I hit ignore and pulled into my garage. I needed time out of my head, time away from the constant push-pull desire I felt for Blue. I headed up to the roof with my tools and wood, relying on the muscle memory to push the thoughts of her away.

The next morning, I arrived at the office with the intention of telling Annaleigh not to disturb me. You'd think I would have this crush under control since I spent every morning jerking off, but no. If anything, the constant fantasies had my lust that much stronger. All it took was the smell of oranges, and I was running to my ensuite like a fucking teenager with his first hard-on.

Taking the elevator, I breathed deep, trying to regain some control—any control. I walked into my office, ready to draw a line in the sand, and rubbed my hand across my face. Fuck, I'd forgotten to shave. Thinking about Blue was becoming an obsession, and it had to stop. I could hear her heels clicking next door, so I schooled my features and walked into Jake's office. No more distractions.

"Annaleigh, today," I said, with a firm direct voice, deliberately not noticing the way her skirt hugged her legs. Her hips were moving slowly with whatever she was listening to, but before my dick could take notice, she shrieked and yanked out her air pods, spilling scalding water all over her blue blouse.

"Holy shit! Hot! Hot! Ouch! What the heck, Max?" she yelled, dropping a coffee mug to the floor and fanning herself.

Her cheeks were flushed, and her chest was red where the hot water splashed. Beads of water trailed down her neck and between her breasts, disappearing down the valley of her shirt. My eyes were drawn to the water clinging to her top and the thin white-lace bra I could see peeking through the wet fabric. I was speechless, my throat tight and dry, while I took in the sight of her wet body. I swallowed harshly and stepped over to her quickly.

"God, I'm sorry! Here," I said, grabbing a towel from beside the coffee station and moving closer to blot her blouse. I reached out, but when I pressed the towel to her chest, she grabbed it from my hand and held it to her neck, sopping up the hot water while hopping from foot to foot. A stream of quiet profanities spilled from her red lips, and I wasn't ashamed to admit the filthy words were a turn-on. I stood stock-still, completely unhelpful, staring as her round, pert, dark-pink nipples stood out against the wet material. Her chest rose, and I could see her pulse fluttering in her neck. My cock strained against my zipper, struggling to get closer to her.

"Max," she mumbled, eyes not quite meeting mine.

"Max!" She repeated my name louder, but I couldn't tear myself away from the site of her wet skin. But it wasn't just her body that had me in a trance. It was how she carried herself around the office, how she radiated warmth, and how she made me want to shift focus and give in to the distraction. No matter what I kept telling myself, I wanted to give in.

"Max!"

"What can I do? I'm sorry, Annaleigh." I apologized again and met her eyes, hoping she was too caught up with the hot water to notice my blatant staring.

"Take your eyes off my tits and go back to your office. Now."

At the mention of her tits, my eyes drifted down again. Not chest, breasts, or boobs, but tits. How that word rolled off her tongue made me want to bury my face in them and feast like a starving man, licking and sucking every exposed inch.

"Maxwell! Out! Now!"

Dammit, she full named me and stomped one red heel down on the carpet to drive her point home.

Knowing there was nothing I could do to dig myself in further, I kept my eyes on hers and pressed an open palm to my zipper, adjusting myself. Her eyes drifted down. She unconsciously sucked her bottom lip between white teeth, but I turned around, not looking back, walked into my office, and shut the door.

I paced back and forth in front of the windows and ran my fingers through my hair. Mature. Real mature. I was angry at myself, mad at the situation, and pissed that the first woman that had held my interest in god knows how long was off-limits. So off-limits. Unattainable. So out of my league. She was too good to get involved with a thirty-year-old idiot with trust issues.

My mind was on a continuous loop: passion, anger, desire, frustration, and need, clouded my thoughts. Minutes passed as I tried to get my anger and cock, under control.

My train of thought crashed at the station when I heard a light knock at my door. With a sigh, I said, "Come in."

She walked in with red splotches on her neck, wearing a new blouse. I wanted to fill the silence, apologize, and pull her into my arms, easing her burned skin with my tongue. I stood behind my desk as she came closer, invading my space. Something was keeping me from pushing her away, and I closed the distance between us.

"Let me apologize again. I didn't realize you couldn't hear me. Are you okay? Are you burned?" I was genuinely concerned, knowing I caused the marks that now dotted her delicate skin.

"I'm fine, really. The redness is already going down." She pulled her hair to the side, giving me a view of her delectable pink neck.

"Stop looking at me like that," she said, glancing at her feet before meeting my eyes.

"Like what?"

"Like you're a lion stalking me. Max, we can't. Please, just tell me you have a weird armpit fetish or foot fungus or that you're into pony-play. Something. Anything."

She braced her hands on my desk and waited for my next words. I should stop this here, end this dance, but I physically couldn't. Whatever my reasons for staying away from this temptress evaporated. It was time to draw a line in the sand, to show her the power she held.

"I despise doing the dishes and like to use all the hot water in the shower," I said, breathing in the sweet citrus scent. She smelled like oranges and spearmint: sweet, delicious, mouthwatering. I would not back down. It was time to own the words.

"But since I saw you in that blue bikini, you're all I think about. I haven't done one productive thing since I started here except fantasize about touching you, possessing you. Annaleigh."

I stepped closer and ran my fingertips from her neck down her arm. Goosebumps appeared where I traced my fingers, and she moved into my touch, closing her eyes. I watched her pulse flutter and wanted to trace my tongue along that curve.

"More, Max." If I hadn't been so close, I wouldn't have heard her. But I did, and with those words, I gripped her waist and pulled her to me.

Feeling her breath against my chest, I bent down to her ear, letting my tongue taste the delicate lobe. Goddamnit, if her whole body tasted like this, I'd never be able to stop. I drew it between my teeth before letting go and blowing. Her eyes were heavy-lidded, waiting for my next words.

"I want to trace my tongue down your neck, biting and licking until my mouth lands between those sweet tits. I want to bite your nipple, hard, sucking it between my teeth while palming the other through that sexy white bra you're wearing."

She let out the softest moan, so much better than what I'd imagined. I wanted all her moans, wanted to hear her sigh my name, then scream it. I longed to see her out of control and lost in the heat of the moment. She leaned into my chest and ran her nails up my shoulders, scraping the skin. I saw the faint outline of her nipples through her dry blouse and almost lost my mind right there.

"I want you on my desk, legs spread, and skirt bunched at your waist while I move my hands up your thighs to see how wet your panties are. They would be soaked, right? See-through and practically dripping down your legs, desperate for my fingers, my tongue, my cock. I would give you everything, Blue, all of me. I'd make your knees weak from coming over and over again, burying my face in your pussy before filling you with my thick cock, again and again."

My tongue moved from her earlobe to the tendon where her neck met her shoulder. I bit down before soothing the sting with a lick and moved my hand underneath her blouse to stroke the smooth skin on her waist.

"God. Yes. There," she said, breathless, sexy.

There were millimeters separating us, yet she pushed herself closer, closing her eyes and tilting her neck to give me better access to her sweet skin.

"He's not here, Blue. You say *my* name."

"Max. Yes."

Her nose nuzzled my neck, and she licked my Adam's apple and spread her legs apart enough for me to put my knee between them, feeling the satin heat I craved through my slacks. She ground against my leg, whimpering with the sensation.

"Tell me to stop, Blue. Give me a reason *not* to taste you right now. Baby, I need to feel you. I need to feel more. I don't want to fight this anymore."

I continued to lick along her collarbone, pulling her blouse aside and teasing her, breathing her in. This was pointless to resist. I needed her—needed to see if the rest of her tasted just as sweet. This wasn't a casual fling. She wasn't someone I would be able to move on from the next morning. This woman was going to ruin me, and I was going to let her.

10

YOUR ENTICING CARESS

Annaleigh

T he truth of what was happening seeped in as I squeezed my thighs against him harder, desperate to relieve the tension growing in my core. Big Dick Energy was right. Max was packing some serious heat. And that heat was currently throbbing against my stomach. His hands worked their magic over my skin, and I used mine to pull his hair while his teeth grazed my shoulder, leaving a trail of sultry wetness behind.

I rocked my core on his thigh, and as he took control, a deep throaty growl spilled from his lips. I suddenly needed him to make those noises against my neck, my stomach, and my thighs. I wanted to feel the vibration all over my body. I craved more skin, needed to run my nails over his abs and lick his chest.

"This isn't supposed to happen," I said, still rocking against his thigh. His large hands gripped my waist and guided me back and forth. I was so close. So close to coming undone for him.

"Then what do we do?" he replied against my neck, licking the skin.

He didn't wait for me to respond, just gripped my waist harder, sliding one hand further under my blouse and dimpling the skin. His fingers toyed with the waistband of my skirt, dipping further underneath and brushing my panties.

If this was what it was like to be his, sign me up.

Right. The. Fuck. Now.

I was ready to lie down and spread myself open for his pleasure.

Max wanted me. Why, and for how long, I wasn't sure, but I could feel the restraint vibrating through his body. I wanted to see him lose control, wanted to feel his raw power consume me.

Everywhere his fingers touched was like an electric current, tingling each nerve ending and making my nipples ache. I arched into him and pulled him closer so I could tease them against his vest. He brought his hands up higher and stroked the underside of my bra, making them heavy with need.

"Tell me," he said, panting. "Blue, let me hear you."

I needed his lips, needed his fingers, needed his touch, needed his everything. I couldn't form a coherent sentence, so I nodded and teased my lips and nose against his neck while working his shirt loose from the confines of his slacks.

"Tired of fighting this, Max. So close. Make me come."

Both of his hands gripped my ass, and he helped me ride his thigh. He thrusted against me and guided my hips, groaning every time his cock brushed my stomach. My legs were turning to jelly as a delicious tingling feeling started to build in my core. My thong was so wet it had slipped between my swollen, tender flesh, making the friction against my clit that much sweeter.

"That's it, Blue. Ride me, give it up. Give me everything, baby."

I brushed my lips along his neck, tasting salt and sandalwood. His five o'clock shadow was rough against my skin. Those long fingers moved from my hips and traced the outside of my breasts, moving closer and closer to where I needed them. His tongue continued to dart along my neck. Stony plains met soft curves. These layers of clothes were getting in the way of feeling his skin on mine.

"I'm going to bury my face between your legs and lick you till your knees quake. I'm going to ruin you, Annaleigh, ruin you for anyone else. I want you to be mine, and I'm done waiting."

I was there, my toes were tingling, and I brought my lips closer to his, ready to give in, desperate to taste his mouth and feel his hot tongue stroke mine as I come.

I craved his lips like a drug, and when our lips were millimeters apart, a shrill alarm filled the air, breaking the moment. I jumped with the noise, putting both hands on his chest and taking a step back. I was throbbing and frustrated, ready to throw his phone across the room and pick up where we were. He leaned in and pressed his forehead to mine, closing his eyes. Letting go, he pushed his hand against his cock, trying to relieve the pressure. If it was anything like what I was feeling, it wouldn't be relieved until he was buried to the hilt inside me.

Max rubbed the back of his neck and moved with his head down towards the desk to stop the inconvenient noise. I stood there, not moving and trying to slow my pulse. There was a very distinct wet spot on his slacks, but I wasn't embarrassed. If anything, I wanted him to look down and see how wet he had made me. Have him see how wet I still was for him, for this.

It was so easy to give in to this, so easy to be his, so easy to want. My body was slick with sweat, and I moved closer to run my fingers back up his vest. He grasped my hand and trailed light kisses over each knuckle, eyes lidded and heavy with lust.

Complicated? Yes. Worth it? Yes. Willing to risk it? Yes.

He looked at me with his bourbon eyes blazing. Whether it was to lock the door, finish what we started, or admit this was a mistake was yet to be determined. If he stopped now, I would most definitely have to lock myself in his private bathroom to take the edge off this sexual tension.

"I have a meeting," he said, refusing to meet my eyes as if he was ashamed of what had happened.

Was this his way of getting over his ex? Was I just a fling to forget? I couldn't be. He felt this pull, this connection, this heat. *Didn't he?*

I stepped back between his legs and fisted his vest between my fingers, bringing my hand up to grip his neck so he would look down and meet my eyes. I'd been twisted and tongue-tied around him since that day at the beach, both of us orbiting around each other about to collide. Whatever this was, he would not make me feel guilty, and he was not going to act like nothing happened. If anything, I would tell him exactly what he did to me and that I wanted to lock the door and finish this. *Now.*

"You do not get to talk to me like that, and touch me like that, then look at me like this was a mistake. It doesn't work that way, Max. I had never even considered getting involved with someone I work with, but now, at this moment, I'm ready to jump in headfirst, for whatever this is. I'm not used to feeling like this, so out of control, so unsure, but I was willing to risk it!"

I fisted his vest harder and could see him grinding his teeth. His eyes were like bourbon ice chips, and I swear one eye was twitching as he mulled over my words. But I wasn't done, I was close enough to feel his hard-on, and I moved one hand down and gave it a hard squeeze. Max hissed and thrust into my hand, making me grip him harder.

"I was ready to drop to my knees and relieve that indecision on your face, Max. I wanted to grip your ass and suck your cock while your fingers pulled my hair. But you will not look at me with regret or look at me like this was a mistake."

I let go and pushed back on his chest; harder than I meant to, but what else was new? I'd been a mess since he started at JMS, a complete one-eighty from my usual self.

Max had left me disoriented, confused, exhausted, and so, so turned on. I wanted him so damn much, but if I'd been this up and down in such a short time, what would happen if we had a falling out? Maybe his alarm going off was a sign. A sign that an office fling was out of the question. A sign showing me that we couldn't pursue this, but we shouldn't regret it.

This was best. Right?

"Fuck, Blue, that's hot. You're in my head, in my thoughts, every day. I came here not wanting any distractions, not wanting anything that would make me lose focus. My ex cheated and lied and screwed me up more than I'd like to admit. I moved here with no desire to start anything with anyone! But here you are, as sweet as sugar, and all I want is to lock that damn door, worship your body, and learn all your secrets. I get hard every time I smell oranges. But this; us, this is a mistake. You're…"

"A mistake." I finished his sentence and stepped further away.

Moments ago, I was ready for him to possess me. But now, something had broken. Whatever tight string of lust that drew us together had just snapped, fraying in a thousand directions.

"I won't be back in the office today," he said, looking at me with a mix of lust and regret.

His hand came up as if he was going to touch me, but at the last minute, he stepped back and ran it through his thick dark hair. Hair that I was pulling moments ago.

"Annaleigh, that's not what I…" He started, but I held up my hand, stopping him mid-sentence.

It didn't matter how he was going to finish. I was going to control the narrative. Frustration, lust, and confusion rolled off him in waves, pulsing around his body and matching mine. His hard-on looked painful, and stress was etched onto his features, like granite.

I closed my eyes and turned around. While his back was to me, I whispered, "I don't want to be at the mercy of my emotions. I want to use them, to enjoy them, and to dominate them."

We could do this. We could stay away. He was right. This was a mistake. But if it was a mistake, why did my chest ache?

Apparently, his ears were just as impressive as the rest of his body because without missing a beat, he turned and said, "Did you just quote Oscar Wilde?" He looked down at me and tilted one side of his mouth up in the smallest smirk, contradicting his coldness from moments ago. Maybe his nickname should be gas-station burrito instead of Broody McAsshole.

Or Icy-Hot.

"Not to you," I said.

"He would never again tempt innocence. He would be good."

I turned back around and tilted my head. Of course, he could quote Wilde. Next, I'm sure he'd tell me he moonlighted saving kittens caught high in trees at night.

"Annaleigh, Blue."

The way he said my nickname, softer than my name, almost broke me.

"Max, you're right. I think we can agree this can't get even more complicated than it already is. I don't want to jeopardize our jobs. We have to set ground rules."

He nodded and hung his head, "Right. No complications. But, Blue, you would never be a mistake, and you deserve everything. You deserve so much more than me."

With that, he traced my jaw with his fingers before brushing past me towards the backdoor stairwell without so much as a last glance. I only wished the tingling on my skin would leave, like he had.

11

ENCHANTED

Annaleigh

I looked at my reflection as I finished my makeup for the Whiskey Gala. My lips were red, and my cheeks were peach. I highlighted my winged eyeliner and gray smokey eyes with a pop of light metallic blue in the inner corner. And after watching a dozen how-to videos, my eyes were sparkling and would stand out through the satin mask. My dress was slate blue and soft satin with a dramatic, plunging neckline, draping front, and train hem. I was wearing long silver earrings that jingled softly as I moved, and my silver heels matched the rhinestones on my mask.

The fabric caressed my skin like a warm embrace, and for a fleeting moment, I imagined Max running his fingers along the lines of the dress. He was on my mind again with dirty, filthy, lovely thoughts. No matter how many times I told myself we were a bad idea, I kept imagining what it would be like if we'd met under different circumstances.

Every time I thought of him, my body betrayed me. I remembered the words he said and the way his hands felt on my body. It was like they were made to touch me, and it was terrifying. So was the way he looked at me, like he could see me, more than anyone else had. With the drinks flowing tonight, I was going to have to work extra hard to remember why we were a mistake.

The town car was due any minute, so I unlocked the door and opened my front curtains to see the street. Baxter jumped on the couch for a better view of any passing squirrels, and I bent down to give him scratches. He wagged his tail in approval, and I sent Jenna a quick text, thanking her for coming over to walk him later.

I was sitting on the couch, slipping on my heels, when Katie opened my front door and came in, bouncing from foot to foot and pointing to the bathroom. I nodded and stood up, putting a reassuring hand on Baxter's head.

She left the door cracked and called down the hallway, "Random question. Is there something going on with you and Max?"

Oh no!

Did Jake know? Did Jake tell Katie? What did Max tell Jake?

The thoughts tumbled out of my head as I heard Katie wash her hands and walk back down the hallway.

"Katie. What are you talking about?"

My hands were clammy, and I stared at my feet, not wanting to say anything until she elaborated.

"So, listen. I brought a date for Max. Leslie, from the club. Remember her from the tennis match last month? He was polite when I introduced them, but then he asked me quietly if you knew he had a date. I said yes because I thought Jake told you. But now, he's silent and weird and angry."

She shrugged her shoulders, and her eyes darted to the window where Jake was standing outside the car with his arms crossed, staring at my closed door.

"And then Max asked me again if I was sure you knew about him having a date. When I said yes again, he shut down. Leslie is on her second glass of champagne and looking at him like he has three heads. Am I reading too much into this?"

"Katie. Max is Broody McAsshole," I said in almost a whisper, hoping to appease whatever was going on in her head and glad our indiscretion was safe.

"What!" Katie said, her voice so high only dogs could hear her. I leaned down and scratched that sweet spot behind Baxter's ears because he was looking at Katie like she was crazy. He licked my hand before jumping back on the couch in search of rogue squirrels.

"Katie, he's my boss," I said, sighing and slipping my phone and mask into my silver clutch.

"And if he wasn't your boss?" she said, looking guilty for even asking.

Not willing to give anything up, I stared at her with a straight face until we heard the town car honk its horn.

"Come on, let's not keep them waiting. I love the dress, Katie. You look so elegant."

Katie wanted to ask more, but thankfully, let it go. I gave Baxter one extra pet and locked the door behind us as we walked out together where Jake was waiting, ever the gentleman.

He held the door open for us and said with a nod, "Annaleigh, you look lovely this evening."

"Thank you, Jake, looking pretty good yourself," I answered, slipping into the car before him and Katie.

"Save me a dance later. We need to talk," he said, giving me a nod and a smile.

He stepped in after Katie and shut the door, straightening his bowtie and lifting his hand to the driver.

I sat beside Katie and kept my eyes on the floor, determined not to look at Max, but that lasted all of three seconds. His eyes were dark, smoldering, and one look at the way he was rubbing his hands up and down his thick thighs had me squeezing mine together, remembering how those hands felt on my skin. He was staring at me so hard I was surprised my forehead had not caught fire. Was he angry because he thought I was okay with him having a date? Or was it something else?

Katie reintroduced us, and Leslie shook my hand as if she expected me to kiss it. Her hands were soft and dainty, and her manicure was flawless. Her dress was red, matching her lips, and it pushed her boobs up to her chin. She didn't seem like Max's type, but what did I know? It wasn't like we'd had long conversations about what we were looking for in a relationship.

But I knew his fingers lit up every nerve in my body, and I knew I wanted more.

"So, you're Max's secretary, Amy, right? Are you here to hold his coat and bring him cocktails?"

Leslie laughed as if she had just told a hilarious joke, and the way she emphasized cock in cocktails made my skin crawl. I didn't want her near Max's anything, especially his cock. No one looked amused, and the condescending voice she used was irritating as hell. Sitting across from us in the car, she gave me a sickly sweet smile, as if she purposely misused my name and title to instigate a response.

Jake rubbed the back of his neck and lightly squeezed Katie's thigh while red slowly crept up her cheeks. It wasn't her fault. It took me three terrible dates before I realized Katie's judgment was questionable.

"Annaleigh, and yes, I am. And don't you have the subtlety of a brick and the depth of a shot glass? It's such a pleasure to see you again," I said with a smile.

Max held his hand in front of his mouth like he was stifling a grin, and I was rewarded with one dimple and a quick flash of his white, straight teeth. Jake focused intently on something outside the window, and Katie looked wide-eyed at Leslie, who downed her champagne, none the wiser.

God, I didn't remember her having the personality of a snobby narcissist. Maybe I shouldn't have taken the bait, but was her comment necessary? I'd like to think I'm only mean to people who deserve it. Kind of like a vigilante bitch; a bitchilante if you will. And if anyone deserved a sarcastic comment, Leslie Fake-Boobs did.

I took a bit of pleasure from watching the confusion on her face, but there was too much Botox in her forehead for her to even furrow her eyebrows.

Petty? Yes.

Guilty? No.

"Right, I guess you'll be getting my drinks as well tonight," Leslie said, either not understanding or attempting to save face.

"Absolutely, Leslie. I'll be happy too," I said with another smile, looking at Katie and widening my eyes.

She glanced at Jake as if she knew this set-up was a mistake. And we spent the rest of the drive in uncomfortable silence.

As we pulled up to the hotel, I took out my mask and slipped it on, watching everyone do the same. Jake got out of the car first and held his hand for Katie. Max followed suit, holding his hand for Leslie, but let go as soon as her heels were on the pavement. He stayed back for a second as if he wanted to hold his hand out for me, but I took one look at Leslie's face and shook my head. Max pinched the bridge of his nose in irritation as Jake side-stepped him and held out his hand to me. I mouthed sorry, and Jake shrugged his shoulders.

The couples were greeted right away, and after a thank you to the doorman and passing over our invitations, I peeled off gracefully to the bar with a subtle nod to Jake, letting him know where I was heading. He tapped his jacket pocket before shaking the hotel owner's hand.

I nodded, walking through the lobby and taking out my cell phone for Jake's text-messaged drink order. I reminded him of our table number before slipping my phone back in my clutch.

The hallways were decorated with black and gray, leading to a beautiful open ballroom with a mezzanine, grand staircase, white columns, and a dark wood ceiling.

The bar took up a good portion of the back wall and had high-top stools made of the same dark wood, giving the entire room a mysterious vibe. I stood at the end, raising my hand to get the bartender's attention and looking over the bourbon selection.

I ordered Jake's drinks and decided on Buffalo Trace for myself, asking for a double, neat with a twist. I looked up a minute later when the bartender cleared his throat and put the drinks in front of me. I rubbed an orange peel around the rim of my glass and dropped it in, studying him. He was a good-looking guy with shaggy blonde hair and bright blue eyes. His shirt was tight, showing off his muscles, and he gave me a wide smile.

"The name's Hugh, and you let me know if you need anything this evening." He winked before turning to help a guy that flagged him down toward the other end of the bar. I smiled back and nodded. He was a great-looking guy but did nothing to pique my interest.

Jake came up a minute later to pick up his drinks, saying thank you before getting cornered by another guest. I shook my head and turned around to face the banquet room with its large chandeliers and black tablecloths.

I focused on the bourbons' golden liquid as I swirled the glass, taking in each color as it dripped down the side. Just as I brought the glass to my lips, butterflies took flight in my stomach. Max's eyes were on me. I could feel them. I could feel him approach. I hated this pull, hated this attraction, hated that I had to watch him with someone else tonight.

His black tuxedo was perfectly tailored to his body, and I took a moment to peruse the way his jacket showcased his broad shoulders as he walked over. The detailed gold mask looked like it was made to fit his face, and my pulse increased the closer he came.

"Exquisite, Annaleigh," he said, his voice raw and husky. *Holy shit, I think my panties just disintegrated.* He dragged his eyes slowly over my body and bit his lower lip as if he wanted nothing more than to trace them against my body. I was ready to let him, my stupid body betraying me.

"You soon lingered above my emptiness. A magical soul whose miracles manifest. At the sight of your aesthetics, my heart knew peace. Doubts dissipated as my knees felt weak."

That was more than a lyric. That was the beginning of a song. As the words replayed in my mind, I looked at Max.

He pursed his lips and stepped closer. "Tell me what you're thinking, Blue."

I shook my head. I shouldn't tell him. "I, um. Thank you for the compliment, Max. You look very suave tonight."

"Hmm," he said, as if he knew I was lying. "Thanks. Whiskey?" He nodded at my glass and reached towards me, tucking a stray wisp of hair behind my ear. His hand stayed a moment longer than it should have, and when he pulled away, he jammed his hands in his front pockets.

"Bourbon," I answered.

"A woman after my heart." He signaled Hugh and ordering a Woodford Reserve on the rocks and a vodka sprite.

"Amateur. That's no way to drink bourbon." I nodded to the ice in his glass after Hugh set down his drinks and held up my own. "It's too good to waste with water."

"I beg to differ," he said, taking a sip. "The ice with the liquors' burn, nothing's better."

"Agree to disagree." I clinked my glass against his, and he drank again, letting the ice rattle. I imagined what it would be like to taste the ice-cold bourbon on his lips before feeling the warmth of his tongue. His eyes narrowed as if he could read my thoughts, and I felt my nipples pucker, begging for his attention.

He glanced down and took in a sharp breath, stepping closer, so my back brushed along the edge of the bar. His eyes narrowed, and he traced one finger up my arm. I looked behind him and saw Leslie standing with her arms crossed. I understood the possessiveness she felt, and I hated how sour the next words would feel tumbling out of my mouth.

"Your date's waiting."

"You don't approve?"

"My opinion doesn't matter, Max."

"Agree to disagree, Blue," he said, mimicking my earlier words. He took another step forward and brushed his thumb along my elbow. My entire body shuddered, and I leaned into him. "I never meant to make you think we would be a mistake. I meant what I said. I don't want to stay away."

How do I answer that?

"Anna! Do you—" Jake said, hurrying towards us and breaking the moment. He just saved me from telling Max, telling Max… something.

"Yes, right here, Jake." I took several of his business cards out of my clutch and passed them over.

"Perfect, thank you." He put them in his jacket with a nod, walking back to Katie and the couple they were talking to a few feet away.

"Ah, Annaleigh," Max said, his eyes darting to Leslie then back to me.

"Here, Max, yours came in yesterday. Now go mingle. Bring Leslie her drink."

He took the cards from my hand, and where his fingers touched mine, sparks danced. He glanced down at our fingers, silently asking me if I felt it too. I did. He knew I did.

"Go, Max. We have to stop. I can't take it. If this were supposed to continue, we wouldn't keep having misunderstandings and interruptions."

"Or maybe the interruptions will make the reward that much sweeter, Blue."

"No, it has to be a sign. This is the Universe telling us it's a bad idea."

"The Universe?" he chuckled. "I didn't take you as someone who believes in signs from the Universe."

"Well, you don't really know me, do you? We hardly know each other. Maybe I believe. Maybe this is life, the Universe…" I lifted my hand in some sort of grand gesture, but he interrupted.

"And everything?"

"Maybe. But enough, Max. It's too much. You twist my insides and get me so turned on I can't think straight. Either we finish this, or you walk away."

He adjusted his lapels and picked up Leslie's drink, glaring at me. I sat my drink down and crossed my arms over my chest, "And Max. If your lips ever touch my neck again, you better not fucking stop."

I didn't mean it as a challenge or a dare, and I wasn't trying to goad him into doing anything. I was just sick of the back-and-forth bullshit.

His eyes got wide, and his pupils went as dark as his tux. He stalked over to Leslie, who was already talking to another masked guest. She took her drink without so much as a glance, and he looked my way, eyes narrowing in frustration. I could read his eyes as well as he could read mine.

You want me, Blue. You want us.
I never said I didn't.
I'd make you scream.
I'd make you beg.
You'd be worth it, Blue.

Those eyes held so many hot, dirty, naked promises as he circled the room with Leslie. When I caught his eyes again, he crossed his arms and licked his lips. Shaking off my frustration, I took a big sip of bourbon, and he smirked at me. I wanted to wipe that cocky smile off his face, but that would have to wait as couples were making their way into the dining room.

I purposely sat across from him at our table and even played the diligent assistant and brought Leslie another drink. When the dessert and dancing started, I stayed to finish my chocolate mousse while Jake and Katie took a turn around the floor. I hoped one day I'd be able to find someone who looked at me the way Jake looked at Katie. Remembering the way Max looked at me, I thought, *maybe,* I already had.

He had drifted off and was deep in conversation with someone across the room while Leslie was back at the bar. Sighing, I took another bite of mousse and pulled Leslie's untouched dessert closer. Might as well take advantage of the opportunity to have more chocolate. Frank Sinatra played in the background, and I hummed along, watching the couples dance. Just as I took a bite, a sweaty hand touched my shoulder, and I looked up to see Benjamin towering over me.

Too lanky with slicked-back blonde-white hair, he put an empty drink on the table and said, "I've had it with the hard-to-get act, Annaleigh."

He sat down and leaned close enough for me to smell the alcohol wafting off him. I reluctantly looked away from my unfinished mousse and decided I needed a more direct approach for his nonsense. The time for being polite was over.

"It's not an act. And we're not going out, ever. You need to back off."

"You better change your mind after I'm named the next Senior Vice President. I'm tired of you turning me down." He picked up a half-empty glass of white wine and downed it in one gulp. *Gross.*

Ugh, his arrogant attitude and assumptions made him worse than his father. I was counting the seconds until he left the table. This man-child was a trust fund kid with freaking logos on his shoes. He was a hard no, even if my thoughts weren't focused on a certain SVP.

"Benjamin, for the last time, I'm not going out with you. Stop asking, now."

I turned away and scanned the room again, finishing my bourbon slowly before glancing back in the hopes he would get the point.

"You know, it's going to be very hard to find a position for you if you don't start playing ball."

He put one sweaty hand on my arm and squeezed.

"What is that supposed to mean?" I jerked my arm away and turned to face him.

"It means you need to reconsider my offer. You don't want my father to hear you turned me down again." He reached out to grab me again, but I pushed my chair back and crossed my arms.

"Really, Malfoy? I'll be glad to tell him myself as soon as I see him. And you'll do well to remember who got a position working here because they earned it, not because of nepotism."

"We'll see about that. Don't make me tell Jake about you making eyes at the guy who stole my job," he sneered, buttoning his coat and standing up. He grabbed his empty glass and stumbled, bracing himself on a chair—twitchy little ferret.

I put my hand on my stomach and took a deep breath, watching him take two steps back and bumping into the table behind ours. He picked up another half-empty glass, drinking whatever was in it before coming back. He pointed a finger at me when I felt a hand on my shoulder. It made me jump, but the hand was warm, firm, and reassuring.

"I didn't realize this event included Analysts, Benjamin. Is there a problem here?" Jake said, his soft brown eyes almost black. I could see how white his knuckles were from gripping the chair beside me. He took a step closer and unbuttoned his jacket. Jake's temper didn't come out often, but when it did, you'd better back off.

Benjamin was close enough to hear him but didn't answer, looking down at me instead. "Not yet. Annaleigh, but we'll talk again soon."

He walked away with his shoulders hunched, darting around guests. I waited until he left the ballroom, then stood up to face Jake and thank him. He smiled and took my hand, leading me to the dance floor.

"What did he say?" Jake asked, spinning me around with a flourish of his wrist as the band started playing Norah Jones.

"Nothing new," I sighed, letting him lead me around the dance floor. "Raymond is looking for a way to push you out and put Benjamin in Max's position. And I get to come along for the ride as some sort of sick consolation prize."

Jake gave my hand a reassuring squeeze and spun me again. "It's time to take this a step further. We're going to talk to Human Resources on Monday."

I nodded, following his lead and swaying with him to the music.

"Good. Thank you, Annaleigh. Now, please tell me why my Senior Vice President is staring at me like I kicked his puppy after running over his grandmother. I had to threaten to send Leslie home with him so he wouldn't stomp over to break Malfoy's nose."

Even with asses like Benjamin, another reason I loved my job was because Jake's knowledge of Harry Potter rivaled my own, and he deserved the truth.

"Max and I ran into each other the weekend before he started. Now, things are… I don't even know Jake. They're upside down. I'm a mess."

I looked up and met his eyes, expecting judgment, but there was only understanding. He looked at me hard as we danced, and for once, I wasn't confident with what he would say next.

"Upside down like you need to disclose a relationship?"

"I don't know. It's more like a reevaluation of my…"

"Priorities?" he said, twirling me around again.

"Something like that."

"Should I be concerned, Annaleigh?"

"No," I said, louder than I should had.

"Maybe?" he prompted, guiding me in the opposite direction. He looked at me, really looked at me, and smiled.

"Possibly."

"Annaleigh, I know you, and I'll support you. Remember, Katie was my tennis instructor, so I get things happen in inappropriate places when you least expect them to happen. But please be careful. I don't want to see you hurt. Either of you."

"Jake," I started as my eyes traveled the room, looking for Max. I found him at the bar with a large drink in his hand. He nodded his head to the left. And when I looked over, there was Leslie, practically making out with whomever she was talking to earlier. He downed his drink and signaled for another as Jake stopped us by the bar.

"Thank you for the dance, Annaleigh. I'm off to spin my beautiful wife around the floor again. Take the town car home. We'll probably stay a while longer."

"Thanks, Jake," I said, giving him a quick hug. He kissed my cheek and shook Max's hand before turning around to find Katie.

The bartender sat another bourbon in front of Max, and I signaled for one as well. Max braced himself with one hand on the bar and took a long drink, crunching the ice and giving me a full wattage smile that showed both dimples. It made the slight crinkling around his eyes stand out. I was not prepared for that smile.

"Look, I'm just trying to get a drink, and you're very distracting." He tilted his head and steadied his feet before downing the bourbon.

"Max?"

"I could buy you a drink, but I'd be jealous of the glass." His crooked grin made his eyes a shade of golden hazel, perfectly matching the bourbon Hugh sat in front of me.

"What?" I dropped in the orange peel and took a sip, smiling at the cheesy pickup lines.

"Are you a Beaver? Because Damn!" Max snorted, and his shoulders shook as he laughed at his joke. "You know, I'm fine being friends, as long as I can seduce you when I'm drunk. Why don't we get out of here, Blue? I bet you're way better to wake up next to than a hangover."

Oh my God! Max was drunk, or at least buzzed enough that his entire demeanor was different. I was completely prepared for a snarly, stoic, silent drunk. But not this goofy, giggly, flirty ball of smiles. I was completely smitten, falling even harder for this man with his layered personality, rugged good looks, and adorably buzzed lean to one side.

He was in no shape to represent the bank, especially now that the food was gone, and the alcohol flowed. I ran my hand down his arm and took his drink. "How much have you had to drink tonight?"

"I'm sober enough to be pissed that my fake date, with her fake tits, is sucking face with someone else. Come home with me, and I'll make you a peanut butter and Smucker's sandwich. I'll bet you'll love it. It's even better with potato chips. I want potato chips too. I want to lick strawberry jam out of your belly button."

"Let's go, big guy," I said, taking his hand and guiding him towards the side exit. He threw a muscular arm around my shoulders and nuzzled my neck.

"You always smell so good. Like oranges and vanilla and sunshine. I want to put you in my dryer with my clothes, so they smell like you all the time."

"You want a lot of things, don't you?"

"I want you to come home with me. I want to hold you. I want a Peanut Butter and Strawberry Jam sandwich. I want my Pimp Chalice."

"Your what now?"

"Sandwich, then the chalice. I'll tell you all the things Blue. All. The. Things."

With that, he booped my nose and stood on the sidewalk as if he didn't just tell me he needed a fucking Pimp Chalice.

When the car pulled up, it took him two tries and lots of giggles before he made it in the back. I couldn't help it. I stood back and laughed, completely unhelpful. When I got in the car, he rested his head on my shoulder with a deep sigh.

"This is nice. You're so pretty."

"Max, what did you mean?" I needed him to finish telling me what he started earlier. Needed to know if he was having second thoughts too.

"What," he replied, turning his head enough to look up at me. "When I said how pretty you are, or when I said that we shouldn't screw, or when I said you deserve more than me? Or what I meant by a PB and Strawberry Jam sandwich because that is life changing."

"All the things Max," I said, using his earlier words and desperate to peel back the layers of his hot and cold mood swings.

"I'm a screw-up. Let my parents run my life. What kind of thirty-year-old does that? Me, that's who. Almost lost my brother, can't let go of so much fucking anger. You're too good for a spoiled mama's boy. I'm no better than that fuckwad Benjamin." He turned his head and tugged on his shirt collar, releasing the bowtie and undoing the top three buttons.

I used the opportunity to inhale whatever shampoo he was using, a scent that was unanimously Max. He continued to nuzzle my neck as we drove, and luckily the driver knew where Max lived. *How could he think he was a screw-up?* This deep, sweet man had more layers than a honey cake.

"Max."

"Don't Blue. Just come home with me."

"I'm taking you home, not going home with you."

"I'll wear you down, especially after you taste my Smuckers. See what I did there? I made a sex joke. I'd love to taste your Smuckers. Why can't I stop thinking about you? I wanted to kill Bennie-Boy for touching you."

"Hush and enjoy the drive, Max," I said, stroking his hair. It was impossible not to touch him, and my rationale for staying away had slipped out the window.

It was the bourbon, had to be the bourbon. Not the man that was slowly running his fingers up and down my thigh while snoring.

Snoring? Ugh and drooling. I rubbed the side of his mouth as drool dripped down my neck, startling him awake with a sexy little snort.

- 12 -

DOUBTS DISSIPATED

Max

R ise and shine. Let's get you to bed," said a warm, bubbly voice. It was the sweetest voice I'd ever heard. And I was so happy, so content, so buzzed. I needed to be closer to the sunshine voice, so I stepped out of the still-running car and tangled myself in the arms of the most stunning woman in the world.

Blue waved to the driver as I wrapped myself around her waist, and she eased us towards the front door. How did I get so lucky?

"Easy there, Casanova. I'm pretty sure these heels have a weight limit."

"Casanova? Trying to nickname me already, Blue?"

"I might as well. It's hard to remember why we shouldn't be together when you're this blissed out. Now, where are your keys?" she said, feeling in the inner pockets of my jacket.

"Not there, beautiful." I reached into one pocket and came up empty. I reached in the other, spun around, found the keys, stumbled, and dropped them on the ground.

She sighed and bent down to retrieve them. With a stretch and a stumble, I smacked her right butt cheek. She made an adorable squeak, and I lifted my shoulders in a half shrug, tucking her back into my arm.

She was shaking her head and fumbling with the lock but got the door open and took a step inside, removing herself from my arms and bending down again. Just as my hand came up to give her left butt cheek the same treatment, she pinned me with a death-stare and unhooked one strap of her silver heel. She slipped it off and did the same with the other, shrinking five inches and breathing a heavy sigh of relief.

"Oh, god. That's good," she said, putting her heels and purse by the door. "Sorry, my feet were past uncomfortable and heading towards nuclear."

"I'm not sorry for anything that lets you make those noises, gorgeous."

She gave me a sly little grin and glanced around my living room, taking in the almost empty boxes and furniture before looking back to the entryway

"Um, Max? You barely have room for another pair of shoes here," she said, looking at my three pairs of sneakers and two pairs of loafers by the door. "But personally, I like a man who knows how important the right pair of shoes are."

She bent down and moved a pair of my sneakers to the side, putting her heels there instead with a wink.

I rubbed the back of my neck and shook my head. *Damn.*

Five days a week wasn't enough. I wanted her every day. Her sighs, moans, screams, everything. I cupped her jaw, focusing on her up-turned nose and rosebud lips. God, this woman.

Why was this a bad idea?

She stepped back and put one hand on her hip, "Point me to the kitchen, and I'll get you Ibuprofen and water while you get your chalice. I'm going to need that story."

"That's my brother," I said, walking in the general direction of the kitchen.

She followed, and it took me three tries to take down the crystal-covered, gaudy beer goblet and hand it to her. She twirled it around, running her fingers over the stones and laughing. Filling it up with water and pushing it to me, she grabbed a beer for herself out of the fridge and opened cabinets until she found medicine while I talked.

"He's always been crazy over the top, doing and saying shit to purposely weird you out. We're rebuilding our relationship, I guess, and when he found out my engagement was off, he sent me this monstrosity. He said something like if I confidently drank this with a hot girl, she would bow to the power of the Pimp Chalice and be at my mercy. Stupid, right?"

I downed the water and pills, waiting for her reaction.

"Well, the chalice works, right? I'm here with you. I'll bet it's wielded its power over many, many women." She made a steeple with her fingers around the beer, smiling with a wink.

"Only the one I can't stop thinking about. I wanted to kill Benjamin when I saw him sitting with you. Please tell me he hasn't done anything inappropriate, Blue."

"I can handle that ferret, Max. So, you were engaged? And what happened with your brother?"

I knew she could handle herself and knew she was deflecting, but I couldn't get the image of him leering at her out of my head.

"Ahh," I said, spinning around too fast. "That's a long story, but the short version is when my brother was eighteen, he had a falling out with our parents and left. My dumb ass believed them when they said it was his choice to leave. He reached out to me, but I ignored him. I was a stupid shit, pushing him away like that. It wasn't until they told me I should take my cheating ex back because she's from a good family that I realized how blinded I'd been and moved away. See? I'm no good for you past a hot, dirty fuck. I'm no good for anyone."

I bowed my head and let out a deep breath. I'd never verbalized the shame I'd felt with Warren, and here I was, spilling my guts to the beautiful girl in blue.

"Wow, Max. I had no idea. How many years has it been?"

"So many I'm too ashamed to even say, Blue. Not exactly something

I'm proud of. All those years we didn't talk… He'd never do something like that to me."

I shook my head and wobbled, pulling my bowtie the rest of the way off and throwing it on the kitchen island. Water, I needed more water.

"Hey. Listen to me," she said, refilling the chalice as if she'd read my mind. I didn't deserve the way she was looking at me like there was nowhere else she'd rather be.

I brought her to my chest, clasping her hands with mine. "No, don't start that pity bullshit. Let's skip the deep stuff and go back to flirting. Sit your fine ass down, drink that beer, and let me make you the best sandwich you've ever had."

I squeezed her hands, backing her up to the barstools at my kitchen island before opening the fridge and taking out the Smuckers Strawberry Jam. Moving to the pantry for bread and chips, I opened the bag and stuffed a handful in my mouth. I got to work with Annaleigh watching, and she pulled the chips closer and helped herself. I liked that she was comfortable in my house, in my space.

"You ready for your mind to be blown, Blue?"

"With Smuckers and flirting?"

"Oh, yes, baby. After all, Smuckers make me wanna fuckhers. Get it?" I said, laughing and pointing the butter knife in her direction.

She smiled and took a long pull of beer, looking way too serious suddenly. "Max. Don't let the past define you. I'm not one to talk because I feel stuck in the past sometimes. But listen, you are an amazing man. And you admitted your mistakes and are now fixing things with your brother, that shows so much about your character."

I was speechless. It was like she had reached into my chest and soothed the anguish in my soul. Before I could come up with a reason she was wrong, she leaned across the island, giving me a tempting peek at her tits, and wrapped her hand around my wrist. Her pink tongue darted out, licking both sides of the knife, tasting the jam, and turning my dick to diamond.

"Blow my mind, Max," she said, dipping her finger into the jar for another taste.

She sucked on her finger, hollowing her cheeks as I plated everything. Dropping the knife, I stepped around to the barstool, thankful her dress had a slit that let her legs spread slightly. I picked up one half of the sandwich and brought it to her lips, loving how her mouth wrapped around the bite.

A large drop of jam dripped from the half I was holding and landed between her breasts, staining them red. Her eyes widened, meeting mine, and she arched slightly, looking down at the trail of jam. We both stared at the jam as if we knew this was a moment we couldn't come back from if either one of us moved. I could see her pulse fluttering in her neck, and her breath turned shallow.

My eyes were burning with lust, my buzz was gone, and I leaned down slowly, letting my tongue follow the jam's path. She gripped the back of my neck and held me between her breasts. The jam sweetened her skin, but the underlying flavor was unmistakably Annaleigh.

"I'm not going to screw you tonight. But, Max, I just need a little more. I can't get your words out of my head." Her grip tightened, and she pulled my hair, arching into my tongue as I traced it along her skin.

"You're right, Blue. I'm not going to screw you tonight. The first time I'm inside you, you'll know you're mine. But baby. Move those hands for me."

I dipped my tongue lower for one more lick, and when her hands left my neck, she moved them to the back of her dress, releasing the clasp and letting the straps fall to her waist.

Fuck, she wasn't wearing a bra.

"Holy shit," I rasped, bending down to take her dark pink nipple between my teeth. I sucked hard, running the pad of my thumb over the other sensitive nub. She was so responsive, working the buttons of my shirt while thrusting her breast further in my mouth.

"Mmm, never letting these tits go."

I nibbled and licked my way to her other nipple, drawing it between my teeth and pinching the wet one between my fingers. Blue was breathing heavier, grinding the air, and making these soft little gasps as I lashed my tongue over her nipples, never staying in the same place. I used my other hand to travel down the supple skin of her back, dimpling her waist and caging myself between her thighs. I ground my hard-on against her, needing more pressure to relieve the ache.

"Oh, Max. So close. That's it."

Close? Christ, I didn't want to get her off just working her tits. I needed more. I wanted to watch her lose control. I released her nipple with a wet pop and made quick work of my shirt, pulling it and my undershirt over my head so I could feast on her tits again. They were fast becoming my favorite obsession.

I growled into her chest, and a giggle escaped her lips, "Something funny, Blue?" I gave her stiff peak a sharp bite. I was rewarded with a louder moan, and she fisted my pants, bringing me closer.

"What in the hell is that?" I followed her finger and groaned into her neck. She was pointing to Warren's housewarming gift.

"Christ, another one of my brother's attempts at humor."

"Is that a cock ring?"

She pushed against me and got up, letting her dress pool around her ankles and walking to an unopened box, picking up the toy on top. Running her hand over the purple silicone, she stood there in nothing but a flimsy black thong, causing me to kick off my pants and shoes with lightning-fast speed.

"I have a purple fuck toy too, but something tells me what's hiding in those briefs is much more satisfying."

A vibrator? She had a vibrator?

I squeezed my balls through my boxer-briefs, trying to relieve the ache.

"Absol-fucking-utely!" I growled, striding towards her, much steadier on my feet. Her body must have a sobering effect. And thank fuck for that because I wanted to remember everything about this moment. She was tracing her hands down her stomach and over her panties as I palmed my cock.

"Keep going," I commanded in a steely voice, watching her stroke the fabric of her panties.

I took the cock ring from her, throwing it on the floor and caging her between my arms. I walked back to the couch until she fell back on the soft cushions. Running my fingers from her calf to thigh, I spread her legs and bent one knee, propping it on the coffee table. I could see a wet spot on her panties and almost blew my load like a damn teenager, knowing she was as worked up as me.

"Is that for me?" I said, pointing at the dampness and leaning down close to lick one delicious globe.

"It's always for you. Every damn day," she said, the words purring from her lips and driving me wild.

"Show me how you touch yourself. Now, I need to see you." Toying with the strings on her panties, she pulled them to the side and exposed her bare, pink pussy. It was glistening, leaving traces on her inner thighs, and I had the perfect view. My hand moved of its own volition, pulling my cock out and stroking from root to tip.

"I need more Max, bring that big cock closer," she whispered, tracing her fingers across her lips and slowly swirling them towards her clit. I wanted to kneel in front of her and worship her pussy with my tongue. But her heavily lidded eyes and the patterns she was tracing with her fingers held me captive. She was so fucking hot, taking control of her pleasure while I watched.

"Faster, Max. Fuck your fist like you would fuck my pussy. Is this what you do at night? Fuck your fist thinking about bottoming out deep inside me?"

I stepped closer, using my pre-cum to slick my hand, and gripped my shaft harder to stave off the impending orgasm.

"Fuck your big." She moved one hand up to pinch her nipple as her hand blurred across her clit. *So goddamn sexy.*

"Every fucking day, I've imagined pounding into that sweet pussy, licking your clit, and you on your knees sucking me off. I want you every way you'll let me. Yes, use your fingers, baby. Imagine their mine stroking you. Hold yourself open for me, show me. Jesus, you look so fucking tight. I don't even know if you could take my whole cock."

She brought her hand down to spread her lips, showing me her swollen clit as her fingers strummed across it.

"Fuck Max. I'm going to come. Come with me," she cried, throwing her head back on the sofa with a scream. Her hips bucked against her hand as she chased her pleasure. I couldn't hold back any longer. Giving myself one more jerk, I growled her name and shot my load all over my hand, slicking the way for the last few strokes. Our eyes stayed on each other as we came down from the high. But it wasn't enough. I needed her. I needed all of her. Every day.

Holy fuck.

Straightening her legs and depriving me of that beautiful sight, she moved to stand up, but before she could, I grabbed her wrist and brought her soaking fingers to my lips, needing to taste her sweetness.

"Mine," I said, sucking them both in my mouth and savoring her flavor. She looked satisfied, sated, but I was still desperate for her touch, craving her skin on mine.

She leaned forward, running a long finger over my release before bringing it to her mouth. "Mine," she echoed.

Fuck, I'm done. I wanted to paint her with my come, mark her like a fucking caveman, show the world she belonged to me. Her look mimicked mine, hungry, desperate. There was no way I was letting her go. I cleaned us both up with a warm kitchen towel and kicked my boxers to the side, pulling her to my chest to caress her flushed jaw.

"Stay, Blue. Stay and sleep. Let me hold you."

She nodded, and I picked her up, wrapping her arms around my neck and carrying her up the stairs to my bedroom. She wasn't delicate, but I needed her close, needed to feel her weight in my arms. I sat her down on the side of the bed, loving how her pale skin looked against my hunter-green comforter, and pointed to the bathroom, watching the mesmerizing sway of her hips in that black thong as she walked.

Fresh-faced and hair down, she came out smiling shyly, and I went in, laying a tee-shirt on the bed for her. I wasn't a snuggler, preferring the bed all to myself. I liked my space, I always had. But right now, I wanted to hold her close and feel her warm, soft body pressed against mine all night. I wanted her body against mine every night.

Walking out, I noticed the tee shirt was still there, and a delectable naked woman was waiting for me. I crawled over her, pressing a kiss to the corner of her mouth and tucking her into my arm.

"Max, that was amazing. I've never…"

"Me either, baby," I said, placing a kiss on each knuckle that still faintly tasted like her arousal. "You're beautiful."

"I don't want things to change, but I can't pretend that wasn't one of the most intense experiences of my life. Where do we go from here? This shouldn't continue, Max. We can't be together. We both know that." Her voice was shaky, breathy. I laid her head on my chest, and she pressed her lips to my neck. Her eyes held uncertainty, and I didn't have the words to reassure her. There were rules for a reason. They discouraged relationships in our workplace, and we both agreed this wasn't a good idea.

"We'll figure it out. Sleep, beautiful Blue."

After a few minutes, her breathing was deep and even, but I couldn't sleep. There had to be a way for us to make this work. I didn't know how to deal with all these fucking feelings, but I knew there was no way I was going to let her go.

RIDGES OF YOUR CHEST
Annaleigh

I slowly woke up, hot, with lyrics bouncing around my head after one of the best nights of sleep I'd had in weeks. Morning light streamed in from unfamiliar curtains, and the mattress felt like a cloud cocooned around my body. Cracking an eye open, I snuggled closer to the source of the heat and the comfort. Max's body was wrapped around mine.

"I never dreamed my words would lead me here to you."

I took a minute to admire the hard plains of his chest and the black ink snaking up one forearm to his shoulder and around his back. It was an intricately designed pocket-watch with its gears visible, starting on his shoulder and branching down his arm. From the bottom of the watch came three feathers, making it look like a dream catcher. The pocket-watch chain wrapped around his collarbone to his back and had a vine woven through it. It was beautiful but not complete. The clock didn't tell a time, and the ends of the feathers tapered to nothing. I traced my fingers down his arm, thinking about how the unfinished tattoo revealed another layer of his personality that made me fall a little harder.

He was breathing heavily and snoring quietly. I didn't want to move, loving the way our bodies fit together. But there was a very pressing bladder issue happening, and it was going to be embarrassing if I didn't get up soon. I inched my way towards the edge of the bed when a firm hand squeezed me, pulling me back. "No, too early. Stay Blue."

"Bathroom," I said, wiggling out of his grip. He released me with one last squeeze and a wicked smirk. After finishing my business, I glanced in the mirror and swiped away the remaining mascara underneath my eyes.

God, it was so intense last night. I'd never lost myself like that, never touched myself in front of someone, never been so obsessed with a man's cock. The way Max stroked himself, brows pinched together, eyes seared with lust. I'd remember that look for a long, long time.

I needed to get my hormones under control. We had to talk, not have round two. But round two sounded better than talking, and my already wet, aching core agreed with anything that brought his tongue and cock closer. I should have put on a shirt. My hard nipples were going to give me away as soon as I opened the door.

What were we going to do? There was no way this could work. I was going to have to tell him this couldn't go any further.

Max was looking sexier than ever with his hair rumpled and no glasses, leaning on one arm with the sheets pooled around his tight waist. He was slowly filling my heart with hopes and happiness, making this seem even more dangerous. I didn't know if the reward was worth the risk, and until I did, we couldn't keep this up.

"Hey, you, get back here," he hummed, opening his arms. "I need you more than coffee."

I climbed on the bed and bent down, resting my head on his chest. I tried not to think about how right it felt there. "Those are high expectations for eight in the morning, but we need to talk about last night."

I gave one of his delicious caramel-colored nipples a lick to lighten the mood and bit my lip when his eyes turned dark. He let out a deep breath and kissed the top of my head.

"For that, I'll need coffee. Come on, Blue."

Max rose to his full six-foot-something frame and stretched before putting on grey sweats that sat dangerously low on his hips. He handed me a T-shirt and put on his glasses, taking my hand and walking downstairs.

He started coffee while I got cream and sugar. An oddly intimate, homey feeling overwhelmed me as if this could be our normal weekend routine. I grabbed my phone from the kitchen island and replied to Jenna, thanking her for walking Baxter this morning.

"So, what are we going to do?" I said, taking a big gulp of coffee to steady my nerves and burning the roof of my mouth. *Wait, was this hazelnut coffee?* He had my favorite coffee. *Was that a sign that I was doing the wrong thing?*

"For breakfast? Because I'm thinking I'll make you chocolate chip pancakes after I show you around my house."

He brought his mouth down to my coffee for a sip, giving me another view of his dimples and smile. His eyes twinkled behind his glasses, and I had to take a deep breath before I climbed him like a spider monkey.

Broody Max was intense and short-tempered.

Drunk Max was hilarious.

Naked Max was unforgettable.

But this Max, morning after Max, was sweet and intimate. This was the Max I was falling for fast.

"No, you ass. About us, this, whatever this is," I said, sweeping my hands in a big circle and almost spilling the coffee.

"Easy. We date," he said with a shrug, as if it was an easy, snap, decision.

"We what?" I had to have misheard him. He couldn't seriously think it was that easy.

"Date Blue. We date. I like you. You like me. I like what we did last night. We should do more of that, preferably right now."

Smirking and taking the coffee from my hands, he put them around his neck, and I stroked his hair, his five o'clock scruff nuzzling my cheek.

He licked my collarbone, leaving wet kisses up my neck. He sucked on the skin, biting down and growling. The bite was sharp and sent a zing straight to my clit. I moaned and tilted my neck to give him better access.

Fuck, that felt good.

Pulling myself away between moans, I said, "What about work? We can't just walk in Monday morning holding hands. There's paperwork and disclosures and…"

My voice trailed off as Max peppered my neck with more wet kisses.

"I'm a selfish bastard, Blue. And I want you, no matter what the rules say. There has to be a workaround. What do you think?"

It was hard to focus as Max pulled the shirt aside and moved his tongue lower. I moaned before pulling away. He stopped and took off his glasses, cleaning them on his shirt.

Shit! He only did that when he was nervous or angry.

"I'm your subordinate Max, it's inappropriate." My voice was quiet, trying to make him understand.

"Do you not want this? Was this just a one-time deal for you?" He put his glasses back on and crossed his arms.

"It's more complicated, and you know it. If we disclose this, I'd probably have to transfer, and I'm not willing to leave my job. I love my job, love the bank, love working with Jake and the other executives. What's the other option? Sneaking around? I won't be your dirty secret."

I rubbed the bridge of my nose, trying to ward off a headache. There wasn't a right answer. I could see him closing himself off, pushing away, and letting anger cloud his handsome features, almost writing off the whole situation.

"Don't look at me like that. What did you expect, Max?" I could feel exhaustion setting in. Stress always made my condition worse. I needed an orange but was trapped by his stern gaze.

"I expected the feeling to be mutual," he sneered, putting his coffee cup in the sink, harder than necessary. "And I never asked you to be a secret."

"No, don't pull that shit with me, Max. It's mutual, so much more than mutual. You don't know how fast my heart races every time I see you. But I'm also distracted and making mistakes. And you said you were too." I stepped closer, but he backed up like he was done with me, done with us.

"Look, forget it. I was in the moment. You're right. Come on. I'll take you home," he said, taking my coffee and putting it beside his.

"Broody Max is back," I said under my breath. My shoulders sagged, and I looked down at the oversized shirt I was wearing.

"The hell does that mean? Broody Max?"

Shit. Might as well own it. This couldn't get any worse.

"Broody Max. You're back to being short-tempered and jumping to conclusions," I said.

He didn't answer. But I wasn't going to end things like this. I wrapped my arms around him, not giving him time to pull away. He stiffened and didn't hug me back, so I held him harder, pressing my face into his chest and breathing him in. Finally, he wrapped his arms around my waist, pulling me closer.

"This isn't easy for me, Max. You don't know how long it's been since I've felt a connection like this. I don't want to write you off. Write us off."

"This isn't easy for me either, Blue. But I guess the right thing to do never is." He squeezed me tighter and ran his hands through my hair.

"I'm not saying no, Max. But I am saying, not right now. I'll call an Uber."

"Like hell, you will… in five-inch fuck me heels and a dress that's still on the floor? I don't think so. Let me grab you some sweats."

He turned around and took the steps two at a time. When he came back down, he handed me a pair before grabbing his keys and wallet. I walked barefoot to his car, holding my shoes and clutch, not knowing what to say.

The drive home was hella-awkward. I hummed along to the radio and gave him directions. He continued the silent treatment until he pulled in front of my house, then he put the car in park and finally made eye contact.

"Annaleigh."

"Max," I started. I wanted to climb in his lap, kiss him, and tell him I was his and that the rest didn't matter. But it didn't work that way. We couldn't compromise our jobs until I talked to Jake and met with Human Resources.

"Don't. You're right. It's too complicated. I was wrong to put you in that position. I'll see you Monday. Thanks for after the gala." With that, he focused his eyes on the front windshield, dismissing me.

Regardless of his shitty but justified attitude, I leaned forward and pressed my lips to his cheek, feeling his warm skin against mine.

"I don't regret anything." I heard him say as I stepped out.

As he drove away, I had the sudden urge to chase the car down and tell him the only thing I regretted was when I said we were a bad idea. I wanted him to hold me close and tell me he'd fight for me, for us, no matter what. I walked to the door with my shoulder slumped, opening it with a sigh and tossing my things on the couch.

Baxter, at least, greeted me enthusiastically, and after a quick change, I grabbed his leash for a jog to get my thoughts straight. The morning air was humid, and the park's path was relatively empty, each side dotted with wildflowers that had sprouted up beside freshly mowed grass.

I listened as my heart beat in time with my feet on the pavement. The path smelled like asphalt and pine trees. Sweat dotted my face, and I sped up, letting the music of Gretchen Wilson drown out everything until I was left with nothing except the therapeutic sound of steady breaths. Words swirled in my head, trying to form something meaningful, something to make it make sense.

"Come back and stay, piece me together."

Bird would be proud. We used to work through tough times by writing poems and lyrics to each other in our letters. From what I remember, Bird's parents were awful people, and writing helped. Sometimes we would write a line or two. Other times it would be pages. But I hadn't had a lyric stick for years. And now, so many stuck around long enough for me to write and remember.

Holy shit.

I stopped and put my hands on my knees. *It was Max.* He was the change. He was the difference. Ever since he came into my life, the lyrics had stuck, bringing music back to help me work through my insecurities.

I took out my phone and jotted down the lyric. The air caressed my face while Baxter watched the ducks lazily swim across the surface of the pond we stopped nearby. He pulled on the leash, wanting to move closer, so we walked to the edge where he sniffed along the ground, looking for squirrels.

"Once just a blank page words drift estranged, but with you at my side, my whole world changed."

What? *Whole world?* Ridiculous.

It felt like my life was one gigantic puzzle. All the pieces were there but incomplete. I was so freaking glad the girls were coming over later to cook Mexican. I needed advice and chips with queso. Lots of queso. I gently tugged on Baxter's collar. We picked up the pace, heading home. For once, the empty house seemed too big for just me, too cold, too alone.

℘ ℘ ℘

"He's such a broody douchecanoe, Anna. Oh, that's his new nickname, BM, Broody Max!" Olivia said with a shrug, finishing the last of the guacamole and helping herself to another taco.

I told them everything, from the office to the gala, finishing with last night. I disappointed Addison by leaving out a lot of the juicy details, but honestly, I wanted to keep those memories for me.

"BM, as in poop? No Liv, gross. He's an immature asshole who is sulking because he didn't get his way," Jenna added, blending more margaritas.

"I disagree, y'all," Addison said. "He's hurt, so he's putting up walls. A guy who was just looking for an easy lay wouldn't have respected your decision not to screw and then held you all night. And I like BM. It works whether or not he's an asshole."

"But did I do the wrong thing? You didn't see his face, didn't see the side of him I saw this morning. Didn't see the intimacy last night." Slurping loudly on my heavy-handed margarita, I sighed and laid my head on the table with a thunk.

"No," came a chorus of voices, giving me a bit of affirmation, but not enough to make me feel better.

"Why am I this miserable if I did the right thing?" I said, raising my head to take another sip. "This can't be real. It's too much, too fast. I never believed in the insta-lust, insta-love, thing, but I sure as hell believe now."

"No babe, it's not too fast. Just because it happened that way doesn't mean the feelings aren't real. If this is meant to happen, no amount of either of you staying away will work," Olivia said, refilling the drinks.

"Then why did I even say no if there's a chance we should be together." I laid my head back down and closed my eyes. "I screwed up. You didn't see how closed off he was. This is my fault."

"No, that's not true! Listen to what Liv said," Jenna cooed. "Why don't you get to know each other better? Build a friendship first. Then see if more is something you both still want."

"Remember what happened with Edward and me?" Olivia said, checking on the cookies she was making between eating tacos. "I accidentally gave him the wrong address for our first date, and you had to literally pick me up off the floor. I was so upset, thinking he stood me up. There is nothing wrong with fast feelings."

"Same for Tommy and me," Addison followed. "We fell fast and hard. But seriously, it's obvious you've already fallen for Max, so why don't you get it out of your system. If it's anything like that mark he left on your neck, you two would have a mind-blowing fuck."

"If we did, there's no way it would be a one-time thing, and like I told him, I won't be a dirty secret."

"So don't be," Jenna said.

"Yes," Addison added. "And you desperately need a ticket to pound-town, especially since you are already dick-matized by Max's Sex Pistol."

"How about he puts his banana in your fruit salad?"

"I'm sure you'll love playing his Sausage-Saxophone!"

"He needs to go exploring in Punarnia?"

"Or go plowing through your bean field?"

"I fucking love y'all but stop. I'm gonna pee. Talk about something else!" I held my stomach and doubled over in laughter, feeling lighter by the second.

"Right back-atcha. Here, drink more feel-good juice," Olivia said with a wink, filling my glass as I tried desperately to stop laughing.

"Well, if we are changing the subject, I got into an argument with Dr. Dumbass the other day," Jenna said, taking a drink.

"Dr. Duvall? The other doctor at the clinic? What happened?" Addison said, changing from the fierce redhead with a dirty mind to an even fiercer friend.

"He said I need to stop taking in every stray animal that comes in and send them straight to the shelter."

"What a jerk! Didn't you say you volunteer your time and always pay the cost of treatment while you work to find them a home?" Olivia added, plating the cookies.

"Yes. But he thinks treating those animals takes away from potential new patients and more money. It's maddening," she said, finishing her drink and pouring another.

"Never question what you're doing, Jenna," I said, taking her hand and squeezing it. "Think of all the animals you've saved, including that ungrateful, brown-eyed boy over there. Maybe you should try to partner with a non-profit?"

"I've been thinking along those lines, actually," Jenna said.

"Cookies are done," Olivia said, "Time to get Chip-Faced!!"

We all groaned at the cheesy joke, reaching for her cookies and laughing.

"These are delicious, Olivia. New recipe?" Addison asked, taking another cookie from the plate.

"Yes, actually. Kristin thought it up," Olivia said, taking a bite of one.

"Edwards's sister? How is she working out?" Jenna said.

"Oh, she's fantastic. But she has so much potential. I wish I had something more for her than a part-time baker and cashier."

"Well, it's awesome that you helped her. Why don't you invite her the next time we all go out," I said, taking two more cookies. There was no shame in my cookie game. I'd jog tomorrow. Or Monday.

"Good idea, Annaleigh," Jenna said. She was the only one eating a single cookie—the only one with apparent self-control.

"I know she would love that. Thanks, girls," Olivia said.

We talked and drank until just past midnight, and even though I didn't have a clear path for Monday, at least I knew my feelings were valid. Not dating and not fucking would have to be enough, for now. Who knows, that decision might last *all* week.

- 14 -

YOU ARE THE ONE

Max

The fucking gala played on repeat all day Sunday, *everything* about the gala. My vision went red when I saw Benjamin sitting with Blue and even more when Leslie snuck off with someone. But I couldn't blame her. I was cold all night and pissed when Katie blindsided me with a date. Even if I had been interested, her first question was about my fucking salary. No, thank you.

I tried to burn off my frustration with bourbon, running, and unpacking, but nothing worked. Blue was right, and it pissed me the hell off. We couldn't walk into the office Monday and assume everyone would be okay with us being together. Hell, I wasn't even sure they allowed it.

I wasn't used to having all these feelings. It was like someone had taken my heart, put it in a blender, and pressed pulse. I should call Warren, but I didn't know what the hell I'd say. I was acting like a maniac. I should be focused on my fucking career. But I'd went against my better judgment and said we should date. What a fucking mistake.

A traitorous voice in my head whispered that I scared her, that she was protecting herself, that she needed time, but the rational part of my mind said to walk away. But after tasting her, holding her, could I walk away? *Did I even want to try?*

Driving to work the next morning, I tried to ignore the damn feelings that threatened to rip my insides to shreds. There was no way I could walk into the office this distracted. I pulled into the parking garage and turned the truck off, closing my eyes and leaning my head back. I blew out a breath and got out. My glasses fogged as I stepped into the heat and walked out of the garage, so I shrugged out of my suit jacket and laid it across my arm, cuffing my sleeves.

I turned left instead of right and walked along the sidewalk, watching the city wake up. Jitterbug Bakery was a two-story brick building with light purple shutters and a brightly decorated chalkboard sign outside advertising specials. I might as well grab a coffee and a peace-offering while I'm sulking. Or more like an: *I'm sorry, I just assumed we would date after one of the most intense experiences of my life*, offering.

The inside of the bakery had black-and-white checkered tiles on the floor, close-up pictures of coffee and cookies, and a dozen booths with red benches. The smell of rich beans and warm blueberry muffins filled the cozy space with promises of sugar and caffeine and made my stomach grumble. I got in line and stared at the endless options on the menu, not bothering to figure out the macros.

"Welcome to Jitterbugs. How can I make your morning sweeter?" the cashier said, giving me a kind smile. She had a pretty face with black hair pulled up in a high ponytail and sharp eyes, reminding me of my favorite grade-school teacher, who could discipline you with a look.

"Good Morning," I said, my eyes glued to the pastry display, still not knowing what the hell to order. "Is that banana nut bread? And what's in the Butterbeer Latte, please?"

Her eyes softened, and she leaned to the side to check the glass display. "Yes. That's banana nut bread with dark chocolate chips, and the latte is a combination of toffee-nut and vanilla."

"Wow, yes. One of each, please. I'll also take an egg-white bagel and a Hazelnut Latte with an extra shot and an orange scone."

"Good choices, we call the latte and scone combo the Anna," the cashier said, turning her head to look at me before ringing up the order. Her eyebrows were pinched together, and she put one hand on her hip, sizing me up.

"The Anna? That's my assistant's name," I answered, reaching into my pocket for my wallet.

"Holy shit, your Broody Max," she said, lowering her voice when the people behind me looked up in surprise.

"Um, yes, I've heard that nickname before. I'm Maxwell Jackson, and you are?" I said, holding my hand out to her.

"Olivia Klein. Owner and head baker." She shook my hand back, hard.

"Olivia, it's a pleasure to meet you officially."

"Annaleigh's one of my best friends. I was there at the beach and with her yesterday."

Damn, this woman got right to the punch line. I liked her immediately.

"Ah, well. Annaleigh is an amazing assistant. I'm truly fortunate to be working with her. And I apologized for that unfortunate situation on the beach," I said, letting go of her hand and passing her my card.

"That, Broody, is an acceptable answer," she said, nodding her head as if I passed whatever test was just thrown down.

"Are you the one I have to thank for that nickname?" I said, taking my glasses off and patting my pockets for my handkerchief. Coming up empty, I sighed and put my glasses back on, giving Olivia a tight smile.

"Nope," she answered.

I couldn't explain it, but I wanted to make a good impression. Olivia had a curious expression on her face like she was holding back.

"Please add an extra cookie and black coffee," I said, slipping a ten into the tip jar. She gave me another knowing look and took a deep breath, meeting my eyes, "May I ask you a question?"

Her words were softer, and I leaned forward, nodding my head. She picked at the corner of her purple apron before motioning me to the end of the counter. I followed her and waited, putting my jacket back on and crossing my arms.

"It's more, right? What you two have? I've, um, known Annaleigh since college and, well…" Her voice trailed off, and she looked at the floor.

I could pretend I didn't know what she was talking about or assured her that Saturday night was a meaningless fling. But the lines between what I wanted and what was right, had blurred. There was no point pretending I still didn't want to make her mine.

"Yes," I said, looking down and clearing my throat. "But I couldn't ask Annaleigh to jeopardize her job or her values. But I think I already did, and it backfired big time."

Shit. Where had that come from? My body had to be in overdrive, making up for the last decade of not having a real, meaningful relationship. But she was right. I'm her boss. Whatever we had was a bad idea. I glanced at my watch, suddenly uncomfortable, with the urge to hightail it out of the bakery without a glance back.

"Talk." Olivia stood with her hands on her hips and stared at me, not blinking. *What the hell was I supposed to say?*

"I don't exactly have the best track record with relationships," I started, not a clue where I was going. Maybe she would roll her eyes then kick me out so I could avoid this dumpster-fire of a conversation.

"You did a lot of screwing around?" she prodded, almost looking for a reason to dislike me.

I glanced around the bakery to see if any curious eyes were on us before continuing.

"Yes. I mean, no. It's more like I came here to start over, and now I'm losing focus."

"Go on," Olivia said, looking confused.

"I wasn't looking for anyone. I'm always in control. Not used to feeling this way. Doubting myself. Distracted. This is too fast, but she's all I think about, and after the gala…"

I trailed off because I knew I wasn't making sense. I rubbed the back of my neck, waiting for Olivia's judgement, but she just continued to stare.

"I met my husband here," she said, sweeping her hand around the bakery. "He started coming in every other day and ordering the same thing, just on the off chance I was at the register. It took him five months and fifteen pounds before he asked me out. We had a disastrous first date that almost never turned into a second one. But afterward, I wanted to get to know him. I wanted to close the bakery early to spend every moment I could with him. The point, Broody Max, is that my focus shifted. I found something I wasn't looking for, and it was the best thing that ever happened to me. Plus, he's a marketing genius, and the bakery is booming."

I stared at her. It couldn't be a good thing my focus was shifting. And in Blue's own words, this wasn't something she thought should continue.

"If the shift or distraction or whatever we have is affecting my work, then it's not a good thing," I said, feeling the frustration all over again.

"Then there's your answer, regardless of what you want. You have to decide what's important." She handed me the coffee and pastries, moving back to the register.

Waving my hand in a half-hearted goodbye, I headed outside, my glasses fogging again in the humid air.

I passed the black coffee to Charlie and the cookie to Elise before settling in for the day, putting the peace offering or whatever on Blue's desk. I could hear Jake through the wall on the phone and was syncing my calendar when I looked up to see her putting her things away.

She had air pods in and wore a red pencil skirt paired with a black and white buttoned blouse. Her blonde hair cascaded in soft curls over her shoulders, and I caught a small smile as she picked up the coffee and wrapped her pink lips around the lid. I stared at her, and it felt like my heart was going to beat straight out of my chest.

Looking up, she mouthed thank you before sitting at her desk with a wink and leaning to open a drawer. There was a noticeable red, raised bite on her neck. *Fuck, that was sexy*, seeing my mark on her, my claim. Her eyes met mine, so I touched my neck and raised one eyebrow in my best Sean Connery impression. She immediately fixed her hair and sat down, sending another wink my way.

Feeling lighter than I had Sunday, my fingers flew across my keyboard, finishing several emails and compiling events. Before I knew it, morning turned to afternoon, and my cell rang with an all too familiar tune. With a sigh, I answered, stepping around my desk to shut the door.

"Father."

"Maxwell," his voice was crisp, and he said my name like it was something stuck to the bottom of his shoe. I wouldn't give him the satisfaction of speaking first, so the silence dragged on until I heard a sharp breath.

"Your mother asked me to call you."

"Please tell her you fulfilled your obligation. Now, if there's nothing else," I said, taking off my glasses and laying them on my desk so I could rub my eyes.

"Don't take that tone with me. We both agreed it's time for this charade to stop. Nicole has kept your penthouse in pristine condition in anticipation of your return. The firm will overlook your recent behavior and allow you to practice if you wish. You will book a return flight no later than…"

"Stop, Father. Enough," I interrupted, running my fingers through my hair and pacing the floor, feeling the familiar rage course through my veins. My speech and tone reverted to proper, professional, cold, and disciplined, everything my father valued.

"I beg your pardon. Do not forget who you are speaking to," he barked.

"I forget nothing. I'm not coming back. Nicole and I are through. I relinquished the apartment to her to do with it as she wished. I do not wish to speak or see her again." I paused and dug my knuckle in my eye, preparing my next words carefully. "Father, I hate we parted on difficult terms. Perhaps—"

"Perhaps you will do your duty as a Smerdon and to this family and not be a disgrace like your brother!"

"A disgrace? Warren is anything but that. You are a disgrace for disowning your son! You are a disgrace because you value your social status over both of your sons' happiness. And I'm a disgrace for letting you and Mother control me for so long."

The anger dissipated as the words sunk in. I was a disgrace. I was in a situation of my making, undeserving of Annaleigh's time and affection.

Pity? Party of one, right this way.

"Maxwell!"

"I'm sorry, Father. This conversation is over." I hung up the phone and sagged into my chair. A blinking icon caught my attention on the bottom of my laptop screen.

Annaleigh.Mackey: Lunch?
Annaleigh.Mackey: Lunch?
Annaleigh.Mackey: I'm bringing you lunch. Back soon.

Damn, I missed her messages. Her ability to compartmentalize was inspiring. I wish I could do the same. Thinking about her helped the anger melt from my mind, clearing my vision. She was the sweet to my surly, the shade on my sunny day, the ice to my bourbon.

A knock interrupted my train of thought.

"Max?"

"Come in."

"Here's a late lunch for you. How was the rest of your weekend? Er, um…"

Her voice trailed off, and she nibbled on her lower lip, placing the containers on my desk.

"Thank you. It was fine. What did you bring?"

"Mozzarella Caprese sandwich with a garden salad. Hope that's alright. I got a turkey on rye. Please take that if you'd rather. I was going to give you the choice but didn't want to interrupt."

"This is perfect. One of my favorites, Annaleigh," I said, opening the container.

"Okay, I'll leave you to it. Remember, you have an eight o'clock meeting tomorrow and lunch with Jake," she said, walking around my desk to hand me a bottle of water.

When she sat it down, I saw the mark again. Reaching out, I traced it with my fingers, running my other hand along her thigh.

"I'm sorry, Blue," I said, pulling her hair so it covered the mark again.

"I'm not," she answered before touching her finger to her lips and walking out.

- 15 -

DOUBT QUESTIONS
Annaleigh

The weeks dragged on.

Max was over-the-top professional, exactly what I asked for from him. But whenever he thought I wasn't looking, I felt the heat of his gaze. Our touches lingered, our eyes smoldered, and my resolve was crumbling.

We were leaving for the conference in Tennessee Sunday morning, and thinking about spending the entire week with Max had me on edge. My nerves vibrated when he was near. He had taken over every empty corner of my mind.

On Friday, I got to the office first and put a quart of strawberries on Jake and Elaine's desk and coffee on Max's, taking a moment to glance around before I sat at my desk to peel an orange and reply to emails. Jake walked by and gave me a two-fingered wave before disappearing into his office for a call, tapping his watch to remind me we had a meeting afterward.

Nodding and adjusting the paper stacks on my desk, my eyes landed on the white envelope Uncle Bob sent me in the mail. I slid the letter-opener under the seal and removed the check and note with a groan. I hated getting these checks, and I hated how guilty they made me feel.

Annaleigh,
Use this check as a reminder of how strong and talented you are.
Spend the money.
Do what makes you happy. Music heals.
Love,
Uncle Bob

I read the note twice and stared at the check, popping another slice in my mouth and thinking about what happened.

After Bird's accident, I got drunk. *Really drunk.* I wrote song after song, telling our story. It started as a cathartic release to get over what happened. The words poured out of me like the bourbon I drank. One drunken Twitter contest, a trip to California, and two double-platinum albums later, and I was left with nothing but guilt. I had exploited our life, our music, and Bird's pain. I didn't deserve the royalties. Running my fingers over Uncle Bob's note, I folded the check and tucked it in my purse.

Hearing Jake's heavy footfalls brought me back to the present. He stopped in front of my desk and smiled.

"How have you been feeling, Annaleigh? Is everything ready for Sunday?"

"I've been good. Thanks, Jake. More tired than usual, but this will help," I said, holding up the orange. "The car will pick us up that morning, and our flight leaves at eleven o'clock. All our Elite Passes are active, and we have that evening free before Monday. I emailed you and Max an updated itinerary earlier. No major changes. Are you sure you're okay flying? We can always drive."

"I'll be fine, thanks. I want to make sure we're rested for Monday, and an eight-hour car ride is not the way to do that. Remind me when…"

"I'll meet you at the baseball field Saturday to drop Baxter off. I appreciate Katie and the kids watching him."

"No problem, you know they love to spoil him. My Martin D-15M will be delivered this afternoon. Are you good to sign for it?" Jake said with a smile.

"Do you even have to ask? You know I'll be glad to sign, as long as I can open and tune it for you, to make sure it arrived in pristine condition, of course," I said, my fingers tingling thinking about the delivery.

He'd ordered another acoustic guitar and had it shipped to the office, hoping to slip it by Katie. But she knew exactly what he was doing and only acted blissfully unaware.

Jake knew most of my history with music, having played at *B's* a time or two with his jam band, Wulfe. He wore dark clothes and sunglasses when he played. Katie thought it was hilarious, telling him it was unlikely he would see a client, at midnight, in a bar.

"Ha, you know it. I'm out for the afternoon. See you Sunday,"

"Sure thing. Thanks, Jake."

By late afternoon, the office was empty, and I felt that familiar tingle at the base of my spine. On top of lyrics sticking, I was getting the itch to play more these days. Maybe Max was what I needed to breakthrough my guilt.

Nope, not going there.

While I waited for the delivery, I stepped into Max's office to water his plants. He handled the renovations like a pro, choosing to keep the sleek black desk and matching table, but adding a soft gray couch on the opposite wall and new high-back leather chairs. It was all hard edges and clean lines, matching his personality. I smiled and moved a letter opener from one corner of his desk to the other, wondering if he would notice, then watered his dragon trees and evergreen, noticing they had fresh fertilizer.

He'd love my terrace. I had it divided into four sections: flowers, fruit, ivy, and succulents. There was also a large hammock that I loved to lie in and read. I closed my eyes, and for a second, I could picture Max and me laying together in the hammock, sharing a bottle of chilled wine, watching the stars, and talking. I'd love to know about his family, his hobbies, his favorite foods, his likes, his dislikes, and his ticklish spots.

Damnit.

The buzz on my desk was a welcome distraction, and I thanked Charlie for the call before meeting the UPS driver at the elevator and signing for the guitar.

I was a glutton for punishment, taking the package and walking back into Max's office just to feel close to him and be near his space. But he had the most comfortable office chair, high back, and black leather with plenty of spring for leaning back to stretch and to play.

I sat down and carefully opened the guitar. The fretboard was polished heavy wood, and the color was a deep mahogany brown. I ran my fingers up and down each steel string, tuning, listening, breathing in the sounds. The strings should be replaced soon with the guitar being so new, but for now, I couldn't wait to play.

Music was a language ingrained in my soul, and strumming the strings was oddly hypnotic, a place I could get lost in the notes and melody. Uncle Bob was right. Music was a place where I could heal. Maybe Bird's accident wasn't my fault.

I began in A-minor, listening as the sounds washed over me and feeling at peace. Softly singing, I started with Cat Stevens' *Wild World* and moved onto *Something* by The Beatles.

Closing my eyes, I played Dave Matthews Band next, swaying slowly as the words to *Crash* flowed then morphed to *Crush* soon after. Maybe that's what this was with Max. Just a crush that had gotten out of hand. Way out of hand.

Damnit.

"You're beautiful," said a quiet and all too familiar voice from the doorway.

I had a hard time sharing this part of me with anyone. And now, Max was standing at the door, staring at me like I had just bared my soul to him. Maybe I had.

"Don't stop," he stepped into the room and walked closer. "Please.

Keep going. You look... Sound... Sing, Blue."

I didn't answer. Instead, I closed my eyes again and switched to F, playing one of my grandfather's favorites, *Blue Gardenias*, by Nat King Cole. I could feel him coming closer, his presence thickening the air in the room. But something was different. There was no nervousness, no worries. I felt at peace. I played the last chord and opened my eyes, smiling.

"How long have you been playing?" he asked, coming closer and bending down in my space. Max was looking at me like he'd never seen me before. And he hadn't, not this side.

"Um. Since before I could walk."

"Why are you blushing, Blue? Do you not want me here?"

"Yes. No. It's rare I play in front of anyone anymore. Mostly, I listen and sometimes write."

"Why?" he asked, leaning against the desk. The guilt tightened like a vice in my chest, but Max reached out and traced his fingers up my arm. His touch was soothing, calming, and I leaned into him.

"I was in a band, years ago," I said, laying the guitar back in the case. "My best friend had an accident during our last show one summer, collapsing on stage. I was too caught up in the music to see the warning signs."

I looked down at the floor, then out the window. Anywhere but those bourbon eyes. But talking to him, my thoughts flowed freely, like something inside of me recognized something inside of him. Something familiar, something that calmed my mind and soothed the guilt.

"You blame yourself?" he said, leaning closer. He wasn't judging, wasn't offering advice, and wasn't trying to fix anything. He was just here, listening, giving me what I needed. I'd missed his touch, so I leaned in. As if he knew, his fingers started the pattern again, tracing up and down my arm.

"Yes, and no. I blame myself, and I blame the music," I said. "If I hadn't been so caught up in the next show, the next song, the next lyric, I could have seen the signs. I feel like it was a deciding moment in my life.

A sign to show me consequences."

"I don't know, Blue. Maybe it was just an accident. But you shouldn't stop doing something that makes you as happy as you look now," he said, looking at the way my hands caressed the strings in the case.

"I understand the hurt, but you can't let it define your life. You can't let it define your happiness. Trust me, don't let it consume you." He traced his knuckles along my jaw, and I sighed, moving closer.

"What if I don't deserve it, Max?" My words were a whisper, a plea, a desperate attempt to move on from the past and to a future with him by my side.

"You deserve it, Annaleigh," he said, brushing his thumb against my lips.

This moment would stick with me. This man was not the wrong decision, and he was not someone I could walk away from either. I wanted to hear his hurt, hear his story, and hear his heart. And I wanted him to hear mine. Somehow, I wanted to give us a chance.

"You deserve everything, Blue. Deserve more than me."

"Max. I think I made a mistake. With you, with us."

"Maybe Blue. But you need to be sure."

With those words, he kissed my forehead and then the corner of my lips, letting his strong, long fingers run through my hair. He didn't break eye contact this time, and I wanted nothing more than for him to open his arms so he could hold me, so I could feel his strength surround me.

But I was the one that said no. He was respecting my wishes, my mistake. Not knowing what else to say, I watched him walk away.

"I'll see you Sunday. I'll be the one in jeans," he said, stopping at his office door and turning around.

"And I'll be the one in blue. Good night, Max."

16

WHISK ME AWAY

Max

A high-pitch, soft whistling roused me from my daydream as the plane made its descent into Nashville. During the short flight, Annaleigh dozed off, resting her head on my shoulder. The soft whistling was coming from her nose as she slept, and her hand rested on my thigh. I squeezed her lightly and brushed my thumb over her knuckles, "Baby. Wake up."

"Humm. Five more, Max. Not sleeping well."

Why wasn't she sleeping? Was she as restless as me? Honestly, I selfishly hoped so. These last weeks had been torture. Getting serious with someone was not something I had planned, and if I was honest, we're not serious, *yet*. Her desire to keep everything professional stayed at the forefront of my mind.

But her skirts kept getting shorter, and every time we talked, I learned more, fell harder. She was like a drug, and my world revolved around getting another hit.

Her book laid open on her lap, and judging from the paragraph I saw earlier, she likes to read contemporary romance—sexy, dirty, romance. I adjusted myself in the small airplane seat as she snuggled in closer, burying her hand under my Henley to stroke the dark hair on my abdomen.

Fuck, she felt better than I remembered.

When the car pulled in front of her house this morning, and I saw her in leggings and a baseball shirt, my resolve crumbled. She had an orange juice in her hand and her hair tied in a messy bun. I wanted to claim her lips. Consequences be damned.

"Come on, Blue. Open your eyes." I shook her lightly, and her slender fingers scraped hard across my stomach as she stretched her legs. I thrusted my hips up, hoping she got the memo before the entire plane saw what was happening in my jeans.

"What? Oh, Max, I fell asleep," she said, looking around. Her hand stayed underneath my shirt, and I was afraid to move, not wanting her to take it away.

"Yeah, I figured that out. We'll be landing shortly," I said, reaching out to twirl a strand of hair that had fallen loose from her bun. I had to touch her. This fucking sucked.

"Oh. Right. Sorry, I'm not sleeping well." She removed her hand from under my shirt and pulled it back down in an oddly intimate gesture. Her eyes didn't reach mine as she stretched her arms up over her head. I got a tantalizing peek at her toned stomach before she lowered them and looked around. Jake was in front of us, and our other partners weren't arriving until mid-week.

"Why aren't you sleeping?"

"I don't want to talk about it," she said, facing the window and biting on her thumbnail. I reached over and took her hand in mine so she would look at me.

"Why not?" I asked again.

"Because talking about it won't fix anything." She was vague on purpose. I could see it in her eyes, in her face.

"Why not?"

"You are infuriating. You know that, right?" she said, pulling her hand away and straightening her bun.

"Maybe I'm just trying to get to know you a little better." I shrugged my shoulders and took a sip of water, passing over her orange juice.

"Well, don't," she said, finishing the bottle. I watched her throat swallow and her pulse flutter. "I'm sorry. I don't mean to be short, Max."

"So make it up to me and tell me why not?"

The fasten seatbelt sign clicked off, and the pilot welcomed us to Nashville. Blue stood up, grabbing her carry-on and brushing past me with an exasperated look. Sighing and rubbing her temple, she turned and said, "This gets harder every day, Max."

"Well, not yet. But with the way your hand was moving, it wouldn't have been long."

She smiled, and it lit up her whole face, breaking the tension. She giggled softly, putting her hand in front of her mouth as a quiet snort escaped her lips.

"To be continued, Blue," I said, grabbing my carry-on and following her out.

The drive to the Atlas Hotel was uneventful. Annaleigh stayed glued to her phone, and Jake looked green around the gills. I was glued to her and the gentle sway of her hips as we walked inside. She handled our check-in with ease, all while texting with Luke, one of the other VPs, who was having an issue with a client.

Annaleigh dropped off her suitcase before letting herself into the joined suite Jake and I were sharing, unpacking a small bag and her laptop. Jake immediately went to his room and shut the door. The adjoining suite had two rooms and a bright common space with a small kitchenette, table, and couch. I walked over to the windows and opened the curtains, seeing the Nashville skyline. Annaleigh set up her laptop at the table and walked to the kitchenette. An orange appeared in her hand, and she peeled it while she heated water in the coffeemaker. Rummaging around in the smaller bag, she took out several tea bags and a small container of honey.

"I think you have a problem," I said, nodding to the fruit as she put a slice in her mouth.

"It's better than the alternative. Obsessed much?" She bit into another slice, licking the juice from her lips. *Damn, that was sexy.*

"Yep, I am. What's the alternative?" I crossed my arms, sitting down at the table and staring as she eyed the different tea bags, willing my cock to calm the hell down.

"Humm, good to know. I have hypocalcemia," she said, shrugging her shoulders and choosing a bag before tearing it open.

"What's that?" I said, leaning forward and wondering why the hell it took me so long to ask her about the damn oranges.

"I have low calcium. It's not a big deal, but I don't want to depend on medicine."

"But it seems like you depend on those oranges," I said.

She stopped seeping the tea and put her hands on her hips, taking a deep breath. "It's under control."

She turned her back and focused on the tea. I crossed my arms and squared my shoulders, anything to keep me from standing up and moving closer. She poured the boiling water from the coffee maker into a large mug.

"Want to tell me why you can't sleep, Blue, or is that under control too?" I sounded like a dick, but these last few weeks had sucked, and I needed to know what she was feeling.

"Okay, Max. You want to know?" She started, resting a hand on her hip and seeping the tea. Her eyes were hard, and her back was stiff like she was primed and ready for an argument.

Huh, maybe I didn't want to know, maybe it had nothing to do with me, and I was a selfish bastard for thinking it did.

"I haven't slept through the night since I stayed over with you. I forgot what it was like to have someone hold me. I'm questioning if I made the right decision with us. Actually, I'm questioning lots of things about my life right now. Happy?"

She looked defeated, and it took every ounce of willpower I had not to hold her, touch her.

Her shoulders slumped forward as she stirred. *Thank fuck.* She felt the same, even if she hated to admit it. She needed to know it had been the same for me. She needed to know I wanted nothing more than to make her mine. I opened my mouth to reply, but Jake opened the door and crossed the room, sitting down across from me and holding a tin of almonds.

"Here. Sip Jake. Easy." She put the tea in front of him with honey and a spoon, and I finally noticed that his hair was plastered to his forehead, and he had dark circles under his eyes. Lifting the mug with shaky hands, Annaleigh placed her hands over his and helped bring the tea to his lips.

"Slow. Easy, Jake," she said, and he nodded his head.

"Thank you," he whispered back, his usual confidence and bravado gone. But he still took one hand from the cup and pushed the almonds towards her.

"You shouldn't have sat by yourself, but it seems to be better this time," she said, picking up the almonds and eating one while surveying him. The concern in her eyes and the way she kept one hand on his bothered me, and I flashed back to the awful words Raymond said about her.

"Maybe, but it would have been worse if we drove," Jake said, interrupting my train of thought. "I get horrible airplane sickness, Max. Sorry, you have to see this side of me. Whatever this magic tea is, it always helps."

"Damn Jake, I hate that for you," I said, my eyes focused on where she was still touching him.

"It will pass soon," he replied, taking another sip and weakly smiling at us.

Annaleigh finally moved her hand and crossed her arms, studying Jake's face as the tea turned his color back to normal. Her phone rang, and she picked it up, walking across the room and mouthing to Jake to keep drinking. I could only hear her side of the conversation, but it sounded like Luke was having an issue with his password. Jake reached into her laptop bag, and before I could ask him what he was doing, he took out a small, black notebook. Holding her phone between her neck and shoulder, she took it from Jake with one hand and pushed his mug forward with the other.

"No, Luke, it's percent then star. Sure. For who? Update the Business Risk Rating? Yes. Okay. I have to go, another call. You too. Talk later."

She looked at the phone and frowned before putting it up to her ear again.

"Hi, Mom. Yes, Nashville. What? No…" She walked into Jake's room and shut the door without a glance at either of us. Whatever her mom said upset her.

I'd been in awe of the working relationship between those two, but it was finally sinking in why she loved her job so much and didn't want to jeopardize it. Annaleigh and Jake complimented each other's work habits, and she kept everything running smoothly, even from afar.

Christ, I was such a dick.

Why would she give this up? I ran my fingers through my hair and stood up. I needed to take a shower to decompress, but first, I was going to ask Jake more about those damn oranges.

"So, hypocalcemia?" I said, taking a deep breath and rolling my shoulders.

"Yeah. She gets exhausted and bad muscle cramps but doesn't like to take pills," he said, pushing the tea away.

"Oh," I said, looking at the almonds. "And I take it those have calcium. Why doesn't she like to take pills? Or find other ways to get calcium besides the oranges."

"Humm. She's a nurturer, Max, and doesn't want anyone to see her weaknesses. She has enough on her mind this week without worrying about her calcium levels. As I'm sure you've seen, I'd fall apart without her. She single-handedly can run that office from miles away. I'm just the lucky fuck that gets to reap the rewards," Jake said.

"What does she have to worry about this week?" I asked, desperate for any bit of information.

"That's not my place to share, but I see the way you look at her, Max."

His tone was light, but his eyes were sharp, daring me to disagree. This was dangerous grounds, and my next words needed to be thought-out.

"Mom, please," Annaleigh said, interrupting us and opening the door a little harder than necessary. Her face was flushed, and her foot was tapping. Turning my head to her, I shamelessly listened, hoping to understand more. "I won't change my mind. Yes, I talked to Bird last week, but it didn't come up. Okay, I will. Yes, I love you too. Love to Dad. Bye, Mom."

She closed her eyes, taking a deep breath before coming back to the room and sitting down at the table with us.

"Is it tomorrow?" Jake asked, pushing the almonds closer again. She absentmindedly took one, chewing softly before standing up and pouring more hot water into his cup.

"No, Wednesday."

"Ah. What's on the schedule this week?" Jake asked, not pressing her and reaching for the tea again.

"Wednesday and Friday, we're free after lunch with a return flight first thing Saturday. I've sent itineraries to your emails and have your presentations in my room."

"What's Wednesday, Annaleigh?" I said, eager for her answer.

"It's the anniversary of when Serin's *Beautifully Broken* album hit Double-Platinum."

Of all the things for her to say, that was most definitely the least expected. An Album? She was being sarcastic. Why would anyone be upset over an album hitting Double-Platinum? Didn't that mean it sold several million copies?

"Serin? The Popstar? Are you serious?" I asked.

"Yeah, Max. The Popstar. I'm glad we have that afternoon off," she said, brushing me off and sitting beside Jake. She powered up her laptop and hummed until Jake interrupted her.

"What are your plans that day, Annaleigh? You better be leaving the hotel." He was kneading his shoulder and finishing the last of his tea.

"Oh yes, we're in Nashville! I'll be visiting the Country Music Hall of Fame and going on the Walking Food and Pub Tour. You two have that Food and Wine Tasting, right?"

"Right, I can't wait to talk about wine flavors for hours with stuffy executives."

"It's tannins Jake, and you're a stuffy executive," she said with a wink.

"I remember you saying you listen to country music," I said, wanting to bring the topic back to her.

"Oh yes, especially with being born and raised in the South. Okay guys, I'm heading back to my room to relax before tomorrow. Text when you're ready to go to dinner, or if you would rather reconvene in the morning."

She pushed the mug of tea to Jake before packing up her bag and walking out with her laptop. As she waved two fingers behind her, the door clicked shut, and I was alone with Jake, ready for his continued line of questioning.

"Okay, Max. I'm going to decompress. We'll hook up for dinner later," he said, getting up and walking back to his room. He closed the door with a click, leaving me alone with nothing but the lingering smell of oranges.

17

VOICES ECHO
Annaleigh

The Country Music Hall of Fame was better than I thought. I had a taco from Bajo Sexto and bought too many souvenirs. It was easy to see why people called this place the Smithsonian of Country Music.

I skipped the Walking Food Tour and went straight for the Pub Crawl, making it to three bars before heading back to the hotel to give my emails a once over and change before dinner. There was a bar I was eager to check out to watch live music and line dancing. And I had killer cowboy boots I was dying to break in.

My laptop and notes laid spread out over the conference table, taking up the entire space since Jake and Max were away for the afternoon. Nothing was urgent except an email from Raymond asking me to call him. I sent him an instant message on our server instead, not wanting to hear his condescending voice.

Annaleigh.Mackey: What can I do for you, Raymond?
Raymond.Whitney: Seven p.m. Saturday.
Annaleigh.Mackey: I don't understand.

Raymond.Whitney: Benjamin will pick you up then.
Annaleigh.Mackey: No, thank you. Please keep all correspondence professional.
Raymond.Whitney: Seven p.m. Sharp
****Raymond.Whitney is Offline and cannot receive messages****

Fantastic. Now I needed to make myself scarce Saturday night. *Hang on!* How did he know where I lived?

Oh. Hell. No.

Accessing my personnel file was a clear misuse of power and intimidation. I saved the message and stuck a sticky-note on the corner of my laptop, reminding me to tell Jake before I headed back to my room to get ready, pushing Raymond and his idiot man-child out of my mind.

I put my hair in two French braids that fell below my bra and jeans that were practically painted on my body. My new brown cowboy boots with teal stitching matched my white blouse had a a scoop neck and cap sleeves. I tucked my ID, credit card, and room key behind my phone and a spare red lip gloss in my pocket before closing the door.

I leaned against the back of the mirrored elevator and closed my eyes, resting my head on the cool glass. Between the plane ride and now, I'd decided something. Something important, something big.

I wanted Max.

I remembered his heavy-lidded eyes beneath his thick lashes and those bourbon eyes that saw into my soul. He awakened something in me I thought I'd lost, bringing music back to my life. He made my lyrics stick and lessened the guilt. I was a better person with him, and he needed to know.

As I walked down Broadway Street, music drifted from the open doors, and the air buzzed with excitement.

Wait.

That was my phone. Looking at Bird's name, I swiped right, and I held the phone to my ear, "Happy Anniversary," Bird said.

"Thank you," I replied, stopping on the street and putting one hand on my hip.

"Stop being a martyr. I can hear it in your voice. This is an important day! Time to stop with the self-flagellation and move the fuck on."

"I'm getting there." I looked up at the sky. The bright lights of Nashville had dulled the stars, but they were still there, ever present, like the lyrics that swirled in my head.

"May our voices echo from the heaven's above to the melody of your enticing caress."

"That's a bullshit cop-out, and you know it," Bird said, dragging me back to the present. "You told our story, using the lyrics you wrote to heal. It should have given you closure, but all it does is drag you into a pit of depression. The fucking money doesn't matter. You saved me! You're my best friend! You were there when I got married, for Christ's sake! Who knows where I'd be if it hadn't been for you," Bird said.

I could hear the exasperation in Bird's voice, and suddenly, it made sense. It was time to stop letting this guilt consume my life and infiltrate my chance at happiness.

"It's time to move on, lady. Quit pitying yourself and be proud of what you did! The line must be drawn here!"

"Did you just quote Jean Luke Picard?" I said, smiling at the cheesy reference.

"Hell yeah, I did. So, what's it gonna be? You love to sing and write; you love to play. So, you know what you should do?"

"Sing, play, and write?" I said, tugging on the end of one of my braids and pacing back and forth. The neon signs of Broadway Street blinked and popped, and it was like a lightbulb had gone off in my head. Bird was right.

"Bingo! I'll never quit. I still play every weekend, and every time I do, it reminds me of what could have happened. I won't be the reason you quit. Stop blaming me, stop blaming the music, and stop blaming yourself.

You know I love you, Annaleigh, but just because I did a shitty thing and fucking OD'd doesn't mean everyone close to you will hurt you. You are a fucking catch. You're sweet, gorgeous, and have the kindest heart I know. You're a little quirky too, but that just adds to your charm. Give yourself more credit and open your heart."

The line was silent, and I thought about the words. "Open my… You know, I think I needed to hear that, Bird. I sort of had a breakthrough a few weeks ago and started writing."

Sighing, I looked up, taking in the unfamiliar surroundings in the city. "Are you serious? What happened?"

"I, um, met someone, Bird. He's grumpy, and loyal, and not afraid to tell me how he feels."

I pictured Max's face and his smile showing both dimples. The smile I liked to think was only for me. The smile I hoped he would make when I tell him how I felt.

"Babe. I'm so proud of you. I hope he knows how fucking lucky he is to have you. I have to run, but let's talk next week and plan our visit."

"Sure, plan on staying with me for at least a night. Baxter misses his sleeping buddy."

"You got it. Talk to you soon. Love you, babe."

"Love you too. Bye Bird."

I hung up the phone as Bird's words sunk in. One simple conversation had me finally understanding and letting go of almost six years worth of guilt. Guilt that had consumed me and infested everything in my life. I'd let it poison my love life, my happiness, and my music. I hadn't been in a serious relationship since college, and if I was completely honest, I'd never gone all-in with another person.

A giant neon guitar reflected on the sidewalk and drew my eyes up. *Hank's Honkytonk* had snuck up on me, and I stopped abruptly, stumbling in my boots. I walked up to the door as the sound of Luke Combs drifted to the street. The bouncer was a tall, bald guy as wide as a brick house with thick, corded muscles and tattoos snaking up his arms to his neck. He motioned me forward without a word and checked my ID before waving me in.

Call me crazy, but having tall, bald, and muscular at the door was reassuring. I was sure he could stop trouble with one stone-cold glance. Making my way up to the bar, I raised my hand to get the bartenders' attention and perused the liquor.

"Hey there, pretty, the name's Ace. What can I getcha?" The bartender said with a smile.

He was wearing tight jeans and a white tank with an armband to hold his bottle opener. He had messy hair and a beard, pulling off the classic cowboy look with ease. His hand tapped on the bar as he waited with a crooked smile.

"Jack and Coke, please Ace. And please send the bouncer by the door a refill."

"You got it, doll. What's your name?"

"Annaleigh," I said.

"Annaleigh? Nice to meet you. Drinks coming right up."

With a nod and a turn, he walked away, returning a minute later with my whiskey.

"Here you go, Little Lady. Bouncer Billy has his coke and is grateful. Nice looking out. You starting a tab?"

"Yes, please." I passed him my card and looked around. The walls were decorated with old hubcaps and guitars. Tables surrounded the perimeter of the dance floor, making a nice sized space where several couples were already two-stepping to the live band that had just finished a Morgan Whalen song.

"Hey Ace, you seen Jess?" A big guy holding a Gibson said, leaning over the bar and grabbing the soda gun. I tried to focus on the couples' dancing, but with them talking right beside me, I couldn't help but overhear.

"No man. She's still not here?"

"No, she's a no show. Without her, we are going to have to cut our set short," the big guy said, taking a drink of his soda and shaking his head.

He took off his hat and wiped a hand across his brow before looking at the stage.

"Sucks, Spencer," Ace replied, polishing the bar with a clean rag and eyeing the people sitting at the other end.

"What does Jess do?" The words were out of my mouth before my brain caught up, and both men looked at me like I was crazy.

"She sings and plays the guitar. Why? You going to be her replacement?" Spencer laughed, shaking his head and refilling his glass before turning towards the stage.

"Sure," I said with a shrug.

"What?" They both replied.

I finished my drink and turned on the stool to face Spencer, crossing my arms.

"I can play the guitar and sing. What's on your setlist?"

Sucking on the straw with my brows raised, I waited for an answer as they looked at each other and then back to the stage.

"We have Darius Rucker, Lady A, Eric Church, and more coming up. Here," Spencer said, taking a folded piece of paper from his back pocket and handing it to me before reaching down for the soda gun again.

"I'm familiar with everything on here," I said, looking over the list. "What do you think, Spencer?"

"You know what, sure, Little Lady, why the hell not. Let's start with *Hole in the Bottle* and see how you jive with the rest of the guys."

"Deal. And I'll use your Gibson for it," I said, reaching out to shake his hand.

"Betsy here?" he said, patting the guitar with clear affection. "No, ma'am you won't, but there's a Gretsch if you're interested."

"Falcon?" I asked.

"Rancher," Spencer replied.

"Done."

With a fresh drink from Ace, I followed Spencer to the bar to meet the guys in his band. Spencer was handsome with dirty blonde hair that touched his collar and curled on the bottom, dark eyes, and a body that made you do a double-take. His black T-shirt clung to his skin, showing his muscles underneath, and his tight jeans left little to the imagination. He had a huge belt buckle and hat to match.

Normally, a man like that would get my lady parts in a tizzy, but feeling him pressed against me, introducing me to the band, so close I could smell his aftershave, wasn't having any effect at all because it wasn't the spicy sandalwood and leather smell of Max. I was going to stay like this, obsessing over every detail, until I told him I felt.

I tried to focus on the brightly lit stage, with room for half a dozen people and every country music instrument you could ever want to play. After Spencer finished introductions, we warmed up while the jukebox cranked out a few early nineties songs for the crowd.

The tables were overflowing, and the sounds of boots and heels scraping the dance floor filled the space. My mind emptied, bringing back the familiar rituals. My muscle memory took over as I played a riff and warmed up my vocal cords.

"Not that I'm not grateful, Anna, but you can play guitar and sing lead vocals to all the songs in our set with no practice?" One guy asked. Jack, I think.

"Jack, was it? Yeah, I can. As long as I'm familiar with the song, I don't have an issue playing it."

"Damn, I'm looking forward to hearing you then," he said.

"Then let's do it right!" I said, turning to face the crowd.

It was surreal, not hearing the ritual from Alice's Monsters echoed back to me, but weirdly, it was like closure.

A loud voice cut through my thoughts, introducing my new temporary band, The Gravel Tracks. I stepped up to the mic, pulling a spare cowboy hat I found low and waving my hand in greeting.

"Hello, Nashville! I'm Anna, and I'm happy to be filling in tonight. Let's start this set out with a song about not missing a man but needing a refill!"

With cheers and whoops from the crowd, I sang, tapping my foot in time with the beat and leaning into the mic, breathing in the familiar smells of beer and sawdust. The lights were bright, but I could see people dancing, drinking, and clapping along. It was invigorating, infectious, and made me want more. But as I was singing, a creeping thought made its way to my brain, like spilling a drink down the stairs.

I wanted to share this with Max.

I wanted to come home to him, have him hold me at night, and have coffee with him the next morning.

As the last notes finished, Spencer sauntered up and taped the setlist to a speaker at my feet. Leaning close, he bent down and talked to the audience, draping an arm around me.

"So, what's the verdict on this little lady? Should we keep her around for the night?"

Resonating cheers filled the space, and I raised my hand in thanks as Spencer winked and moved to my right. We began another song, and with a fresh drink beside me, I focused on the music, strumming the chords and letting the sound melt over me, letting go of the past and ready to embrace the future.

- *18* -

SENSUAL DESIRE
Max

Annaleigh was on my mind and in my space all week long, running the day-to-day details with perfection and ease. Her laptop was open on the conference table, covered with blue sticky notes, and Jake was talking with Katie on the phone in his room. I thought about the week and reached down to adjust the laces on my Balmain black and white sneakers. I took point for each focus group and presentation, and the response was better than expected.

Running my fingers through my hair and tugging on the short strands, I tried to stop thinking about her words on the plane. She hadn't been able to sleep. I'd been sleeping fine but leaning heavily on the bourbon, trying to forget how my arms felt around her.

Stretching my legs underneath the table, I kicked the side, rattling Annaleigh's laptop. I steadied it, noticing a sticky note that said: *Benjamin 7 pm Saturday.*

My hackles rose as I adjusted my glasses and read it again. My palms got sweaty, and I could feel my temper rising. *What the hell was happening Saturday?* Was this the real reason she didn't want more with me? Was she already involved with that dick-weasel?

I was mulling the words over when Jake opened the door and walked out looking like he belonged in a bad western movie. Right down to his scowl, bolo-tie, cowboy boots, and huge belt-buckle. He was walking bowlegged, like the boots were too tight and the jeans were too stiff. I pressed my hand over my mouth to stop him from hearing me laugh. But I couldn't help it.

"Not a word," he said, adjusting himself and picking up a hat from the sofa.

"I'm glad Katie doesn't want any more kids because these damn jeans are cutting off the circulation in my balls."

"Man, if we weren't in Nashville, you'd get your ass kicked!"

His scowl got impossibly harder, so I snapped a picture for posterity, making him laugh along with me.

"Ah! Now we have evidence I wore this monstrosity. Let's get out of here before I change my mind," he said, patting his pockets for his wallet and phone.

"Where are we heading?" I asked, standing up and doing the same.

I tucked my handkerchief in my pocket and put the sticky note back, resisting the urge to crumble it up and throw the laptop across the room. I had no right to be pissed, but I was. I wanted to demand to know what the note meant, then kiss her so hard my name would be the only thing on her lips.

"Annaleigh sent a list of the best bars to visit. I think she said she was going to a place called *Hank's*. Let's start there."

"Sounds good. If I have to look at you in that get-up all night, I'll need a beer," I said, shaking out my hands and cracking my neck.

"At least you're not wearing this. And I thought you'd want to be wherever she was."

"What?" I said, putting my wallet in my pocket and not listening to his words, too caught in that damn note.

"Are we really going to play this, Max?"

He pinned me with a stone-cold look, daring me to disagree. It was times like these that reminded me why he was the Bank President. Jake had an innate ability to read the situation and adapt accordingly.

I didn't know what to say. I was the one who stupidly asked her to date, asked her to compromise her position with the bank. But I sure as fuck was reconsidering things if she was too.

"Jake," I said.

"Let me stop you right there, Max. I'm talking to you now as a friend, not your boss. I've seen the way you look at her, and it's obvious she reciprocates. But since she is your employee, and it's an inappropriate gray area with human resources, you better be sure if you are going to pursue her, and the way you're staring at me says you will. Just know, you better always have her best interest at heart. Because if things go south, I've known her a lot longer than I've know you."

With that, he slapped my shoulder, hard, and strode to the door, not giving me a chance to respond.

But I should. I put myself between him and the door. His eyes widened, and he stood back, crossing his arms and narrowing his eyes.

"As my friend," I swallowed. "And boss. I would never intentionally do anything to hurt her. But Jake, man-to-man, I'm trying my damndest to fight this, but I don't think I can. And if she's in, I sure as hell am too."

Jake didn't respond, just nodded his head and turned to open the door, hitting me in the face with his ten-gallon hat. The elevator ride was silent, but by the time we reached Broadway Street, he was back to the easy-going guy I met one night at a dive bar in Chicago.

Hank's was nuts to butts with a phenomenal band playing, and a sassy, hot lead singer strutting around the stage with a cowboy hat pulled low and skin-tight jeans. Jake and I took the crowd's distraction with the band to slide into the last empty high-top table closest to the stage. My head was on a swivel, looking for a flash of blonde hair.

"Max. Max," Jake repeated until I looked up and ordered a draft from the server that walked over.

"You found her yet?" he asked with a smirk, as if he had already spotted her and was waiting for me to catch up.

Still looking, an achingly familiar, smooth as silk voice floated through the air, like a warm blanket. It sounded like home. The voice was amplified, and I turned towards the stage just as Annaleigh lifted her hat and whooped with the crowd's cheers.

Holy fuck! I was mesmerized as she traded one guitar for another and sauntered to the microphone closest to our table, leading the band in another song. It wasn't anything I recognized, but my foot still tapped along with hers.

Annaleigh's face was flushed under the lights, sweat glistening on her neck and arms. Her lips were red, and she was nibbling on them as she played, leaning in to harmonize with the chorus about wagon wheels. I waited, staring at her, hoping she'd see me. Every time she looked our way, her eyes seemed to pass right over, then focus back on her guitar.

"Goddamnit," I growled, taking a long pull of the beer the server dropped off. Even in his ball-gripping jeans, Jake had a gigantic smile plastered on his face and shook his head before looking back at the stage.

"You knew about this?"

"No, I didn't," he said, crunching on the ice of his gin and tonic.

I followed his eyes back to Annaleigh, taking in every feature, every detail. She looked so happy, so in her element. I tapped the side of my glass as she sang about keeping it together when you're falling apart and wondered what happened that would make her not want to be as happy as she looked right now?

"Why did she stop, Jake?"

"She almost lost someone she loves," he said, tapping his fingers on the table like he was strumming a guitar.

"She's told me a little. Was it her fault?"

"No, but that doesn't matter. She blames herself, always has. Lately, though Max, she's gotten better. More open, more trusting. Katie and I both have noticed a difference."

"What about Benjamin?" I asked, going back to that fucking blue sticky-note.

Jake's voice was muted in the background as Annaleigh started a duet about not going downtown anymore, standing awfully close to the cowboy singing with her. The cowboy's hand reached out and brushed her arm. *Too intimate.* My eyes narrowed, and I glared at him, but he only pressed himself closer.

"What about him?" Jake said, holding up his empty glass to signal for another one. I did the same and tore my eyes away from the stage to ask Jake the question that had been on my mind since I overheard Raymond and Benjamin at his office.

"Did they ever date? Her and Benjamin?"

"Date? Are you crazy? No, Max, I can confidently say they never dated. She's way too fucking smart for that. Why?"

"I saw something on her computer about Benjamin and seven o'clock Saturday. It made me curious," I said, shrugging my shoulders and looking away.

"I'm sure you're mistaken Max, Annaleigh would never go near someone like him."

Jake didn't elaborate, only sang off-key as they finished the song and stopped for a minute. The too-close cowboy was speaking to the crowd, but I only had eyes for Annaleigh. She slid up to the bar, and another cowboy leaned down and touched her arm while she ordered.

Jake stood and let out a sharp whistle, causing half the place to stare. Hat tilted, she turned and waved, heading over, forgetting her drink at the bar.

"What a surprise! I thought the wine tasting was all afternoon," she said, leaning down to give us both a half hug. She smelled like whiskey and sweat. It made me want to grip her by the back of her neck and pull her down to my lips.

Standing, I motioned for her to sit, but she waved me off, staying in between us with her hands on her hips.

"Thanks, Max, but we have two more songs."

"The tasting got out early, so we thought we would start with one of your recommendations," Jake said, looking for our server.

"I'm glad you did. Nice outfit, Jake. Authentic. Now the real question is, who is drunk enough to line dance with me when the set is done?"

"Not there yet, Little Lady."

"Little Lady, Jake?" she said, giving him a playful shove in the shoulder.

"Gotta get in with the times." He shrugged his shoulders, finally getting a server's attention and ordering a soda.

I watched their carefree exchange, jealous of the relationship they'd built over the years. Nursing the last of my beer, I reached out and touched her leg, pulling her attention away with a smile. But a bartender came up to the table between us and gave her a sly grin.

"Hey Anna, here's your drink. You guys doing alright?" The bartender said, setting her drink down on the table.

"Thanks, Ace. These two need shots, and please send Bill another coke," she said, pointing to us.

"You got it, doll." With a wink, the bartender walked away.

"How did you wind up on stage?" Jake asked.

"I was at the bar talking to Ace and overheard the lead singer say one person couldn't make it, so they would have to cut the set short. I volunteered. How's it sound?" she said, tapping her fingers against her thigh.

"It sounds like you were made for the stage, Annaleigh. I'm glad we're here," I said, taking her hand and squeezing it.

She squeezed my hand back, "Aw, I'm glad y'all are here as well."

Ace walked back up with a tray, "Shots all around. And Bill says thanks. Your tabs on Spencer tonight, as thanks for filling in."

With a two-fingered salute, he walked away, leaving Annaleigh to pass out the shots.

"Who's Bill?" I said, looking at the shot.

"The bouncer."

"You bought the bouncer a drink?"

"I bought the bouncer a soda. Well, technically, Spencer did."

"Oh," I said. *Why was she buying drinks for other guys?*

"Max. I'm a girl, at a bar, in a strange city, by myself. Common sense says get to know the bartender and the bouncer, just in case. Sending Bill a drink means he's more likely to remember my face, and Ace will remember the generosity," she said with a shrug, pushing one glass towards Jake.

"That's really smart."

"Um, thanks, Max. Always a ton of surprise. Now drink up, two more songs, and I'm dancing with one of you."

She downed the shot, pointing to ours, and chased it with one last sip of her drink before going back to the stage. Taking a hand from the too-close cowboy, he whispered something in her ear, and she laughed, taking off her hat to reveal two sexy as hell braids trailing down her back. This time, instead of moving to the mic or picking up a guitar, she sat at the piano and adjusted the seat.

"Oh, come on! She plays piano too?" I said, slamming the shot back too fast. Damn, it burned. "She's too goddamn perfect."

Dragging my hand over my face, I scrubbed my five o'clock shadow and watched the stage. She was in her own world, where the music made her smile harder than anything I'd ever seen. The too-close cowboy was singing about being in love with loving someone. The tune was catchy, and I couldn't help but tap along again.

"Yeah, she plays piano too," Jake said, ignoring my other comment. "She can pretty much play anything she picks up. There's a technical term that I don't know for what she can do, but that's what it boils down to."

"Wow, and she just stopped because someone got hurt? Sounds like a copout. What, they fell or something? Why would that make her quit?"

Ace returned with two more shots. But I pushed mine away, not wanting to drink anything else. I could feel Jake's eyes boring into mine as I watched her hands dance across the keys.

"That's a shitty thing to say, Max. You don't know the whole story.

Hell, I don't know the whole story. And I won't pretend to understand her reasons."

Shaking his head, he downed the shot and slapped his hand on the table.

"That's all for me. Are you going to dance with her?"

"No, man. I'm not."

"Okay, Max," he said, clearly not believing me.

Annaleigh's voice cut through my foggy haze as she brought the piano mic to her lips.

"Thanks for listening to us tonight, Folks! I'm Anna, and these handsome boys behind me are The Gravel Tracks. Usually, they like to finish with a classic, but tonight they gave me the reigns to play one of my favorites. I was recently told I shouldn't stop doing something I love just because of the past. And it made me think about adjusting priorities and love. And when I think about love, I can't think of a better song than *Whatever It Is* by the Zac Brown Band. Thanks again for letting me play tonight, y'all!"

The song started, and her body slowly swayed as she played. Her eyes were closed as the too-close cowboy sung. Those were the words I said to her that afternoon in the office. Did I help? Did I make her think about love?

The song ended, and she stayed on stage, talking to the band. This was too much. I had to get out of here. I was getting too many mixed signals, and the combination of liquor and beer wasn't sitting well.

Standing up to leave, I didn't notice her until I smelled oranges and felt her fingers stroke across my back. With a breath, I turned to tell her goodnight when she pulled my hand to the dance floor.

"Come, Max." Her words sparked all kinds of dirty thoughts. "Dance with me." Leading me into the crowd, I resisted for a minute, but she turned with a blissed-out expression on her face. "Please."

It wasn't a question. It was a request. An invitation to touch her, out in the open, where everyone could see. I took her hand and pulled her closer, stepping to the far corner of the floor, away from the crowd. Holding her tight, I pressed my hand against her back, drawing her so close there wasn't room for a sheet of paper between us. Clasping her other hand in mine, I brought them to my chest and moved. I recognized this tune, Garth Brooks' *The Dance*, but the words turned to background noise as I held her.

"You amaze me," I said, drown into her orbit, her universe.

"Thank you for dancing with me, Max."

"I can't seem to say no to you," I said, swaying with her.

"Do you want to say no to me?"

"No, Blue. I don't."

"Good," she said, laying her head on my chest, "Because I think I made a mistake, Max. Ask me again."

"Ask you what, baby?"

I didn't mean to call her baby. The word slipped out before I could catch myself. But she didn't seem to mind. We were barely moving now, locked together. The song had changed to something faster, something about a body and a back road, but we were in our own world. The bar, the music, and the crowd faded away as she spoke, her voice nothing but a whisper against my chest.

"Ask me on a date, Max. Ask me to be yours," she said, looking up at me.

"Anna. Blue, are you sure?" My hand moved from her waist to the back of her neck, tilted her head up so she couldn't look anywhere else. She needed to be sure. If she wasn't, this couldn't go any further.

"No, but I want to be. I'm tired of fighting this," she answered, standing up on her toes. Her hand fisted my shirt, and she pulled me down, brushing her lips against my cheek. Her kiss was soft, as if she was waiting for me to push her away or pull her closer.

"You need to be sure, Blue. You won't be my secret," I said, breaking away.

"I never asked to be a secret. I asked to be yours. I'm sorry, Max. I shouldn't have said anything. I'll go," she said.

People circled us, smiling and line dancing across the floor, but she pushed further away. Her smile was gone, and her eyes were glassy. I froze, playing back the last thirty seconds in my head to figure out where it went wrong. But like waking up from a dream you couldn't remember, she drifted away in the background, leaving me grasping at nothing.

No!

Not this time. I was not going to let her walk away. She was moving quickly, running out of the bar, eager for distance. I followed her outside and lost her in the sea of bodies before spotting her about twenty feet in front of me, walking as fast as she could in those boots. I ran towards her, pushing past bystanders until I caught up and grabbed her elbow.

She turned to pull away, but my grip was firm, and I pushed her to a narrow passage between two buildings. Smaller than an alley and shrouded in darkness, I slammed her against the brick wall, suddenly aware of how close we were. I caged her in my arms, giving in to the staggering amount of adrenaline coursing through my veins.

"Not again, Blue. No more running away. You want this, and so do I. It's time to stop playing games."

Her pulse fluttered, and her eyes widened, but there was no time for over-thinking as I launched myself toward her lips. Nothing made sense except threading my fingers into her braids and kissing her like she was oxygen. Energy crackled down my spine, chasing out all rationale except her. This moment was more important than a hundred thousand others, more important than anything I'd ever felt.

Unforgettable.

Mine.

Annaleigh fisted my shirt and gasped, pulling my face to hers. I swallowed the sound and swiped my tongue across her lips, demanding entrance. I could feel her need mirroring mine and the heat of her body as she pushed herself closer. She was so unbelievably beautiful, knocking the breath from my lungs and leaving me dizzy with need. She was all soft curves and smooth skin, with lips I wanted to lose myself in every day.

Trailing one hand down her back, I gripped her waist and kissed her wildly, using my teeth and tongue to taste her.

And holy shit, her mouth tasted like whiskey, spicy and sweet. I was addicted to her taste, addicted to those sweet cherry-stained lips. I pulled away sharply and pulled her further into the darkness. This time, when her back hit the wall, she dragged me down to her level and threw one leg over my thigh.

I bunched her white blouse around her waist, and I pushed my hand under the material, feeling her hot, toned skin on my fingers. Lightning ripped down my hand where our skin connected. I nipped her bottom lip, stroking her tongue, her taste bursting across my lips. She was everything I wanted. My chest was rapidly rising and falling in sync with hers. She was so right, so familiar. I wanted to see her, see all of her. Know all of her. Make her mine.

Desperate little moans escaped her mouth as she kissed me back with such ferocity, I hoped my lips always carried her burn. I was hard as steel, my cock surging towards her core that was pressed so perfectly to me. One thrust. Two. Three. I was desperate to relieve some of the pressure. My palm grazed higher, finding the fabric of her bra and stroking the cotton and lace.

I wanted more skin, needed more contact. But this wouldn't go further unless she knew she was mine. Forget her past pain and forget whatever bullshit was going on with Benjamin. She was mine, from her beautiful body to her breathtaking soul. Slowing the kisses, I pressed lingering ones along her lips and jaw before grasping the base of her neck and pressing our foreheads together.

"I'm asking you again, Blue. Whose are you?" I dropped my voice low. Pulling on her braids lightly to tip her chin, so her seafoam green eyes met mine. I needed her to see there was no hesitation, no second-guessing, no going back.

"Yours," she answered.

Breathless. Beautiful. She brought her hands to my face and ran them over the curve of my jaw, so much gentler than I was with her.

"I need more, Blue."

"Max, I need more too." She used that moment to grind on my cock, making my eyes roll back in my head. Pushing her harder against the wall, my hands slipped under her ass, and she wrapped her legs around me, giving me blessed, sweet relief. But she deserved more than a hard brick wall. It took every ounce of strength I had to stop. I lowered her to the pavement, my legs all but numb because all my blood was currently in my cock.

"I will not fuck you against a brick wall, Annaleigh."

"You don't want this as much as I do?" she asked, voice husky with lust.

"Trust me. You do not know how much willpower this is taking. I want nothing more than to fuck you against this wall, then take you back to the hotel, get you naked, and lick every inch of your body."

To show her how serious I was, I took her hand and pressed it against my cock, letting her feel me. She cupped it and squeezed, making me groan. Pulling away, I took her hand in mine and led her back to the street, looking left and right before heading back to the hotel.

"Go out with me this week."

"Okay," she said, with swollen lips and flushed cheeks.

"Good baby." I squeezed her hand, not letting go as we walked, wanting to savor every alone moment I had with her.

"You were stunning tonight. I remember you saying today would be rough, mind if I ask why?"

Broadway Street was emptying, so I slowed down as we walked, wanting to hear her story and needing to adjust myself. My slacks were cutting off circulation to my cock.

"Yes... I mean no," she said, taking a breath and glancing down as I rearranged myself. She bit her lip and gave me a sly smile before continuing. "Remember how I said someone I know got hurt?"

"Yes, I do," I stopped to give her my full attention and my cock time to chill the fuck out.

"Well, I blamed myself. I told you that, and I still do. Anyway, in the accident's aftermath, I got drunk. Really drunk. Like ugly-crying, snot-bubble, sloppy drunk."

"I'm sorry I missed that," I said, bending down to kiss her neck.

"Ass!" she giggled, pulling away and slapping my shoulder. "A damn broke that night, Max. I put our life on paper. I stayed up all night, writing and editing, then drinking and writing more. The next morning, I stumbled on a Twitter post from Serin, the Popstar. She was advertising a lyric contest, encouraging fans to send them in for a chance to be featured on her next album."

"You entered?"

"Yes, I entered. Then forgot about it and passed out. About a month later, someone from her entourage reached out. I had won and was flown out to meet her."

"What an accomplishment, Annaleigh, but why was that a bad thing? You sound like you're embarrassed or ashamed. Tell me more," I said, taking her hand back in mine.

"Well, Serin is really down to earth. She just called off her engagement and had writer's block. She asked if I had written more than the song I entered in the contest, so I showed her everything from that night. It was unbelievable, Max. She loved it and said it was just what she was looking for. She ended up using everything I had written for an album."

"Blue, holy shit."

"Yeah?" she said as if she didn't believe it was a huge fucking accomplishment. She wrote an album! *My girl wrote an album!*

"That's phenomenal, babe."

"The album's called *Beautifully Broken*, and it ended up being her most successful one to date, going double-platinum," she said, looking down.

She still looked guilty, and it finally clicked. "You feel like a sell-out," I said.

"Yes! Exactly Max! I sold what happened, used our story. Every time

I get a freaking royalty check or hear a song on the radio, I feel so guilty I can barely breathe."

"Did the person mind that you used their story?"

"Bird? Not at all. Wouldn't take a penny for it either," she said, throwing one hand in the air.

"You're the bravest person I know," I said. "You put yourself out there, opened yourself up, and shared your soul. I could never do something like that."

We were right outside the hotel, but I wasn't ready to go in. I wasn't ready for this night to end.

"I get where you're coming from, Blue, but if Bird doesn't blame you, you need to let go of the guilt. Don't let it consume you," I said, running my hands up her arms.

"I know. Tonight helped. It helped so much. And you help, Max," she said, reaching up to kiss me.

She took my hand and pulled me through the doors. We walked through the lobby to the elevator. Her floor was below ours, and I held her hand tighter as we stepped in. She pressed her body to mine and put her head on my chest like she belonged there.

All too soon, we were at her door. I didn't want to let her go, so I took my time, running my hands up her arms and over her collarbone. She leaned into my touch, pressing a kiss to the side of my mouth, but I turned my head to catch her lips.

"It was a privilege watching you play tonight. Thank you for telling me about the album," I said, breaking away and running my nose along her neck. My cock was back to full attention, and I was so tempted to push her inside her door and finish what we started in the alley.

"Thank you for listening, Max. Goodnight."

"Night, baby," I said, pressing my hands to each side of the door. With one last smile, she turned, and I didn't walk away until I heard the distinct click of the lock, silently hoping Jake was asleep so I could handle this fucking hard-on.

As much as I wanted to learn every nuance of her, I still hadn't felt her under me, and it was slowly driving me insane. But she was worth the wait. My blue balls just needed to get the memo. I adjusted my cock on the elevator, grateful all was silent when I opened the suite door.

My phone pinged from my pocket, and I stopped in my tracks, sucking in a harsh breath and scrubbing my hand across my face when I saw the message.

Blue had sent me a picture. It wasn't dirty, and it wasn't of her delicious tits or smackable ass. It was a picture of her pointer and middle finger, soaked with her wetness, glistening in the flash of her phone's camera. Underneath was one simple word that was my undoing, sending me sprinting to the backroom, desperately unbuttoning my pants to grab my cock.

Yours.

God, this woman—she was everything.

SHADOWS FLICKER

Annaleigh

On the plane heading home, we had our hands threaded together underneath a sweatshirt on my lap. He was so warm, and I selfishly kept my shoulder pressed to his, wanting as much contact as possible. We were going to give this a try—give us a try. I was content. Happy. Ready to move on. With him. I wanted to shout from the rooftops that we were together, but there were still so many uncertainties.

But I pushed those aside and focused on the present. Talking to Bird, singing at the bar, and afterward with Max had filled something in me. It was hard to explain, but it felt like I was whole. I laid my head on his shoulder, glad no one was near us. Max leaned down and kissed the top of my head, so gentle, so intimate, making me fall a little more.

"Can I ask you something?" he said, removing his hand and taking his glasses off.

"Yes, of course." I sat up to meet his eyes.

"On my first day, you said you would always be honest. Is that still true?"

"What? Yes, of course." I couldn't read his expression, but his eyes were dark, and he had a crease between his brows. I reached over and squeezed his hand, nodding for him to continue.

"Well, if we're being honest, yesterday, before the bar, I saw something on your laptop about Benjamin."

"You were looking at my laptop?" I said.

Oh, no! He saw that damn sticky note. Jake was furious when I told him, and Max would blow a gasket if he knew.

"Did you ever go out with Benjamin? I saw his name and tonight at seven o'clock. Is he the reason you were hesitant the morning after the gala?" Max asked, putting his glasses back on and reaching out to twirl a strand of hair that escaped my bun.

My palms were sweating, and I could feel the color rising in my cheeks. I could not start this relationship with lies, but I was so embarrassed about the meeting Jake and I had with Human Resources after the Gala.

"Oh my God, Max. No. That morning, in your kitchen, all I could think about was how right it felt, being with you... like we were in sync. And honestly, it scared the shit out of me. You're my superior, my boss, and I don't want to compromise either of our jobs. Please know, nothing is going on with Benjamin, and there never has been."

I reached up and grasped his hand, bringing it to my lips. The corner of his mouth tilted up a millimeter, so I squeezed harder, doing my best to reassure him.

"Then what is happening tonight at seven o'clock?" he pressed.

"Nothing," I said.

That was the truth. My lights would be off, my doors and windows locked, and my car parked around the corner. Nothing was going to happen tonight.

"I plan on being in the tub with a frosty glass of something alcoholic," I said, smiling as best I could.

"You sure about that? Are you not telling me something?" he said, pulling his hand away. I could hear the irritation in his voice. It was like he knew I was holding back.

"Listen, Max," I said, "We've, um, never been together. But after an incident at the Gala, and we had to involve Human Resources. I can't say anything more than that."

I looked at my feet, then out the window. If he could wait until the investigation was over, I could tell him about the stupid messages and incidents with Benjamin. But patience was something Max had about a teaspoon of, and I could see him closing off and jumping to conclusions.

"Fine," he said.

"Fine," I answered.

We stayed silent as the plane landed, and as I passed Jake ginger drops for his nausea. We stayed silent as he waved us away and high-tailed it to the bathroom. We stayed silent as we waited for him and when we walked to baggage claim. The longer the silence went, the worse I felt. I had to get out of there. It felt like the walls were closing in. With a thank you and a wave to them both, I flagged down a taxi and left. I wouldn't have been able to stand the silence of the town car home.

But the silence followed since the Rosenberg's weren't bringing Baxter back till later. I threw my bag in my room and headed up to the roof with a beer. I sent a quick text to Katie asking her to make sure she was here long before seven. Sitting down in the hammock and swinging slowly, I opened my phone and stared at the screen, trying to decide if I was going to text Max. I took a long pull of my beer and started typing.

Annaleigh: I should have been honest upfront.
Max:...

Three dots appear and disappear four times, but nothing came through. Was he having second thoughts? Replaying the last week in my head, I sipped my beer, passing the time, until my phone beeped. I looked down to see a chat from the girls asking about the trip.

Olivia: How was the trip?

Annaleigh: Long, but had a good time.

Addison: Did you finally fuck BM?

Jenna: GIF of rabbits humping

Annaleigh: Please stop calling him that. And No. But...

Addison: He gave you the best orgasm you've ever had?

Jenna: He confessed he's madly in love with you and is leaving JMS so you can be together?

Olivia: He has the biggest dick you've ever seen, and you were so intimidated you ran away?

Annaleigh: NO, BUT... We kissed. It was more than a kiss. More like he fucked my mouth with his tongue.

Olivia: Oh, that's hot

Addison: GIF of flames

Addison: Did he finally give you a HOT load of his High Fructose Porn Syrup??

Olivia: HIGH FRUCTOSE PORN SYRUP??? REALLY??

Addison: You're welcome :-)

Jenna: I thought you weren't going to get involved?

Annaleigh: So did I. But it seems like I have no self-control around him.

Addison: There's a big difference between a casual fuck and a relationship.

Annaleigh: I know. We're going to try. I'm crazy about him.

Olivia: Wow

Jenna: Is he worth your job?

Annaleigh: It's a gray area with HR.

Addison: You didn't answer her question.

Annaleigh: I know.

Jenna: Does Baxter have an upset stomach from being away this last week?

Annaleigh: Katie is bringing him back later.

Jenna: Ok, let me know.

Olivia: SOOO. What are you going to do now?

Annaleigh: Right now? Take a bath. About Max, I want to get to know him. Date him. Spend time with him. But I'm second-guessing myself at every turn.

Addison: You need to go all in.

Olivia: I agree.

Jenna: I think you need to spend more time together outside of work before making any more decisions.

Addison: Either way, we're here for you.

Olivia: GIF of hugging

Annaleigh: GIF of hearts

The next girl's night, I was going to tell them about Bird and my music. It was time to heal. It was time to move on, and they were right. It was time to go all in. I picked a handful of ripe strawberries and headed down the spiral staircase to take a bath.

Cracking another beer and filling my clawfoot tub, I stripped and lowered myself into the hot water. I watched the bubbles get higher, pressing the cold bottle to my forehead and breathing in the vanilla bubbles. When I got out, I was going to smell like a giant cupcake. My eyes got heavy, and just as they drifted closed, my phone rang. Max's name flashed across the screen. Smiling and biting my bottom lip in nervous anticipation, I answered.

"Hey, you," I said, picking up the bottle and taking the last sip.

"Hey, Blue. I'm glad you picked up."

"Me too. I'm glad you called."

"We shouldn't have left things like we did. And I want you to know that I trust you, Blue. And there's a reason I pushed you about Benjamin," he said. I heard him let out a big breath. He was probably taking off his glasses to clean them.

"What happened?" I said, sitting up higher.

"What do I hear in the background? What are you doing?"

"Oh, I'm about to get out of the tub," I said.

Before I stood up, my phone beeped with a video call request. Smiling, I answered, seeing Max's face light up the screen.

"That's better. How you doing, Blue?"

He was shirtless, laying sideways on his couch. The low-slung gray sweatpants he had on left nothing to the imagination and were making my mouth water. As he brought a rocks glass slowly to his lips, his eyes dipped down to the bubbles covering my body.

"Please continue explaining, Max, don't mind me," I said with a wink, propping the phone on the side of the tub and reaching for my beer. His eyes narrowed as he drank, as if he had all the time in the world.

"You are so fucking gorgeous, baby."

"Well, those sweatpants are doing lots of things for me right now."

"Really?" he said, trailing his hand down his stomach to his waistband. Pulling my lower lip into my mouth, I followed his hand, wishing it was my tongue.

"I had an altercation with Benjamin last week," he said. "I probably should have told you after it happened."

"Wait. What?"

It was like a cold bucket of water had been dumped on me. Snapping out of the moment, I leaned closer, pushing aside the site of his naked torso and closely cropped dark hair.

"I overheard him, and Raymond saying some very unflattering things and confronted him in the hallway about it," he said, standing up and blowing out a loud breath.

"Oh, Max. I remember seeing your bruised knuckles. You hit him?" I focused on his features. His brows were drawn together, and he was clenching his jaw.

"He deserved it," Max spit out.

"But why would you stoop to his level?"

I watched as Max's expression hardened. "Annaleigh, he was insulting you. Insinuating you were nothing but an easy lay and that you slept around. Even if I wasn't infatuated with you, that's unacceptable. I made it clear he was to leave you alone. I want to know if he continues to contact you like he did at the gala, or whatever that message was about tonight." His tone was venomous.

"Max, as grateful as I am that you stood up for me, please don't do that again. I couldn't stand it if it was my fault you were in trouble. Did you report him?"

I knew he hadn't. If he had, Jake would have acted. Benjamin deserved whatever Max did and more, but this was not the way to handle it.

"Report him? No, I didn't. Does he have a pattern of harassment?" Max asked, bringing the phone closer to his face.

"Um. Yeah, he does." I bit my lip and looked down. I watched his eyes widen and nostrils flare. He was downright pissed, the phone almost vibrating with anger.

"I knew it! That's it. I'm coming over," he said, standing and looking around. He let out a sharp breath and ran his hand through his hair.

"Max," I said, "No. Don't come over. My lights are off, my car's parked around the corner, and Baxter will be back soon. Nothing is going to happen."

"Annaleigh. I practiced law in Chicago and would never break your confidence. If Human Resources is dragging their feet, you have options. You have rights. I can help. Talk to me." He was using his alpha voice, his possessive bedroom voice that demanded submission and respect. The deep throaty way he spoke was such a turn-on, I could almost feel my nipples hardening under the warm water.

I sat up straighter, and his eyes flicked down, his long eyelashes blinking slowly as he took in his fill.

"Answer me," he growled, staring at my boobs. I picked up the phone, wanting to reach out and stroke his jaw, feel his scruff, and reassure him.

"Max, trust me. It's fine. Nothing is going to happen, and I'll see you Monday. And for the record. You are, without a doubt, the only man I want and the only man I would risk my job for."

"I trust you," he said, "But I don't fucking trust him."

"Neither do I. And thank you, Max."

Sitting back on his couch, he spread his legs wide and ran his hands through his hair again, messing it up to look sexier than before.

"My last relationship wasn't healthy, and I don't want to start ours with dishonesty. I know we're different, but not knowing the whole story with that twatwaffle seems like dishonesty."

"Max?"

"Hum?" he said, looking at the floor, then back at the phone.

"You said relationship."

"Yes, I did. I meant it when I said I didn't want a casual fuck. I mean, I want to fuck you so bad my eyes cross every time I see you. But I also want to date you, take you out, and do all the relationship things."

"I'd like that, Max."

"Me too, baby. Pick a day this week, and we'll go out or stay in. Whatever you want."

"That sounds great."

"Good. I'm going to go for a run. Are you sure I can't come over? I don't like this."

"I'm sure. Thank you, Max."

"Will you call me if anything happens?"

"Yes, of course."

"Okay, Blue. Goodnight."

"Night, Max."

I hung up the phone and pulled the plug on the tub, standing up and wrapping myself in a fuzzy blue robe.

Slipping on a pair of yoga pants and an oversized T-shirt, I walked to the kitchen to search the fridge for dinner. I took out the ingredients for a spinach salad with chicken and put everything on the counter when the doorbell rang. The blinds twitched as I peeked out, relieved to see Jake holding Baxter's leash. I flipped on the lights and opened the door, only to be bombarded by a fur missile that brought me to my knees.

"Where's my good boy," I said, kneeling to scratch behind his ears and cooing to him like the big baby he was. "I thought Katie was bringing him by."

"She was until I caught up on my emails and remembered you might have an unwanted visitor tonight."

"Um, right. Thank you, Jake."

"Of course. My neighbor's a cop, and he's parked down the street just in case."

Jake looked at his watch, then back at me, bending down to pat Baxter's head.

"Isn't that excessive?" I said, looking at the clock on the wall.

How had it gotten so late?

"No. It's not. You've never given him your address, right?" he said, walking over to the blinds and peering down the street, waving his hand to his neighbor. Shadows flickered across my living room as Jake pulled the curtains closed.

"Right," I said, going to the pantry to fill Baxter's food and water dish. He eagerly gobbled it up before trotting to the corner and sinking into his doggie bed.

"That means he accessed your file and violated your privacy, and as of Monday, there will be consequences. I didn't want Katie here and, in all honesty, you shouldn't be here either."

"Thank you for taking this seriously, Jake."

"It's my job, Annaleigh, and we have more than enough documentation. It's time his actions have repercussions. But, more than that. I care about you. My family cares about you. This is not something you have to face by yourself. Is someone staying here tonight?"

"No."

Maybe I should have asked Max to stay. But if Max and Jake had both been here, we'd be having a different conversation. A conversation I wasn't prepared to have yet.

"I'd think about that if I were you, just in case. Also, depending on if he shows up, we need to talk about a restraining order," Jake said, taking a seat and pulling out his phone.

"A restraining order? Really?"

"That's a last resort, but you need to be aware of all the options. I'll be pushing to have him fired, and you need to be protected."

His phone pinged, and he looked down, then back at me, head nodding towards the door before a fist banged. Loud. I froze, my body going stiff, and Baxter's hackles went up. Jake moved to the opposite window and peeked out, giving me a nod to let me know it was Benjamin.

Pointing to the door, Jake nodded and moved back. My heart racing, I breathed deep and opened it. Baxter was at my side, and I leaned down to take hold of his collar. Benjamin was holding a bouquet of flowers, and his cheeks were flushed as if he'd been drinking.

"There you are, not dressed up, I see. Eager to stay in, Princess?" he said, holding the flowers out for me.

Princess? Ugh. Gross.

"You look extremely unapproachable right now, but aren't you going to ask me in?"

"Not a chance. The only reason I opened the door was to tell you this is an obvious violation of my privacy, and if you do not cease all contact, you will force my hand."

"Oh, you like it forceful? That can be arranged," he said, throwing the flowers on the ground. He pushed forward, attempting to get in, but Jake threw the door open and used a loud, badass voice that even made me cower.

"This ends now!" he boomed, putting himself between us. "For too long, I have put up with your narcissistic, arrogant ass! You are to report to HR first thing Monday morning for disciplinary actions. You will cease all contact with Annaleigh immediately. Now, get the hell out of here."

Jake shut the door harder than necessary, but Benjamin blocked it with his shoe. The door bounced back, and Jake caught it, leaning forward so Benjamin couldn't come closer.

"So, you're fucking him too, Princess? Don't worry. I don't mind. I'll leave now, but this isn't over. Not by a long shot."

Jake made the mistake of taking the bait and opening the door, ready to fire back an insult. But he let his guard down for a second, and Benjamin cocked his arm back and landed a cheap shot on Jake's chin.

"Son of a bitch!" Jake yelled, flailing his arms back and knocking over a vase, shattering it on the tile. Benjamin walked away, kicking the flowers as Jake tried to go after him. But I stepped in front, putting my hand on his chest.

"No, Jake! He's instigating you. Come on, let me look. Be careful of the glass."

Baxter was whimpering and pacing back and forth, not wanting to come closer. Tiptoeing around the glass, I locked him in the backroom until I could get everything swept up. Jake was fuming. It was rare he got angry, but when he did, it was bad. Running his hands harshly over his thighs, I could hear the constant stream of curse words escaping his lips.

Getting some ice from the freezer, I wrapped it in a towel and handed it to him before getting a broom. I loved that vase. My parents got it for me when I moved here, but better a vase breaking than one of us. Baxter was still whining, but I needed to take one more pass with the broom before letting him out. Jake was still mumbling as I finished, so I grabbed two glasses and poured us each a few fingers of bourbon, pushing the glass towards him with a weak smile.

"Thank you," he said, taking the glass.

"Sure. Let me see your chin."

He moved the ice away as I examined the bruise, running my fingers over his raised skin and thankful it wasn't worse.

"I'm so sorry, Annaleigh. I shouldn't have let you open the door."

"Stop. I cringe to think what would have happened if I were here alone."

"What can I do? Is everything cleaned up?"

"Yes, everything's fine," I said, my body sagging against the counter in exhaustion.

"I should have helped you clean. I'm sorry about the vase. I'll replace it."

"Oh, it's fine, Jake. I'm just ready for this night to end."

As if karma gave me the middle finger, my doorbell rang, and I dropped my head in my hands with a sigh.

"Shit, what now?" I said, laying my head down on the table.

"That's my neighbor, the police officer. You need to file a report. This is grounds for a restraining order," he said.

"Okay, I guess you're right."

I walked forward slowly and answered the door, waving him in. My mind was numb as I remembered the details, wanting nothing more than my bed. Officer Hansen had a serious expression and kind eyes, listening to every detail. He was intimidating as hell with his growly voice and tattoos, but his mannerisms put me at ease. He assured me that someone would patrol the street tonight in case Benjamin decided on a repeat performance. Jake picked up where I left off, filling the officer in on several of the incidents at work and promising to send documentation Monday.

With a shake of his hand and a card, he left, giving me a copy of the report. Filing it away in a kitchen drawer, I walked Jake to the door, wrapping my arms around him in thanks. He nodded and left, apologizing once again.

I opened my kitchen drawers until I found my bear mace and brought it upstairs with shaky hands, Baxter on my heels. But it didn't make me feel safe. I put it on the nightstand and flipped the light on in my closet, bending down to retrieve my small gun safe. I touched the fingerprint access and was rewarded with a soft click as it opened, revealing my Ruger LC380. I closed the lid and laid the safe by the mace, but it didn't help either.

I peeled off my clothes and crawled into bed, wrapping myself in the warmth of my comforter. The only thing I wanted was Max. I picked up the phone and called him. It barely rang once before he picked up.

"What happened?"

"Will you come over?" I said, burrowing myself further in the warmth.

"I'll be there in ten minutes, Blue."

"Good."

He hung up, and I stayed in bed, willing my heart to calm down. My phone chirped nine minutes later, and I walked downstairs, opening the door with my blanket still wrapped around me.

Max swooped in, lifting me up in his arms and closing the door with his foot. I laid my head on his chest and pointed to the stairs. He nodded and leaned down, kissing my head. The bed was cold when he laid me down, and his eyes went dark when he saw the mace and safe.

"I'm going to walk Baxter and check the doors and windows, Blue."

I nodded, and he leaned down, pressing a kiss to my lips. I grabbed the back of his head and pulled him closer, driving my tongue into his mouth. He thrust his tongue against mine, running his hands up my stomach and over my breasts. The world made sense when his lips were on mine, and when he drew my bottom lip in his mouth and nibbled, I moaned. His tongue caressed mine, and he slowed down, peppering my mouth and neck with wet kisses.

"Keep the bed warm for me," he said, standing upright and patting Baxter on the head. "Come on, buddy, let's go for a walk."

Baxter tilted his head to the side, then licked Max's hand and trotted after him. A wave of exhaustion washed over me as I closed my eyes for a second then stood up, stripping and pulling on Max's shirt from after the Gala. It still smelled like him, and it grounded me until Baxter trotted back in and put his front paws on the bed.

"How's my good boy? He did so good protecting his mama."

Baxter whined and scooted forward, so I patted the bed, and he jumped up, turning in a circle before plopping down at the foot. He usually slept in the big doggie bed on the floor, but tonight, the bed would fit us all. Max came back, set a glass of water on my nightstand, and plugged in my phone before stripping down to his briefs. He climbed into bed over me, pressing another kiss to my lips before pulling me into his arms. I rested my head on his chest and threw one leg over his, tracing my hands up his stomach. There was a rumble deep in his chest, and he pulled me closer.

"Thank you."

"Baby, nothing could have kept me away. I shouldn't have listened to you. I should have been here," he said, nudging Baxter with his foot.

"You're here now, Max."

"I am, and I'm not leaving again. Now sleep. I've got you, Blue," he said, with another kiss on my head.

And I did.

- *20* -

BY MY SIDE
Max

Monday morning was here again. And this time, walking into the office, I was just as pissed as before. I trusted Annaleigh. *I did.*

Who I didn't trust was that little shit, Benjamin. I purposely didn't ask her about what happened Saturday, hoping she would confide in me. But she didn't. She fell asleep, wrapped around me like a koala bear. I barely slept, listening for anything that sounded suspicious. Baxter kept his eyes on me all night like he knew something might happen to his Mama.

Maybe she didn't trust me, or maybe there was more to the story than she was letting on. The urge to protect her, to keep her safe, and to learn all her secrets was overwhelming. I was angry at myself for constantly having my thoughts stray since it was clear I needed her like oxygen.

My mind kept ricocheting between needing Annaleigh to validate my feelings and clocking Benjamin. I hated how jealous I felt. But jealousy wasn't the right word. It was a deep, possessive need to know her inside and out, to know every nuance of her body and mind.

Why the fuck were relationships so hard?

Relationship.

This was the start of a relationship. I'd said the word before, but it had finally sunk in. A distraction I hadn't wanted, had morphed into something I couldn't do without anymore. I didn't want to be alone. I wanted her to stand with me, beside me.

Restless, I stood and paced my office. The warm sun reflecting off the river through my windows hit my face, and I cracked my neck, letting it soak into my body. I grabbed my coffee cup and walked into Jake's office, turning on the machine. Syncing my calendar, I scrolled through my appointments until the smell of coffee roused me, and I filled my cup, determined to get some work in while the office was quiet.

But Raymond was standing in the hallway with his arms crossed over his chest. His cheeks were puffed, and his chest was bowed, the intimidation clear. Mimicking his pose, I spread my legs and stared back, glaring at him across the space.

What in the ever-loving hell...? Benjamin must have gone to his father, complaining about the big, bad new kid picking on him. Raymond broke contact first and walked into his office, slamming the door. The sound reverberated through the office. *Geezus*, nothing like getting in a pissing contest before eight o'clock in the morning.

I was three steps from my office when Jake came barreling around the corner like a force of nature, tie askew and hair sticking up in every direction.

"Max!" he barked, radiating anger, "My office. Now!"

Not waiting for a response, he opened his door with such force it hit the wall, sounding like a gunshot in the quiet space. Following without a clue as to what had him so rattled, I took a seat in front of his desk and sat my coffee cup down. He paced back and forth, raking his hands through his hair. His eyes had dark circles, and his normally impeccable shirt was wrinkled.

"Jake?"

He held up a hand, silencing me as he paced. What had him so frazzled, so furious? Stomping over to the coffeemaker, he pushed the button for hot water and shoved a mug underneath, breaking off the handle.

"Goddammit," he said, yanking the pieces from the coffeemaker and slamming them in the trash.

"Max." The word came out as a hiss because of how hard his jaw clenched. "As of this morning, Benjamin and Raymond are on unpaid administrative leave. I'm going to ask you two questions. You need to know that I'm going to do everything in my power to make sure they never set foot through our doors again. I'm confident they'll be fired within the week. But I need your complete honesty, and I cannot comment on anything about any incidents or investigation. Now, did you threaten Benjamin's life?"

His face was a blank slate, eyes burning coals, waiting for my answer.

"I had an altercation with him the week before Tennessee," I said.

Not leaving out a detail, I told him about my quick stop in the office, the conversation I overheard, my threat, and popping that twatwaffle on the lip. When I got to that part, I saw a slight upturn to Jake's mouth and noticed the bottom of his jaw was discolored.

What happened?

"Thank you for your honesty. As your boss, you should have reported him and Raymond right away. I'll need you to speak with HR and recount the incident. You won't face any repercussions. And as your friend, I'm glad you punched the little cockroach."

"Um. Thanks? What happened to your jaw," I said, rubbing the back of my neck.

"I had my own altercation with Benjamin," he said, touching the discolored area. "And that brings me to the second question, the reason for the altercation. Are you romantically involved with anyone in the office, Max?"

"Jake," I started.

Oh fuck. We sure as shit were in a relationship, but it wasn't right to tell Jake anything before discussing it with Annaleigh. How could I word this, so I wasn't lying but also not putting her in a position she didn't want to be in yet?

"Are you romantically involved with anyone in the office?" he repeated. "While we investigate, I need all the facts." He crossed his arms then shook out of shoulders, taking another coffee mug down.

"As of today, Jake. There is nothing I can disclose to you without first speaking about it with other parties who may or not be involved."

"How very diplomatic of you, Max," Jake said. His words were sarcastic, but he was grinning, the tension leaving his body. "Good man." He put out his hand to mine. I stood and firmly shook it.

How was it only Monday?

Running my fingers through my hair, I walked out of his office, willing the time to move faster. Annaleigh was sitting at her desk, talking on the phone and looking edible in a blue dress. Holding her fingers to her lips, she waved them in greeting before looking back at her computer screen. I mimicked the motion, holding my fingers to my lips like I was blowing her a kiss, and smiled.

The bullshit with Raymond and Benjamin wasn't over. I could feel it in the air. I sat at my desk, staring out the windows and drinking my now lukewarm coffee. Standing up for a refill, I saw Jake lean down and speak to Annaleigh so low I couldn't hear. She reached up and touched his chin, where the skin was bruised. He took out his wallet and handed her money. I couldn't see how much from here, but she tried to push it away before sighing and tucking it in a drawer.

"Thank you for Saturday night," he said louder before tilting his head towards his office. She followed and closed the door, leaving me in stunned silence.

What the hell was that? Benjamin and Jake's faces swirled in my vision, and I sent Annaleigh an instant message asking her to come into my office when she had a moment.

This was not how my week was supposed to start, bouncing between self-loathing and confusion. I was an edgy mix of restlessness and exhaustion. I needed to relax desperately, but my mind kept firing synapses in every direction, preventing any semblance of that from happening.

There was a soft knock a half-hour later, and she walked in with red-rimmed eyes and a splotchy face. I turned around and smiled at her before looking back out the windows. Clouds now covered the sun, much like my mood, and I sat behind my desk. She left the door open and sat in one of the grey chairs, crossing her legs.

"How you doing, Blue?" I asked, leaning forward and steepling my fingers. "What happened?"

"Jake dropped off Baxter Saturday, and Benjamin showed up," she said, looking at her shoes. "I met with Human Resources this morning, and it wasn't a pleasant conversation. There were lots of accusations thrown around. I just want to feel something normal." She twirled a strand of her blonde hair and leaned back in the chair, putting her tablet on my desk.

"Did they share the next steps with you?" I asked, cracking the seal on a water bottle and passing it to her.

"Thank you," she said, wrapping her red lips around the bottle and taking a drink. "Based on the evidence they have, they should be fired, but these things take time."

"What can I do?" I said, taking the water back and finishing the bottle. I wanted to pull her in my lap and nuzzle her neck, then pink her ass for the frustration I felt. But this shit wasn't her fault, and no matter what HR said, she should trust me enough to share.

"Honestly, Max. You know what you can do?" she said, standing up and locking my door with a click. She walked towards me, looking like an innocent vixen, and spun my chair so it was facing the windows. Then she sunk to her knees with a naughty grin on her face and her bottom lip stuck between her teeth.

The way she was looking at me as she dragged those teeth over her lips was enough to send my heart rate higher, practically beating out of my chest. Seeing her on her knees, looking up at me with wicked intent, had my cock pushing against my slacks, desperate for contact. My mindset focused on her red lips. My fantasy was coming to life before my eyes.

"Mr. Jackson, sir," she said, twirled that same piece of hair between her fingers. "It's been a doozy of a day, and I need something to take my mind off of things. I need to be bad." She started a tortuous climb of her fingers up my thighs, spreading them apart and looking up at me doe-eyed.

"Is this what you need, baby?"

The words came out a growl as I leaned forward to grip the back of her neck, making sure her eyes stayed on me. Even if she wasn't on her knees, looking like a goddess, I'd give her anything. I'd fall to the ground and worship every inch of her body until she was nothing but a puddle on the floor.

"Take it away, Max, all the drama. Let me feel you. All of you. Right now."

Not waiting for me to process the words, she leaned forward, dragging her fingernails across my cock. It surged towards her as she worked my belt loops, drawing out the moment and keeping that goddamn lower lip between her teeth. I was gobsmacked, staring at her as she worked the button and zipper. Tilting my hips, she lowered my slacks and caressed my hard-as-steel cock through my briefs. My breath caught in my chest as she leaned in, nuzzling my erection with her nose.

"I've fantasized about this, Blue. You, on your knees, sucking me off. My cock hitting the back of your throat as you take me deeper. I want you so fucking bad, right here. No one the wiser. The door closed and locked with your red lips wrapped around me. You drive me crazy."

"Humm," she moaned, the sound even hotter with her on her knees.

I worked my fingers into her hair as she lowered my briefs, my cock jutting out proudly to bob against my stomach. I needed to feel her silky tongue slide over me. Her eyes traveled down, making my hips almost jerk to bring her closer. But this was her show. I was just the lucky fucker along for the ride.

She wrapped one hand around the base of my cock and stroked up slowly, twisting her hand slightly. She pumped me until a drop of pre-cum oozed out, and her tongue darted out, lapping it up, almost causing me to lose it before I felt her sweet lips. I wanted to trace my cock around her lips, painting myself on her like a caveman, marking her on the outside like she'd marked me.

"I love the taste of you, salty-sweet and oh so sexy. You make me feel naughty and powerful. I'm addicted."

The way she purred those last words pushed what little control I had out the window. Gripping her hair harder, I tilted her neck so she was looking up at me again.

"Take what you want. You fucking have all of me, Blue."

Instead of going for my swollen head, she sunk lower, moving her hand and licking the base of my cock before drawing my balls into her mouth. She sucked gently, while her fingers circled the head and her tongue moved between each one. Flattening her tongue, she licked me from base to tip before swirling her tongue and doing it again.

Whispered moans escaped her lips as she worked. I kept my grip loose, letting her set the pace. Bracing one hand on my thigh, she wrapped the other on the base of my cock and plunged her mouth all the way down. This time, my hips thrust forward, and my grip tightened.

"Holy fuck. Your mouth is so hot."

Her hand and lips were working in tandem, and she bobbed her head faster. Every time she raised up, I saw a red lipstick ring around my cock. My breath was coming in quick gasps, and sweat beaded my forehead as she worked faster and faster. As I gripped her hair harder, a growl slipped out, and my hips thrust up again.

Bobbing down so far, I felt the back of her throat. She released me with a wet pop, looking up with flushed cheeks and bright eyes.

"Fuck my mouth, Max."

I fisted her hair again, and she lowered herself on my cock until I felt the back of her throat. I held her there, wrapped in her warm, wet mouth. She swallowed and hummed, the vibration traveling down my legs.

"Christ, do that again," I said.

She complied, sucking me down as I held her in place while she swallowed. I watched her intently, making sure there was no discomfort, but she was sucking me off like her mouth was made to take my cock. She did it again and again until I felt my balls tighten and a tingling at the base of my spine. I was close, wrapped around sweet wetness with no doubt in my mind this was where I belonged.

But I wanted more. As painful as it was to make her stop, I pulled on her hair, and she looked up, released my cock with a wet pop.

"Turn around and put your palms on the desk. Now."

I loosened my tie and undid my shirt-bottom, swallowing harshly as she turned around and did just that. I pressed my palm between her shoulder blades and pushed down, bunching up her dress and pulling it over her hips. She was wearing black panties, no bigger than a postage stamp, and I tugged the strings down, slipping them to her ankles.

I ran my fingers from her calves to her thighs and spread her legs wider before burying my tongue in her pussy. I needed to taste her. I flicked my tongue against her clit then gave her one long lick, gathering up her wetness. She turned her head and looked at me, biting that goddamned lower lip.

"Fuck me, Max. I need you to fuck me."

With my pants around my ankles and my cock borderline painful, I retrieved a condom from my wallet and sheathed myself, pressing it to her entrance. She was so wet, so responsive, and if her pussy felt half as good as her mouth, I wouldn't last long. I draped my body over hers and nibbled on her earlobe, "Are you ready, baby?"

She pushed herself against my dick, and in one smooth motion, I thrust deep inside her, both of us groaning with the sensation. *Holy fuck.* This was better than I'd imagined. I dragged my cock back out and slammed home, making her body jerk forward. Office supplies scattered on the floor, but the sound of them dropping was drowned out by the sound of our bodies slapping together. I reached around and rubbed tight, fast circles over her clit, needing her to come, needing to feel her slick walls flutter around me.

I set a punishing pace, grunting as I rutted into her. Her moans were getting louder, and I took my hand off her hip to cover her mouth, gritting my teeth with the effort of not coming. But it was useless. She felt too good, her pussy was too tight, and I felt my balls tighten as they slapped her ass.

"Close. Need you."

The words hissed out between my teeth, and with renewed vigor, I gave one last thrust as her muscles spasmed around me. She moaned around my hand, and my world constricted to only her as I held back a roar, her name on my lips. Black dots danced across my vision as I came, filling her with rope after rope of come. I sagged back on my office chair and quickly tied off the condom before pulling her on my lap.

"I needed that," she said, running her palm up my arm.

"You needed that? Fuck, Blue. You're amazing."

My cock was spent but grateful to be in proximity. I needed those lips—lips that were swollen and smudged. I kissed her slowly, gently, my lips gliding over hers.

Sighing and pressing herself closer, I wrapped an arm around her waist and moved my other hand in lazy circles up her thigh. She deepened the kiss, licking along my lips and leisurely moving her tongue with mine. I trailed my hand higher, closer to her pussy, when she stopped me with a smile.

"Let's not push our luck, Tiger," she said, resting her head back on my chest.

"Tiger?"

"Yes, Tiger. Growly. Possessive. Sexy as hell."

"Ha. Thanks, baby. But you know, tigers are loners. They mate, then leave. At least that's what *Animal Planet* says. I'm not your tiger, Blue. You're not a one and done for me." I grazed my knuckles along her jaw.

"I couldn't do casual with you either, Max. But you need a nickname, a sexy nickname," she said, looking up at me through her long lashes.

"Hum, I'm sure you'll think of something. Now, not that I don't want you to do that every day, but Jake asked about us, and I was vague. We need to talk about that."

I willed my cock to calm down. But being so close to her, he was not having any of it. She shifted slightly, and I clamped a hand on her thigh to keep her still.

She snuggled in deeper, fitting perfectly into my chest. We sat there for a minute, and she hummed quietly. Sometimes I could pick up the tune, and other times the notes were tuneless. I could have sworn I heard her humming The Black Crowes last week. They're my favorite.

"Why don't you come over? I'll cook for you. For us." I said, adjusting myself.

"Cook?"

"Yes. Any night. I'll cook us dinner, spoon feed you dessert, then lick your pussy for hours."

"Hours, you say?" she said, scratching her nails through my hair and pulling the short strands. She looked up and grinned, looking so damn sexy my cock twitched again, ready to get back in the game. "Then how about tomorrow?"

"Absolutely. Come over whenever you want," I said.

"What can I bring?"

"I'm going to eat you for dessert, Blue. But if you wanted to bring actual food, I wouldn't say no."

She reached down and cupped my cock, now at half-mast, before winking and standing to pull up her panties and pull down her dress. Groaning, I stood up and tucked myself back in. Her eyes stayed locked on my hand movements. She licked her lips and turned around to walk out, smoothing down her dress and opening the door.

Before she walked out, I stalked towards her and pulled her hard to me, swiftly kissing her. Smiling, she turned around, and I popped her ass, causing the tiniest squeak to fall past her lips.

Tomorrow. Time couldn't go fast enough. With every passing day, I wanted her more, needed her more. She was like a forest fire. A blinding raging inferno and I was just the kindling, ready to be consumed.

DEVOUR ME

Annaleigh

By early evening Tuesday, my anticipation at seeing Max had reached a breaking point. I went for a jog and packed an overnight bag before jumping in the shower. As I shampooed and shaved, yesterday's meeting stayed in my mind, like a nagging bug you couldn't squish.

I cried. I hated crying. Benjamin had filed a formal complaint with Human Resources, claiming we had dated. He said after our relationship ended, I teamed up with Max and Jake to have his job and reputation threatened. Raymond also filed a complaint saying I'd offered sexual favors for favoritism within the bank.

But I'd been open with Jake about their nefarious intentions, and there was an obvious pattern of harassment and intimidation. It blindsided both of them when shown the evidence, and they were escorted off the property. Jake was furious action wasn't taken sooner and pushed for them to be fired immediately.

Hearing the accusations was horrible, but seeing the printed words was worse. I felt dirty, used, and helpless. Jake had his meeting before mine, then brought me into his office and asked me if I was, or ever been, involved with someone at JMS. I couldn't answer. For the first time in our working relationship, I could not give him an answer. Max was right. At dinner, we needed to get on the same page, then talk to Jake.

Drying off and putting lotion on, I looked at the calcium supplements on the bathroom counter and sighed, popping the top and chewing several. Maybe these would work better than oranges, and the boost of vitamins would help my fatigue. I felt it flare up yesterday afternoon, and a minute later, my leg seized with a cramp that almost brought me to my knees. And not the good being on my knees, like when I was under Max's desk. The cramp was sharp and followed with such exhaustion I barely made it through the day. I went home and slept for close to ten hours. I hated relying on medicine, but I had to take better care of my condition.

Picking out a pair of slouchy jeans and a sleeveless blouse, I took extra care to wear a lacy, revealing matching bra and panty set. Baxter eyed me from the bed, head following my movements as I grabbed a pair of tan peep-toe wedges. I reminded him Jenna was going to stop by later, and I'd be back in the morning. I swear his eyes squinted in annoyance. I ignored his silent judgement and scratched the sweet spot behind his ears. He rolled over, and I gave his belly a once over, earning his forgiveness.

The strawberry shortcake I made this morning was on the counter, with homemade whipped cream in the fridge. The cold cream and strawberries went in my travel Hufflepuff cooler, with plenty of extra in the hopes our evening got sweet. Then dirty.

I took a small notebook out of my purse and wrote down the lyric. I saw the lines I'd written over these last weeks, jumbled and incomplete. But as I looked over the words, I knew there was something there, something big.

Everything had led up to this moment, every touch, every kiss. I wanted to be a part of his story, his life. My phone dinged with a work notification, and I unplugged it, shoving the cord in my purse. The email was from an unknown sender, and when I opened it, the phone almost fell to the floor.

To: Annaleigh.Mackey@JMSbank.com
From: Unknown Sender
Subject: Last Warning
Princess,

This is your first and last warning to stay away from Jackson. There will already be consequences for not listening. You are barking mad if you think I will tolerate this behavior. Stop now, or else.
Yours,

B

It was without a doubt from Benjamin, but the message was confusing. Aside from work obligations, this was the first time Max and I had seen each other personally. The police report was still in my kitchen drawer, so I pulled it out, forwarding the message to Officer Hansen and Jake. Taking things a step further, I left a message for both, feeling uneasy since Benjamin knew where I lived.

Shaking out my hands, I walked back upstairs and took the calcium from the counter. I tossed them in my bag and gave Baxter more tummy rubs before rechecking the windows and deadbolt. There was a discarded plant on the sidewalk that I kicked aside before loading my car, ready to see Max.

He opened his front door with a big grin, showcasing both glorious dimples. Max pulled me in with one hand and grabbed my bag with the other, closing the door with his barefoot. In a pair of low-slung jeans and a dark t-shirt, his hair was perfectly styled in that messy casual look all hot guys mastered with ease.

He led me to his delicious-smelling kitchen and put my bag down, pulling me in for a sweet kiss. I melted into him, putting my hands in his back pockets to squeeze his ass. He bit my lower lip in approval and pulled away, still wearing that same grin, breathing me in and pressing a swift kiss to my pulse point.

"What smells so mouthwatering?"

"Lemon linguine, green beans, and chicken piccata," he said, leaning down to check the pasta. The sauce bubbled and smelled mouth-watering. Max fed me a bite, and I moaned around the spoon.

"Oh, that's delicious, Max. I brought strawberry shortcake with homemade whipped cream for dessert."

"Whipped cream? We'll be using that later," he said, giving me a look that had me positively melting.

"Good thing I made extra."

I opened the bag and lifted the lid, swiping my finger through the cream and bringing it to his lips. He gripped my wrist and took my finger in his mouth, swirling and sucking the sweet cream.

"Delicious."

His bourbon eyes blazed bright with lust, like two overheated coals smoldering in a campfire. Releasing my finger, he turned and handed me a glass of white wine, tilting his head towards a set table in front of his large windows. He put the dessert in the fridge and took a sip of his wine, stirring the pasta on the stovetop.

"Make yourself at home, babe. I'm almost done. When we're done eating, I'd love to show you my…"

"Terrace?" I said, slipping off my shoes.

"Yeah. How d'you know? I don't remember giving the tour after the gala," he said, turning off the burner and throwing a dish towel over his shoulder.

"This floor plan is like mine. Spiral staircase? Porch off the master bedroom?"

"Wow. Yes."

"My place is a few streets over, remember, Max?" I said with a smile and a sip of wine.

"Maybe we are M.F.E.O," he said under his breath, blanching the vegetables.

"What did you say?"

Did he just do that? Did he just quote my favorite movie?

I stared, waiting for him to repeat himself.

"Nothing. Sorry," he said, shrugging his shoulders with a smile.

"No, seriously. What did you say?"

"M.F.E.O. It's from a movie. One of my brother's favorites."

"That's my favorite movie too, Max."

"Then you'd love my brother," he said. "Maybe it's another sign?"

He winked and reached up, grabbing two plates and showing me a delectable peek at tanned, toned skin.

"Here, baby. Help me plate and let's eat and talk," he said, pulling out my chair and refilling the wine.

When I sat down, Max pulled me as close as he could and kept one hand on my thigh. The chicken was tender enough to cut with a fork, and he rubbed slow circles with his thumb as we ate. There were so many things to say, but the words felt like sand when I opened my mouth. Everything made sense when his hands were on me and when he was whispering dirty things in my ear.

"What are you thinking, Blue?" he asked, breaking my train of thought and laying his fork on his plate.

"Well, one, this meal is amazing. And two, us, Max."

He let go for just a second to refill our glasses before scooting his chair back and laying one leg across his thigh.

"I'm glad you brought it up, Blue. I've been thinking about us too, and there are two things I want."

The way he caressed my name with his tongue made me eager to hear his words. I leaned closer, my lips centimeters from his.

He reached forward, tugging on my hand and pulling me onto his lap. His hand glided up my back, and he took a piece of my hair and twirled it around his pointer finger. The movement relaxed his muscles, and I could feel his shoulders slump forward. I put my hands up his sleeves to trace his biceps.

"Two things Annaleigh. I want you, and I want us. I don't want to keep this a secret. You're not something I'm ashamed of or will hide. We're already in a relationship. I want you around in the mornings, and I want to make you chocolate-chip pancakes. I want to feed you oranges and walk Baxter when you're tired. I want you to be mine, Blue. We should disclose our relationship tomorrow," he said, running his nose along my neck.

"We should, Max. We've been fighting this, dancing around each other. It's time to own it. I want to know about your past and what makes you smile. I want to wake up in your arms and share everything with you. I want to be yours."

"Good, Blue. And for you, I'd do anything. Now, where's that whipped cream?"

I was all in, standing up and walking to the kitchen, then peeking back to see his eyes go dark. I slid my hands under the waistband of my jeans, and he sat forward, resting his elbows on his knees with his legs spread, watching me.

I popped the button and wiggled them down slowly, letting him see my blue lace thong. I ran my hands over the strings and up my belly, pulling off my blouse to show him the matching bra. The air crackled, and I opened the fridge and bent down, taking out the whipped cream. I dipped my finger in the bowl and walked back, hollowing my cheek as I sucked.

He grabbed my wrist again and pulled me back onto his lap, sucking on the sweet cream while his other hand traveled up my back. He unclasped my bra with ease, and my nipples puckered when the air conditioning hit them.

Holding my hands together, Max kept his eyes locked on mine and lowered his mouth to my nipple. I arched towards him, desperate, and he rewarded me with a lick. I pulled my hands from his grip, running them up his shoulders to hold the back of his head. Through my lust, I heard my phone ring, but I ignored it. Max licked and sucked with such enthusiasm. I doubted we'd make it to the bedroom. But I was good with him bending me over his dining room table and fucking me senseless.

What started with lust and annoyance had turned into feelings and desires so intense it physically made me ache. I moved my hands from the back of Max's head so he could pull off his shirt, throwing it to the floor. He kissed me again, smashing my boobs to his chest. He tasted like lemon and wine, delicious and addicting. I scratched my fingers up his arms, tracing the lines of his tattoos and moaning.

My phone rang again, and I broke apart to reach behind me. Jenna's name flashed across the screen, but I hit ignore and dove back into kissing him. I could feel him thickening through his jeans, and I rocked myself forward. He gripped my hips and guided me along his shaft, both of us groaning with the contact.

When my phone rang a third time, and I answered, letting some of my frustration out through the clipped response.

"This better be important, Jenna," I growled, pressing the phone between my neck and shoulder while tracing the hard outlines of Max's chest.

"Baxter is sick," she started, ignoring my tone and jumping straight to the point.

My back straightened, and I dug my nails into Max's chest, earning a deep groan. He met my eyes, reading the tension in my body, and reached down to grab his shirt.

"I'm sorry, Jenna, what happened?"

I swung one leg over his and stood up, looking for my shirt until I felt a calming hand on my back.

"He ate something while we were walking. I'm taking him to the clinic now. Meet me there," she said, her voice clipped. I could hear Baxter whining and the noise from her engine. She was already on the way.

"On the way," I replied, taking my clothes from Max and pulling them on. Dessert all but forgotten, I lunged for my keys when Max closed his fist around mine.

"I'll drive. Just tell me the address. It will be okay. Come on, baby," he said, steering me out the door without a glance at the remnants of our dinner.

He kept a firm hold of my hand, helping me in his truck and pushing his speed higher. I was chewing on my thumbnail and tapping my foot on the floorboard as we drove, feeling beyond guilty at not answering Jenna on her first ring.

Max rubbed soothing circles on my palm, not filling the silence with empty promises or mindless chatter. It was times like this I realized how much we complimented each other. He could read me, knowing what I needed to calm my racing mind.

Jenna's practice was ten minutes away, and exactly seven minutes later, I pointed to the back entrance, telling Max to pull in by Jenna's big red SUV. Once the truck was in park, I threw open the door and ran to the back entrance, with Max hot on my tail. Running through the back hallway, I called Jenna's name until I heard her, following her voice to an examination room and stepping in.

Baxter was lying on the table, breathing hard. Jenna was murmuring soothing words softly to him and stroking his back. Around his mouth, the short fur was matted and black. He looked pitiful, and his tail gave two half-hearted thumps when we walked in. I ran my hands along his coat, tears silently streamed down my face, and I felt Max rubbing the same soothing circles on my back. Again, he knew what I needed.

"What happened?" he asked Jenna, pushing up his glasses with one hand and rubbing me with the other.

"Honestly. This was the strangest thing. As soon as we left for a walk, he dove to a spot on the sidewalk and started eating something. In the two steps it took me to get to him, he already had eaten a mouthful. It was a discarded aloe vera plant, but I also smelled coffee grounds, chocolate, and some sort of meat. It was like a cocktail of poisonous things for dogs. I had activated charcoal in my SUV, and he's already thrown up twice. I've given him fluids, and I'm going to keep him overnight just in case. Annaleigh, he's going to be fine, but I knew you'd want to be here."

"Thank you, Jenna," Max said, reaching out to shake her hand. Jenna nodded and shook his hand before bending back down and listening to Baxter's heart. She looked at me and smiled, removing her stethoscope and getting a wipe to clean his mouth.

"He's okay, Anna," she said, reaching out to hug me. I sagged against her, leaving one hand on Baxter. She rubbed my back like Max had, and he reached out to stroke Baxter's fur. His tail thumped a little harder, and he lifted his head to lick the back of Max's hand.

"Thank goodness he was with you. I can't imagine what would have happened if someone else was walking him," I said, squeezing her tight with gratitude. In the back of my mind, something tried to break through, nagging at my subconscious.

"I'm going to go see if his X-ray is ready," Jenna said with one last squeeze. I nodded and held on to Max's hand for dear life. Why would someone be so careless—leaving garbage on the sidewalk that could purposely hurt animals?

Wait. Was this on purpose?

Barking mad.

The email. Benjamin.

I froze. There was no way he could do something like this, could he? Hurting an innocent animal? It was cruel. It was sick. It was me jumping to conclusions, thinking the worst.

"What?" Max said, gripping me a little harder. "You just got tense. What's the matter?"

"I don't think this was an accident, Max."

"Not an accident? What do you mean? He ate something he shouldn't have. It unfortunately happens, right?"

"I think someone did this on purpose—to hurt Baxter, to hurt me."

"Baby, who would want to hurt you?"

"I think Benjamin did this."

"What?" Max released my hand to throw his in the air. "How is that possible? It's time you tell me more. Consequences be damned, Annaleigh!"

I took a deep breath and met his eyes. They were blazing, his understanding and compassion gone.

"He sent me an email earlier saying I'd be barking mad to keep seeing you, then Jenna finds a doggie-doom cocktail outside my house? It's too much of a coincidence. I need to make a call."

"Benjamin? Is that asshole still bothering you?" Jenna said, walking back in and over to Baxter.

"So, everyone knows more about your history with him than me, right? That's great."

Max paced back and forth in the small space, and Baxter raised his head to follow him. Jenna laid a soothing hand on his back, and he settled down, breathing deeper and letting Jenna listen to his heart again.

"Don't get defensive with her, Broody!" Jenna said, crossing her arms. "Wasn't this supposed to be your first date or whatever? Unless you count almost fucking against a brick wall date number one!" She slammed her stethoscope on the table, making us all jump, and put her hands on her hips. Max shook his head and looked down, clenching his fists.

"It's fine, Jenna. I think Benjamin might have had something to do with this."

"That little chicken-shit! I'll poison him!"

She looked between Max and me, and he was grinding his jaw and squinting. His face was getting redder by the second. When I stepped closer, he stepped back.

"I have to make a quick call." The hallway was cold and sterile, and I took out my phone, seeing a missed call and voicemail from Officer Hanson. I paced and listened. The restraining order came through. *Finally,* good news. With the police report and documentation from the bank, they served Benjamin this evening. I fired off a quick text to Jake and called the officer with my suspensions about what had happened to Baxter. Shaking out my shoulders, I took a couple of deep breaths before walking back in.

Three sets of eyes met mine as Baxter lifted his head all the way.

"See Annaleigh? He's already getting better. Why don't you head home? I'll call if anything changes."

"I can stay, Jenna. I don't mind."

"I know you don't, but staying won't do anything except give you an awful night of sleep. I promise I'll call if anything changes."

"Okay, if you're sure."

"Of course, I am. Now say bye and go home," Jenna said.

Max hadn't moved from the corner, but when I said goodnight, he stepped forward and took my hand, using his other to scratch behind Baxter's ears. That earned us both a stronger tail wag. Thank goodness. Jenna was a literal lifesaver.

After spending a few more minutes with Baxter and Jenna, we went back to the truck. I was chewing my lower lip and thinking about what to do next. I was planning on staying with Max, but I doubt I'd be good company. I'd call Addison and see if she wanted to come over or head to my parents' house. My parents might be the best option. Mom would definitely have homemade scones and good vodka.

Max was quiet on the way back to his house but kept a firm hold of my hand. When we got there, he brought my hand to his lips before letting it go. I unbuckled to get out, but he stopped me.

"Stay put. I'll be right back, Blue."

I nodded as he opened the door. *Good.* He understood and was going to take me home. Jake had texted back and said he had another meeting with Human Resources tomorrow, and I replied, saying thanks before laying my head back and closing my eyes.

Max came down a few minutes later and put a large black bag in the back seat before climbing in and taking my hand.

"I'm moving in," he said, meeting my eyes for a second before returning them to the road.

"You're what?"

"I'm going to stay with you for a few days. Just to make sure nothing happens. I'd prefer it if you stayed with me, but when Baxter comes home, I know he'd be more comfortable at his house. My brother's coming down next weekend, but at least this way you won't be alone. How long has this been going on? With the dick-weasel?"

"Um, it started with him asking me out and not taking no for an answer. Then Raymond got involved, and lately, they've both gotten aggressive, and I had to involve HR."

"And Jake knows?"

"Yeah. I told him, and we started documenting each incident."

"Thank you for telling me," he said, letting go of my hand and making a turn.

"Thanks, um, for not getting upset?"

"Oh, I'm fucking furious. But not at you. At them, and at the bank for not doing something sooner."

I could see the anger rolling off him in waves, but at every opportunity, he reached out and reassured me with a touch. My house was unremarkably waiting for us, and the doggie-doom concoction was still on the sidewalk. We walked in, and I tossed my purse on the kitchen island before slumping on the couch with my head in my hands. I was not some weak damsel-in-distress. I take charge and kick ass. But through this ordeal, all I'd done was wait. Wait for Human Resources. Wait for the restraining order. But it was time to stop waiting. I was not a pushover.

Max dropped his bag by the door and looked around before walking to the kitchen. I heard him opening and closing cabinets and water running.

Oh, Max. He was making me tea. I stood and walked to the kitchen, pressing my front to his back and wrapping my arms around him. Tensing for a moment, he breathed deep and ran his hands up my arms before turning to face me and pressing his lips to mine.

His kiss was reassuring, and he moved his lips against mine in practiced perfection. This wasn't a precursor to sex. It was loving and intimate. When we broke, I wrapped my arms around his neck and laid my head on his chest. We swayed slowly back and forth, like when we danced in Tennessee until the kettle whistled. I took down lavender tea with orange honey while Max found the broom and dustpan. He walked outside to clean up the sidewalk mess, and when he came back in, he grabbed the bag and walked upstairs.

I found him in my bedroom. He was sitting on the edge of the bed with his head down and his elbows on his knees. I took a sip of tea and put the mug on the dresser before kneeling in between his legs. Rubbing my hands along his thighs, he looked at me. I could see the worry lines around his eyes. His cheeks were splotchy, and his hands were sweaty.

Running my hands down his stomach, I pulled off his shirt. He didn't stop me as I pulled him up and unbuttoned his pants, stripping him down to his briefs. I did the same and pulled him into the bed.

"I don't like this. What if he tries to hurt you next, Blue," he said, squeezing me tighter against him.

"He won't. We won't let him, Max."

I traced the light dusting of hair on his stomach and felt my eyes get heavy as sleep pulled at me. It could have been my imagination, but I thought I heard Max whisper, "I've fallen for you, Blue," but sleep pulled me under, my tea forgotten on the dresser.

- 22 -

COME BACK AND STAY
Max

It was amazing how fast something new turned into something I didn't want to be without. I was usually awake before our alarm went off, listening to Annaleigh's cute whistle-snore. She was like a sexy little lumberjack in training, and I'd spend a few minutes holding her before getting up. The irony wasn't lost on me that a man who hated to snuggle, now preferred to wake up next to someone, and used words like *ours* to describe an alarm clock.

Sometimes Annaleigh joined me on my morning run, but mostly, it was Baxter and me. The lick-monster came back two days later, healthier than ever. Jenna worked her magic and earned herself a well-deserved bottle of wine and spa day. She assured us there was no permanent damage, and Blue said he was back to normal when I *accidentally* left a hot dog on the kitchen table, and it mysteriously disappeared two-point-five seconds later.

After our run, there was coffee, kisses, and kibble. But my favorite part of our new morning routine was that most days, I had a very wet and very limber shower partner. God, I remember yesterday, the way she licked her lips and sunk to her knees, taking my cock in her sweet mouth. I buried my hands in her wet hair and growled when my cock hit the back of her throat. She responded by digging her fingernails into my ass and swallowing. One of her hands trailed down my thigh to her clit, and she bobbed up and down on my cock, rubbing her pussy. I came so hard my knees shook, and she screamed my name as she came with my cock in her mouth.

Oh shit!

And now I was hard again. I was always hard around her. I palmed myself and stepped out of the shower, wrapping a towel around my waist. I breathed in the citrus smell and looked down at Baxter, who was lying on the bathmat. He looked up, tilting his head.

"Cut me some slack, bud. I can't smell oranges without my dick getting hard."

He wasn't amused and hustled out of the bathroom to judge me from the bed. Laughing to myself, I dried off and wiped off the mirror to shave.

We still drove separately to JMS. We were going to hold off on telling Jake until the shit with Benjamin was over. But we still had a secret sign, like the Bat-Signal. We used it when we wanted to kiss. It was cheesy as fuck, so damn cute, and totally my idea. I did it at least a dozen times a day.

I hated going home tonight, but Warren was coming to town tomorrow and staying with me for the week, and nothing had happened on the Benjamin front. There wasn't a reason for me to stay except the constant desire to always be around her. But I had to sand and stain the bench I was working on and at least move the dirty laundry to the closet. I couldn't fucking believe I'd almost missed being a part of her life because I was a stubborn idiot.

We were going to *B's* after work for burgers and to listen to her cousin Alex play with her band, Lace and Whiskey. When I asked if she was going to sing, she smiled and said not tonight, but probably over the weekend. I was glad she had plans since I should focus on reconnecting with Warren. It wasn't the right time to introduce him to my girl, no matter how much I wanted them to meet.

My Girl.

It was the phrase I repeated more and more. After spending time in Tennessee, I'd listened to Country Music, and *My Girl* by Dylan Scott described my feelings to a tee.

My girl was in a band. My girl lit up a room when she walked in. My girl wrote an album that went double-platinum. My girl was a partner in a bar. She shrugged it off as if every person got album royalties and invested in local music. She'd had these big, beautiful things happen in her life and one night took it away. I wanted to shake the hell out of whoever Bird was for ruining her passion.

But it was coming back. I could see it in her eyes when she sang along with the radio or when she talked about her old band. There was a light in her eyes that wasn't there before, because she was embracing her passion.

Closing my car door, I grabbed an orange and took the back entrance stairs two at a time. The boardroom door was closed, and Annaleigh was sitting at her desk chewing on her thumbnail and tapping one red heel on the carpet.

I could feel a crackle of tension in the air. Something was different. Something was off in a bad way. She was fidgety and nervous. Her features barely changed as she met my eyes. I touched my pointer finger to my lip in our little secret code for a kiss and furrowed my brows when she didn't mimic me.

"What's going on?" I asked, moving closer to her and running my fingers along her jaw. She leaned into my touch, like she always did, but didn't smile.

"I don't know. Jake stormed in here earlier, canceled our meeting, and locked himself in the boardroom. I've heard him raise his voice, but he's alone in there."

"I'll go see what's going on."

"No, Max. Don't do that."

"Why? I mean… are you sure?"

"I am," she took her thumb out of her mouth. Her poor nail was chewed down to the quick and touched her lip.

Giving her a wink, I touched mine back and handed her the orange before walking into my office. I turned on my computer and checked my emails. The first one was from an unknown sender, sent at four am this morning. As I scanned the words, color slowly crept up my neck, and I tugged at my tie that was suddenly too tight.

To: Maxwell.Jackson@JMSbank.com
From: unknown sender
RE: Out of Time
Mr. Smerdon,
Consider this payback for daring to touch what is mine. I would advise walking away, or next time you'll be sorry. Remember, she was mine first.
Yours,
~B

Mr. Smerdon?
Shit!
Benjamin did a piss-poor job of trying to hide his identity, sending this to me over the bank's server. I wanted to handle that little chicken-shit myself, but since he knew about our relationship, I needed to loop in Jake. And I needed to tell Blue my last name. I should have done that weeks ago. I wasn't hiding. I only wanted to distance myself from their influence.

Undoing the top button of my shirt and loosening my tie, my mouse hovered over the forward button, almost missing the attachment. Knowing my luck, it would be a freaking computer virus, but I couldn't help myself. I opened it.

What the hell?

Benjamin and Annaleigh were sitting at what looked like a bar, awfully close. Intimately close. His arm was around her, and she was staring at her drink, smiling. It looked like they were on a date. I didn't know what was worse, seeing proof she might have lied about their relationship or knowing someone was spying on them. Closing out the picture, I stood and motioned for Annaleigh to follow me back into my office. She stood and gave me a tight nod.

"Leave the door open," I said, as she sat down and put one hand on her stomach.

"Benjamin knows about us," I said, turning my computer around to show her the email without the attachment open.

"We need to tell Jake," she answered, not missing a beat. "And then go to HR and disclose us and report this."

"I agree. We should have done this last week."

"As soon as Jake is finished, we will," she said, standing up and looking determined and sexy as hell.

But I had to ask one more time; I had to make sure she was telling me the truth about Benjamin. I took off my glasses and blew out a breath, lowering my voice. She had to lean in to hear.

"Annaleigh, baby, just tell me one more time you've never been involved with Benjamin."

She tilted her head, and I reached out to twirl a strand of her hair. As she opened her mouth to reply, the connecting office door was thrown open, and Jake came barreling in, his face a mask of fury. Annaleigh jumped and froze, eyes wide with worry, when she saw his face.

"Both of you! In the boardroom! Now!" he said before slamming the door closed. Our eyes met, and Annaleigh shrugged her shoulders before walking out of my office.

We walked inside and sat, looking at Jake who was standing at the front, holding a manilla file folder. His posture was aggressive, and he paced back and forth, almost daring us to speak. I looked to Annaleigh and back to Jake before taking a breath to talk. Before I could, I felt a featherlight touch on my thigh.

"Let me guess," Jake started before either of us could begin the conversation. "You want to disclose a relationship."

"Um. Yes. We would. And there's something else," I replied, looking at

Annaleigh. She kept her eyes on him as he paced the boardroom.

"Jake, we started officially dating last…" she said.

"Sunday. You started dating last Sunday."

Jake finished her sentence and took two pieces of paper out of the folder, passing them to us.

"Didn't you?" He leveled us both with a glare, and Annaleigh nodded. I followed suit and dipped my head in acknowledgment. We didn't officially start dating until the night Baxter got sick. But we had been involved long before that.

"Sign this. It's a relationship disclosure for HR."

We both took the paper and looked it over. It was a standard document to protect the bank and us if things took a bad turn. Looking at Annaleigh and nodding, we both picked up pens and signed the bottom, sliding them back to Jake. He put them back in the folder and took out several more pages. He sat down beside me with a sigh, looking between us before running one hand through his hair.

"They fired Benjamin earlier, and Raymond resigned. Another employee came forward with harassment charges, and the board had an emergency vote this morning. With that being said, Annaleigh, they're questioning your allegations."

"Questioning? I don't understand, Jake," she said, leaning towards us until I could see an adorable crease on her forehead. I shouldn't be thinking of how adorable she was in a situation that was quickly becoming ominous, but it was hard not to because she was fucking adorable.

What the hell was wrong with me?

I go from questioning her, then back again every time we had a roadblock. Maybe Nicole mind-fucked me more than I cared to admit.

"These were waiting for me this morning. Neither of you is going to be happy, and frankly, I'm so damn pissed I can barely see straight, but we've handled it. You're going to look at these, and then we are going to have a quick conversation about honesty."

Jake tapped the papers and pushed them forward.

Annaleigh and I both reached for them at the same time and turned them over. The color slowly drained from my face as she put her hand over her mouth, lowering her head and closing her eyes. When she opened them again, her face was hard, like she was forming a plan before I could process what I was seeing.

Fuck me.

No wonder Jake was fuming. It was pictures of us, in my office, the day we had afternoon delight. In one photograph, we were embracing, lips millimeters apart, and my belt was undone. On the other, my hand was dangerously low on her hip. The timestamp in the corner was clearly before we disclosed our relationship.

Jake covered for us, literally saving our asses by having us fudge the date. Annaleigh made the same conclusion a few seconds after me, and her eyes got wide before she took in a big breath.

"Save it," Jake started, raising his hand to silence her, something I'd never seen him do. "I don't want to hear excuses or apologies. I asked you both point-blank if you were together. The moment that answer changed, you should have come to me. But instead of doing that, you sneak around and lie, and I had to lie to Human Resources! I don't want an apology from either of you, and I don't want excuses. I want you to both think about how bad this could have been and the consequences of your actions. I'm leaving for the day, but on Monday, we all start over. Open communication. This will not happen again, because I will not cover for you again. Is that understood? Now, what else did you want to tell me, Max?"

"I got an email from someone. Benjamin, I'm assuming."

"What?" Jake said, looking for confirmation from Annaleigh, who nodded slowly.

"Yes. He threatened repercussions for me for, um, daring to touch what is his."

"Send that to me right away, and I would contact the police if he made a threat."

"Okay," I said, reaching out to touch Annaleigh's thigh under the table.

She grabbed my hand and squeezed, then said, "This has to end."

Her voice was quiet and shaking. I could see the worry pouring out of her. And I *obviously* still didn't know the whole story.

"I know," Jake answered. "I'm going to speak with HR and reach back out to my neighbor. This will stop now, Annaleigh."

"Thank you," she said, her voice still barely above a whisper.

Jake looked at us with empathy, but mostly like a disappointed dad who caught his kids out past curfew. And fuck if I didn't hate putting him in this position. Standing up, I put my hand out to shake his. Annaleigh did the same, her face flooded with relief and embarrassment, much like mine.

"Jake. Thanks, man. We appreciate you giving us the benefit of the doubt."

He nodded and shook my hand. Probably a little harder than necessary, but at this point, he could do the *Vulcan Nerve Pinch* on me, and I'd smile and say thank you very much.

"Yes. Jake. This means so much," Annaleigh said.

Jake let go of my hand and stepped to her. She was staring at the floor but met his eyes. He reached out and put his hand on her shoulder, patting it softly. She leaned into him, and that uneasy feeling crept into my stomach again. It was intimate, almost too intimate, and I didn't like it.

Why was Jake so quick to cover for her? For us? Had he done it before? Did he cover something up with Benjamin? With him and Annaleigh?

Jake walked out without a word, and I heard the click of his door shutting before soft fingers traced their way up my arm, calming my wayward thoughts. Looking down at her, I forced myself to smile, and she returned it.

"I feel like I was just sent to the principal's office," she said, walking out of the boardroom and sitting down at her desk with a sigh.

"And then sent to my room without supper," I added, leaning against her desk and taking off my glasses to clean them with my tie. She reached out and took my glasses, opening her desk drawer and taking out a handkerchief.

"I'm humiliated, Max. Those pictures. What we did. I can't even imagine what Jake thinks, and what he had to do. What are we going to do? What's going to happen?"

I followed her hands as she cleaned my glasses, not having the words to reassure her. We dodged a damn freight train today, but I kept thinking about that email saying this wasn't over.

"Well, for starters, I'm going to peel this orange for you, so you feel better," I said, touching my finger to my lips before picking one up from her desk. "Then, I'm going to say what a shitty situation this is. But we'll move forward, together, and handle whatever happens."

Shrugging my shoulders, I handed her another slice, hoping to portray the confidence I didn't feel. Between the email, the pictures, and the intimate touching with Jake, I had the confidence of a fruit fly.

"You don't think we should cool down? Take a break?" she asked, looking down at the floor.

"No. I don't. We should go to *B's* later and then enjoy the rest of the weekend."

"I guess you're right, Max. I'm glad your brother is visiting, but I've gotten used to you being around in the morning."

"I like being around in the morning, Blue. I like being in your space. Let's try to put this behind us."

I handed her the rest of the orange, and she nodded, touching her finger to her lips. It felt like it should be five o'clock, but it wasn't even ten. Scrubbing my hand over my face, I walked into my office, shut the door, and dove into the growing pile of paperwork on my desk, wishing we were already at *B's*.

- *23* -

OUT OF SYNC
Annaleigh

I was so embarrassed I could barely see straight. What in the world was I thinking? The words on my computer screen were blurry, and my thumb was throbbing from where I'd chewed the nail. There was no way I'd be able to do anything productive. But there was always mind-numbing filing and shredding.

My chair squeaked as I spun it around, standing up to brew a cup of tea. I hated to bother Jake, but I needed my lavender honey from his office. The mug felt heavy in my hands as I moved forward and knocked on Jake's door.

"Come in," he said, standing beside his desk and packing up his laptop. He stopped and looked at me, putting the cords away and putting his hands on his hips. I walked over to his machine and got the water started before turning to look at him. His face was unreadable, and once again, I didn't know what he'd say.

"Jake. I'm so sorry we—I put you in this position. Please know I am still willing to take full responsibility for my actions and never would expect or assume you would cover for me, for us. I'm so ashamed."

"Come here, Anna. Sit down."

He motioned to the chairs in front of his desk, crossing his arms in front of him and still pulling off that disappointed, dad-look with practiced ease.

"I understand why you two didn't come to me sooner. This situation with Benjamin is awful, and disclosing a relationship with a superior while another employee wrongfully accuses you of sexual misconduct just looks bad. But we have worked together long enough that you should have trusted me."

"You're right, Jake."

"I know. There's a reason I have the corner office," he said with a smile. "Go finish making your tea. And just so you know, I could make your hair curl with the stories I could tell you about when Katie and I started dating and all the tennis lessons we missed."

He used air quotes for tennis and rubbed the back of his neck, smiling.

"But what happens when this gets out, and people talk? I'll be a laughingstock, dating my boss. They'll question my ethics," I said, standing up and watching the hot water fill my mug.

"I won't sugar-coat this for you. You're right. They will. But when have you let what people say bother you? You're damn good at your job. Without you, this place wouldn't be half of what it is, and you know it. The real question is, will you let what people say get to you? Or will you rise above it and show them how wrong they are?"

Letting his words sink in, I steeped the tea, adding honey and blowing on the top. Jake put his hand in his pocket and took out his keys, then patted his jacket and shirt pocket, looking for something. Putting the tea down, I walked over and picked up his phone, handing it to him with a smile. He nodded and slid it in his pocket, leveling me with his mastered dad-look again.

"Thanks. See what I mean. This place, and me especially, would fall apart without you. Now don't sweat this, Annaleigh. HR didn't ask for copies of the pictures, and I've already called Officer Hanson. He's added this evidence to your file to see if this warrants an arrest. Try to put this behind you and enjoy the weekend. Plus, people do crazy things when they're in love. Trust me, I know."

With another smile, he picked up his laptop bag and slung it over his shoulder before he walked out.

In love?

That was crazy talk. We just started dating and hadn't been together long enough to be in love. In like maybe, and definitely in lust, but not in love. And regardless of what Jake said, I was worried about what people here thought.

What if the bank wasn't the best fit for me anymore? *Was this a sign?*

The tendrils from the tea swirled, and I focused on the steam, weighing my options before popping a handful of calcium chews and putting in my air pods, willing the day to move faster.

It didn't.

The day passed at a snail's pace. I could count on one hand the times I'd left the office before five. But today, I did exactly that. I shut down my computer as fast as my exhausted hands would let me and took Max's as we walked to the lobby.

"So, it's true then," Elise said, almost sneering. "You two are together."

"Hi Elise," I said, with a smile, trying not to let on how drained from the day I was feeling. I didn't have the energy to deal with her drama. "Yes, Max and I are dating. Have a pleasant weekend."

"I'm sure it won't be as good as yours," she said, focusing back on her computer as we walked by and pressed the elevator. When the doors opened, she mumbled something loud enough for me to hear. Shaking my head, Max followed me into the small space and pulled me close.

I melted and wrapped my arms around his waist, laying my head on his chest and feeling his muscles, letting his strength soothe me. Everything felt better when he was touching me, holding me.

Was this love?

"What did she say, Blue?" he asked, leaning down and brushing my hair from my face.

"She said if fucking someone was the way to an EA position, she would have tried it years ago."

"What the hell?"

"I know, Max. People are cruel. It just makes me think, you know."

"Think about what?"

"Maybe it's time to move on to something else, to look for a new opportunity."

"That's bullshit," he said, squeezing me harder. "You know how valuable you are to the company. Don't let people determine how you live your life. I'll leave the bank before I let you do it."

"Let me? Come on, Max. Think about it. This could be a good thing."

"Doubt it. Why should you change to accommodate other people?"

"But what if we break up and end up hating each other? How could we still be impartial? How could we still work together?"

"Right, but what if this goes all the way? You always assume the worst, Blue."

He shook his head and let go when the elevator doors opened, walking out together to our cars. "We're driving together to B's. I need you close, Blue," he said, opening the door to his truck and pinching my butt as I stepped in.

He started the truck, playing the familiar music of Old Dominion. Smiling, I reached over and took his hand as he pulled out of the parking garage.

"Didn't take you as someone who listens to Country Music."

"Well, ever since I heard this super sexy chick sing at a country bar, I've been switching things up."

Bringing my hand to his lips, he kissed it and winked before focusing back on the road.

"Oh? Sexy chick, you say? I'm a little jealous," I replied, distracting myself.

And there was no better distraction than listening to Max when he talked sweet or dirty. *Especially dirty.*

"Don't worry. I only have eyes for you, Blue."

"I'm glad. So, your brother's coming tomorrow? Tell me about him."

"Oh. He's a great guy, a few years younger than me, and happily married. Warren is really into music. I remember growing up. He was always playing music or writing, and all set to go to college when my parents…"

I felt him tense, and he let go of my hand, white-knuckling the steering wheel.

"What happened, Honey-Bun? I'm here."

He smiled at the corny nickname, blowing out a deep breath and lifting his shoulders in a half shrug. I reached across and pried his hand from the wheel, taking it in mine and rubbing slow circles on his palm.

"You always know what I need, Blue," he said, pulling my hands to his lips.

"Growing up, our parents were more like social coordinators, trying to cram us into the perfect All-American family. We were expected to practice law at our father's firm and marry well. I tried to fit into their perfect bubble, letting them control every aspect of my life, molding me into their idea of perfection. Warren fought their control, and they tolerated it until he graduated high school. He left the night he graduated. My parents told me it was his decision, and I fucking believed them. I was a jaded asshole."

"Because you believed your parents?"

"Yes, exactly. My brother's gay. The night he came out to them, my father wrote him a check and said he never wanted to see him again. Can you imagine? He had his whole life ahead of him. I still don't know the whole story. He tried to reach out over the years, but I never answered. Years later, when I walked in on my ex-fiancé cheating, he was the only one I called. I hadn't realized how much I'd missed him. He has this way, you know, this way of putting everything into perspective. He's always been my best friend, and I'll never forgive myself for losing sight of that. We're playing golf tomorrow. We have a lot of years to make up for," he said, taking his hand from mine to adjust his glasses.

"I'm glad he's visiting so you can reconnect."

Max's story sounded so familiar, parents not accepting children, brothers divided. It was heartbreaking. Max's brother did a brave thing. Forgiving him. Letting him back into his life.

"Me too, it's a long time coming. I was such an idiot."

"I can tell you blame yourself. And believe me, I know a thing or two about that, Max. I'd like to meet him one day. The way you talk about him sounds so familiar. But honestly, your parents… I'll skip that family reunion."

"Yeah, there's no love lost there. I argued with my father the other week and have been avoiding calls from him and my mother since then. Speaking of parents, there is something I need to tell you," he said, turning into the bar and finding a place to park.

"Sure, of course. Let's head in and grab a table." I picked up my purse and stepped down from the truck. "Are you ready to meet some of my family?"

"Of course, I am. And even more ready to have a drink after our day."

We walked hand in hand, and he opened the door for me. The crowd was small since it was early, and as always, the familiar sounds and smells drew me in. I loved this place. We chose a table near the stage, and I waved to UB behind the bar. He gave me a two-finger salute before turning to pour a beer. Max scooted his chair closer to mine and handed me a bar menu before glancing over it.

"I'm glad I'm checking this place out. I've wanted to since that day at the beach when I made an ass of myself. It reminds me of the bar where I first met Jake back in Chicago. So, what's good?" he asked as a server came over to get our drink order.

"Oh," I answered, taking a moment to peruse the menu. "Everything. But the burgers are the best. There's always a new one on special. I think this week it's provolone with guacamole. And that's Uncle Bob behind the bar."

Max turned his head and nodded in greeting and Uncle Bob returned the gesture.

"Damn, that sounds good."

"Right! My aunt comes up with the best combos."

"It's a shame I'm going to miss hearing you play this weekend." He gave me a mischievous smile and cocked his head to the side like he had a secret.

"You know I'd love to meet your brother, but I don't want to take away from you two catching up."

The server dropped off our beers, and I took a long pull, glancing around the familiar space.

"Have you come up with something better than Honey-Bun yet?" he said, unbuttoning the top buttons of his shirt.

"Ugh, no. The girls call you Broody Max, BM for short. You didn't exactly make a good first impression. I believe my vote was Sexy McGrumpy."

"Humm. Max McHotness, maybe. Or, Sex-God is always an excellent choice."

"Oh, I'm sure my mother would love to hear that one."

"Fair point, Blue. How about… The Man Who Rocks Your World?" he said with a smile, putting the beer bottle to his lips and taking a drink.

"So, you rock her world?" Uncle Bob's deep voice said, stepping up to our table and crossing his arms over his barrel chest.

Just as I thought Max was going to snort beer up his nose and sputter through a response, he smiled, stood up, and held out his hand.

"Oh, I'm sorry. Would you repeat that, please? I was too busy staring at your gorgeous niece," Max said with ease, not at all put out by Uncle Bob's playful jab.

"Ha! Good man! Pleasure to meet you. The name's Bob." He shook Max's hand enthusiastically and stepped over to give me a quick hug.

"Bob. The pleasure is mine. I'm Maxwell Jackson. Please call me Max."

"Thanks, Max. It does these old bones good to hear you say that."

"Old bones?" I said, "Stop that! You are not old."

I tried to level him with an intimidating stare, but it must have come across as more of a grimace, or maybe a sign of constipation, because Max jumped back in the conversation, squeezing my thigh.

"Quite the place you have here. I look forward to coming back soon to hear Annaleigh play and look forward to watching Alex tonight. Annaleigh says she's a terrific drummer."

Releasing Max's hand, he smiled and moved to stand between us.

"Thank you, Max. And yes, hearing both of them play is always a treat. You're welcome here anytime. And Annaleigh, there is something I want to talk to you about."

"Sure, what's going on, UB?" He dropped his eyes to the floor before meeting mine. I put my hand over Max's and hoped he wouldn't bring up the check again. I deposited it last week. Probably.

"Your aunt and I have been talking. We wanted your thoughts on taking a more active role here, at the bar."

"A more active role? Like you want me to handle the books?"

"Um, sure. If that's what you're comfortable with," he said, his body language clearly saying that was not what he had in mind.

Was he short a bartender? Or did he need help with scheduling the local bands?

"I take it, that's not what you were thinking. What did you have in mind?"

The question lingered in the air while Max used his thumb to trace patterns on my hand.

"Well, we would like to do some traveling now that Alex is moving away. I'd love to go back to Norway, and Diane wants to go to Scotland. With both of us being so active here, it would be hard to leave for more than a long weekend."

I still didn't understand. It almost sounded like he wanted to retire, but that couldn't be right. Opening this place had been his dream for so long. The silence dragged on for a minute or five as Lace and Whiskey warmed up.

"Um, I'm going to go get us another beer," Max said, breaking the silence and kissing my cheek before grabbing my bottle and walking up to the bar. Nodding to him, I looked back to Uncle Bob and took a deep breath.

"Are you thinking of retiring?"

"Maybe. If not that, then at least slowing down. I had a career, and this has become a second one. And even though I love every second, I don't want to wake up and be seventy years old with regrets."

"I honestly figured Alex would eventually move back and take over."

"She loves this place, yes. But not like we do, Annaleigh. Diane and I were wondering if you would consider stepping in and managing *B's*. You've been instrumental in making this place thrive."

"But…" I played with my cell phone and stared at the floor, not knowing what to say.

Take over the bar?

"I know. I know. You love your job. I'm just throwing the option out there should you want a change of pace. It's a lot of nights and a lot of tedious details, but if there is anyone that loves this place as much as we do, it's you."

"Can I have some time?" I said, looking down to stare at the floor.

"Of course. I'm not asking for an answer this week or even this month. It's just something for you to think about for the future. I mean, this could be a sign, right?"

"A sign?"

"Yeah, a sign. Or destiny, or whatever. Just don't dismiss it before giving it some thought. Oh, and Max seems like a good guy, and you look happy. It's nice to see you smile more."

Max came back with two more beers and set one in front of me before sitting back down.

"Back to behind the bar. Good to meet you, Max."

He reached out to shake Max's hand and clap him on the back before smiling and walking away. I took a sip of beer but couldn't taste it. Max put his hand on my thigh, as I processed what UB asked.

"Come back to me, Blue. What's going on?" he said after the server dropped off our burgers.

I rubbed my forehead and shook out my hair, picking up the beer for another drink.

"He's thinking about retiring, Max. He, um, asked me how I felt about taking over for him."

"Oh. That's intense, Blue. Especially after our day. I take it that wasn't even on your radar?"

"No, it wasn't," I said, cutting my burger in half and taking a bite. "I'm not upset or anything, just thrown for a loop. I mean, one day, he's talking about this new local band that's coming to practice, and the next, he's saying he wants to travel. I'm all for travel, and I understand where he's coming from but give a girl some warning."

Lace and Whiskey played their first song, and we ate and watched. Max's head was bobbing to the music, and my fingers tapped chords on the table. I ate half my burger but pushed the rest away, no longer hungry.

"Are you feeling better? Want another beer?"

"I'm good on the beer, thanks, Max. It's been a lot to process today. And honestly, I'm not feeling great. I made an appointment with my doctor to see if my hypocalcemia might be best treated a different way. I don't think the oranges are cutting it, and the calcium chews aren't working."

"Hmm. I'd miss the oranges if you gave them up. They make you smell editable," Max said, leaning over to give me a swift kiss. "Why'd you decide to call your doctor?"

"Well. Bird, mostly. But also, you."

"Elaborate for me."

Max raised his hand, asking for the check, and passed over his credit card. He finished the last swallow of his beer before focusing on me.

"It's strange. But a good strange. Ever since we met... it's like my mind is clearer. I've been writing lyrics and playing more. It's almost like you filled something I was missing. Something to help me heal. Then Bird all but kicked my ass while we were in Tennessee, and I stopped feeling guilty. So mostly, I'm saying, in a very roundabout and vague way, is that I'm happy, Max. You make me happy. Incredibly happy."

He smiled and took my hand, leading me out of the bar as we waved to Uncle Bob. The night was balmy, and even though I was tired, I hated I was going home alone. He turned down the radio when we got in his truck and rubbed his hands together, pulling onto the road.

"When I first moved down here, Blue, the last thing I was looking for was a relationship. I was so jaded by Nicole. I think I still am sometimes. It's hard to trust, and I'm always thinking the worst. But being with you, I feel like this is how it should be. Maybe not with all the extra drama that comes with us, but what a real relationship should be. And just so you know, I am totally and completely bamboozled by you, Blue."

"Thank you, Max. You make my heart so happy. But I'm not sure if that's the right context for bamboozled."

"What? Yes, it is. Max, smart. Max know words," he said, doing his best Tarzan impression before hitting his chest with a loud thump that echoed in the truck.

And then I pictured him in nothing but a loincloth, and I had to press my thighs together to keep from crawling over the console and straight onto his dick like a nymphomaniac. Looking over, he gave me a sexy wink that did nothing but made my panties wetter.

"Whisk me away on the ridges of your chest."

"So tomorrow," Max said, "Warren and I are going to clear the air and start over. But it's nerve-wracking, knowing we weren't in each other's lives for so long. Plus, I'm halfway between wanting to find Benjamin and bloody his nose and wanting to lock you in my bedroom until we are one-hundred percent sure he's handled. I am *not* used to… not being in control."

"I love it when you go all possessive, Growly Alpha on me."

"Growly Alpha? Will that make the list of potential nicknames?"

"Maybe… And did you say your brother's name is Warren?"

"Yeah, Warren. I've told you that before, I think. Why?"

"Just another freaking coincidence. My brain is weird."

Get it together, woman!

I twirled a strand of my hair, letting his brother's name sink in.

Stop looking for signs that are clearly not there!

"Okay, way to be clear as mud," he said with a laugh, pulling up beside my car and walking around to open the door for me. I moved to step out, but he stepped between my legs and leaned in, running his stubble against my neck. Sandalwood and clean cotton clouded my senses, so I tilted my neck, and he peppered me with kisses until he reached my lips. He brought both hands to my face and kissed me slowly like he had all the time in the world.

I leaned into him and sighed, loving the taste of beer and mint as his tongue stroked mine. I loved the way Max kissed me. Slow, sensual, and oh so passionate.

All too soon, he pulled away and pressed his forehead to mine.

"Remind me why I'm going home alone tonight," he said, giving me several quick kisses in a row, making me all but lose my train of thought.

"I don't remember. Not when you kiss me like that."

"Good, baby. Because I want another night with you. Do you need anything from your car?"

"Not a thing, Max. Come home with me."

He kissed me again, long and slow, stroking his tongue with mine as his fingers traced up and down my arms. Rational thought all but left my body when we kissed. Bird, the bar, and Benjamin faded to background noise. When we broke away, and he closed the truck door, I was so close to saying I love you. The words were on my tongue, and they felt so natural, so right. But love? In such a short period?

Faces swam across my vision, like more missing puzzle pieces, and something tried to push its way through my subconscious. But every time I thought it was getting closer, it slipped away.

Max turned the radio louder, humming to the music and tapping his fingers on the steering wheel. I watched the streetlights speed by and reminded myself that everything wasn't a coincidence, and everything wasn't a sign. I had a smart, sexy, growly man that was all mine, and I was his.

- *24* -

PIECE ME TOGETHER
Max

"Sliced it, Bro," Warren said, taking a sip of iced tea and turning his head with a grin. "You going to go for two over par again? Or this time, try for three?"

His lanky frame shook with silent laughter as I glared up at him. I rarely looked up at anyone, but at six foot four, Warren towered over me by several inches.

I whispered 'asshole' loud enough for him to hear before stepping away so he could take his shot. He re-tucked his bright pink polo, lined up, and drove the ball straight down the fairway.

Asshole.

He smirked and brushed nonexistent dust from said pink polo, shrugging his shoulders as if he could see the steam coming out of my ears and didn't fucking care. He walked down to our cart without waiting for me to reply. I was too mad at my piss-poor game for a comeback, so I resorted to our same old golf razz, just like when we were teenagers.

"Doesn't matter. I still have a better short game than you."

I followed him over and slammed my driver back into the bag before sitting beside him and crossing my arms over my chest. I didn't find my rhythm in the front nine, and the back nine was going the same way. The freaking water hazard on the seventh hole did me in, and I haven't hit the ball right since.

"Maybe. But it's only because this is all you corporate types do, right? Play golf? Some of us have real jobs, Maxie."

Warren stepped on the gas, and we headed down the path in search of my ball. He used my old nickname, and even though I hated when he called me that, it felt damn good. It felt like I had my brother back. We fell into step as if it had been weeks since we had seen each other, not years.

"Ha! Some days, but it's still better than sitting in a cubical, playing video games, dick."

I scanned the fairway for my ball, and it mocked me from a bunker. I grabbed another club before stomping over in the hope I could make it to the green.

I turned around and looked at Warren, who walked behind and picked up the rake before he answered.

"Video games? Is that what you old men call line editing software manuals these days?"

"Just shut up so I can blow this damn shot, and you can finally give me a rundown of these last years."

"Whatever you say, Maxie."

I blasted the ball from the bunker, spraying sand in every direction. Surprisingly, the damn ball made it to the green, and I fist-pumped the air like a spoiled kid who finally got his way.

I got this!

Finishing the hole, only one over par—thank you very much—we packed it up and headed to the clubhouse. I was in a great mood, even though my final score was three damn digits.

We dropped the cart off, and I changed into my bandana-chain Amiri sneakers before heading to the bar and taking a seat by the window. I fired off a quick text to Annaleigh in the locker room, and as I sat down, she sent me a selfie of her and Baxter. I noticed her bright eyes and smile first, and those gorgeous tits second. She was teasing me with her low-cut shirt, and I loved it. The table gave me cover as I reached down to adjust my dick, and Warren stared at me with a stupid grin on his face.

"I see you still have a sneaker fetish," he said, looking at my black and white shoes. "Now, want to tell me what that text was about?"

"Want to tell me first what's happened in your life these last few years? Not sugar-coating any of the bad shit?"

Just as Warren was about to talk or tell me to fuck-off, the server walked over with a smile and an introduction.

"I'll have a pulled pork BBQ sandwich and sweet potato fries with a draft IPA. Um, no. Soda, please."

"Miss? It's Meghan, right?" Warren said with a glance at her name tag. "What my much older brother means is an IPA, not soda. And I'll have an Arnold Palmer with a lobster Po-Boy sandwich and a salad, please."

Meghan nodded, walking away, and Warren glared at me like I had done something wrong.

"Don't do that, Maxie. Don't order soda because you don't want to drink in front of me. I'm good. I'm clean, have been for years. Now, are you going to tell me what made you grin like a guy who found his father's stash of porn?"

At the mention of our father, we both paused, and he cleared his throat.

"Tell you what. I'll tell you why I'm grinning if you hold nothing back about what happened."

"Deal," Warren said. We clink our glasses together, and I took a long pull from the IPA, enjoying the hops.

"You first, man. I'm straight dying about what has finally removed the giant stick from your ass." Warren rubbed his hands together like he was waiting for juicy gossip, ever the Drama King.

"I'm dating someone. Someone the opposite of fucking Nicole."

"Yes! I knew it! I told Tay that's what it was. That man owes me a back rub. Sweet! I'm going to need to meet and vet her for you—only the best for my big-bro. Now, you sure you're ready for this, Maxie? I will not sugar-coat this shit for you."

"Hit me." I finished the IPA and set it down, crossing my arms and bracing for his story.

"So, picture it. Almost seven years ago, on the eve of my High-School graduation." He paused for dramatic effect and swept his hand across the table. I leveled him with a scowl that had him crack another smile and shake his head.

"Damn, you remind me of Father when you scowl like that."

I schooled my features and was about to tell him not to compare me to that megalomaniac when he kept talking.

"Yeah. Anyway," he said. "That night, after graduation, I went to them. I had known I was gay for years, probably my whole life, and had finally made peace with myself and who I was. I knew it would be hard and knew that I wouldn't fit into their idea of our perfect country-club family. I had hoped to have an open conversation. But nope, I should have known. Mother started crying and wouldn't even look at me. Father took a more direct approach. He threw his drink at me. The glass shattered on my face and gave me this nice little souvenir."

Warren pointed to a thin scar on his left cheek and took a drink of his Arnold Palmer, probably pretending it was whiskey. Or maybe glad he wasn't dependent on whiskey. Looking off towards the green, he rubbed his hands on his shorts and took a breath.

"Holy shit, Warren."

"Yeah. Holy shit is right. Father told me to get out, that I wasn't his son, that I was dead to him. I nodded or yelled. I honestly don't remember and said I'd be gone as soon as I pack. Father said no. He wrote me a check and dropped it on the ground, and said to leave right then. No clothes, not even a fucking toothbrush. He never wanted to see me again."

"I remember that weekend, man. I'd been on the other side of the house, without a clue as to what happened. Father stormed into my room that night, completely trashed. He was screaming about how you'd left and demanded my cell phone. I'm positive he blocked your number. I called you the next day, and it said out of service. I should have known. What did you do? Where did you go?"

If a bomb had exploded on the green, I wouldn't have been able to look away. Guilt swirled across my vision, but I held in it. This wasn't about me.

"I went straight to the bus station. Thank fuck, I had my phone and a little cash. I called my best friend, you remember? The one I went to music camp with every summer. Her father answered, and I was blubbering, barely able to string together a sentence. He got me a plane ticket that night to them. I had something like four layover stops, but I left everything. You, my friends, and all of my things except what I was wearing. A fucking blood-stained polo."

"They told me you refused to grow up, to go to college, and that you only wanted to play music. And me, the perfect son, believed them."

"I swear to all the gods if you start with that pity, whoa is me, I'm so sorry bullshit, I will stop and not tell you anything else! They screwed us up both so bad I'm surprised we're normal. We both could have tried harder." He pounded his fist on the small table, causing it to shake and several people to look our way. Meghan appeared with another round of drinks, dropping them off tentatively and walking away.

Warren pointed at my beer and said, "Drink, and tell me about your girlfriend before I finish my sob story."

I couldn't help but smile when I thought about my Blue.

"Warren, man. I'm a fucking goner. She's it for me. I know it. And gorgeous. She makes me want to do better, be better. You'd like her. We'll have dinner this week. I wish you could meet her tonight. I'm so proud of what she's done."

"Count on it, Maxie. I always wanted to go on a double date with my big brother. But not tonight. We already have plans." He clasped his hands over his heart and batted his eyelashes like an idiot, and I almost snorted my IPA. Damn, I'd missed him.

Our food came, and we took time to eat and watch groups walk in from the eighteenth hole, both absorbed in our thoughts. He finished his Po-Boy and reached over, grabbing a handful of my fries and stuffing them in his mouth.

"So anyway," he started, spraying pieces of sweet potato in my direction, accidentally on purpose. "I moved in with them and started working part-time, taking night classes in creative writing and editing until I got my degree. Then I overdosed, went to rehab, got married, and currently am living happily ever after with two cats and a goldfish from a County Fair Tay won three years ago. That goldfish was a buck and is now the size of a fucking baseball."

"Nope. Nice try. Remember, I walked in to find a yoga instructor balls-deep in my now ex-fiancé. Tell me all the dirty details, let me apologize one more time, then let's move the hell on and plan that double date."

I raised my hand for another IPA and took my last fry from his plate.

"Fine, douche. You asked for it. I moved in with them above the garage. Her and I started the band we always talked about, and I got to know her family. Things were great, really great, Maxie. But then they weren't. I got depressed. I was done with Chicago, done with our parents, and pissed at you. Pissed at them. I think it was two years after I moved in that I broke my ankle. Nothing serious, I just tripped walking down the steps, but I got a prescription for pain meds."

Warren met my eyes, and they got glassy. Hell, mine did too. This is what I needed to hear. The noise from the bar faded out, and I gave him my full attention. Meghan dropped off my last beer and the check. I gave her my card without a glance.

I held my breath and his voice got quiet as he went on, "When the meds ran out, I started drinking. It was easy enough with our band playing every weekend. I had so much anger, so much resentment. Nothing helped, not even therapy. The pills numbed it all and made everything bearable. No one noticed. When the pills ran out, two beers turned into a six-pack before we even went on stage. Then straight liquor and anything else I could get my hands on. One show, our last show, I bought some pills from some random guy at the bar. I took a handful before the show and passed out on stage. It messed her up pretty badly. Tay too. After that, her parents checked me into rehab. I didn't realize how fucked-up I was. But Maxie, you want to talk about an amazing fucking family. They were waiting for me the day I got out. They saved me. She saved me. Tay saved me. I got my shit together and started dating Tay. He got a job out of state, so we moved to Georgia. Things are good now."

Warren stood up as I finished my beer and motioned for me to follow, but then paused and looked behind me, cocking his head at someone. I turned around but only saw the back of a blonde guy's head disappear behind a corner. Turning back to me, he shrugged his shoulders and put his hands in his pockets.

Scribbling my signature on the receipt, we walked to my truck, and I threw him the keys. He got in and moved the seat back with a sigh before he pulled out of the club. My head was buzzing, and something was pushing at the edge of my thoughts, something familiar. It reminded me of when I first met Annaleigh, right before I realized she was my new assistant.

"I'm sorry, War. Sorry for everything. For not realizing sooner the shit our parents pulled, for not answering when you reached out, for not being there when you went to rehab, and for not being there when you got married. I don't know if I'll ever be able to make it up to you, but you, us, we're brothers. I'll never make that mistake again."

"I know you won't, Maxie. Now, are you ready for your surprise?"

"Yep. Hit me."

"You're meeting her and her family tonight."

"I'm what?" I said, wondering if the beer had affected me more than I thought.

"She lives here, and the bar we used to play at is here too."

"She lives here? This is where you lived? How did I not know that?"

Warren turned the radio up and tapped along to Anderson East while he drove.

"Well, bro-tato, there's a lot you don't know. But no more," he said, reaching over and punching me on the shoulder. "Right. So tonight. You, me, Tay, and her family at her Uncle's bar. You're going to listen to your little brother's band play, and you are going to meet her. I'd set you up if you both weren't with other people."

Stopping at a red light, I stared out the window, then back at Warren, hearing him talk but not listening to his words. The beers were stronger than I thought, or maybe I was seeing signs everywhere too. Warren was still talking, and I turned to him, feeling sick as the realization pushed its way through the beer and took root in my brain.

"When I talked to her the other week, I got the feeling she was screwing her new boss. She works at a bank downtown, keeping all the executives in line. Help me razz her, will you? Her voice gets all squeaky when she's mad. It's hilarious. Oh, and when we're done with the set, y'all are going to get drunk, and I am going to take very incriminating photos to be used as blackmail one day."

I was speechless. There was nothing left to say and only one thing to ask, and I already knew the answer. Swallowing harshly as Warren pulled onto the street in front of my house, I asked, "What's her name, Warren?"

"Oh. Annaleigh. Annaleigh Mackey."

You have got to be fucking kidding me!

- *25* -

GLIMMER OF FADING LIGHT

Annaleigh

L eather pants.

Why in the world did I think leather pants were a good idea?

My size eight ass was screaming, and I looked in the mirror before peeling them off and throwing them in the back of the closet. The *oh so soft* spandex pleather leggings with pockets that glimmered in the light called my name, and I shimmied into them without having to hold my breath. My purple tank top that had: *Stay Humble or Be Humbled* written in big block script matched perfectly, and I tied the look together with tall black boots and heavy-handed, dark makeup.

Baxter was on the bed, halfway sitting on a stack of letters from Bird. I pulled one from under him before popping one last slice of orange in my mouth. *Different last name.* It wasn't the same person. It couldn't be. Bird's last name was Smerdon. And his brother was Mark or Matt. Something like that. Not Max.

The name was in one of these letters. I'd look later or ask Bird tonight. *Duh.* This was the Universe's way of having everything come full circle. It was not another coincidence.

Warren. Wren. Bird. *It was not the same person.*

Tucking my scarlet lipstick and phone in my pocket, I scratched Baxter one last time, grabbed my JIVA10, and loaded it up before heading to *B's*.

I was so excited I could barely stand it. It'd been too long since I'd seen Bird. I missed his face. I missed his laugh. I missed his voice. I missed my friend.

I pulled into a parking spot too fast and barely turned the wheels straight before shutting off the engine. My black guitar case was in the trunk, and I slung it over my shoulder and pushed open the door, then straight-up screeched like a girl with front row tickets to One Direction.

There he was, my Bird. He stood on the stage and absolutely owned it tuning his bass.

His hair was blonde, shaggy, and longer than I remembered. He was wearing a black mesh shirt and ripped, skinny jeans with several new tattoos peeked through the holes. And oh my god, was his nipple pierced? Yep, I could see the shiny bar. *Kinky*. His eyeliner was so natural you barely noticed, but it brought out his honey eyes. Familiar eyes.

Achingly familiar.

Not missing a beat, he put the bass down and jumped from the stage with his lanky arms open wide. I ran to him and jumped, wrapping my legs around his waist like a python and squeezing for all I was worth. He stumbled but kept one hand on my ass and wrapped the other around my waist, squeezing back tighter.

"I have missed you so freaking much!" I said, my voice high enough to shatter glass. He gave me one last squeeze before he set me down and clasped his hand in mine, turning me to Taylor so I could give him a huge one-armed hug. Taylor glanced at Bird and raised his eyebrows, nodding in my direction, silently passing something between them.

I looked between them and said, "What? You two are doing that weird married mind-meld thing."

Bird grinned and squeezed my hand, "What can I say, babe. I'm a man in love." He winked at Taylor. *Something was off. They both looked guilty.*

"And I've missed you too. So much. We should have done this a long time ago."

"Damn straight, we should have. Thank you for kicking my ass into gear in Tennessee. I needed it."

"Happy too. After all, even though the love of my life is standing beside you, I can still appreciate a nice ass."

"Glad to know your personality is still intact," I said, and playfully jabbed him in the stomach.

"Ugh, easy. I work too hard on these abs for you to bruise them. And. Um. A little issue has been brought to my attention that's going to take you by surprise. I have had a, well, an interesting afternoon. An interesting, awfully long afternoon."

"What? You can still play, right?"

"Play? Of course, I can, better than you, as usual," he said, poking me back. "But you, honey, need to take a deep breath and turn around. There's someone you should meet."

"Drama much?" I said, keeping hold of his hand while turning around.

It was... Max.

What was he doing here?

He should be with his brother. Smiling, I walked forward with one arm outstretched, but Bird's hand stayed firmly grasped to mine, pulling me back. Grounding me. As if he knew my world was about to be turned upside down.

Oh God, it was true. Max's Warren was my Bird. The color drained from my face with the realization, and I barely heard his next words.

"Honey," Bird said, much softer than his usual boisterous voice. "This is my brother, Maxwell Jackson Smerdon."

My brain must have done a complete short-circuit and reboot because I didn't remember sitting down and drinking the amber liquid that was in my now empty glass. Someone was holding my hand, but the hand was clammy and sweaty.

It was my hand. I was clammy and sweaty.

If I had opted for the skin-tight leather pants, they would be a permanent part of my sticky body.

How had we not known? Was I really this closed off and vague to the important people in my life? Did I not share enough to make the simple connection that Max and Bird were *brothers?*

Max was the man that made my sweet friend cry the hardest when he showed up at my parent's doorstep. I could see the pain in Max's face, like he knew what I was thinking, knew I was there for Bird at a time he wasn't.

My heart was beating fast, and my mouth was dry. I pointed to the glass, and more liquid appeared. The thing that had been pushing against my subconscious was now clear as day, and doing a tap dance across my vision, along with tiny black spots wearing top hats and tails.

My entire body felt like it was nothing but pins and needles, tingling everywhere. Moving my hand to the glass, I brought it to my lips and took a slow sip. I tasted the bourbon this time, and when I put the glass down, I looked up, and my eyes darted between two very important men in my life.

"Blue?" Max said the same time Bird said, "Honey?"

"How did we not know? Or maybe I knew." I said, looking down to see Bird's hand still in mine.

"What?" One of them answered. I couldn't tell which one. Even their voices were similar.

"It was you." Max moved his chair closer to me and touched my thigh. "It's always been you." His voice was so low I had to lean forward to hear, and his teeth were clenched together with each word spoken.

"I'm going to go make-out with my husband and figure out our first song while you two sort this out," Bird said, letting go of my hand and standing up.

Uncle Bob, Diane, Alex, and Taylor were all on the stage, far enough away that they couldn't hear, but close enough for me to see the sympathy. Max grabbed the chair between my legs and pulled it swiftly towards him, making me stare up in surprise.

"You were there, Blue. There when I was too stubborn to be. There when he needed you." His strong fingers traced my jaw, leaving my skin tingling. I was confused. Max's touch was calming, but he was also the man that broke Bird's heart.

"It wasn't enough." I sniffed and picked up the glass again. "I didn't see the signs. Didn't know he started using."

"You were a teenager. I'd be worried if you saw the signs. We can play the blame game all night, but what would that solve? If Warren can forgive me, and I can forgive myself, you can let go too, Blue."

He picked up my bourbon and drank the rest before pouring more from the bottle of Macallan on the table.

"Hey, honey. Do you want to start by playing *Poison*?" Bird called from the stage, trying to draw my attention away from the freaking tsunami of a situation. And oblivious to how I was feeling because I didn't share enough and probably had the emotional range of a teaspoon.

"Oh, sure. Max has only heard me sing country and jam a little at the office. Let's start with a song that has me practically dry-humping your leg for the last ninety seconds."

"Don't forget about when you rip my shirt off. That's my favorite part of the song," Bird said, wagging his eyebrows

"Gah!" I stood up so hard the chair fell over and threw my arms in the air. "Don't be a dick, or I'll rip that nipple ring out!"

"Oh, kinky. Does Maxie know about this, you dirty girl?" Bird winked then looked at Max, "Maybe we should have told her this afternoon. We've had time to process this. She hasn't."

Bird was looking over me like I wasn't there and having a conversation with Max, who still had an unreadable expression on his face. But it wasn't unreadable. It was hurt.

"All afternoon? All afternoon? Do you mean to tell me you two had known about this all freaking afternoon while I've been at home stuffing my face with so many oranges I'll probably sweat juice and wondering when my ass got too big to wear my leather pants comfortably?"

"Calm down," Bird called, stepping down from the stage. He came closer, but I held out my hand, and he stopped. Everyone on stage stared at us like some sort of twisted triangle, and Alex lifted a thumbs-up in our direction.

"Calm down? Oh, my god! You calm down, you stupid flamingo, with your stupid long legs! I just found out the man I am *in love* with is also the man I swore I would dropkick in the balls one day. Sure. I'll calm down. Consider this calmed down!"

I was pacing now, so it took me a minute to process that I'd just admitted out loud that I loved Max. Not to him, and not in a reasonable, calm voice. But I'd said it. *Foot-meet mouth*. I hadn't even admitted that to myself. Max was still sitting, calmly, at the table, not facing me. Maybe he hadn't heard. Please, I hope he hadn't heard. This was not the time to share that piece of information. I'd prefer to do it when we were naked. Or on a date. Or in a blizzard. Pretty much anywhere but right here. Bird strode up to me in one step with those damn long legs and bent down to stick a finger in my face.

In my face.

"Flamingo? Really? You know you suck at nicknames, right?" Bird removed his finger and smiled, standing at his full height and crossing his arms across his chest. He was intimidating and had better hair, but damn it, I was not overacting!

"I get it, I do, but no need to be bitchy. And honestly, you're calm compared to how the man, you are apparently in love with, acted earlier." His voice dropped low when he said in love, giving me hope maybe Max hadn't heard.

"Earlier? At least you had an earlier, coming in here all cool and calm. Meanwhile, I have citrus sweat pouring off my boobs and down my butt-crack!"

"Wow, I never knew I missed so much being into guys. But I promise you, Taylor smells much worse than citrus boob sweat. And I'm kinda into it." He made a bow-chick-a-bow-wow noise and blew Taylor a kiss.

"Ugh! Stop. I need a minute. Back off, buckwheat. I'll be in the beer cooler."

"You still suck at nicknames," he called after me.

I stomped to the cooler in the back, piling my hair on my head and fanning my face. When I opened the heavy door, the cool air hit my overheated body, and I rummaged around until I found a twist-top beer. I closed my eyes and took a drink before putting the cold bottle against my forehead.

The door opened again, but I didn't open my eyes or turn around. Warm, strong arms wrapped around me. Arms I fit into. Arms I belonged in. I turned around to see Max. He took the beer from my hand and finished it before laying it on the floor.

"Hey there, Sparkle-Pants."

"Sparkle-Pants? You bragging that you're like the king of nicknames or something?"

"No, but I'll take that title. I just wanted to talk without an audience."

Max put his hands in his pockets and shuffled from foot to foot. I focused on the steady hum of the air conditioning and the cases of beer lining the walls, hoping there was a way for us to come to terms with this.

"When did you know, Max? I can't tell how you're feeling."

"Um, when I stopped blaming myself and actually listened to Warren's story, I knew. It's been a long afternoon. And I don't know how I'm feeling, Blue. Tired maybe? When did you know?"

"I didn't admit it to myself until Bird introduced you, but I think I knew when we left here the other night. Do you want to leave?"

I stepped back and rubbed my arms, chasing away the tingling feeling.

"Yes. No. I feel like this entire thing wouldn't have happened if we had an honest, non-vague conversation about our past. I'm tired of being the last to know everything. It's maddening," he said, shaking his head.

"Are you putting this all on me, Max? It's not like you were very forthcoming about your last name." I sagged down, not even angry, sitting on a full case of beer and letting the cold seep through my leggings. Maybe he should put this all on me.

"No, not at all. I meant to tell you my last name but didn't. I despise being a Smerdon, knowing the power and influence that comes with the name. When I moved here, I wanted to leave that name behind, leave my old life behind. That's on me, and we should have had this discussion weeks ago. But this has to stop. No more secrets."

"I agree. And I get why you wanted to leave that name behind. But wow, Ace."

"Ace? Really? Still working on that nickname, Blue?" He smiled at me, and his features softened.

"Ugh, nothing works. And what's worse is I don't really feel like singing."

Max rubbed my shoulders, and the tingling feeling was back. He leaned in and cupped the back of my head, tangling his fingers in my bun and pulling it out.

The cold air was supercharged, and when his lips touched mine, electricity cracked from my mouth to his. I parted my lips and let him tease along the seam with his tongue, tasting the bourbon, tasting him. He deepened the kiss, and I sighed into his mouth, pulling his hips to mine.

Holy Wow. Max knew how to own a woman's mouth.

He explored my mouth, teasing my tongue with his and keeping a firm grip on my hair. His hips dug harder into mine, and he sucked my bottom lip into his mouth, reminding me of how well he could work that tongue over every inch of my body.

The leisurely kiss quickly turned possessive, and I pulled away to press my forehead to his, "Max, so good."

He gave me a wicked grin, glasses fogged with our combined heat, and surged in again with renewed vigor, nipping, sucking, and licking my lips, jaw, and neck. I wrapped one leg around him as if he was my personal playground and sexy as fuck. He kissed me hot and hard, his tongue devouring mine, claiming me, as if I had any intention of going anywhere.

He pressed our foreheads back together and untangled his hands from my hair, breathing deep before giving me one of his signature panty-melting smiles. And said panties were definitely close to spontaneously combusting.

"Now that's bull-shit. I haven't heard Warren play in years, and the sight of you on stage in those skin-tight, sparkle-pants is not something I want to miss. Though I will need you to elaborate on the dry-humping of Warren."

"Oh. Yes. Well, that's exactly what I do. It's a whole routine we always used to end our shows. We practiced it in the garage for months before we even tried it on stage."

"I'll need to see that Blue, and remind myself my brother is a happily married man."

"Would it help if I told you I pull a red scarf out of my boobs and 'pretend' to strangle him at the end?"

"Wow. That's intense. And yes, that helps. Thanks."

"Anything for you, Hot-Stuff."

"Ugh, give it up, Sparkle-Pants. Technically, my name is Maxwell, so Max is a nickname."

"Never. Just you wait, I'll find the perfect one." I rubbed my arms. The adrenaline and sweat had finally dried up. My teeth chattered, and Max turned around and led me out of the cooler. We walked hand in hand to the front room, where five pairs of eyes turned toward us.

The lights looked hazy, and someone had taken my JIVA10 and put it beside the microphone on stage right. The wood creaked as I walked up the side stairs to the stage, with Max behind me.

"Here, have an orange," Uncle Bob said, walking forward and handing me a slice before giving my cheek a kiss. "You two kids, okay?"

"Yeah, I think so. It was a lot to process. It still is."

I stepped closer on the creaky wood stage to run my fingers over my guitar and smile at the band, my band. Max looked on with one hand in his pocket and his head on a swivel, taking in the setup.

"Tell me about it. Your mom flipped out."

Uncle Bob reached out and shook Max's hand with a nod before turning back to me. The blue spotlights were already calling. I was finally ready.

"Oh, UB. You called mom?"

"Duh, they both are planning on coming by later." He chuckled to himself and shook his head, handing me another slice.

"That's right, I'd forgotten."

"Understandable, given the drama. You ready for them to meet Max?"

"Doesn't seem like I have a choice." Finishing the orange, I opened and closed my hands, shaking them out and tapping chords on my thigh.

Bird walked behind me and smacked my ass with a crack that made me squeak. "Come on, guys. I'm itching to play. Let's do this!" He clapped Uncle Bob on the back, and then Max, shooing them towards the stairs.

Max leaned forward and gave me a PG kiss, very different from almost mounting me in the cooler. I wondered if he would take me back and give me an orgasm or two—just a little something to take the edge off.

"I know what you're thinking, Blue. And don't you worry, I'm coming home with you tonight." He was leaning down close, breath whispering against my ear. "Those boots are giving me all kinds of ideas." His fingers traced a line down my arm, and I pressed myself closer. I could never get close enough. This man could perpetually be inside of me, and I'd still be pulling him down harder to feel more.

"Thank fuck," I said back, giving him a sly smile. With one more kiss, he saluted Bird and the band, following Uncle Bob and Aunt Diane off stage.

Walking over, I picked up my guitar, adjusted the strap, and ran my fingers over the dark, polished wood. Max sat at a high-top table by the bar, legs spread and hands resting on his knees, looking hot as sin.

"So, you love my brother?" Bird asked, sauntering up to me with his bass guitar slung low.

"I am very much in like with your brother." Strumming a few cords to warm up my fingers, I smiled and felt my cheeks grow hot with the obvious lie.

"Okay, keep telling yourself that, babe. Now, should we open with *Poison*? I know how much you love Alice Cooper." I nodded, and he stepped up to the microphone. Bird adjusted it, before testing out a few lyrics before giving Uncle Bob a thumbs up.

I nodded and smiled, blowing Max a kiss before the stage lights turned up and his face faded away. Taylor strutted over, handing me a red scarf, and I tucked it in my boobs before giving him a fist bump. Alex stepped up to my other side, and the four of us looked at each other, smiling.

"Do it right!" I started, bringing my hand in the middle.

"Or not at all!" Bird added, putting his hand on mine.

"Own the stage!" Alex said, flipping her drumstick up and catching it before putting her hand in.

"And chicks dig scars!" Taylor finished, slapping his hand on top.

This felt right, and I felt whole.

Ready to let go of the guilt.

Ready to love.

We finished our set, and the lights dimmed, finally giving me a clear picture of our small audience. I was sticky and sweaty, feeling freer than I had in years. My parents were smiling and waving, and my mom was snapping pictures.

Shaking my head, I waved back and walked over to put my guitar away. Bird was already jumping off the stage to greet my parents with Taylor close behind. I scanned the space for Max but came up empty, wondering if he had stepped out for a minute. Grabbing my almost empty water bottle, I finished it before going down to greet everyone.

I was still looking for Max as I hugged my parents and chatted with Alex. It wasn't until Uncle Bob walked over shaking his head that I knew he'd left.

"Max said he needed some air, Annaleigh. And that he would call you later."

Bird slid over beside me and bent down to my ear.

"Don't let this worry you. He takes time to process stuff. He was like this growing up too. And you should have heard him talking about you this afternoon. Trust me, that man is head over heels in love with you."

Bird pressed another drink in my hand, but I pushed it away and got water. It was close to midnight, and I was fading fast. Less than a half-hour later, we said our goodbyes, making plans for brunch.

Taylor walked me to my car and kissed my cheek. Sliding into the front seat, I started the engine when a car came barreling down the street with its high beams on, practically blinding me. I thought I glimpsed white blonde hair as the car sped by on the road. I shielded my eyes, and it took a minute before I could see enough to pull out of the parking lot. *Douche.*

The drive depleted the last of my energy. When I got home, I gave Baxter some scratches and left a trail of clothes to the bathroom. I filled up the tub and sank under the mountain of bubbles. I didn't bother to check my phone. Max knew my number. He could call me when he got his head out of his ass.

He needed time to process. Hell, I needed time to process. But these bubbles felt too good, and I was too tired to be mad. Sinking down further, I let the stress melt away.

- *26* -

INSECURITY'S CHAINS

Max

I was questioning everything.

Everything.

And it didn't help that I think I saw Benjamin when Warren and I walked into the bar. Maybe I was delusional. It was a very real possibility. I was sure Warren would agree.

Or Bird.

Whatever the fuck his nickname was. Too many important moments in my life started with the words, Annaleigh Mackey. Not that there was anything wrong with that, but damn, ease up on the coincidences.

I was driving with no destination, making turn after turn, following the white lines on the road. Muscle memory took over, letting my head mull over the night. Seeing her on stage, playing with the band, was better than the office, better than Tennessee. The way she moved. The way she played—doing what she loved. It was amazing to watch. Her smile stretched across her entire face, and she looked happier than I'd ever seen her.

I don't know why I left before the set was done, but the air in the room was suddenly stifling. I left her family, and I left Warren when I high-tailed it out of the bar. Uncle Bob clapped me on the back like he understood, but it still felt like I was running away from my issues.

A light turned red, and I sent a text to Warren apologizing before I threw my phone down, grimacing in the dark. I leaned my head back, waiting for the light when Warren's text came back.

Warren: It's time to stop running.

He was right. I was so desperate to make her mine, to be in her space. And when I was, seeing her in her element, seeing her beautiful and glowing with happiness, I ran.

The light turned green, and I rolled down my windows and turned up the radio. That same song from the retreat was on, *Whatever It Is.* I hummed along and listened to the words, looking around to get my bearings. Straight ahead was her house. Of course, it was. My subconscious was light years ahead of my brain, already knowing exactly what I wanted.

I pulled into a spot on the road and turned off the engine. It had only been a few hours since I'd last touched her, and I already needed more. Running was stupid. It stops now. All these feelings threatened to overwhelm me, but for once, I let them come, fully accepting what I admitted to Warren earlier.

I need her.

I want her.

I love her.

And it's time to tell her.

Here the hell we go.

I stomped back up her stairs and knocked on the door. Probably harder than I needed to, but right now, the only thing I needed was her. Glancing at my watch, I realized she might be sleeping. But a minute later, she opened the door a crack. She gave me a once over before opening it wider, then turned around and walked away. I got a glance of her make-up-free face.

She looked more beautiful at this moment than she ever had before. She looked like the woman I loved. She was so fucking gorgeous it hurt.

We didn't speak. I kicked the door shut and stalked straight towards her. She was like a baby zebra, helpless. Ready for the taking. Ready to be devoured.

Baxter trotted up to me, sniffed my hand, and demanded scratches. I bent down to pet him, and his tail shook so hard his entire body moved. Content with the attention, he licked my hand and disappeared into the other room. Good. He didn't need to see what I was about to do to his mama.

Grabbing her arm, I pushed her against the kitchen island, eyes never leaving hers. I was ready to tell her all the things, tell her she was it for me. But when I saw the sexy little crease between her eyebrows and the way her eyes sparkled in the light, all the words I had prepared to say evaporated to nothing.

Wondering for half a second if she was angry, I caged her in my arms and crowded her space. But she was gazing at me as if I was the sexiest thing she's ever seen. She was so delicate but so strong, and I was sure my heart would beat out of my chest if I didn't taste her, if I didn't tell her.

I leaned in and traced my nose along her neck, breathing her in. "I missed you, Blue."

"Then you shouldn't have left," she answered, crossing her arms but leaning into my touch. So beautiful. So sassy. So mine. Pressing my lips to her neck, I growled and licked a line up to her earlobe.

"No, I shouldn't have. Tell me how to make it up to you, Blue."

She made a sexy little moan and arched her neck, giving me better access.

"You can stop leaving when things get hard, Max. That's not how this works. We have to talk to each other and open up like you said."

I was not expecting her to call me out, but she was right. Righter than I'd like to admit. Breathing her in and sucking on the tendon where her neck met her shoulder, I answered with a growl. She reached up and gave my hair a sharp yank. I hissed and bit down on her neck before meeting her eyes.

"I know, Blue. No more running for either of us. And no more passing blame. And there is something you need to know," I said, palming her breast and letting my thumb slide over her nipple.

Fuck, she wasn't wearing a bra, just a flimsy blue T-shirt and shorts. I traced circles over her nipples, loving how they pebbled under my touch. Her eyelids fluttered shut, and a soft moan escaped her lips. The little movement of my fingers made her squirm.

"You're it for me, and you're mine. No more running. I'm going to spend every day showing you how much you mean to me and every night worshiping your body."

"Good. I like you around in the morning. I like you around all the time. I'm yours, Max. And you're mine," she said, letting go of my hair and running her hands underneath my shirt.

"Damn right. I was thinking of fucking you on the terrace tonight, but the living room works just as well."

"Max," she whispered, and those breathy little moans went straight to my cock.

I felt vulnerable and exposed. In the years I'd been with Nicole, we'd never had this intimacy, never had this connection. It was like I'd lived my life in total darkness, and she woke me up with flashes of blues and purples. All the colors were because of her, because of how she made me feel. My heart squeezed like a vice. Painful with a feeling so new, so wonderful, it enveloped my entire body.

"I need to kiss you."

I kept kneading her breast, and when my mouth found hers, her velvety soft tongue thrust softly against mine. Her hands continued their trek under my shirt and up my abs, making me break away for a second so I could pull it over my head. Every second I wasn't touching her was a second wasted. She did the same, taking her shirt off, revealing those perfect tits.

I kissed her again. I couldn't stop kissing her. But the second I saw the goosebumps on her bare flesh, I broke away and lowered my head, lapping at one perfect nipple. She arched forward, and I pressed one hand against her back, pulling her closer to my eager mouth. I sucked on her nipples, taking long pulls and lashing my tongue.

When I came back to her lips, I pushed my cock against her and wondered why the hell we weren't naked. She dove for my pants, desperately working the buttons, but I gripped the back of her neck, taking control, and pulled her lips back to mine, making her hands stop their feverish pursuit and grip my shoulders. I wasn't in any state to appreciate her flushed skin or her soft curves. The only thing that mattered was getting her closer.

I reached into her shorts, pushing them down and letting my fingers trace her perfect pink slit, teasing her clit, not touching her exactly where she needed it. The second my fingers got close, her hips thrust towards me in a silent plea for more.

I agreed. This was why I was here, why I was carrying her over to the couch and laying her down. She spread her legs wide, and I wasted no time kicking off my pants and grabbing a condom from my wallet.

"Are you ready for me?" I rubbed my hands down her smooth thighs, and she took the condom, rolling it down my length.

"Oh my god, yes," she said, tipping her legs open further and beckoning me closer with a finger. I leaned down and gave her one long lick, needing to taste her. Her hips bucked against my face, and I smiled, licking my lips.

"I love this pussy, baby," I said, nuzzling her thigh, "I love this body."

I lowered myself on top of her, fitting perfectly between her legs, and aligned my cock with her entrance.

"You were so damn sexy tonight. I loved watching you play, watching you move on that stage like you owned it."

I slowly pushed in one glorious inch at a time, feeling her clench around me. Taking her hands in mine, I lifted them above her head, pinning them down and leaning forward to claim her lips. I kissed her like she was my air, like it was the only thing to do to keep on living. I poured myself into the kiss, hoping she understood what I was trying to say without words. Her entire body shivered under me as I sank home, knowing this was where I belonged for the rest of my life.

Holy fuck. The words sank in, and I knew it was true. I belonged with her. I was made for her. Every moment of my entire life has led up to this, being inside the most beautiful girl in the entire world and knowing that she was mine. Forever.

I slowly and methodically plunged in and out of her warm wetness, letting go of one of her hands to skim down her neck to her breasts. Running my palms over one nipple then the other, I watched them pebble under my touch.

"Don't leave me again," she moaned, tilting her hips up to meet mine. I understood what she was asking, what she needed.

"I won't." *Groan.* "I promise." *Thrust.* "I need you. I need us. I won't ever leave you, Blue."

"You have all I am, Max," she said, reaching up to run her fingers down my face. Her touch was electric, like flames licking up my skin.

We were both tiptoeing around the words, not saying them *yet*. But we both felt it; both knew it was real. Annaleigh's head fell back, and she closed her eyes, gripping me with her delicate walls. She was quivering around me, and I could feel her desire, her need. It matched mine.

Letting go of her other hand, I lifted her and wrapped both arms around her waist, smashing her breasts to me and loving the feeling of her hard nipples dragging across my chest. I watched her closely as we slowly built the pace and found our rhythm. I moved faster, and she met me thrust for thrust, our hips smacking together.

"Close, Max. More. Harder." Her words were breathy and pained as she gripped my shoulders and chased her release.

Snaking one hand between us, I rubbed her clit in tight, fast circles, laying her back down and pushing her hard into the cushions. She was so warm and tight, and I wasn't going to last much longer. We were shaking the whole couch when I felt her body tense.

"I feel you. That's it. Come for me, Blue. I'm right there with you, baby."

I didn't want this to end. But when I felt her tighten around my cock and come apart, lightning shot up my balls, and my cock swelled. She was gripping me so tightly, so sweetly, I couldn't hold back a second longer. Growling her name, I exploded, coming so hard I almost blacked out. She threw her legs around my waist, connecting us, binding us together.

Collapsing on top of her, I wrapped my arms around her and buried my face in her neck, leaving hot, open-mouth kisses in my wake.

"Mine, Blue. You're mine," the words were a promise, a commitment.

"I was never anyone else's," she answered, relaxing her legs and pulling me to her lips. She tasted like mint and bourbon. She tasted like home.

- 27 -

LEAVING BLISS BURIED
Annaleigh

All too soon, morning light streamed in the curtains, and I felt a distinctly rough tongue lick my hand. Said hand was currently the only part of my body not touching Max.

God, I loved waking up with him. I barely remember making it upstairs and falling into bed last night. I only remembered him pulling me close and holding me tight. He made me feel cherished. He made me feel desperate. He made me feel loved. It felt like things were back to normal, back to the way they were supposed to be. I pulled my arm back underneath the covers and tried to stretch.

Max had one leg thrown over mine and his arm across my chest, resting on my breast. I could feel his breath tickle my neck, heavy and even. He was still very much asleep and looked so peaceful, like all the weight he carried had melted away. Tracing one hand up his arm, he didn't shift an inch. Maybe I could scoot away and let him sleep longer.

Baxter put two paws on the bed and whined, nudging his face under the covers. "I know, bud, I'm getting up," I said, stretching one leg to the edge of the mattress.

I was almost free when Max's cell phone rang. All three of us jumped with the noise, and Max untangled himself from me long enough to look at the screen before laying it back face down.

"Morning, beautiful," he said, reaching over to drag me closer and run his stubble over my neck. I felt something thick and hard pressing into my back, and I rubbed my ass against it, earning a thrust and a growl. "I like this Blue, waking up with you, being in your space. Feeling your tight ass pressed against my cock."

Baxter let out another whine, and Max groaned. "Okay, bud. I'm up. Bathroom, coffee, then walk," he said, planting a wet kiss on my neck.

With a squeeze to my thigh, Max got up, pulled on a pair of sweatpants, and went to the bathroom, leaving the door cracked enough for Baxter to follow him in. *Hilarious.* Not only had we broken the dreaded bathroom barrier, but I was also sure Baxter was glad there was another guy around that peed standing up.

I stood up and stretched, pulling on Max's shirt. His phone rang again, and I glanced over to his side of the bed. His mother was calling. It looked like she'd been calling since yesterday.

He walked out of the bathroom with Baxter hot on his heels and came up beside me, wrapping his arms around my waist. "Let me take the boy for a walk, then let's crawl back in bed, baby."

"Hmm, yes please," I said, scratching my nails up his arms. "Your mom called again. Shouldn't you answer?"

"Nope," he said, kissing my neck and grabbing his glasses. I knew they had a terrible relationship, but her persistence made me uneasy. As if he knew what I was thinking, his expression softened, "If she calls again, I'll answer. Now, what should we do today?"

"Today? Don't you and Bird, um, Warren have plans later?"

"I told you, baby. I'm not leaving. Whatever plans we have include you."

Smiling, I nodded, just as his phone rang again. His posture stiffened, but he smiled and gave me another open-mouthed kiss before leaning down to pick up his phone.

Answering, he held his phone with his neck and put on his glasses, sitting on the edge of the bed. Wanting to give him privacy, I headed to the bathroom and then downstairs to make coffee. As I tiptoed around, I heard him raise his voice. I hoped his mother wouldn't cause him any more stress, but I remembered all the horror stories Bird used to tell me about how manipulative they were.

It was still early, so I opened the back door and let Baxter out for a quick potty break. He did his business, running back inside and up the stairs to pester Max for a longer walk.

I started a dark roast brew first, taking out the cream, then reached in the cabinet for my hazelnut K-cup. His hard footfalls came down the steps. Slow and methodical, with Baxter hot on his heels, tail wagging. He was raking his hand through his hair. His face was blank, and his skin was pale.

"What's the matter? What happened?" I handed him the coffee cup, but he pushed it away, gripping my wrist like I was his lifeline. His hair was sticking up in every direction, and his glasses were askew.

"It's my father. He had a heart attack." His voice was flat and emotionless, much different from the erratic expression on his face.

Oh no.

I put my hand on his chest and laid the coffee down, taking his other hand in mine. Guilt and anger clouded his vision, and his hand felt limp and sweaty.

"I'm so sorry. What happened, Max?"

He pulled his hand away and looked at the floor, defeated.

"My mother said I needed to get back to Chicago immediately. God, she said it was my fault, Blue. Said he was all worked up because I wasn't answering the phone. What the hell is the matter with me? I should have tried harder. I am ungrateful."

Holy fuck, his parents were manipulative.

What kind of mother would do this to a child? I remembered one story Bird had told me. His father lied about an illness to trick him into coming home after he ran away as a teenager. I should give them the benefit of the doubt, but any parent that would choose status over children didn't deserve the benefit of anything.

I pulled his head down to mine and kissed his forehead. He was clammy and shaking. Taking a shuddering breath, he wrapped his arms around me tight, and I hugged him back just as hard until his heartbeat matched mine.

How could he not question his mother's motives?

"Max, baby, no. This is not your fault, not at all. Your mother was wrong to put this on your shoulders. Are you sure that's what she said? Would you like me to go with you?" I said, talking to his chest and feeling him tense.

Pulling himself from my arms, he threw his hands in the air and scrubbed them over his face. "Am I sure? Yes, I'm fucking sure. My mother wouldn't lie about something like this. I have to go to the airport and see if I can catch a flight today. You stay here."

I could see the anger in his eyes. He was furious at himself, questioning all his choices up to this moment and lashing out at me. Baxter followed him as he paced the room, clenching his fists and taking deep breaths. I paced with him, twirling my hair, and wondering how much I should push. I could clear this up with one simple phone call, and I had no issue eating crow if I was wrong.

"Max, are you sure your mother is telling the truth? Maybe you should call the hospital."

All of his guilt and anger broke through the surface, but I had to question him. Something wasn't right. But the closer he moved to the door, the more rational thought left him.

"This is bullshit! There is no time to call the hospital. I have to go straight to the airport," he said.

"Shouldn't you shower? Pack? Call Warren? You told me you wouldn't leave, Max."

I leaned into him and brought my hands to his face so he would look down and meet my eyes. But he shook himself from my grasp.

His face was hard, like always, but it was his eyes that had me biting my tongue. They were fiery, hard, unyielding. It was like he'd snapped.

"Are you not listening to me? My father had a heart attack. Jesus, I'm not leaving forever," he said with a voice still emotionless. I almost wish he had yelled. This dead, monotone voice he was using scared me. "My mother is making me feel guilty enough, I don't need it from you too."

He was halfway up the stairs before he looked back like he wanted to say something else. His emotions were getting the better of him, and that was understandable, but speaking to me like that was not.

"You need to stop it right there, Max," I said, crossing my arms before he could say anything else. "I get you're stressed, but you need to think hard about your next words and the direction this conversation is going. There are some things you won't be able to take back."

For one moment, I saw my Max shining through his dark eyes, and I moved closer to him. But in a blink, he was gone, and the angry beast reared its ugly head again.

"Trust me. There are many things I wish I could take back, Blue. I'll call you later," he said, running up the stairs.

In a blink, he was back, with his shirt rumpled and his shoelaces untied. His eyes softened for a moment, and he reached out and stroked my cheek with his fingers.

With a half-hearted wave, he ran out of my life as fast as he ran into it. I closed the door and sagged against it until Baxter nudged my hand again. I was seriously neglecting my dog-mom responsibilities today. My fur-baby needed a longer walk.

I ran up the stairs and grabbed my phone, sending a quick text to Bird in hopes he could talk some sense into Max. Regardless of his relationship with his parents, if his father was sick, Bird needed to know.

I rooted around for a sports bra as I thought about last night. We were so damn close to saying I love you. I wondered if that was screwing with his head. It sure as hell was screwing with mine.

But he was worth it; we were worth it. That was what mattered. I let my insecurities go last night in his arms, and there was no question, I was in love with Max Smerdon. And I needed a nap. Maybe I could bribe Baxter with raw-hide and take one after our walk.

I finished getting dressed and took a quick sip of coffee, bending down to get Baxter's leash when the doorbell rang. *What did Max forget?*

I walked to the door and opened it, ready for a kiss and an apology. But no one was there. I stepped onto the porch, looking left and right. But the street was empty. Baxter licked my hand, and I grabbed my phone and key, locking the door and heading to the park.

The air was warm and breezy, but my skin felt itchy like something was wrong. Baxter stayed pressed to my side like he could sense it too. We paused before turning the corner, and Baxter stopped, his hackles raised. I gripped his leash and turned around, my breath catching in my throat.

Benjamin's squinty eyes looked at me, unfocused and leering. His shirt was wrinkled and untucked, and his hair was a mess. He was swaying, and I could smell the alcohol wafting off him. But his eyes scared me the most. He looked like a rabid dog about to attack.

We'd only been walking for five minutes? How long had he been following us?

Baxter growled low, baring his teeth with raised hackles. I wrapped my wrist around his leash, pulling him tight to me. I could feel my palms getting slick, and my tongue felt too big in my mouth. My phone was tucked in my leggings, and I inched my hand closer as my eyes darted around for someone, anyone close.

"Put that hand by your side, or I'll show you what's behind my back," he said, bringing his hand to his lips like he was blowing on the barrel of a gun. Baxter growled, and I had no choice but to listen, lowering my hand to the side.

My mind was racing, and I tried desperately to remember Baxter's training. He was a big marshmallow, far from an attack dog, but there was a command they taught us. Something to use in an emergency. It was a

Russian word, no German, and I racked my brain while Benjamin swayed. My feet felt like two cement blocks, and I willed them to move, knowing I could outrun this asshole.

"Your boyfriend stormed out of here pretty fast. Did you finally tell him about us?"

He moved closer, and I managed to take one step back. My heart was pounding in my ears, and terror narrowed my vision. "I was hoping you'd be fired after my little side piece took those pictures, but me getting fired works just as well. It's not like I have to work. Now we can be together."

"You are delusional!" I hissed, taking another step away. I wasn't trying to be quiet. I wanted to get noticed, wanted someone to see what was happening. I kept a firm hold on Baxter's leash, making sure there was no confusion with my next words. "I would never be with you! We have never been together. You violated the restraining order, and I will press charges. Leave me alone, now!" I was practically yelling, taking a step back with each one he took forward. My eyes darted in every direction, and I saw a runner on the other side of the road, willing him to call the police.

"No, Princess. I'm not leaving. I love you. I did all this for you! You can even keep the stupid mutt!"

He spread his arms wide, like he was making some grand gesture by following me at nine in the morning, drunk. Not only did he admit to having his side piece or whatever take those pictures, but he also all but admitted he was the one that hurt Baxter. This was getting out of control fast. I knew what I had to do. I slowly unwrapped my hand from Baxter's leash, giving him slack. The grass was squishy with the morning dew as I bent my legs and prepared to run, stepping back to the sidewalk. Baxter pressed harder to my side, teeth bared and growling as if he knew what I was about to ask him and was ready.

My vision was crystal clear, and everything slowed down. I knew what was going to happen before it did. Benjamin reached behind his back at the same time I yelled, "*Fass!*" as loud as I could. Baxter lunged, snarling, all traces of my sweet marshmallow gone, and sunk his teeth into Benjamin's scrawny leg with a vicious growl. Benjamin's eyes got wide, but I wasn't sticking around a second longer.

I took off running, letting go of his leash and pumping my arms, focusing on my porch. I heard Benjamin scream, and I looked over my shoulder, tripping in my flip-flops and face planting on the sidewalk. I let out a sharp cry, my hands shaking with adrenaline.

"Baxter! To me!" I yelled, scrambling up and making it to my porch a second before he did.

I braced both hands on the door and slammed it shut, leaning against the cold wood. My hands were shaking as I called the police, sliding down the door and wrapping one arm around Baxter. After I hung up, I whispered and cooed praise to him as the adrenalin wore off, holding my other hand to my chest. My wrist was throbbing. I closed my eyes and took several deep breaths, then looked down at my leggings. They were torn where I'd fallen, with several scratches bleeding onto the black fabric.

I slowly stood when I heard sirens, stepping to the window with a groan. I saw Benjamin lying in the grass where Baxter bit him, clutching his leg. I wasn't a vengeful person, but if anyone deserved an injured leg, it was him. Actually, since he tried to hurt my dog and get me fired, I'd say he deserved two broken legs, a fractured rib, and a punch to the jaw.

The sirens got louder, and I focused on the noise until I heard pounding on the door. When I opened it, two police officers rushed in as my vision narrowed and the room spun. The last thing I remember was Baxter's whining from the kitchen.

ભ ભ ભ

The hospital lights were too bright, and the room was too cold. After an X-ray of my wrist, the doctor said it was sprained, and my calcium levels were too low. I felt so called out.

I was bandaged and sore, with bruised knees and a raging headache. A nurse came in a short time later with several prescriptions, and I was ready to go home with as little drama as possible.

I called Bird since he and Taylor were planning on spending the night tomorrow and asked them to come pick me up. I'd rather the girls come over to help me shower and such, but it was nice that Bird stomped in and took charge. I needed my bed in a bad way.

He charmed the nurses and handled the discharge paperwork, getting me out of there with no fuss. Officer Hanson came by for my statement and told me Benjamin had ten stitches and was handcuffed to a hospital bed awaiting transport to jail.

Officer Hanson also assured me that Benjamin would not make bail since he admitted he had been following Max and me for weeks between his hysterical wailings. *This was finally over.* The only thing left to do was call Max and tell him everything, after maybe kicking his ass for being a jerk, asking about his father, and telling him I loved him. I just needed to rest my eyes for a minute first.

The next time my eyes opened, I was being pushed out in a wheelchair. Bird was hanging up the phone with a scowl on his face, and Taylor had pulled the car around to help me in the front seat. Bird sat in the back, fingers flying across his phone. Seeing his phone reminded me I needed to call my parents and text the girls. The hospital had shitty reception. Digging it out of my purse, I saw a missed call from Max. I called him back, pressing the phone to my ear, and listened to the rings.

"Hey Blue," he said, his voice sounding like dark chocolate. Hearing him soothed me. I missed him. I wanted him to cocoon me in his arms and whisper sweet words.

"Hey, you, how's your father?" I said as Bird put a reassuring hand on my shoulder from the back seat.

"I don't know. I'm heading to my old place to shower. I'm sorry for the way I left."

"Thank you, Max. I'm sorry for questioning your mother's motives." I put my hand on Bird's and squeezed.

"You had every right to, I snapped at you, and that's never okay. I miss you, baby."

"I miss you too. Max, I need to tell you something."

My phone buzzed and I looked down to see a text from Jake. I replied I'd call him shortly, then pressed the phone back to my ear.

"Blue? Blue?"

"Hey. Sorry about that, Jake was texting."

"Yeah. Nice to know your boss is more important than your boyfriend," Max said, his voice low.

"What was that?" I asked, almost daring him to repeat himself.

"Nothing. Let me call you back in five, the elevator has shit reception."

"Okay."

"Thanks, Blue. Bye."

I hung up the phone and let go of Bird's hand, watching the palmetto trees that dotted the medium.

"I'm glad he apologized." Bird said, "He's always been a hothead, a trait he, unfortunately, picked up from our father."

"Yeah. But hothead or not, his comments can be downright mean sometimes. I'm just glad this is over, Bird," I said, trying to push his attitude aside. "Now I can tell him what happened, support you both through whatever is going on in Chicago, and we can come out stronger."

"Our father didn't have a heart attack."

"What?" I must have misheard him.

"I called the hospitals. He's not there."

"Then what's going on? Why didn't you warn Max?"

"I tried. But like I said, he's a hothead." Bird shook his head and stared out the window, tapping his fingers on his leg.

I waited for Bird to elaborate, but he didn't. Taylor looked at Bird in the rearview mirror, and they had a married mind-meld conversation. I hated being the last to know everything. I hated being kept in the dark. I sat there, silent and brooding, until the phone rang again.

"Hey you," I said, resting my head back and pressing a palm to my cheek.

"Hey, Blue," Max said. I could hear keys rattling, and he drew in a long breath. "I've been meaning to tell you something. Something I realized. I should tell you when we're together, when we're naked, or when I'm holding you. But I think the words are more important than the moment. And I can't wait a moment longer. I should have never left without telling you, and even if I'm not holding you, I don't want to wait a moment longer."

I held my breath and put my hand across my mouth. He was going to tell me he loves me. I could feel it, down to my bones. He was going to tell me, and I was going to shout from the rooftops, that I love him more than chocolate, more than my favorite guitar. I love him. I want him by my side.

But first, I shouldn't have to explain myself, or justify talking to Jake, especially when it's my *job*. And some small, nagging part of my brain wanted to reassure him before we said anything else.

"Max. You know better than anyone that my job is more than nine to five, right?"

He sighed loudly before answering. "Yeah. I know. But he covered pretty quickly for us, you know. It makes me wonder if he's done it before."

"Done it before? Are you serious?"

"Yes. No. Who knows. Just seems like we got off easy. And you didn't answer the question."

"I shouldn't have to answer!" I said, getting madder by the second. I took a deep breath, ready to give him a piece of my mind, but there was a voice in the background. A high, silky voice, almost purring. It sounded like nails on a chalkboard and made my skin crawl. But it was the words the voice spoke that cut me to the core, and I pressed a hand over my mouth, whimpering.

The words, *her words,* wrecked me. Gutted me. I didn't know what to think. I didn't know what to feel.

Bird leaned closer, hearing every word, and I shifted in the seat, trying to hold back tears. He reached for the phone, but I jerked forward and cried out, trying to stop the sobs.

"In this moment, you broke us," I whispered, sobs making my voice quiver.

"What?" said Max, sounding worse than when he was monotone. He sounded breathless, panting, worked up.

"I said, in this moment, you broke us, Max!"

"Annaleigh!" he yelled, but I hung up the phone and leaned back, letting my tears fall. I missed the good old days of being able to slam the receiver down. Maybe that would make me feel better. But truthfully, I wasn't mad. I was hurt and tired. So tired.

"What a stupid fuck," Bird said, reaching over to rub my arm.

We pulled up to my house, and Taylor parked, both of them helping me in. Tears streamed down my face, and Baxter whined when we got inside.

"Oh god. How could he have done that? How was I so naïve? I love him so much. Or I did. I do. I don't know."

"He'd be a fool to let you go. I don't know what his deal is, but I know he loves you. If he is this stupid, Taylor and I will kick his ass, even if he is my brother. I am taller and younger, after all."

"And you have better hair," Taylor said.

"That I do, baby. Now you need to sleep and let us handle all the things. Tell us what to do," Bird said, looking to Taylor, who nodded in agreement.

"Oh, guys. Thank you. I need to call my parents and the girls. And Jake. How could I keep working at the bank? How can I go there and see him every day? And the prescriptions I got need to be filled, and... and..."

"Honey, you need to sleep. The girls will be over tomorrow, and Tay and I will handle everything."

Taylor helped me upstairs, and propped several pillows on my bed and handed me the remote. I turned my head and smelled the pillow. It still smelled like Max. More tears fell, and I wondered if I'd have any left by the time morning came. I didn't want to sleep in the same place he held me hours earlier, the same place we all but admitted we loved each other.

Taylor pushed Tylenol in my hand and a glass of water. I swallowed it down and laid back, staring at the wall.

"Sleep, Annaleigh. And you know what you need to do."

"No. I don't."

"Well, you're going to get out of bed every morning and breathe in and out all day long. Then, tell me, what will happen?"

"Taylor."

"What will happen next, Annaleigh?"

"Then, after a while, I won't have to remind myself to get out of bed every morning and breathe in and out," I said, lying back on the pillows.

"That's right. Now sleep."

I nodded and turned my head, smelling the pillow and trying not to fall into self-doubt. Anger slowly replaced my hurt, and I threw the covers off and held in another moan. I didn't want to smell him. I didn't want reminders of us. I held onto the anger. It gave me strength, and I grabbed a blanket from the linen closet.

Stripping the bed as best I could, I curled up on the bare mattress and wrapped myself in the blanket. But that didn't fix it. Max's masculine scent has permeated the bed down to the mattress.

I felt like I was about to tumble over a waterfall, with no way to stop the undertow from pulling me down. I'd had some bad relationships, but nothing like this. I knew it was because I'd never loved anyone like I loved Max. Like I love Max. I'd never given myself so fully to someone else, and he broke us. I was shattered to a thousand pieces.

There was nothing to do but sleep. Everything would be clearer when I woke up. I'd call Jake, ask to transfer, call the girls, eat too much ice cream, and breathe. I had to remind myself to breathe. *In and out.* Maybe tomorrow I wouldn't have to remind myself anymore.

LEAVING ALL WE BUILT BEHIND

Max

I walked out of the airport and hailed a cab, checking the voicemails on my phone. There was one from Warren and one from Jake. I fired off a text to both. I'd call them back once I checked on my father. My mother had gone silent since I told her I was heading to the airport, and that had me so damn worried. She asked me to go to my old place and shower before calling her.

The Chicago air was stale and smelled nothing like the ocean. It smelled nothing like home. The city I was born and raised in was no longer familiar and no longer where I wanted to be. Tall, cold buildings dotted the skyline, and car exhaust permeated my wrinkled clothes. Ugh, no. That wasn't car exhaust. I smelled.

But I didn't care. I'd much rather head straight to the hospital, but the last thing I wanted was to cause my mother more stress. And with every step I took, I smelled oranges. Oranges, sweat, and guilt. A shower could help, and there might be clothes left in the closet.

A cab pulled up, and I rattled off the address as Warren's name flashed across my phone. I was sure Annaleigh told him where I'd gone and how

I'd left. The phone was wedged between my ear and shoulder, and I put my glasses on my head and dug my knuckle into my eye to stave off a headache.

"I don't have time to talk right now, Warren. I'm heading to my old place to take a shower before going to the hospital."

I rubbed my hand over the scruff on my face. Maybe I could find a razor stashed somewhere in the bathroom.

"Good. I'll be brief, you stupid ass," Warren said.

"What the hell, man?" I bit back, "I know it was a shit way for me to leave this morning. I left a message for her as soon as I landed."

I put my glasses back on and sighed, waiting for him to argue back.

"First. Shut up, Maxwell."

Shit. He used my real name.

"Two," he continued, voice getting louder. "I called Northwestern and Rush. He's not there. Mom's lying. You're walking right into whatever shit they have planned."

Whatever I was going to say vanished with those words. Was father already discharged? Had he died? Several scenarios were running through my head, except one where I was wrong. I was not fucking wrong.

"And third. I know what you're thinking, and you are wrong, Max. Don't let them manipulate you. And you better call her again to fix how you left things this morning. But hey, I still love you. And remember, I'm a men's large when you're shopping for 'Warren was right presents,' and I like shiny things. Seacrest out."

Warren hung up before I could argue. I tried to close my eyes but was too geared up between worry, guilt, and my cab driver, who was driving like a fucking maniac. The breaks squeaked in the cab as I kept hold of the *oh-shit* handle until we pulled up to the high rise. The air was smoggy when I stepped out, and I walked in, straight to the concierge, barely lifting my hand in greeting as he handed me a key.

I paced the lobby, my sneakers squeaking on the floor when Annaleigh's name flashed across my phone. I stopped, answering, "Hey Blue."

I needed her, needed her to calm me, soothe me. I needed to cocoon myself in her orange scent and blonde hair. But first, I needed to apologize. I let my temper get the best of me, *again*. There was never an excuse for speaking to the woman I love like that.

"Hey, you, how's your father?" Her voice sounded shaky, weak, like something was wrong. Way more wrong than the way I left her.

"I don't know. I'm heading to my old place to shower. I'm sorry for the way I left."

"Thank you, Max. I'm sorry for questioning your mother's motives."

"You had every right too, I snapped at you, and that's never okay. I miss you, baby."

"I miss you too. Max, I need to tell you something."

I waited for her to talk, but the line stayed silent. I took the phone from my ear to check the connection, but the call hadn't dropped. I said her name once, twice, before she answered.

"Hey. Sorry about that, Jake was texting."

Jake was texting? My father had a heart attack and we were in the middle of a conversation, but *Jake was texting?*

"Yeah. Nice to know your boss is more important than your boyfriend," I said, almost growling into the phone.

"What was that?" she asked.

I thought for a second and decided not to repeat myself.

"Nothing. Let me call you back in five, the elevator has shit reception."

"Okay."

"Thanks, Blue. Bye."

A doorman jogged after me and followed me into the elevator, pushing the button for the penthouse.

"Good evening, Mr. Smerdon. Welcome home," he said with a tip of his head as the doors opened. I turned around, about to correct him, but didn't bother. It wasn't worth it.

A sense of dread washed over me the higher we rose, and as I walked down the hall and stood outside. The last time I opened this door, I walked in on Nicole getting plowed by her yoga instructor. This time, I'd do to it talking to Blue.

"Hey you," she said.

"Hey, Blue." I tossed the spare keys in the air and caught them, drawing in a long breath. I didn't want to be here, but I stepped inside anyway, almost gagging on the sticky, cloying smell of perfume. The place looked the same. White and red with clean lines and hard edges. Fresh lilies were in the foyer, and the living room lights were on. The sticky-sweet scent got stronger the further I walked in, but all I could think about was telling Blue I love her, then taking a shower.

Forget going upstairs. I kicked my shoes off in front of the spare bedroom on the first floor and dug around in the linen closet, finding a towel, washcloth, and soap. I didn't see a razor, but the faster I got out of here, the better.

"I've been meaning to tell you something. Something I realized. I should tell you when we're together, when we're naked, or when I'm holding you. But I think the words are more important than the moment. And I can't wait a moment longer. I should have never left without telling you, and even if I'm not holding you, I don't want to wait a moment longer."

I smiled into the phone and paused, not really sure where I was going. I wanted more than anything to tell her how much I love her, but something kept needling me, preventing me from blurting out the words. Before I could figure it out, she started talking.

"Max. You know better than anyone that my job is more than nine to five, right?"

I sighed loudly before answering. "Yeah. I know. But he covered pretty quickly for us, you know. It makes me wonder if he's done it before."

"Done it before? Are you serious?"

"Yes. No. Who knows. Just seems like we got off easy. And you didn't answer the question."

"I shouldn't have to answer!"

Shit!

She was right. She shouldn't have to answer because I should trust her. I *do* trust her. I love her. My love for Blue filled up every deep, dark spot that Nicole ever tarnished. I scrubbed a hand over my face again, ready to tell her sorry, *again*, but a voice cut through the silence. The cloying smell made sense, and I could hear my heart thundering in my ears.

"Hey baby. About time you got here. I've been waiting all afternoon," the voice purred. Not just any voice, her voice. The owner of that disgusting perfume, Nicole.

She was wearing slinky, red lingerie, putting her tits on display. Her bleach-blonde hair hung across her shoulders, and she toyed with the string holding the lingerie together.

She was faker than I remembered. Her skin was so tan it looked orange. *How was I ever with someone like her?*

My thoughts were all over the place as Nicole strutted over in heels so high she could almost look me in the eye. I held both my hands out, keeping her from coming closer, but she reached out and ran one red, manicured fingernail up my shirt.

"What the hell are you doing here, dressed like that?"

"How else would I greet my fiancé? I've missed you, Max. Come here and let me remind you what you've been missing," she said, reaching out to touch me again.

She leaned closer, all silicone and collagen, and I barfed in my mouth a little, the bad airport food bubbling dangerously in my stomach.

"What do you think? Like my outfit? I know red's your favorite color. Put the phone down and let me do that thing you love with my tongue."

I shivered in disgust and stepped back.

Fuck! My phone! Blue!

I backed up until I was pressed against the door, raising the phone to my ear.

"What?" I said, not hearing her words.

"I said, in this moment, you broke us, Max!"

"Annaleigh!" I screamed, but she had already hung up.

Oh, no! No! No! No!

"No way in hell, Nicole. I don't have time to deal with your bullshit. Father is sick, and I have to go. See yourself out," I said, trying to push past her and hold back the anger that was simmering below the surface.

"Oh, silly. He's as healthy as a horse. But your mother and I were talking and decided there wasn't another way to get you home."

"He's not sick? Are you fucking kidding me? How could you do that? What the hell's the matter with you all?"

Warren was right. *Oh fuck.*

I walked right into their trap.

"Don't be mad, baby. But you needed to come home. There wasn't another option. You wouldn't return my calls. But I forgive you, and we can pick up where we left off."

"We are through, Satan! Don't you ever come near me again."

I needed to get the hell out of here and back to the airport.

I had to call Warren. I had to call Blue. *God, I was an idiot.*

"Please, baby. Come here," she said, crooking her finger at me.

She cocked her hip to one side and pulled the string of her lingerie, but I bolted out the front door and slammed it in her face, barely grabbing my sneakers. Anger and humiliation burned any lagging exhaustion from my body as I headed to the elevator. I pushed the button and heard the penthouse door open as she strode down the hallway, not caring that her tits and ass were on display.

"Stay the hell away from me, Nicole!" I pushed the button again, pressing my phone to my ear, calling Blue. It went to voicemail.

"I will not stick around forever, Max! You better not make me regret waiting for you!"

"The only thing I regret is not leaving your plastic ass sooner," I called back.

The door opened, finally, and the attendant looked between us, his eyes widening.

"Mr. Smerdon? Ms. Phillips?" he said, uncertainty clouding his face.

"Shut up! Don't let him get on that elevator!" Nicole said, walking as fast as she could in those heels.

The attendant ignored or didn't hear her, and I stepped in and pressed the button for the lobby. Taking the spare key out of my pocket, I threw it down the hallway. She followed it with her eyes as the doors closed. *Thank fuck.*

"Goodbye forever, Satan," I said, sagging against the door. The attendant didn't make eye contact, but it was hard not to notice his smile. I tried not to smile back, but soon we were both laughing.

I had to call Blue, tell her what happened, then call Warren and get back to the airport, but I couldn't stop. I was laughing harder than I had in months. It was freeing, or my sanity was slipping. Probably the latter. And I still smelled oranges. Maybe I was having a stroke.

I shook his hand and pushed him some bills when we got to the lobby, cramming my feet in my sneakers and hailing another cab. I pulled my phone back out when I slid in the cab and called Warren. It rang once, twice, three times before he picked up.

"The fuck do you want? It's been a long damn day, and I'm laying on the couch with a boxer who keeps trying to sniff my butt."

"Warren! Fuck! Blue heard Nicole. She was waiting for me. You were right! This is a huge misunderstanding!"

"Misunderstanding? I don't think so, dick! We were on the way home from the goddamn hospital when she called you, Max! I heard everything! How could you say those things? How could you get back together with *her?*"

"Warren, no! Nicole was waiting for me. I left! Damn it! I would never go back to her! I love Annaleigh! Wait. Are you with her, and did you say hospital?"

My heart dropped when I heard that word. The crazy cab driver was swerving in and out of traffic, and I willed him to go faster, to get me the fuck out of this godforsaken town and back to Blue. My ears were roaring with a blind panic... *if anyone hurt her.*

"Yeah. The hospital. Max. It's bad." Warren's voice got low, and I heard rustling and a door opening. "She had an accident."

"Oh God, and I wasn't there. I left. What happened, Warren, please?" I held my breath, my hand balled into a fist, waiting for him to answer. I felt sick, dirty, unworthy.

"You fucking swear you had no idea Nicole would be there? And you didn't mean all the hurtful shit you said?"

"No! I should have listened to you, to her, and never left. Please. Warren. Tell me. I need to know."

"Yeah, man. Okay. She was walking Baxter, and Benjamin confronted her."

I sucked in another sharp breath, growling, terrified as he talked.

"Baxter bit him, and she got away, but she tripped and is bruised up pretty bad."

"I'll fucking kill him. I'll quit the bank and open up my own firm to make sure he is charged with assault..."

"He's been arrested, has stitches, and won't make bail. Now, who's a good boy? Are you? Yes, you are. Such a good protector and mama's boy. We need to cook you a steak tomorrow, don't we?" Warren said, baby-talking Baxter.

The cab driver's eyes flicked to me in the mirror, and a maniacal giggle spilled out of my lips before I could stop it.

The airport food might make a second appearance after all, "Fuck, Warren."

I took off my glasses to rub my eyes. They felt like sandpaper.

"Fuck indeed, Maxie."

"Can I fix this? Talk to her?"

"She's sleeping. And I don't know."

"Thank you for being with her. Please keep her safe. And thanks for answering, Warren. I'll text you when I'm back home."

"You do that, Maxie. And for the record, I'm rooting for you."

"Thanks, man. I love her," I said.

"I know you do. You just have to convince her that you do. Love you, bro. Talk soon."

"Bye, Warren."

I was silent for the rest of the drive. My brain was in overdrive, fueled by my mistakes. All my mistakes. I laid my head back in the back seat of the cab. All the feelings that had been fighting their way to the surface broke through, coming together to make one thing crystal clear.

It was time to man up and become the man my father never was, the man she deserved. No more letting my temper get the best of me. I was going to jump in headfirst without a life vest, diving into the deep end of obligations and responsibilities. She deserved someone who loved her and trusted her. Someone who listened to her.

She deserved a place where she could be the amazing person she was without anyone second-guessing her. She deserved someone a hell of a lot better than me and my fucked-up psyche. But if she'd let me, I'd make it up to her.

Hell, I'd stand in her driveway John Cusack style with a boombox. Did they even make boomboxes anymore? Didn't matter. I'd write her love letters or meet her on top of the empire state building. Whatever it took. She was mine, and I was hers. Nothing else mattered. *Operation Get Her Back* was about to begin.

29

MY EMPTINESS
Max

The next thirty-six hours went by at a snail's pace. Thank fuck my bourbon didn't judge. I was going to have to make another stop at the liquor store if this kept up. Annaleigh wasn't answering my calls. She was answering my texts, but little good that did.

> *Max: Can I come over?*
> *Blue: No.*
> *Max: Will you answer the phone?*
> *Blue: No.*
> *Max: Are you okay?*
> *Blue: Yes.*
> *Max: I'm sorry.*

My thumbs had permanent indents from pressing my phone screen so hard. Warren was at least answering me with full sentences. *Operation Get Her Back* might as well be called *Operation Epic Failure*. But she couldn't ignore me at work. It was a shit thing to do, but I was prepared to lock her in my office until I could apologize and explain what the hell happened with Nicole.

But she didn't come in to work on Monday. The office felt empty and cold. Even her plants looked wilted and sad like she had been their sun. I knew she was my sun, lighting up every dark corner of my life. Elise wasn't at work either. A new girl was sitting at the reception desk. I introduced myself, but her name didn't register, and when I got home that evening, I sent another round of texts.

Max: Are you sick?
Blue: No.
Max: Can I do anything?
Blue: No.
Max: Can I call you?
Blue: No.
Max: I'm sorry.

When I got one-word answers again, I drowned my feelings in bourbon and passed out on the couch.

She didn't come to work Tuesday either, and I made more of an effort with the new receptionist. The new girl, Lydia, said that Elise was fired for being in cahoots with Benjamin. She used the words cahoots and did air quotes for added effect.

Tuesday night was more bourbon and more one-word answers. I should take it as progress that she wasn't telling me to fuck off, but clearly, this wasn't working. I needed help. I texted Warren, and he reluctantly agreed, putting him at five percent Team Max.

By Wednesday, I was using every technique I could muster to keep my emotions in check. And I wasn't the only one who was a walking disaster without Annaleigh. I had listened to Jake stomp around his office for an hour before he knocked on my door. His personality had done a complete three-sixty. He was short-tempered and angry.

I got it. I was a jerk. But I was a jerk that deserved a chance to make things right! He walked in with a scowl on his face and an indent between his brows.

"Do you have any idea where these Promissory Notes are, Max? They have to be mailed today, and I don't want to bother Annaleigh in her condition."

He handed me a blue post-it with names and loan numbers. My heart broke when Jake stressed the words 'her condition.' I should be with her, comforting her, holding her, letting her know I'd never put her second again. But I was here—a useless shell of a man without her.

"Um, yeah. I witnessed her notarizing these," I said, standing up.

Jake followed me to Annaleigh's desk, and I opened her second drawer, taking out a stack of documents with her familiar blue post-its. I handed the docs to Jake and picked up a piece of paper lying underneath.

It was a list of about a dozen nicknames, some crossed off, and some circled. *Ace, Tiger, Babe, Broody, Sexy, Tight-Ass, Baby, Boo, Cutie.* And the list went on. I ran my fingers over her blue curly script before tucking the list in my pocket. She was taking her nickname search seriously. At least if she never forgave me, I'd be able to look back and see how good I had it.

"I'm a fucking lunatic," I said under my breath, walking back to my office and slumping down in my chair, turning it to face the river. Jake followed and cleared his throat, tilting his head to his office. Standing back up, I sighed and rubbed my hands over my face, pulling off one, no two, pieces of tissue from where I cut myself shaving. I slumped down in front of Jake's desk and stared at the floor.

"You ready to stop wallowing in self-pity? It's not like you were ever good enough for her," Jake said, sitting down and linking his arms behind his head. He leveled me with a glare, the intimidation clear, but I seriously wasn't in the mood for him. I wasn't in the mood for anything.

"Wow. Thanks, Jake. Way to be impartial," I said, sarcasm dripping from my voice.

I took off my glasses to clean them on my tie, but they came away with more smudges than before. Coffee stains dotted my tie. My *blue* tie. I loosened it, pulling it over my head and throwing it towards Jake's trash can.

I missed.

"I never said I was going to be impartial, Max. I specifically remember saying I would side with her if things went South. I don't know the whole story, so are you going to tell me why our EA refuses to give me a date for when she'll be back to work? And are you going to ask me to help you fix this fucked up situation? Or continue to sulk around the office like a kid that had his favorite toy taken away?"

Jake stared at me until the words sunk in. *Holy shit!* He'd help me!

"What? You'll help me. What do you want to know?" I said, standing up to pace his office. I shook out my hands and rolled my shoulders, pouring out everything that had happened these last few days—from Warren, to the band, to freaking Nicole, and my epic screw-up. I was wildly waving my hands as I paced, trying to make him understand.

"So, yeah. I planned to talk to her here, but she hasn't shown up. I don't want her to slam the door in my face, but something has to give," I said, slumping back down in the chair. "Jake, I'm spiraling."

"You mean to tell me your big plan was to talk to her here?" Jake said.

"Yes. I mean, no. She won't answer the phone. I don't know. She deserves an apology and an explanation for my overreaction. She deserves everything."

Jake reached in his top drawer and took out a manilla folder, laying it in the middle of his desk. With a tap of his finger, he pushed it forward.

"I'm overstepping big time here, Max, but I feel like you need to know the whole story. Pick up the folder and say, 'you're welcome.' "

"What is this, Jake?"

"Answers," he said, crossing his arms across his chest.

I sat back and picked up the folder, flipping to the first page. It was complaints. Some dated more than a year ago, and they were all from Annaleigh about Benjamin and Raymond. *Holy shit.* I kept flipping until

I got to the printed conversation that happened in Tennessee, and not far after that was a copy of two police reports, one from Annaleigh, another from Jake. Flipping further, I saw a restraining order.

Oh, God. The next papers had my hands shaking and sweat beading on my forehead. Phrases jumped out at me, *possible fractured wrist,* suspect taken into custody, history of abuse and threats, *arrest record.* I was sick reading the words. She called me after it happened, she tried to tell me. But I accused her, and Jake, of being deceitful. I put down the folder and put my hand over my mouth, taking off my glasses and laying them on Jake's desk.

"HR forbade her from discussing this until the investigation was complete. But it's over now. Benjamin had a prior for assault. I don't know how the fuck he covered it up and was hired in the first place. But this is his second offense. He's not getting off this time. And she'll be fine, but I'm not too sure about you. I don't think I've ever seen someone deteriorate so fast in seventy-two hours. You wore that suit yesterday," Jake said, taking the folder back.

"It is going to take more than talking to fix this," I said, hanging my head. "Especially after what I said."

"No shit, Sherlock. Now, get the hell out of here," Jake said, "You have literally been useless this week."

I bolted up like a man on a mission, because I was. I wouldn't argue with Jake about being useless. It surprised me it took him three days to kick my ass into gear. I was going to go to her house and would stand on her doorstep until she answered.

Stepping forward, I shook Jake's hand, and he clapped me on the back. I sprinted down to my truck and fired off a text to Warren to let him know I was coming over. He responded almost immediately with *about time,* making me push my speed higher through the city.

Operation Get Her Back was back, baby! No, that sounded stupid. Operation Blue? Operation True Love? *Operation True Blue!* Maxwell Smerdon, marketing genius!

I needed a nap. Or another cup of coffee. No, I needed Blue.

I turned the radio on and *Whatever It Is* was playing. It was a sign—a sign I was doing the right thing, something I should have done as soon as I got back from Chicago. It felt like each moment I went without seeing her; the further she slipped away.

Different reactions she could have crossed my mind as I drove, from her slamming the door in my face, to us slow kissing in the rain, to us becoming exhibitionists and screwing on the porch while her neighbors watched and cheered us on.

I was fine with being an exhibitionist, as long as having a cheering section didn't give me stage fright. It was like that movie with Kevin Bacon where he imagined his wife's parents at the foot of their bed with headlamps, making sure their technique was right to get pregnant.

Um, no. On second thought, no exhibitionist antics are in my future. But thinking about that movie gave me a clear picture of Annaleigh with a swollen belly and a bright smile, softly singing *You Are My Sunshine* in a room with pink curtains and a white rocking chair.

Our daughter would wear glasses like me and have Blue's love of music. Her favorite color would be green, and she would have long fingers for playing the piano. She would be strong-willed and short-tempered, perfect for running her own company. She would be everything good about the two of us and be surrounded by so much love.

We'd move somewhere with a big yard and a garden. Baxter couldn't handle her spiral staircase, and neither could a kid. *Damn.* I might as well stop for a pair of New Balances. But hell, I'd wear them to the office every day if it meant winning her back. Silk vests and dad shoes for the win!

My man-ovaries, or fatherly instinct or whatever, was kicked into overdrive. *Let me win her back before I go planning our life down to a white-picket fence*, I thought, peeling out of the parking lot. Blue didn't need to hear my fantasies or my excuses. She only needed to know I love her, and I was going to fight for her.

Turning on to her street, I snorted, imagining her coming home to find me waiting in nothing but a vest and dad-shoes. She would compliment how white my sneakers were and how much she loved my dad-bod before we went at it like frenzied rabbits. Then we would take our multi-vitamins and be in bed by ten.

Warren's rental was parked in front of her Highlander, and I pulled my truck in and jogged to her doorstep. Knocking harder than I should, I tapped my foot and waited. She answered the door with red, puffy eyes.

"What are you doing here, Max?"

Her hair was piled on top of her head, and her blue robe was thrown over her shoulders. She was wearing an oversized T-shirt and shorts and had a brace around one wrist. Her knees were scraped, and there were dark circles under her eyes. Seeing her like that, not smiling, looking defeated, shattered me. I wanted to take her in my arms. But when I stepped forward, she stepped back. Baxter pushed his way beside her and whined, and I reached out to scratch behind his ears. He licked my hand and pressed himself against Blue, looking between us.

"I should have been here the minute I came back from Chicago. I never should have left. It was a set-up, and I was a fool for falling for it. You are the only one I want, Blue. And I'm so sorry for ever making you doubt it. I'm sorry for ever making you think you were not the most important woman in my life. I'm sorry for not being here when you were hurt, for not being able to stop him and keep you safe."

"Thank you. But that seems to be our story, doesn't it? Misunderstandings and apologies. It shouldn't be this hard. We shouldn't be this hard," she said, moving to shut the door.

"No. I shouldn't have overreacted. And that fucker Benjamin is exactly where he belongs. Blue, baby, can I come in? There are things I need to say."

I braced both hands on her door frame and leaned into it, smelling oranges and vanilla. My heart was beating with caffeine and adrenaline, and I was lightheaded smelling her, being near her again.

She didn't move, and I knew her next words before she said them, "Not right now, Max. The place is a mess, and I'm tired."

I stepped closer and traced my knuckles along her jaw. She closed her eyes and sighed. *Bingo!* This wasn't over by a long shot. She just needed time.

"I understand. I'll text you later, is that okay?"

She nodded, and when her red-rimmed eyes met mine, I saw everything I wanted. I saw my future. Leaning forward, I cupped her jaw and lightly brushed my lips against hers.

"Blue," I said, "Our story isn't misunderstandings and apologizes. Our story is love, so much love that neither of us knew what to do with it all. But I'll show you every day. I'll show you that you're worth it. And loving you isn't hard. It's the easiest thing I've ever done once I got out of my way. Leaving you is something I'll regret for a long time and something I'll never do again."

She backed up and put her hand on the doorknob. I leaned forward, hating that I couldn't pull her into my arms, and brushed my lips against her cheek this time. "I was an asshole, baby. And I'm so sorry."

That brought a small smile to her beautiful face, and I bent down to Baxter, rubbing his head and whispering my gratitude. When I stood up, she was smiling, and I felt like I'd won the lottery.

I started my truck and looked back to her house, seeing the drapes twitch. Scrubbing my hand over my patchy hatchet shave-job, I pulled back onto the road and headed to my next stop. Phase one of getting her to acknowledge my existence and apology went better than expected. Phase two of bringing people over to Team Max was going to involve groveling.

The bakery was slow, and I was wracking my brain with what to say when I stepped up to order. I pushed my glasses on my head and dug a knuckle into my eye. "Large hazelnut latte with an extra shot and a half-dozen orange scones, please."

Blindly reaching for my wallet, I kept my head hung, jerking up with a start when Olivia slammed a coffeepot back on the warmer. The look she gave me made my balls shrink to the size of marbles, and I instinctively covered my dick.

"What the hell are you doing here, Broody?" she said, putting her hand on her hip.

I felt sorry for any kids she has one day. Her mom-look could stop a hardened criminal in their tracks. Smoothing the wrinkles in my shirt, I stood up straighter and squared my shoulders, handing over my credit card with somewhat steady hands.

"I was hoping to talk to you, Addison, and Jenna."

Her face didn't change, and she tossed my credit card back to me before tilting her head to the end of the counter. I nodded and followed, knowing my balls were going to have to drop back down to make it through this conversation.

"I don't think so, Broody," she said, pushing the coffee and scones to me. She crossed her arms and pursed her lips, "Now, if there isn't anything else, some of us are working."

I reached out and touched her arm, and she flinched like my hands were hot pokers.

"Listen, I'm not leaving until I can talk to you. I want your support. I won't stop till I get her back. I'll come back every day if I have to. I'll be over there waiting," I said, tilting my head to a small table towards the back and grabbing my coffee and scones.

I was a glutton for punishment as I sat, sipping the sugary-sweet drink. I pulled out my phone and flipped through several pictures of us. One stood out from the rest. It was at the bar, right before she sang. We were looking at each other, smiling with our hands clasped together. I could count on one hand how many pictures I had where I looked that happy. As I stared out the window, my eyes glazed over, watching people walk by the storefront. An idea started to form—something to show her how sorry I was.

I was gripping a third cup of coffee when I heard voices moving closer. I didn't take my eyes from the window, willing my heart rate to slow down.

"How long has he been here, Liv?"

"Going on three hours. I feel sorry for him. Thought it was time I called y'all to meet me here."

"Good idea. He looks more miserable than Annaleigh."

"Well, duh, Addison. Look at him."

"You know, I can hear you," I said, kicking out the chair beside me.

One sat down, and the other two pulled up chairs to the tiny table. Someone took the coffee I was white-knuckling and replaced it with water, and someone else pushed a plate of fruit toward me.

"Yeah, we know you can hear us, Broody. And figured you'd suffered enough. We needed to make sure you were serious about getting her back."

"Of course, I'm serious about getting her back. And thanks, I think."

I took an apple slice and popped it in my mouth, meeting the eyes of her three best friends.

"You're welcome," one said.

She was wearing a red power suit with matching heels and nails. Ah, this must be Addison, the real estate mogul. Sitting next to her was Jenna. She was wearing a dark shirt and purple-rimmed glasses. She had her hair in a low bun, and her back was ramrod straight.

Olivia took off her apron, laying it on the table before crossing her arms, with the mom-look back in full force. All three of them were staring at me with mastered mom-looks. I wondered if they practiced at home, trying to figure out what would intimidate the most.

I took a swig of water before talking. "So, I'm an asshole."

"Obviously," Addison said.

"I assume we are not supposed to disagree with you?" Jenna added, swiping an apple slice from my plate.

"Um, right. I've apologized, but it's not good enough. I don't know if I'll ever be able to do something good enough."

"Not with that attitude, Broody. Can you be done with the pity party now, please?" Jenna said, pushing the fruit closer.

"Yeah, you're right. I'm so tired. I have an idea, but I'm going to need your help, ladies."

"You look like hell, and so does she. Talk to us, Broody," Olivia said, her eyes softer than before.

"I'm not going to sit here and make excuses or tell you I only acted the way I did because I was worried about my father. I should have listened to her, trusted her, and never left her. Walking into that situation with my ex was a mistake. Not running to her the second I got back was a mistake. Not being here when she got hurt, when there was a chance I could have prevented it, was a mistake. But I love her. I need her. I'm miserable without her. And I'll do whatever it takes to get her back. To show her I can be the man she deserves. I just want her back."

I guzzled the rest of the water, and Addison pushed an unopened one to me. I didn't want to go into more detail. It hurt enough to admit that much out loud, to say all the ways I'd failed Blue. Letting the silence stretch, I cracked the seal on the second bottle.

"What? You can't all be speechless," I said, pushing the leftover scones to the middle of the table.

"You've surprised us, is all, Broody. We, um, didn't expect you to say that," Addison said. Olivia and Jenna looked at each other and then Addison, something silently passing between them.

"Yes, well, it's been brought to my attention that my communication skills sometimes lack. So here I am, all open and honest, sharing my feelings like a grown-up. And here's what I'm thinking for *Operation True Blue*," I said, rubbing my hands together.

"*Operation True Blue?*" Addison repeated, laughing with the words.

"You are so damn perfect for her. I can't even stand it," Olivia said, looking over at Jenna and smiling. "Broody. We are ready to help with *Operation True Blue*."

I smiled so hard my face hurt. I felt like I could pull this off. Opening my phone, I turned it around, showing them the design I scribbled.

"Oh, wow. You really know her."

"You can build this?"

"We love it, Broody."

Rubbing my hands together, I dove in headfirst, explaining the idea and ready to win back my Blue.

30

NO SONG RESONATING

Annaleigh

O kay, guys, I'm going to escort the canine on a leisurely stroll around the neighborhood," I said, trying *not* to notice how achingly bright the sun was, like it was mocking me in my self-pity.

"Well, look at you all dressed and awake. Um, awake, maybe. But don't you think it's about time you took a shower? Your last several meals are on your pajama top." Bird said, looking up from the couch.

He had been working on line-editing a software manual between stealing kisses from Taylor, who was working at the dining room table. Those two were so freaking cute. They made me sick. I had to get out of this house and away from their love fest. I owed myself at least three more days of wallowing. Maybe four.

They had been tiptoeing around me, trying to give me space. It was maddening the way they looked at each other, passing glances and having conversations without words. It made me miss Max. Everything made me miss Max.

"Huh?" Taylor said, "Why don't you just say you're taking Baxter for a walk?"

As soon as Baxter heard the word walk, his tail went crazy, wagging so hard his entire body shook, and he ran to the front door and back again. On the third trip, he stopped and looked back at us with an annoyed expression, then ran back and forth again.

"That's why, smartie," I said, shaking my head and bending down to grab his leash. I groaned and sucked in a breath, shaking out my wrist. It felt better, but my whole body felt like I got hit by a Mack truck.

"Nope. Back to recovering. We'll take the mutt after getting you some Tylenol," Taylor said, standing up and walking to the window.

As if he heard them say mutt, Baxter tilted his head and plopped down by the door in anticipation, tail still wagging.

"Ugh, I guess. Thanks, guys."

I sat down beside Bird and rested my head on his shoulder. Taylor handed me Ginger-Ale and medicine, and I swallowed it down.

"You ready to talk about this yet?"

Taylor picked up the glass and took it back to the kitchen before leveling me with a hard stare.

"No. How can I talk about something I don't know the answer to?"

"But you love him, right?" Bird said, rubbing my leg.

I didn't answer, just nodded, so he kept talking.

"Then there's your answer. Seriously, babe. It's obvious he loves you and you him, and he apologized several times. And do I have to remind you of the flowers and chocolate and letters he's sent? Why haven't you kicked Taylor and me to the curb so you two can have hot, dirty make-up sex? I mean, I know Maxie isn't a power-bottom, but I'm still fairly confident he rocks your world."

"Um, do I want to know what a power-bottom is?" I said, deflecting his logic.

"Not unless you're ready to go down the rabbit hole of gay terms," Taylor cut in with a wink.

"Yeah, okay. I'm going back to bed."

"Maybe shower first," Bird said.

I picked up a still full bottle of wine and turned to head up the stairs. Before they could stop me, I leveled them both with a glare, "It's my pity party, and I'll drink if I want to."

They both raised their hands and stayed silent. I heard them whispering *again* as I trudged up the stairs, but I tuned the words out.

I left a trail of clothes to the bathroom and started the water in the tub, grabbing an empty glass from the nightstand.

"We've had our run, hearts sang their song. My words shun bright, you were my sun. But leaving all we built behind, has frozen my heart in despair's time."

Even my lyrics were miserable. Crumbled blue post-its littered the bedroom. I picked up a handful and stuck them to my vanity, smoothing out the edges and reading the words over again.

The bathroom door stayed cracked, and I poured an obscene amount of bubble bath in the tub and the same amount of wine in my glass. The liquid went down too easy, and I closed my eyes, trying to figure out what the hell I wanted.

"Where is she, Bird?" I heard Addison ask as she walked through the house. Something about her voice always carried. It was a combination of her fiery red hair and even fierier personality. Fiery? Fierier? I think those were real words.

I wasn't ready to face her yet. There were several voices, and knew she had Olivia and Jenna with her. *Great, a united front.* I wasn't ready to face any of them. My wallowing was far from over.

I sunk further into the tub and finished the last of my glass, reaching down to refill it and press it against my forehead.

"She's doing a little self-care right now," Taylor called after them.

I heard footsteps coming up the stairs and sunk lower, closing my eyes.

"Annaleigh! Are you drunk in the tub?" Jenna called before opening the door and walking in. Addison and Olivia followed, and I heard Bird yell about taking Baxter to the park because of the amount of estrogen invading the house.

"I'm not drunk, y'all," I said, reaching down to show them the bottle. It wasn't even a quarter gone. Or maybe there was a quarter left.

"That's because Taylor replaced the liquor with apple juice two days ago!" Olivia said.

"I thought it tasted different. But I'm not in the mood to talk about anything yet."

"We don't care," Jenna said. "This behavior is unhealthy. Your body is not going to heal like this. You need a proper balance of protein and carbs."

"I have brownies too. Max brought them over yesterday. Or the day before. I don't know."

Sighing, I laid the glass on the edge of the tub and scooted up so I could see them all better. Addison was wearing her trademark power suit, green today. And Jenna still had her lab coat on. Olivia had flour on her shirt and her apron tied around her waist.

"Isn't it the middle of the day? Why isn't anyone working?" I reached for my drink again, but Addison picked it up and downed the whole thing without so much as a wince. *Damn*, that girl could throwback with the best of them. *Wait*, it was only apple juice.

"Yes, we all should be working. But it's time to talk about this and figure out what you want."

"Liv, if I knew what I wanted, I wouldn't be here, would I?"

"Time to get out. Here," Jenna said, handing me a fluffy towel.

The girls walked out, talking to me from the bathroom door. "We are going to make a list of all the pros and cons. Then, we are going to make an informed decision and clean this room."

"So practical, Jenna. But I don't think one of your lists is going to solve this." I said, standing up and pulling the plug in the tub.

"This is worse than we thought," I heard Olivia whisper.

"I know," Addison echoed. "Has anyone heard her talk in *Seinfeld* quotes yet?"

"Not yet," Jenna said. "She hasn't done that since Bird overdosed."

I pretended like I didn't hear them as I walked out of the bathroom. Sitting on the bed in my towel, I took in the candy wrappers and potato chip bags. My room was not that bad.

"Don't question the logic if it helps you to make a decision," Jenna said, walking in my closet. She came out with an oversized sweatshirt and yoga pants, handing them to me with a nod.

"Stop judging me," I said, taking the clothes from Jenna and pulling them on.

But that was a dumb thing to say. Of course, they should judge me. I was a wreck. I had made a blanket nest on top of my mattress, trying to get rid of Max's smell, and there were three half-empty now goopy pints of ice cream on the hardwood floor. I'd lost count of the number of empty chip bags that littered the room.

Sleepless In Seattle was on repeat, and pieces of paper were balled up and scattered on the floor, evidence of me trying to put my feelings into words. I almost texted Jake to put in my notice, but I stopped myself before hitting send. Jake deserved more than a half-drunk text message. I think that was before they took away the liquor because I definitely woke up with a killer hangover.

In the throes of one of my crying sessions, I shamelessly thought I could write enough songs to quit the bank, so I'd never have to see Max again. But when I thought about that, I cried even harder. Then I'd sleep, and the process would start all over again. I groaned and plopped down in the middle of the bed, tossing a half-eaten bag of Hershey kisses on the floor.

"It's time to move out of this wallowing, self-pity phase," Addison said, crossing her arms.

She took off her heels and sat on the edge of the bed. Jenna and Olivia did the same.

"Consider this a *Southern Charms* intervention, Annaleigh," Olivia said, tossing a pair of dirty socks on the floor.

"I second the motion," Jenna said.

"It's only been two days, y'all, plenty of time to still wallow," I said, leaning back on the pillow.

"Um, no. It's been almost a week. We are getting you out of this house today, end of story."

"It's been almost a week, Liv?"

I looked at Olivia, then Jenna. They both nodded, and my head swam. A week? How had I been in this house wallowing for a week? I remembered people visiting: my parents, Uncle Bob, my girls, and even Jake and Katie. But Bird and Taylor ran interference, and I mostly stayed in the bedroom.

"Should we go to *B's*?" Jenna said.

"No," was the unanimous answer. Good, I was not prepared for *B's*.

"Maybe I should start by cooking a real meal," I said. "Or ordering one."

"That's the smartest thing you've said today," Addison said, standing up to collect more dirty laundry.

"Could we maybe go out another day? I feel like I need to get my head on straight and become a productive member of society before venturing out."

"That's acceptable. As long as we get you cleaned up and delete your browser history." Jenna said.

"Huh? Why?"

"Because we need to see how far you've gone. Here," Addison said, tossing the phone to Olivia. She opened the history and sucked in a breath.

"Oh, Annaleigh."

"What has she been googling?" Jenna asked, collecting trash from around the room.

"Self-help books, job searches, cat adoption, vacations for one, how to write song lyrics, and Maxwell Smerdon."

"What? I could have been googling vibrators."

"At least that would flood your body with endorphins," Jenna said.

"Tell us what the problem is, the real problem, and we'll help you work through it."

I sighed and sat straighter, redoing my rat's nest of a bun and picking nonexistent fuzz from the sweatshirt.

"I can't stop thinking that our relationship shouldn't be this hard. I knew deep down he would never cheat on me and go back with his ex. But hearing her in the background and knowing he could be so easily manipulated terrifies me. What's going to happen the next time? He broke us. Or maybe I broke us by keeping him at arm's length from the beginning. I don't know anymore."

"Okay, I get it," Jenna said. "You have every reason to question your choices and your relationship, especially after what happened."

"Right, you're insecure about your feelings and obviously making some questionable life choices at the moment," Olivia added, picking up a magazine about career options in Alaska.

"And this," Addison said, waving her hand at me. "Is not okay. Whatever you feel for him is real, or it wouldn't hurt so much."

"Edward and I were in therapy last year," Olivia said.

All eyes turned to her, and she looked down, throwing a magazine about singles cruises into the ever-growing trash pile.

"I didn't know that Liv," Addison said.

"I know, no one did. We were arguing over dumb stuff and couldn't see the forest through the trees. It helped to have a third party talk with us, to help us communicate. It made us stronger. And love is hard. Really hard. You have to work at it every day. You have to put someone's needs above your own. But Annaleigh, I love him more every day. Even on days, I want to kick him."

"She's right, you know. You have to trust him enough to see you at your worst and have him help you be your best," Jenna said, shrugging her shoulders.

"So the question is," Addison finished. "Do you love him enough to fight for you both?"

I didn't know how to answer her. I loved Max so much it made my chest ache from not being with him, touching him, kissing him. But was it enough?

I stood up and picked up one a piece of paper, smoothing it out and reading the words. I stuck it on the vanity, with the rest of the post-its. A tiny idea started to take root. A scary, but possibly brilliant idea. Or an epic failure. Either way, it was the best idea I'd had all week. But until this point, taking a bath was the best idea, so the bar wasn't exactly high. I looked at my girls and back at the paper, smiling slightly.

"I don't know what that face is about, but whatever it is, tell us," Jenna said, taking the crumpled paper from my hand and reading the words.

"A sudden spark lit like stars in the sky. Within me, stories find a life renewed. Enchanted by the soul buried within your eyes."

I didn't know if I was crazy, or drunk, or both. But there was one thing I knew. With my best friends by my side, I could get through anything. They would always be there to pick up the pieces.

COMPLETE ME WHOLE
Max

Dear Blue,
    I hate hummus. It tastes like overcooked vegetables mixed with beach sand and lemon juice. But I love homemade macaroni and cheese with Ritz crackers on top. The first time I had it at a friend's house, I ate so much I was constipated for a week. During my first week of college, I craved that macaroni in a bad way, so I bought a crockpot and boxes of Kraft. The problem was, I didn't add enough water, and the crockpot caught fire. The entire dorm had to be evacuated. I haven't attempted to make macaroni and cheese since, but I'd make it for you.

    This one time at band camp… Just kidding, I've never been to band camp. But I have been to chess camp. It was the three most boring weeks of my life. I wandered off one day when we were taking our "mandatory" daily hike, looking for an escape route. Little did I know, I trampled through poison ivy and had to be taken to the hospital for a steroid injection in my ass. Needless to say, I am now a wicked good chess player.

Love,

Max

cɔ cɔ cɔ

Dear Max,

The secret to an unforgettable macaroni and cheese is sour cream. Weird, right? But it helps to thicken the cheese and gives it the creamiest texture.

I love a good steak, but it has to be cooked right. And by right, I mean medium rare. People who eat steak well done might as well eat hockey pucks. And I hate mushrooms. Like hate mushrooms. People are not meant to eat fungus! Can you imagine how much trial and error went into determining what mushrooms are good and bad: "Listen up, guys... The mushrooms in Pile A killed Steve, the mushroom in Pile B you can eat, and the mushrooms in Pile C make you taste colors." Nope.

I also think I'm the only person in the South that doesn't like sweet tea, don't tell anyone. ;-)

My favorite color, obviously, is blue. But did I ever tell you why? As a kid, I loved beige. I know, I'm weird. But beige is the color of beach sand, and beige is the color of my grandmother's lace wedding dress. The very first time I sang on stage, there were these blue lights that pulsed in time with the bass. It was this electric, neon, gorgeous blue that calmed my nerves. It's been my favorite color since.

When I first started a garden on my terrace, I attempted to make my own compost. It was an epic disaster that resulted in a warning from my HOA and a hefty fine. Now, garbage goes in the trash, and I buy dirt like a normal person. I still maintain that the smell was not that bad.

Thank you for the flowers, and the beer, and the chocolate. But most of all, thank you for your letter. It made me smile.

Love,
Blue

cɔ cɔ cɔ

Dear Blue,

All of your secrets are safe with me. The first time I french kissed a girl, I cut my tongue on her braces. It hurt like a mother, and I talked like I had a lisp for days after. When I told Warren, he fell on the floor laughing and said that's why he was never kissing girls.

I tried wearing contacts, several times in fact, but the thought of putting something in my eye freaks me the hell out. I don't see how you put on makeup, especially that wingy thing you do around your eyes. I had to order special sunglasses because my regular ones would slip down my face when I ran. The first pair that came in were hot pink, and I couldn't return them. They may or may not be in my truck in case of a sunglasses emergency.

I drink bourbon: one- because it's the best liquor known to man. And two- because it pissed off my dad. He was always a scotch man, and doing stupid shit like that kept me sane all the years I was under his thumb. That's also why I never got Lasik. You're weird, and I'm petty... It's a perfect match.

When I was in high school, I got a monster zit right before prom. I snuck into my parent's bedroom, looking for something to put on it before we had photos taken. I accidentally grabbed self-tanner, and my eleventh-grade prom photo has a bright orange dot right in the middle of my forehead.

Walking away from you was one of the stupidest things I've ever done. I'm sorry I let you down.

I miss you. So damn much.

Love,

Max

❧ ❧ ❧

Max,

When I was in middle school, I got suspended for flicking off my teacher. My mom had gotten me a Mood Ring. I wore so much it turned my finger green. I freaked out, not having any idea why my finger was green, and raised my middle finger in the air, waving it like crazy at my teacher. He thought I did it on purpose.

I drink bourbon: one- because it is the best liquor known to man. And two- because I never liked martini glasses. Drinking a Cosmo from a rocks glass just seemed like sacrilege. The first time I had a neat glass of Buffalo Trace, I knew I was a bourbon babe for life. But nothing beats a chilled glass of Moscato in my hammock with a good book.

When I was in high school, I desperately wanted to save my wrist corsage from Prom. I decided the "smart" thing to do was press the still alive flowers in between the pages of my yearbook. Not only did it not work, but the flowers ended up sticking to the pages and rotting. I had to throw both away.

I started taking medicine for my hypocalcemia, and I feel better. But I think I need to cut out the oranges. I swear my face had an orange tinge the other day.

When I first got Baxter, he had fleas. Even though Jenna assured me they would not get in my house, I was paranoid and had the place bug-bombed. Thinking about any creepy-crawly critters makes my skin itch. I had to stay at Jenna's house for a week because the smell was awful! Speaking of Jenna, she talks to her plants and plays music for them. It's adorable. I tried leaving the radio on for Baxter, but he knocked it off the coffee table. I think he prefers solitude.

Yes, you should have never walked away.

You've never given me a reason not to trust you, and I knew, deep down, you were not back with her. But after the night we had and the way you left, it hurt. You brushed me off like I was nothing, like we were nothing. It hurt, Max. Your words hurt.

I miss you too. I miss you so very much.

Love,

Blue

ೞ ೞ ೞ

Blue,

Don't stop eating oranges. I'll feed you slices and worship your orange skin every day. You are not nothing. We are not nothing. You changed my life. You are everything. You show me the beauty in everyday things, and you've made me a better man. I'd like to come over Saturday. I owe Baxter a steak for protecting

the most important woman in my life. What do you think?
Yours,
Max

ↁ ↁ ↁ

Max,

The girls and I are going out, but I'll be back by dinner. I have news. Big news. See you then.
Yours,
Blue

ↁ ↁ ↁ

Operation True Blue was coming together, and the girls had gotten Blue out of the house. I enlisted Warren and Taylor's help, and they came over Saturday after Blue had left.

Six days. It had been six days since I'd left. Six days since I'd held her. Six days of emptiness. I read her last letter again and ran my hand over my short beard before tucking it back in my pocket.

"You think this is going to work?" Warren asked, tapping his foot on the floorboard and turning up Cheap Trick.

"I sure as fuck hope so," I replied, pushing my glasses up and making a right turn onto her street. "Where are they going again?"

"Manicures, I think, and then to *B's*. I kinda zoned out when they started talking about different shades of pink."

Warren motioned to the spot behind her Highlander, and I pulled in and saw a familiar wet nose pressed against the living room windows.

"Okay. Let's get the tarp laid first and clear the furniture before we unload. The installation guys will be here in an hour."

"You got it, boss-man," Taylor said, handing me her keys.

Unlocking the door, I bent down and gave Baxter some love. Her place smelled like oranges, and it made my dick twitch. I adjusted myself and looked around. I missed it here, missed being in her space. Baxter pushed against my hand, and I patted his head.

"You gonna help me win your mama back, buddy?"

His tail thumped the floor, and he cocked his head as if to say, "Duh, dad."

An hour later, a huge delivery truck pulled up, and three guys introduced themselves and got started. I wished I could have been more hands-on, but I couldn't wire for shit. Building the platform and railing was one thing, but there was a strong possibility something would catch fire if I did the wiring.

Halfway through installing the railing, I went to the kitchen for water. Blue had two crockpots simmering, and it smelled delicious. My stomach gave a loud gurgle, and I pulled out my phone to order pizza for lunch. Baxter stayed on my heels, and I grabbed the new dog bed I had for him and put it on the platform.

"What do you think?" I said, cooing to him like a baby. "Come lay here, buddy."

I patted the bed, and he stepped up and sniffed it before plopping down. *Nice.* The last thing I needed was for him to hate the idea.

"You know, Maxie," Warren said, sitting on the couch and passing a water to Taylor before taking one for himself. "I think this is going to work."

"Me too," Taylor added. "You really outdid yourself. I'd forgive you."

"Thanks. I'm going to escort man's best friend around the pavement. One of you sign for the pizza when it gets here."

Warren and Taylor had the biggest shit-eating grins on their face, "What? You can't say the 'w' word, or he will get so excited you can't put his leash on."

"Oh, we know that, Maxie," Warren said, holding up finger guns. He was the only guy I knew that could make finger guns look cool. *Idiot.*

"Why are you assholes looking at me like that?" I said, looking between the two of them. "You both have the same sappy-ass expression."

"No reason," Taylor said, telepathically communicating with Warren.

Shaking my head, I nodded to them both and walked out. Baxter eagerly headed towards the park, and I checked the time. The lift would be done in another few hours, and Blue would be home not long afer. The only thing left for me to do was show her how much I love her, and that I was a better person with her by my side.

- *32* -

STAY FOREVER
Annaleigh

I knew the old saying went, *if you love someone, set them free*, but I was calling bullshit. If you love someone, you stand by them. You support them. You wake up at two o'clock in the morning and sit with them because they couldn't sleep. That was love—not worn-out cliches and empty promises. And if this time apart had taught me anything, it was that Max was showing me, love. Big, scary, imperfect love.

The girls and I were on our way home from *B's* after a nice lunch, and I felt better. They were chatting about Jenna's surprise houseguest, and I had never seen her so animated. She was waving her arms around in the front seat, babbling about thunderstorms and boundaries. I glanced at my pink nails and listened to her barely breathe in between sentences. She reminded me of how I used to talk about Max, not that I'd ever say that to her.

Palm trees dotted the median, and the sunshine mixed with the smell of the ocean were like jumper cables, kick-starting my heart and making me feel alive. All the negative energy that had been weighing me down was disappearing as the minutes ticked closer to when I'd see him. But it wasn't just Max. It was Bird, Uncle Bob, the girls, and *B's*. It was everything. I'd changed the direction of my life and embraced the music I thought I'd lost.

And I had my own way to show Max how much I loved him. A way for no one to question our relationship. A way for both of us to grow together.

I quit my job.

Not in a dramatic, spectacular, hair-flipping flourish. But with quiet discussion and a guilt-free conscience. Jake and Katie had visited again so the kids could see Baxter, and we had a long chat. I told him about the opportunity at *B's,* and he agreed. This was the right decision, the right opportunity. And Uncle Bob was thrilled, hollering to Aunt Diane in the kitchen and pulling out a stack of travel brochures from under the register before I had finished accepting.

I was going to stay at JMS until Jake hired someone else, and I'd already started prescreening applicants. On top of that, I was looking for a Bar Manager so I could focus on the local bands, and I'd set up meetings with several non-profits. I couldn't wait to share the news with Max, and I rubbed my hands on my thighs as we got closer to home. My body was filled with nervous anticipation, and my foot bounced in time with the song on the radio.

Addison pulled her Honda in a space by my house and turned around, "What time is he coming over again?" she said, tapping her red nails on the steering wheel.

Olivia and Jenna looked on, and I smiled ear to ear.

"He'll be here before dinner. I'm making his favorite with plenty of leftovers. Y'all are coming in for a drink, right?"

"You know it," Olivia said. "How do you think he'll handle the news?"

"Oh, probably an overreaction at first. But he'll understand," I said, waving my hand and taking off my sunglasses.

"What makes you so sure he'll understand?" Jenna asked, closing the car door and pocketing her phone with a groan.

I thought for a second, then shrugged my shoulders, "I just know." I couldn't tell her how I knew, but I did. Not seeing him every day was going to suck, but listening to office gossip and petty comments would be worse.

"Good, Anna. I'm glad. You deserve all the happiness," Jenna said.

"We all do, Jenna. Come on, ladies. I have Moscato chilling. Let's go get our drink on."

I motioned for them to follow and unlocked the door, tossing my purse and phone on the couch. The house smelled like brown sugar and barbecue, and Jenna started talking a mile a minute again as I went to the kitchen to get glasses. When the last one was down, a throat cleared behind me, and I turned to see Max walking out from the downstairs spare bedroom.

His faded jeans were low-slung, and his blue t-shirt hugged his chest. The black ink of his tattoo snaked down one arm and moved when he flexed. His hair was a mess, and his jaw was scruffy. I stopped short and stared. From his tan skin to the blue sneakers that matched his shirt, I took in every detail, memorizing him. And those glasses. Those tortoise-shell glasses that fogged when he kissed me so hard I couldn't breathe. It was all I could do to keep myself from flinging the cabinet door shut and jumping in his arms.

"Hey, Blue. Hope you don't mind me gate-crashing. I couldn't wait to see you."

He ran a hand through his hair, messing it up more, and came closer, pressing a sweet kiss to my cheek. He smelled like spicy mint, and a low moan escaped my lips before I could stop it. I was speechless, just like the day we met on the beach. And Max rubbed the back of his neck, stepping to the side as Bird pushed through.

"Sweet, about time you got here," Bird said, rubbing his hands together like he had some big secret. I looked between them, and Bird smirked, pulling Taylor to the living room with a wink.

He greeted the girls, and I heard them talking, but Baxter's sharp barks drowned out the noise. Usually, he was waiting by the door, and I glanced around looking for him.

"Is Baxter barking? Where is he?"

"He's up here, Blue. I think he wants to go on the terrace. Come on," Max said, taking my hand and pulling me further in the house and up the stairs. I go along, feeling his hand, warm and strong, engulfing mine with a gentle squeeze.

I sighed, stopping and pulling back when we got to the second floor. "You know he has a hard time with the staircase."

I was all for Max carrying Baxter to the terrace like the big baby he was. Especially if it meant showing off his massive guns and maybe even taking off his shirt, but I'd rather talk about us and share my news first.

"I know he does, baby." Max turned and cupped my face, leaning down to run his nose down my cheek. "Fuck, I've missed you. I was kind of hoping we'd be alone, but I don't want to wait to say this. I realized last night that my words are nothing but empty promises."

"Um, what?"

He buried his face in my neck and chuckled, running his fingers up my back. I wrapped my arms around his waist and rested my head on his chest. One of his hands trailed higher, and he gripped my neck, turning my head to meet his eyes. I could hear laughter from downstairs and knew we had an audience, but I didn't care. I was content standing here, in his arms. But he let go and rolled his eyes, glancing down the stairs and pulling me further down the hall. "No. Um, that's not what I meant."

"Max," I said, "From the start, we tried fighting this, and it didn't work."

"No, it didn't."

"So, we tried keeping us a secret, and it didn't work."

"Right again, Blue."

He blew out a breath and crowded my space, but I didn't move. I tilted my head and looked up, releasing one hand to rest it on his scruffy cheek. His beard was rough, and he turned his head to kiss my palm.

"Then we tried being apart, and it didn't work."

"That was a fucking failure, Blue," he said, nuzzling my hand and laying his over it.

"So really, there is only one thing left to do."

"There is?"

"We go all in," I said, wrapping my arms around him. Bourbon eyes met mine, and he smiled, leaning down, so our mouths were centimeters apart. "Max. I'm crazy about you. I can't keep my hands off you, and even when we're tangled up in each other, it's not enough. I want more. I want to be closer. I love you. You healed my soul and brought music back. This week has shown me that I can live without you, but I don't want to. You make me whole."

"Oh, Blue. Thank fuck. I love you too. Come here."

I pressed my body against him, wrapping my arms around his neck as he lifted me up and spun me around. The hole in my chest where guilt lived for so long was filled. It was filled with love. I missed him. Missed him so much I was hanging onto him like a barnacle, but he didn't seem to mind. He held me up and buried his face back in my neck.

"I've been miserable this week, Max. But something big happened. I quit JMS."

"What? Why? Did I drive you to this, make you think you had to? Oh, Blue. No. Not a chance. Nope. I'm calling Jake."

Max put me down and reached for his phone, running his other hand through his hair. I stopped him with a touch, putting both of mine on his chest.

"I'm going to take over *B's*. I'm going to work with nonprofits, bringing music into rehab centers. And I'm going to sing, Max. And play. And write. You did that. You brought my music back. And it makes me love you even more. This is a good thing."

"But..." he started, searching my face for doubt, for uncertainty. "That's... Blue, I'm so proud of you." Max brought my hand to his lips and kissed each knuckle, shaking his head.

Baxter let out another loud bark, trotting over and pushing in between us.

"Aw. Hey, bud. How's my boy," I cooed, bending down to rub his back.

"He wants to go to the terrace. Take a look."

"What?" I said, turning around to face the staircase.

It took me a minute to process what I was seeing. It was a stairlift, almost like the one my great-aunt had but customized. Instead of a chair, there was a wooden platform with a large blue dog bed. Baxter ran back and jumped in the bed, turning in a circle before plopping down and barking again.

"Max? You did this?"

Max kept a firm hold of my hand as I walked over, looking at the lift. I ran my hand over the light wood of the platform and the railing. *How had he done this in just a few short hours?* Baxter was in his element, ready to go for a ride.

"I love it, Max. It's perfect." My voice was shaking with all the other things I needed to say, but Max knew, leaning down to press a kiss to my lips.

"I'm glad, baby. I wanted to show you how I felt. Want to take the boy for a ride?"

"I do, Max. Let's go."

We took the stairs with Baxter riding behind us, and when we got to the terrace, he ran around sniffing every plant. I leaned into Max, running my hands underneath his shirt, not believing it was possible to smile so much in a day. Max whistled, and Baxter cocked his head, running back to the stairs and sitting down in anticipation of another ride.

We walked down to the first floor with Baxter behind us, stealing glances and smiles. Through the hall and into the living room, we held on. I never wanted to let go. Everyone's eyes were on us, so I pulled Max down for a wet kiss and was rewarded with that full dimpled smile.

Bird gave Addison a high-five, and she held up a wine glass with a silent toast. Olivia poked her head out of the kitchen, pulling off an oven mitt to give us a thumbs up.

"You two are so disgustingly cute. I can't stand it," Jenna said, shaking her head and reaching out to pet Baxter. He sniffed her hand, then rubbed against her thigh, making her stumble backward with surprise.

"You're next, lady!" I said, pointing to my eyes, then hers. She held up both her hands in mock surrender and walked back to the kitchen.

"Um, low blow, Jenna," Bird said, pulling Taylor to him and wrapping an arm around his waist. "Have you forgotten the standard all couples should aspire to? Hashtag goals right here, baby!"

He leaned down and kissed Taylor, shoving a hand in his back pocket with a grin.

"I don't think you're supposed to say hashtag, Bird. But fine. Max and Anna, you take second place on the cuteness," she said. "And one thousand apologies to the couple that takes the cake."

"Noted," Bird answered, following Jenna into the kitchen and rubbing his stomach.

"The macaroni needs another hour or two," Olivia said, stirring the cheesy goodness and leaning over the adjust the temperature on the BBQ.

"Macaroni?" Max said, rubbing slow circles on my back. I laid my head on his shoulder and breathed him in.

"Yeah, Broody. I made macaroni."

"With ritz-cracker crumbs?"

"And sour cream."

"Blue," was all he could say before I pressed my lips back to his, smiling.

"Ugh. Come on, gang. Let's give these two time to catch up. Beers on me," Bird said, grabbing the keys to Max's truck and waving to us.

"You two!" Addison said, grabbing her purse. "You have one hour before we're back. Make it count!" She wiggled her fingers and followed Bird out the door.

"One hour?" Max said, waving one hand to our little group and grabbing mine with the other. "Make it an hour and a half! And someone put the crock pots on warm!"

I barely heard the front door shut, and the cat-calls Taylor made as

Max pulled me back up the stairs. I was right on his heels, desperate for his touch and giggling like crazy.

He dragged me into the bedroom and slammed the door. In an instant, he pushed me against it, and his lips were on mine, our mouths frantic, tongues dueling. The noises we were making were obscene, and I absolutely loved it. And him. So much.

Max's mouth broke from mine long enough for him to pull his shirt over his head. God, I had forgotten how massive he was. How long had it been? Days? Weeks? Decades? All I knew was it was too damn long. He was all thick arms and tan skin rippling with defined muscles. He jerked my head back as his tongue dove into my mouth, possessively. He was gorgeous and wearing too many clothes. Hunger, powerful and vibrating in my veins, threatened to explode out of every pore in my body.

"I need you to know something, Blue." He cupped my cheek and ran his thumb across my lip. "I know we had a bit of a rocky start, but I wouldn't change a thing. I love you, Blue. I love your beautiful smile and your strawberry shortcake. I love your big heart and your loyalty. And I love how you make me feel like I could move mountains. I think I've loved you since that moment on the beach. And we don't have to do anything. I'm content to just hold you, to kiss you."

His tongue darted out again, and he licked my earlobe, making me shiver.

"Did you not, um, want to?"

He reached out and grabbed my hand, pressing it to his cock and hissing when I squeezed.

"No. Fuck no, Blue. I've been on a desert, an island, in a drought without you. But I just got you back, and I want you to know that I'm willing to wait for you. To earn you. To deserve you. Whatever you need, baby. Tell me."

He pressed his forehead to mine, and relief poured through me and my eyes stung with tears. We were real. This was real. This was love.

"Max," I said, drawing my lower lip in my mouth. His eyes got dark as he watched the movement, hanging on my next words. "Take your pants off. I need you inside me. Right, the fuck, now."

He gave me a wicked grin, and those huge arms picked me up and carried me to the bed, and sat me down. He leaned down and wiped my tears, kissing the tracks they left on my cheeks. I wrapped my legs around him, spreading them wide as he pulled my bra straps off my shoulders and popped both breasts free from their cups.

He groaned and held both tits in his large hands, licking each hard peak as my head dropped back and the throbbing pressure between my legs made me almost explode. I was aching, desperate, and flooded with warmth.

I braced myself against the edge of the bed and rubbed my core up and down his length. That drew his attention away from my tits long enough to pull my shorts and panties off. He shucked his jeans as I took off my bra, freezing me with a lust-filled look. He licked his lips and leaned down to lick my inner thigh, letting his dark, short stubble tease the sensitive skin.

I loved it. I loved him. But my body was not prepared for the way he looked at me. Like he would have walked a hundred miles through the arctic cold to feel my heat pressed against him. I wanted nothing but the moaning, panting cries of our bodies slapping together, struggling to get closer. To feel. To live. To love.

"You taste so fucking good. I'm going to spend every day worshiping this body."

He kissed and licked, moving closer and closer to my core. When his tongue finally darted across my clit, my hips arched off the bed, and I grabbed his face, pushing him into me, begging for more. His tongue was magic, and when he added two thick digits, I almost passed out from pleasure. I held on to the bed as if my life depended on it, and he sucked on my clit, pumping his fingers in and out of me. My legs were trembling as he owned my body, bringing me to the brink then holding me as I was about to shatter.

"I love this pussy," he said between licks. "I've missed you, Blue.

Missed this. Let go, baby. I've got you."

I could feel my core building, racing towards relief. I tried to hold back, wanting to prolong the pleasure and come on his cock, screaming his name. But he wasn't having it. He kept pumping his fingers in and out, curling them to hit that magic spot. He paused his licks for a second and looked at me, face covered with my juices and smiling with lidded eyes.

"Come on, beautiful. Come on my face and let me drink you down."

With one last lap, he sent me spiraling over the edge, coaxing out every drop of pleasure until my thighs were shaking. *How did he know how to reach down to the deepest, most intimate parts of me and make me feel alive?* And I came, screaming his name and holding on like he was the only thing keeping me anchored to this world. Maybe he was.

He slid his fingers out and licked his lips while I tried to catch my breath. His cock jutted out proudly between us, and I wrapped one hand around it, bringing him down on top of me. His cock was everything. Hard and thick and dripping with pre-come, pulsing in my hand.

His eyes tracked my movements, taking me in. I had no idea what was going on with my hair, and my thighs were shaking, but whatever he saw, he liked, because he smiled and leaned down, fitting perfectly between my legs. I brought his fingers to my lips, tasting him, tasting us, needing him.

His look was filled with molten lust, but also love, so much love. I could see it radiating off his body, and god did it feel good to be loved, to be desired.

"You ready for me, beautiful? Ready for more?" He leaned off the bed and pulled a condom out from his discarded pants, but I took it from him.

"I'm clean, Max. And on the pill. I want to feel you."

"Fuck, Blue. Yes. I'm clean too. But I've never…"

"Me either," I said, dropping the condom on the floor and pulling him closer. My core tingled with anticipation, and I chanted, "Yes, Max. Please."

He held my legs open, and his lips curled into a wicked grin. "I love fucking you, Blue. But more than that, I love you. So much."

He moved closer, every inch of his body hard and thick. I opened my mouth to reply, but he thrust inside—bare, hot, and nothing between us. My body stretched to accommodate him, filling me to the breaking point. He drove his cock in and out, abs flexing, and looked at me like I was his entire world. He was everywhere, hands moving up and down my chest, kneading my breasts and lightly pinching my nipples. And his eyes. His eyes never left mine.

He held my legs further apart and chased his pleasure, moving one hand down to circle my clit. The first orgasm was just the prequel, the beginning, and Max was playing my body like he had years to master it. He thrust harder, and I whimpered, my core tightening and tingling with his every movement.

My eyes fluttered closed, and I let the sensations wash over me, his hands on my body, his skin pressed on mine. By the time the second orgasm ripped through me, I was trembling, panting. Opening my eyes, I watched the groove between Max's brows deepen as his hips jerked harder before he pulled out and palmed himself.

"Knees," he ordered.

I sat up on shaky legs and flipped over, bracing myself on the bed and sticking my ass in the air. I looked over my shoulder and bit my lip. He traced his hands over my ass before pulling me towards him and thrusting in again. I arched my back and dropped my head to the pillow as he drove in fast and hard, his hips smacking my ass as he went faster. I was moaning incoherently, and he was growling with every thrust, both of us bared down to our most basic instinct, feeding off each other's lust.

Picking my head up, I looked back at him, "Harder, Max. Fuck me harder."

I didn't think it was possible, but he did, reaching forward and grabbing a handful of hair, so I arched further. We slammed together, and he let go of my hair to reach between my legs to rub my clit in tight, fast circles. I could feel another orgasm barreling towards me as he pounded me from behind.

Max Smerdon, Sex God.

The pressure intensified, and my legs started trembling before my entire body shuddered, and I started coming. It began in my toes and raced up my legs, and I felt the moment Max came too. His cock swelled inside of me, and he dug his hand into my hip hard, groaning my name.

"That's it, Blue. I love you!"

I tried to reply, but it came out as a muffled scream, and we fell over the cliff together. I was panting, shaking, and couldn't do anything but sink to the bed. Max gently pulled out, bent down, kissing my back and caressing my ass before walking to the bathroom. He came back with a washcloth, and after cleaning us up, he crawled in beside me, pulling me to him so I could lay my head on his chest.

"I'm completely fuck-drunk, Max. What did you just do to me?"

"No, baby. It's what you did to me. You changed me, Blue. I'm better because of you."

I moaned into his chest and ran my fingers through his dark chest hair before leaning up for a kiss. I kissed him until our breathing slowed, tracing my tongue along his neck and nipping his shoulder. He bucked with the sting and hauled me closer, threading our hands together.

He looked at me like I was his world, like I was the only thing that mattered. With his forehead pressed to mine, he cupped my face, thumbs stroking the red marks his beard left. I could still feel him in me. In a place deep down in my soul, a place he belonged.

"Think we can convince them to stay away longer?" I said, snuggling in deeper.

"Not a chance. You have dinner and dessert. Besides, the faster we eat, the faster we can get back to more of this."

He traced his hand over my breast and down my stomach, giving me the smile that made me fall harder each time I saw it.

"I'm glad I made enough to feed an Army. Alright, Broody. Let's go."

We both got up slowly and got dressed, opening the door to find Baxter lying outside. He looked up and cocked his head as if he knew exactly what Max had done to his Mama.

"Come on, bud," Max said, bending down to rub his head. "I brought a nice ribeye for you."

We were walking down the stairs, and I was admiring the view when Max stopped suddenly, making me bump into him.

"Did you call me Broody?"

"I did. What do you think? It was your original nickname, after all."

"I think," he said, giving me another smile. "That as long as I can call you mine, I'll love whatever nickname you give me, Blue."

With one last kiss, we went into the kitchen with Baxter hot on our heels. Just as we put the last condiment on the table, the door swung open, and the girls plus Taylor and Bird came barreling in.

"You two better be decent because we are hungry!" Bird called, walking into the kitchen and giving Max a sharp smack on the ass.

Edward came over a short while later, giving Olivia a sweet kiss and a smile. I could see the love reflecting in their eyes, remembering Olivia's words. Max was worth it, we were worth it, and every day I'd show him how much I love him. As if he knew what I was thinking, he met my eyes and touching a finger to his lips. Smiling, I did the same.

Later that night, we were relaxing on the terrace with strawberry ice cream. Max and I were laying in my hammock, arms and legs entwined, with Baxter at our feet. He was twirling a strand of my hair with his eyes closed, and I was humming. His normally hard edges were smooth and relaxed. I ran my hand up his side, and he shivered and laughed, pulling away.

"Easy, Blue. That's my ticklish spot."

He winked and leaned down for a kiss, "I love you."

"Hmm. I love you too, Max."

And I did; I was so in love with this man. I'd finally found what I'd been missing and what I'd been looking for, and I found both in him.

"What are you humming, Blue?" he asked, throwing one leg off the hammock to gently rock us back and forth.

"Us, Max. I finished a song, a song about us."

"You wrote us, baby? Will you sing it to me? Please?"

I started humming the melody that had been on my mind, squeezing Max's hand and turning to face him. It was our song, our happiness, our love. A song about how we'd found each other. I'd poured myself into the words, the music.

And as I sang, Max traced shapes on my palm and rocked us. When I got to the chorus, I realized he was tracing hearts. Over and over. He was tracing our love, our happiness, and our life.

"Here I lie beneath the whisper of night,
shadows flicker in the glimmer of fading light,
Fingers silent at the cold touch of keys,
No song resonating within me.

But you soon lingered above my emptiness.
A magical soul whose miracles manifest.
At the sight of your aesthetics my heart knew peace,
Doubts dissipated as my knees felt weak.

In moments of time, will I ever be ready?
Heartbeats out of sync, will we ever be steady?
Eyes deep as the ocean, willingly I'll drown,
Would you save my breath or sink me down?
Once just a blank page, words drift estranged,
But with you by my side, my whole world changed.

I never dreamed my words would lead me here to you,
A sudden spark lit like stars in the sky,
Within me, stories find a life renewed,
Enchanted by the soul buried within your eyes.

Let me perish in the depth of your love,
Whisk me away on the ridges of your chest,
May our voices echo from the heavens above,
To the melody of your enticing caress.

Devour me to your most sensual desires,
For you are the one that ignites my fire.
Yet doubt questions to turn our page,
leaving bliss buried in insecurity's chains.

We've had our run, hearts sang their song,
My words shun bright, you were my sun,
But leaving all we built behind,
Has frozen my heart in despair's time,
Oh would you return and stay forever,
Come back and stay, piece me together,
Complete me whole, now and forever.

In moments of time, will I ever be ready?
Heartbeats out of sync, will we ever be steady?
Eyes deep as the ocean, willingly I'll drown,
Would you save my breath or sink me down?
Once just a blank page, words drift estranged,
But with you by my side, my whole world changed."

When I sang the last note, Max cleared his throat with glassy eyes, bringing my palm to his lips.

"You're right, Blue. That's us. You pieced me together."

I sighed with his sweet words, content and knowing we had a lifetime of happiness ahead of us because with him by my side, my whole world changed. I found my music. I found my happiness. I found my love. I found them all with him.

The End

EPILOGUE: NOW AND FOREVER
Warren / Bird

A Reasonable and Respectable Amount of Time Later...

What? You thought you'd be reading some sweet, sappy, romantic happily ever always from Max or Annaleigh's point of view? Think again, you lucky ducks. You get me: the infamous, the amazing, Warren "Bird" Smerdon.

You're welcome.

So here we are, a reasonable amount of time later, back on the same beach, where their love story began. My BFF, the gorgeous Annaleigh Mackey, is sitting on her blue lounge chair, under her blue umbrella, with her three friends and me—the sexist guy on the whole damn beach.

Sorry ladies and gentlemen, I'm taken. *And expecting!* That's right, Taylor and I are pregnant! Our surrogate is due next month, and I am going to be the bestest father this world has ever known! So get ready!

But anyway, back to our story. Max is a mess. An absolute mess. And it's hilarious. He's been planning the perfect proposal for months. Months! I suggested shaving: "will you marry me" into his chest hair, but he kindly told me to fuck off. Whatever. It's not like Annaleigh is going to say no. Not with how obsessed they are with each other. It's disgusting.

No, it's not.

It's adorable, and they both deserve all the happiness this world can give them, especially since he's been working so hard to pull off this proposal. I've found a dozen crumpled pieces of paper around his house with things to say when he asks her.

"What are you thinking about over there, Bird?" My beautiful best friend asks, peering over her blue sunglasses and putting down her latest romance book. "You narrating our life in your head again?"

"Maybe. But mostly thinking about how much you've grown, and how happy we all are."

I leaned over and fist-bumped Jenna, trying not to cut myself on her freaking huge engagement ring. Like seriously, we all know you're marrying the growly, tattooed cop your magical vay-jay-jay has tamed—no need to draw blood.

I mean, I'm sure my balls have some magical properties, but Taylor isn't sporting a rock the size of his face. Though actually, that's not a bad idea. We both have simple gold wedding bands, but Taylor deserves the world. He'd look even hotter with a huge rock on his finger. Maybe something in black onyx to celebrate the baby. Is that a thing? I'll start a new trend if it's not.

"I'll drink to that," Addison says, bringing me back to the girls and the beach, and lifting her bottle to clink it against Jenna's.

Olivia raises her bottle of water and steadies herself, keeping one hand on her pregnant belly. I reach over, so she doesn't have to move as far to clink her water to my soda. I always thought it was bad luck to toast with water, but it's not like this is their wedding day. I'd be seriously underdressed if it were. I glance down at my green bathing suit and shrug my shoulders.

All of us are peering to the shoreline, waiting for the show to start, with Annaleigh none the wiser. She is sipping her IPA, humming under her breath to the radio, and tapping her foot in the sand. I rub my hands on my thigh and take another swig of soda, looking toward the shoreline just in time to see a dog running our way. It's too far away for me to tell if it's Baxter, but I let out a low whistle, so the girls look up. I tilt my head toward the dog, and we all hold in a collective breath as they move closer.

I spot Max's neon pink sunglasses before I recognize Baxter, and clear my throat, smiling. Baxter must spot us because he starts barking, and Max picks up the pace. Annaleigh looks up, tosses her book to the side, and runs toward them with a huge grin on her face. Max wraps one hand around

Baxter's leash and the other around her, lifting her up for a wet kiss. He sets her down and lifts a hand in greeting.

"What are you doing here, Broody? I thought you were stuck at home all day working on the new project specs for Jake?"

"I was Blue. But something more important came up."

"It did? Is everything okay?" she asks, running her hands up his arms. Baxter pushes himself between them, and they both reach down to stroke his fur. Content with the attention, he plops down on the sand, tongue lolling, to watch the sandpipers hop along the seafoam.

"Oh. Um. Yes. Everything is fine, Blue. But there's something I've been meaning to talk to you about."

I hate spying, but I'm desperate to see Max's plan come to fruition, so I slowly step closer so I can hear them better. The girls follow, but Annaleigh barely notices, only having eyes for my bro-tastic, big brother.

Max shifts nervously from foot to foot and looks at his watch, then at me. I give him a small nod and covert thumbs up. He looks at his watch *again* and blows out a loud breath. Addison snickers from somewhere beside me, and I kick sand in her general direction. She rolls her eyes and shrugs her shoulders before looking back at the happy couple.

"Are you sure you're okay, Max?" she asks, reaching up to press her palm to his forehead. He dodges her hand and nods.

"Yeah. I'm good. Better than good. Great, actually."

This time Olivia lets out a little giggle, and Max glances at us and shakes his head. Annaleigh looks back at us too, and I square my stance and cross my arms, trying to get the girls to shut the hell up so Max can handle this. They get the message, and Jenna mimics locking her lips with a key while Addison flicks me off.

"Blue. Baby. Listen. For days, weeks, months, I've been searching for the perfect words for you. I've read poetry, listened to song lyrics, and watched every Hallmark movie in existence. But none of those were right. None of those were us."

She tilts her head to the side, waiting for him to continue as he glances at his watch again.

That girl can always pick up on his emotions because she lays one hand on his chest and brings the other to his cheek.

"Broody. I don't know what's going on, but listen, the only thing I want, and the only thing that matters, is you and me. It's us, baby. Not words, actions, remember?"

She moves her hand, putting it on her heart, then his, and bringing her pointer finger to her lips. He does the same and grips the back of her neck so their foreheads are touching.

"You're right, Blue. Words are useless and empty if actions don't back them. And today, right now, I'm going to show you. One year ago, on this very beach, you changed my life. You opened my eyes and showed me a world filled with gorgeous blues and beautiful music. A world I never want to leave because it a world where I am yours, and you are mine. And it's time to make it official. I've loved you since that day on the beach a year ago, and I want to spend every day for the rest of my life loving you."

Max stops to take a breath and glances at his watch, letting go of Annaleigh's hand. She covers her mouth with glassy eyes, and all of us have smiles a mile wide. He reaches in his pocket, and my eyes get a little glassy as he pulls out a black velvet box and drops to one knee in the sand.

"Annaleigh Mackey. My Blue. My love. Mine. Will you make me as happy as I am today for the rest of my life? Will you marry me?"

I fist pump the air, and Olivia straight up squeals. But no one, *no one*, is smiling harder than Annaleigh, who drops to her knees beside Max and kisses him for all he's worth. He drops Baxter's leash and wraps both arms around her, kissing her back just as hard. His hands are in her hair, and her hands are around his neck, and I'm man enough to admit my eyes are a little watery watching them.

Baxter trots over to us, hoping for attention, and Annaleigh breaks away long enough to say, "Yes! Yes! Oh Max, Yes!"

They dive back into each other, kissing, laughing, and saying sweet things. We can't stay away from them a second longer and are all running to them as soon as they stand back up. I swear the Universe dims down to just the two of them, and even as Anna hugs us, one hand stays firmly grasped in Max's, like he's her center.

Addison reaches out and grips Max's shirt, tugging him hard into the hug and then playfully punching him on the shoulder.

"You did good, Max," she says, bringing Anna's hand close to look at the ring. I've already seen it, and Addison is right. Max knocked it out of the park. It's a platinum band with simple teardrop diamond, surrounded by blue sapphires. The sunlight catches the sapphires, making them sparkle even brighter, but it's nothing compared to the happiness in their eyes.

He rubs the back of his neck and smiles before I pull him into a bear hug, pulling him away from Anna and lifting him up.

"I'm so fucking proud of you big-bro!" I say, putting him down and slapping him on the back. I grab her and do the same, not squeezing as hard, of course.

"Proud of you, lady. And so happy for you both."

"Thank you, Bird," she says, letting go and reaching out to take Max's hand again.

The girls are clinking drinks and already talking about the wedding, so I turn back to my brother and best friend, seeing them grasp hands again.

"Max. This was perfect. I couldn't imagine a better proposal. I love you."

"I love you too, Blue," he answers, letting go to pull his T-shirt off. He flexes his bicep so she can see his tattoo. It takes her a minute to see what he's done, but when she does, she puts her hand over her mouth and starts the waterworks all over again.

The face of the pocket-watch finally tells a time, the exact time he proposed, or close enough to it. And one of the feathers is complete and colored in with different shades of blue. She traces the ink up his arm to the back of his neck and pulls him back down for a kiss.

"That day at the beach a year ago, Max, it felt like my heart started beating."

"Mine too, Blue," he said, reaching out to tuck a wisp of hair behind her ear. "And this is just the beginning. You ready to get out of here?"

"Yeah, I am. Take me home, Broody."

He presses a sweet kiss to her temple, then pats me on the back and takes Baxter's leash. The only thing that would make this moment better would be if they were walking off into the sunset with Bryan Adams playing in the background or if Taylor was here.

I check my watch and give them a final wave, taking my phone out of my pocket to send him a heart emoji. He returns it a second later, and all of a sudden, with all this love in the air, I need to hightail it back to him. Because if this crazy love story has shown me anything, it's that actions speak louder than words, and sometimes, love really is all you need.

ACKNOWLEDGEMENTS

There are so many people who helped this book become a reality, and I'd like to take a few moments to thank them for making Max and Anna's Happily Ever Always possible.

For Sheri. You were the first person I shared this crazy idea with. Thank you for listening.

For Jen and April, my amazing alphas. Thank you for letting me obsess over every detail and for reading a very, *very* rough draft. We will forever be: *the three best friends that anyone could have!*

For Jessica Snyder. Thank you for reading the first few chapters and giving me invaluable guidance. You gave me the confidence to keep writing, and I am forever grateful.

For my sister Meghan. Thank you for your unending support and for always having my back. You helped me power through writer's block and gave Max and Anna the ending they deserved. You always know how to make life brighter.

For Traci, my aunt, and amazing beta reader. Thank you for not getting weirded out reading the sexy stuff, and for emotionally supporting me through every freak-out and every *a-ha* moment. You have always been my biggest cheerleader, and you make my heart smile.

For Meghan and Amber. Your developmental edits were on point! You are both detail oriented bad asses and I can't wait to work with you again!

For Rebecca Colvin of Just Ask Her Productions. Thank you for being there, for supporting me, and for teaching me all the things. Our friendship is something I treasure, and I would not be where I am without your guidance. You are truly an amazing soul.

For Kris Guiao. Thank you for the amazing cover, beautiful formatting, and for working with me and my million questions and overthinking brain.

For Brett and Danielle. Thank for you for proofreading a book that is *way* out of your usual genre. And Brett, I'm sorry about almost making you crash when Danielle got to *that* plot-twist!

For my ARC Readers. Thank you for being patient and for your worthwhile comments. I am humbled and grateful for each and every one of you.

For my husband, and my parents. Thank you for believing in me, supporting me, and for not letting me give up when things got sticky. And a special shout out to my marvelous mom for reading the first chapter and immediately shoving a laptop in my hands!

For my Reader's Writing Romance FB Group. Thank you for the fantastic advice and all the helpful suggestions.

For Erica Walsh. Your graphics are on point! Thank you for helping to make the release the best it could be!

And finally, to my Mormor. You are the voice in my head when I want to give up, and the woman I strive to one day become. I love you.

DID YOU LOVE THIS BOOK?

Thank you for reading **_Had To Make You Mine_**! I hope you enjoyed Max and Anna's story as much as I enjoyed writing it!

If you loved this book, please consider leaving a <u>review</u>. Even just a few words can help Indie Authors reach a wider audience! As an author, your feedback is vital to our success and will help other readers decide what their next favorite book will be.

If you'd like to get notifications of new releases, sneak-peeks, and special offers, please join my Facebook Group, <u>Kat Long's Between the Covers</u>, and sign up for my (non-spammy) <u>Newsletter</u> at <u>www.katlongromance.com</u>.

ABOUT THE AUTHOR

Kat lives at the beach with her Happily Ever After, a daughter, and two irritating but lovable cats.

Before she started writing contemporary romance, she graduated with a Master's Degree in School Psychology from The University of West Alabama. Now, by day she works in Commercial Banking and by night she's a Writer.

Books have always made her heart beat faster, and she started writing her first novel after dreaming up an Alpha-Marshmallow!

Her characters are sexy and clever, but in real life Kat's the ultimate over-thinker. Let's face it, her inner monologues would *not* make good reading!

She flips for a good romance and gets giddy anytime there's HEAT.

When she's not reading or writing sexy stories, she's probably researching her next book, watching Animal Planet in yoga pants, trying not to over-water her succulents, drinking too much coffee, and wondering if the real meaning of life is forty-two.

Readers make her world go round!
Keep in touch with Kat Via the Web:

www.KatLongRomance.com
https://linktr.ee/KatLongRomance

SNEAK PEEK

Here's a Sneak Peek of <u>Love Under Construction: A Love Falls Novella</u>
Free with Kindle Unlimited

I have a secret—a secret so scandalous, so outrageous, and so down-right dirty that the mere mention of it sends grown men cowering into the shadows—a secret so diabolical, so shocking, that the fact I even consider saying the words out loud should leave you feeling lucky.

And afraid. Very afraid.

Are you ready?

Are you sure?

Take a moment. Have a seat. Get a drink; maybe two. Prepare yourself for the bamboozlement, the shock, the bewilderment—what? That is too a real word; my word-a-day calendar in the bathroom says so. It's not like my cactus and I have a lot to say to each other when I'm in there.

My reputation is on the line for even daring to allow the words to cross my lips. The core of my very being could be disrupted, destroyed, burned beyond recognition.

Have I drawn it out enough?

Is *everybody* paying attention?

This is your last warning to turn and run away.

No?

Okay. Here it is. Don't say I didn't warn you.

It was a dark and stormy night…

Just kidding: I'm hilarious.

I, Maddox Hart (nickname Mads), owner of *Hart Construction*, owner of a reputation that will make your toes curl: for being a badass, a hardass, a pain in the ass, and any other ass words you want to add, I'm a (sigh)—I'm a (bigger sigh), oh for fuck's sake! I'm a hopeless romantic—I love, love.

There (deep breath), I said it. It's out in the open for the world to see. Fuck. I feel better.

By day, I run the most successful business in this town. I run my company with ruthless effectiveness and unyielding perfectionism. Construction is a tough business, with lots of room for error. When we started offering Handy-Man services, general repair, and upkeep to the books, my standards got even higher. Go ahead, judge. I didn't get where I am by being a pushover. I hold myself and my crew to the highest standards and have no issue with making the world bend to my will if they fail. But at night, it's a different story. A softer story.

At night, I like nothing more than watching *HGTV* under a quilted blanket, with hot tea and chocolate chip cookies fresh from the oven. And yes, before you ask, I made the cookies. And the quilted blanket. I knitted the shit out of it. The bubble stitch pattern will knock your socks off.

It's my downtime, my happy place, my peace. Do I still burp too loud when drinking beer with the guys and laugh when I fart in the shower? Abso-*fucking*-lutely.

But when I'm at home, after I sign the invoices and check the sites, I can finally drop the facade like a wet blanket. Drop the facade, and just enjoy the peace and solitude. Well, the peace? Yes. The solitude? No. That's the real issue. The root of the problem. The stone in my Timberlands. I'm lonely.

After I hit the big three-zero, I did some soul searching. The kind of serious soul searching that resulted in matching sweaters for half the local nursing home residents and a hat for every baby in the nursery—sent anonymously, of course. I didn't get the nickname Mads because I walked them in myself. I'm not a fucking idiot.

The problem is, my accomplishments don't mean shit if there's no one to share them with when I get home. Yeah, I have an oversized apartment, but it's too damn big for just me. I should have a house by now and a family with a dog and matching Christmas sweaters, all made by yours truly. And yes, before you ask, the dog has a matching sweater too, duh.

You see, most women take one look at me and think I'm their walk on the wild side. I get it. I'm a dominating force, always have been. That's one part of my life that's not a facade. I demand complete control, and in return, will spend tortuous hours giving nothing but pleasure. But on the two occasions I let down my stonewall facade, it backfired. Badly.

So I'm done—done with casual dating. Am I complaining about my past affairs? No. But I'm sick of it—sick of not having a connection, sick of not having someone to spoil, sick of not having someone to love.

I want someone I can spend hours worshipping in the bedroom and then wake up next to in the morning. They say, "True love is your soul's recognition of its counterpoint in another." It's time I find her. It's time to find a girl I can knit socks for because she has cold feet. It's time to find a girl I can laugh with, a girl I can draw a bath for, maybe even a girl that would make me chicken soup if I was under the weather. Oddly specific, right? But hey, a guy can dream. I guess if dreaming about knitted socks and chicken noodle soup is wrong, I don't want to be right.

I'm ready to settle down. In all honesty, I've been ready for a while, but no one seems to hold my interest. Well, that's not entirely true.

One woman sure as hell holds my interest, but she's as tight as a tick and doesn't even give me a second glance. And believe me, I've tried. I've tried more times than I'll ever admit.

When you grow up here in *Love Falls*, you get to know everyone. Except her. She's been a mystery since she first moved here. The bits and pieces I've gathered have done nothing to bank the inferno in my stomach when I'm in her presence.

And once again, before you ask, I know there's a shit-ton of irony when a guy with the last name Hart lives in *Love Falls*.

Want to know what her last name is? Ha! Not yet. There's a reason my family doesn't call me Mads. They prefer Drama King on account that I sometimes, maybe, occasionally, draw things out and overreact. Might as well live up to the nickname.

Anyway, I think I'm finally ready to tell you where my story begins. Ugh, maybe my family isn't as off-base as I thought with the nickname. Whatever, it's not like I'd ever admit that to them.

Now, it's time to sit back, relax, have that drink, and enjoy the ride.

My story began as I rushed through my routine, the same as every other morning. There was nothing special about the bitter January day as I poured my cold-brew in a thermos and pulled my apartment door shut. Before I could help myself, I glanced across the hall at her door, and saw it was still closed.

Shaking my head, I checked my watch. I knew she was probably a minute or two behind me, just like every other morning, but I couldn't linger. There were three sites I needed to check today, and then I needed to process payroll and reconcile the books.

Wanting to see her, I walked a step or two slower than normal, but her door never opened, and the exit door mocked me like a joke I didn't understand. When I reached my mud-splattered truck, I stepped up and started it before looking back one more time, willing that damn door to open.

When it was obvious I was out of luck, *again*, I reached over the console to grab my phone for my appointments, but it wasn't there. I groaned loudly, closed my eyes, and hit my head on the headrest. My phone, like my life apparently, was in on the joke. I knew it was lying upstairs on my counter on top of my lunch, homemade chicken-cordon-bleu over wild rice and mixed vegetables.

I got out of the truck and slammed the door, stalking over to the apartment entrance. I tried to wrench the door open, but it had more resistance than normal. So I yanked harder, and was rewarded with a high-pitch squeal on the other side.

No. Please no. Don't tell me it's her—come on! And please don't tell me I hit her with the damn door. I peeked around the door, and yep, there she was on the floor.

"I'm so sorry! Here, let me help," I said, reaching out to lift her up and feeling glad it didn't look like I did any serious damage. She pushed my hand aside and stood up, running her hands down her skirt and giving me a look that could melt steel.

"Not necessary. Excuse me," she said, her tone as cold as the ice colored dress she was wearing. White-blonde soft waves framed her face, and once again, I was drawn in by her full red lips, and *those eyes*. The first time I met her, it was her eyes that made me stop and stare. She had such soft, kind eyes buried under a harsh, unforgiving personality. She had the kind of eyes a man could get lost in. The kind of eyes a man could stare into forever.

"Sure," I said, attempting to redeem myself by holding the door open for her.

She was pinching her eyebrows as if the last thing she wanted to do was look my way. And she didn't, not even making eye contact as she breezed past in ridiculously high-heels. Like how was she even able to stand up by herself in those things? Damnit! She was walking away, again. Maybe this time I could make her say more than three words to me.

"Wait a minute!" I said.

She stopped and turned around, cocking her hip my way and oblivious to the way my hungry eyes took in every inch of her body.

"I'm so sorry, Maddox," she replied, finally looking at me with both rage and boredom. "I've checked my schedule and can't possibly give a damn until next Monday."

Foot—meet mouth: jaw—meet floor. I had nothing. Not a comeback or witty response. Just a blank expression as I watched her throw those hips around before climbing into her car and peeling out of the parking lot.

Taking the steps two at a time, I threw my apartment door open and grabbed my lunch and phone before cramming a hat on my head to keep me from pulling my hair out in frustration. Getting back in my truck, I followed her lead and peeled out of the parking lot in the opposite direction, just as pissed as she seemed to be.

I sped to work, hating that I probably wouldn't be the first one there. Yep, the universe took another sucker punch, right at my kidneys. There was a beat-up Chevy already in the lot and a light on in the front office. I cracked each knuckle as I walked inside, my mood worsening by the minute.

"Hey, Mads. 'Bout time you showed up, man."

"The hell's that mean, Rob?"

"Damn, Boss. Nothing. I've, uh, never beaten you here before."

"It won't be a habit," I said, throwing my hat on my desk.

I snagged my lunch and shoved it in the employee fridge. Rob followed and didn't flinch. He's used to my moods by now. It still wasn't a reason to rub my lateness in my face. Being late wasn't an option, no matter how distracted I was.

"Where will you be today?" I asked him, scrolling through the appointments on my phone.

"I need to check on the progress the guys are making at *The Tasty Freeze* and do a final walkthrough at *Pop's General Store*. We also got a request to fix the drive-through at First Bank. If you're going to check it out first, take the deposit with you."

"What?" I said, looking up and glaring at him, "Why didn't you go last night?"

"I got caught up talking with Pops. By the time I got away, the bank was closed," he said with a shrug.

"What the hell, Rob? Why are you my foreman if you don't do the damn job?"

I towered over him, and he stepped back, crossing his arms and staring back just as hard.

"Christ, Mads. I'm here early to take it first thing. And you're welcome, by the way. Not only has Pops already paid in full, but he finally convinced Buster to let us fix his well and re-shingle his roof."

"What? Really?" We'd been after Buster for years to do some much-needed upkeep on his house. Huh, Rob came through, not that I'd admit that to him, but the bank deposit still happened to be his damn job.

"See what being personable can do?"

"Why would I need to be personable when you handle it so well?" I pointed out, taking my hat off and running a hand through my hair. Ugh, I needed to get it cut soon.

"Damn. That's pretty close to a compliment, Mads."

"Don't be a dick, Rob. Give me the check, and I'll take it to the bank since you didn't do your damn job."

"Again. You're welcome," Rob said, doing stupid ass finger guns before turning to walk out of the office.

"Fuck off," I said that last part with a smile, knowing I'm damn lucky to have Rob. But I still was not going to give him a big head.

With a two-finger salute, he left the check on top of the bank bag and grabbed his keys. I needed to knock out the reconciliation of the books before licking my wounds and going to the bank. Maybe I'll go at lunchtime, and she'll be out, even the Bank Manager has to eat, after all. But knowing her, all the sustenance she needed was the tears of men she had rejected. But enough of these damn distractions. I flopped down, taking a big gulp of coffee as the chair creaked ominously underneath my 225-pound frame, and started working.

By early afternoon, my stomach was rumbling, all traces of my lunch eaten, gone. With no more excuses, I grabbed the bank bag and headed out. The drive didn't take long enough, and the *First Bank* got too close too fast. Parking, I took in the older brick building with two drive-through lanes.

The work order said some idiot hit a support beam, revealing rotted wood. My team had to replace everything before the drive-through collapsed.

I walked around and zipped up my jacket in the icy wind. Someone did a piss-poor job taping off the area, and they were damn lucky the beam hadn't already snapped. I checked over it all, making notes along the way, before heading inside.

The teller, Amy, greeted me with a smile, and I grunted, taking off my gloves to hand her the bag. Purposely, I didn't glance at the corner office where I knew she was sitting. Hopefully, my posture was relaxed, but I was grinding my teeth so hard they might not make it to my next dentist appointment.

"How's it going, Mads?"

"Good, thanks," I said, tensing my whole body and hoping no one noticed.

I despised small talk, so I pulled out my phone and plugged in the estimations for the repairs while Amy handled the deposit.

"Ice Queen just opened her door. Watch it," she said, motioning to the other teller. Pete, I think that's his name, nodded and straightened his shoulders.

"I wish she would go back from where she came. No one likes her," Pete muttered, visibly disgusted at the open door. Amy nodded in agreement, and they both peered past me like I was in on some big secret.

I slowly turned around, feeling the back of my neck tingle. She was at her desk, staring right at us as if she had overheard the conversation. The most curious expression was on her face. Almost sadness? But she couldn't hear them, right?

"Ice Queen?" I said, drawing attention from them both and hating that I was getting sucked into the gossip. I had heard the name Ice Queen before. Maybe I could gossip a little, and these two could help me unravel her mystery. Here we were, the three of us clucking away like hens. Goddamnit, I might as well go for a manicure next.

"Oh, you know the rumors, Mads. She came in, all the employees were fired, and now she runs this place with an iron fist. I'm afraid to ask for a day off," Amy said.

"Remember when she first hired us? Brought us those donuts, as if she didn't just fire three of our friends?" Pete added, rolling his eyes and glancing back at the still, open door.

"Did y'all give her a chance?" I asked.

"We're still here, aren't we?" Pete said with a smile, passing back my receipt and bag. Well damn, that shut them down quick. So much for gossiping. At least I can forgo the manicure now.

"Right," I waved. "Bye, guys."

"Bye, Mads," they echoed.

Confused, I turned and headed to the door. It didn't seem like they had given her much of a chance. But what did I know? My reputation revolved around being an unyielding dick seventy-five percent of the time. She was still staring but had moved around her desk to stand in her doorway, right by the exit and in my line of sight.

"Hey, Lily. Sorry again about this morning. I hope you have a good day."

"Are you stalking me now?"

"You wish, pretty lady." Smirking with a wink, I used the opportunity to take another uninterrupted peruse of her body, taking in her luscious curves and white-blonde hair all over again.

A flash of amusement crossed her face, and I swear her lips turned up in the smallest smile, and her eyes sparkled before she schooled her features and the ice wall returned.

"Holy shit, Maddox, I just rolled my eyes so hard I checked out my own ass," she said.

Comments like that made my hand twitch, thinking of how pink I could make her hot little ass. I swear this woman would have me wrapped completely around her pinky finger with just a few sweet whispered words. Still, with each sharp barb and thinly veiled insult, she slipped deeper beneath my usually thick skin. She's not a conquest. She's a reward, a reward that should be treasured, savored, worshipped.

"Wow. I sure am glad I have boobs because I'd hate for you to have to look me in the eye while I'm insulting you."

I purposely took my eyes away from hers to stare directly at her tits, especially since she already thought I was. "You know, Lily, I feel like you wouldn't even be able to be nice if a unicorn shoved a fairy wand up your ass while Judy Garland stood there singing *Somewhere Over The Rainbow*."

"Then I suggest you move right along, you flying monkey."

"You...Lily... Later." I stuttered like an idiot but did as she asked, walking out the door without a glance back.

I let her words roll off of me until I got to my truck. Slamming the door, I ran my hands through my hair, and I threw the bank bag on the seat, looking back. I could see straight through Lily's window. She was standing by her desk, staring out but not seeing anything. Her expression was unreadable, and her features were soft with worry. She reached up, and I watched her wipe underneath those baby-blue eyes and lower her head.

What was with that crying gesture? The Ice Queen, huh. I think the hard-ass act was a front, and I knew just a smidge about putting on a hard-ass front.

Screw this. There were two more sites to visit and at least a few hours of paperwork back at the office. Attempting to remove the stick from her ass would have to wait, and it wasn't like she wanted anything to do with me. And, honestly, I didn't think I could handle another rejection of my softer side. The grumpy, hard-ass vibe worked, and it guarded my heart. It was better that way. Turning left out of the bank, I hit a drive-through for some food, knowing I'll be lucky to be home before dark.

Made in the USA
Middletown, DE
29 May 2021

40677630R00213